LEST YOU BE JUDGED

a novel

DAVID HUTCHISON

FRANKLIN *f* PUBLISHING
GREENFIELD USA

ISBN 9781079735727

For Kate H. and Matthew H. with love.

Gordon H., for his tireless, and knowledgable, encouragement.

and

Alexis H., for being in my life. Namaste.

ഈ

*This is the law: blood spilt upon
the ground cries out for more.*

DEATH WAS THE LAST THING on Judge Pride's mind, but it was waiting for him patiently.

"Another brandy, judge?"

Replete, and lost in thought, the old judge said nothing, but gazed through the rain-streaked windows up to the illuminated castle, floating like a fairytale fort on an island in the night sky. He'd quite taken to having his evening meal at the Advocates Club. Despite semi-retirement, it kept him in touch with the gossip and chatter of his own kind, that select community of judges and lawyers, fellow practitioners in law.

Though no longer sitting in the High Court, his temporary bench suited him fine; he was still practising. And, even if the cases were not those grand ones he used to hear, he was still sitting in judgement over others, lesser people than himself. *His* voice, *his* take on the law, still carried weight. The extra money was to his liking too.

His plans for retirement had been well considered and, if those jumped-up fools in the City hadn't over-played their hand, well, he would be pottering in France now. He sighed. Who knew how life would turn out? Nobody ever knew for certain what was round the corner . . .

"Judge Pride?"

Leave me *alone*, was the first thought that came to mind; the man's fussing – his very presence – was spoiling his thoughts, spoiling his evening. "No," he snapped, "I'll be heading home."

Pushing away from the table, his fingers splayed against the heavy white linen, and he got to his feet unsteadily. One too many brandies.

As the server helped him into his coat, he looked out at the castle again. When had he been first taken by this splendid view, this symbol of the city's power and authority? With a start he realised it must have been more than fifty years ago. He'd been a green lawyer then, devilling for Hector McKenzie, and the old man had proposed his membership.

McKenzie – an awful man with no *real* breeding, but a collection of select clients – had been of some use at the time. How time passes . . .

He became aware of the expectant server at his shoulder. "*What?*"

"I asked whether you wanted me to get you a taxi."

"No . . . I'll walk."

"It's a pretty rainy night, judge."

He ignored him. Pretty, indeed; where on earth did the Club get these people? Glancing at the man by his side, he saw an obsequious nobody who would've been in short trousers when he'd first stood here, all those years ago.

Wrapped up, he left the club, stepping out into the sleety rain and noisy Friday night crowd on Princes Street. Strings of underdressed girls and packs of girlish boys whirled and whooped past him like jungle savages. Rain doesn't seem to bother these common folk, he thought, it won't bother me.

Reaching the corner, he headed up the gentle incline towards George Street.

The driver of the car double-parked on Frederick Street watched the judge pass, allowed him to get a distance ahead, then slowly followed, ignoring the horn blast from a car that had sped up at the rear and swerved past.

On George Street the judge took in the vulgar Christmas lights and milling young crowd that now frequented the bars of this once quiet, refined street and shivered. The mundane is taking over the world; all it takes is a little money for these little people to think they have a life.

As he stepped out to cross the street the car turned the corner. The driver flicked on the main beam and stamped hard on the accelerator. The needle of the rev counter briefly hit the red zone and, with the engine whining in complaint, the wide tyres spun on the wet road, then gripped.

Judge Pride was half-way across the street when the speeding car ploughed into him. His legs were broken before his head smashed off the bonnet and he was catapulted through the air, already dead when the heavy car crushed his body to the road.

With the accelerator now floored, the car fish-tailed in the wet before leaping forward, broad-siding a parked vehicle and almost hitting a young couple who were dancing in the street, a dangerous prelude to a night of youthful sexual adventure.

When the first patrol car arrived, the young policeman listened to the eye witnesses and radioed-in a hit and run. It was a damaged, large, dark blue, possibly black, Ford – then again, possibly a dark navy Nissan – headed west.

One thing people *were* sure of: the car had been going too fast; the old judge had never stood a chance.

ONE

STEEL TURNED INTO POLICE HEADQUARTERS at Fettes, feeling as if he'd never been away. Truth be told, time off meant nothing to him; he'd spent the Christmas break spinning his wheels. Now it was 2000, a new year, a new decade, a new century, and he glanced up at the building, looking for some kind of change. It, too, had been new once, but across the street Fettes College, "the Eton of the North" that preceded it by a hundred years, stood in lofty, permanent rebuke. It was Monday.

Stepping from the warmth of his car, he pulled his jacket tight against the bitter cold wind, and feeling sharp acid in his stomach, reached deep into his pocket and found the comforting shape of a roll of Rennies.

A young policeman held the door for him. "Morning Chief Inspector."

Steel nodded; the constable looked no older than his son. He let the thought slide; he hadn't seen his son in years – he wouldn't look quite so young now.

Making his way along the corridor he saw the figure of Chief Superintendent Grieve approaching, balancing a coffee precariously on a pile of folders. Steel sighed; he wasn't five minutes in the door. It was impossible to avoid him, and in any case Grieve, who moved along the corridor like a slow earthmover, had him in his sights. "Morning Mike, well met. Happy New Year, eh? . . . Good break?" and without waiting for a reply, "My office. A word with you."

Allowing Grieve to pass, he followed him to his office. Apart from a potted plant on the window ledge which Grieve would fiddle with, and a framed photo of his daughter with her two sons, it was a spare room with three filing cabinets, a coat stand and nothing on the desk other than a computer screen, a sophisticated phone and an uncooperative Anglepoise which, Steel knew, exasperated Grieve every day. *He* would have broken it irretrievably to get a replacement.

"Now then," Grieve said, gingerly lowering the folders with their coffee on to his desk and settling his bulk into his seat, "sit down Mike. I'm glad you had a good break." He took a sip of coffee, pulled a face and shuffled through the folders. Finding the right one he looked up, "In your absence we found you a new bagman."

Steel said nothing and waited. He knew he'd lost a good Detective Sergeant in Brian when he had passed his exams and moved on. A replacement was necessary.

Grieve swivelled the folder round on the polished surface and slid it across the desk. "Robin Moss. Comes to us from Merseyside with good words."

Steel leaned in, flicked the folder open, and skimmed the front page. "What, a graduate on Accelerated Careers? I'm not going to be a mentor."

Grieve gave him a thin smile. "Like you have a choice, eh?"

"These rising stars are in and out, Bob. What's it now, under four years and they're off? There can't be any *real* learning in that time, and pretty soon they're on their way to a knighthood and you and me are saluting them."

"You're a dinosaur, Mike. Besides, Moss comes to us as a recent DS – Phase Two of the Development Programme, if you actually read anything that comes across your desk. There's already *been* real learning experience, and Merseyside isn't exactly soft experience either."

Steel sat back with a sigh. Brian had been a good Sergeant with plenty of years under his belt; now it was going to be uphill with a fast-track career policeman, having to show him the local ropes, wasting valuable time before real policing kicked in. He looked up to see Grieve containing his humour. "What?"

"Turn the page."

Steel flicked the page, and seeing the ID photo his head jerked up. "A *woman?* You're joking."

Grieve's laugh filled the room; Steel was making his morning. "As I said, a dinosaur. We employ women these days . . . I hear some of them have become doctors too."

Steel ignored the jibe. "Robin?"

"Ah, yes . . . I'll admit to being caught by that. Anyway, she comes to us very highly recommended. Leaving aside the graduate and Accelerated Career bits, she's apparently bright on the street, took part in a few important collars as a DC, speaks a couple of languages, knows Tai whatsit-"

"Aikido actually. A first kyu, I believe," huffily correcting him; he *did* read everything that came across the desk, if only with a brief glance.

Grieve held up a hand. "Whatever. Liverpool says she's a good copper and that's all we – you – need at this stage."

Steel took in the face filling the five by seven glossy before him. Apart from the open almond shaped grey-green eyes, which had met the photographer's lens evenly, he could read nothing there. She was easier on the eye than Brian, but, good copper? Time would tell. Hopefully, not *too* much time, for everyone's sake.

A knock at the door interrupted his thoughts.

Grieve glanced at his watch. "That'll be her now."

"Do I stand when she comes in?"

"Just behave yourself, that's all I ask – as a copper, if not as a human . . ." and he tailed off. "You need a bagman; Moss is it," and called out, "Come."

Steel stood to meet his new DS thinking, Bag*woman*, surely.

The young officer entered and Steel gave her a quick appraisal. Slim, in her early thirties, with fringed chestnut hair cut round a strong featured face in a short, not unfashionable, style, and dressed in a dark blue trouser suit – work wear, not boardroom – over an off-white blouse, with a small gold cross at her neck. Attractive rather than pretty, he thought, and the Job hadn't etched any hard lines on her face. Yet. The only blemish he could see was the three inch scar that ran along her left jaw.

7

She leaned in to shake Grieve's extended hand, knowing she was being assessed. "Good morning sir. DS Moss reporting for duty."

"Morning Sergeant. You found us alright then," and with a small tilt of his chin, "This is your new DCI, Mike Steel."

Moss turned to him. Her handshake was firm and she made direct eye contact. "Pleased to meet you, sir. I'm looking forward to working with you."

Steel caught only the slightest trace of a Liverpudlian accent and thought she was presenting herself well. Then he remembered – the Accelerated Careers Development Programme carried several Leadership courses with it. She'd studied well.

"I've gone over your file at length Sergeant," Grieve said, "*and* I made a couple of calls. People down there speak well of you. You'll find Lothian and Borders a wee bit quieter than Merseyside . . . though, quiet's the way I like it."

As Moss knew, her file would comprise her performance at Hendon Police College in addition to her experience in Liverpool. She had learned fast, making Sergeant at the first attempt; her superiors would have made their notes in their own way, saying to Grieve what they wouldn't commit to paper. There would be no negatives with the positives, but file and comments were not for her eyes or ears. "I'm just hoping for the broadest experience sir."

The phone on Grieve's desk purred into life. Annoyed by the interruption, he stabbed a button. "Yes? What *is* it?"

"The Chief Constable on line three for you, sir."

Grieve picked up the handset. "Yes, sir . . . Well, I have DCI Steel with me, right now", then "*What?*" followed by "Very good, sir . . . of course, sir."

Replacing the handset with care, as if handling something incendiary, he looked up at Steel. "Get yourself to Barnton Meadows – Lord Mitchell of Warrender has been found murdered. And Mike, that was the Chief on the phone and I'll be reporting to him directly. You understand me. Tread gently – no heavy feet on this one, eh? – and let's see whether we can clear this up quickly."

Turning to Moss he said, "There's paperwork and a lot of *et cetera* we'll get to later. Stick close to Steel, amongst all else he's a good copper . . . hopefully you'll learn something in your time with him."

Moss, saying nothing, nodded and got to her feet.

TWO

THE DRIVE TO THE CRIME SCENE would be quick; a straight shot west on Ferry Road, through Davidson's Mains, north towards Cramond and then on to the other world of Barnton where, although it didn't exactly mix, Edinburgh's old money rubbed shoulders with the new.

While the newer housing clinging pretentiously to its outskirts had hijacked the name, Barnton itself was home to those – more often than not, generations of families – who owned, and ran, the city. It was a place of real wealth, real power but, in Edinburgh's way, its face was private; there was no show, no ostentation.

Steel saw Moss taking in the streets as they drove. "You'll find Edinburgh's quite different from Liverpool, you know."

Moss nodded. "Lord Mitchell . . . who and what was he?"

A High Court judge, which is going to make it difficult."

"How so?"

"You worked murder before?"

"No, sir."

Steel grunted. "Well, murder's a passionate crime and that, normally, makes it easy – we'd be looking for someone close whose passion has overflowed, has made them snap – someone slighted, a wife, a lover. Here we have decades of the judge's criminal cases and to add to that, we've got pressure from on high too."

"The Chief Constable?"

"Well, you heard. Grieve was certainly called by the Chief, but at this stage I don't know whether someone had called *him*."

"Sorry, I don't follow."

Steel gave her a quick mirthless smile. "You're getting to move in rarefied air for your first day here, Moss. Me? I *try* to see every victim the same way – everyone was some mother's child – but compared to an old down-and-out who dies after taking a kicking on a Friday night, this'll be big . . . front page. And, who knows, maybe the Chief Constable and Lord Mitchell holidayed together, were in the same Lodge, or their wives played bridge together. Maybe all three, but I hope it's none of them; it ends up as interference whichever way it arrives."

Moss absorbed his words; more, she absorbed her DCI's point of view. She was well aware crime may be democratic but policing it never was; thin resources would almost naturally flow to high-profile cases.

They reached the heart of Barnton, where most houses were set well back from the street, hidden from view. "This seems like a different world," Moss said.

"In every way possible. If you haven't got a soft touch, you'd better find it fast. In this area, we may not be dealing with someone who knows the Chief Constable, but you can be damned sure they'll know someone who does. Think politics."

Turning a corner they saw the judge's house marked by two police cars at the gateway, their lights slowly flashing, and an Incident Command Vehicle already in place. As they drove up Moss saw, despite the stark winter trees, that this was one of those houses where you could barely see the roof from the street. Steel parked beside the ICV and they went inside.

The Sergeant working communications looked up. "Morning, sir."

"Morning Ken. What do we have?"

"The body's in an upstairs back bedroom, and the pathologist – it's Knox – is in there now with the Crime Scene Examiners. I've sealed off the whole property to its perimeter and we'll start going through the grounds for a fingertip search once the Examiners are satisfied with the house. So far there's no sign of a break-in."

"Who discovered the body?"

"Lady Mitchell," and looking at his screen, "at eight twenty-five. She'd been visiting grandchildren in Crail over the weekend. Fife Constabulary is confirming."

Steel nodded. "When did we get the treble nine?"

"O-nine hundred, sir."

"Thirty-five minutes later? Anyone else in the house?"

"Living there? No, just Lord and Lady Mitchell."

"Okay, thanks Ken. I'll have a look," and he reached for the mandatory coveralls. "By the way, this is DS Robin Moss, she comes to us from Merseyside."

The Sergeant stood to shake her hand. "You'll find it's pretty awful over there I'm afraid, but welcome to Lothian and Borders, Robin."

Steel and Moss crunched up the long gravel drive, taking in the house. It was a large, three storey, ivy-clad, honeyed sandstone house, built for a large family, with tall windows piercing the face and small windowed turrets at either end. "Mock Scots Baronial I believe," said Steel. Moss glanced, but couldn't tell whether he was being humorous or not.

Inside, they climbed a wide dark oak stairway which rose off the vast entrance hall, and at the first floor went down a panelled corridor, lined with heavy framed oil paintings of ancestors and hunts on the Scottish moors, and reached the bedroom. On entering, the first thing Steel noted was its size – it was at least three times the size of his living room – next, there was the smell: a combination of blood and faeces.

In silence, several Crime Scene Examiners were patiently taking stock of the room, checking all likely surfaces for fingerprints before retracing their steps for the unlikely ones and photographing every square foot. Their painstaking method reflected the cast-iron rule that every contact leaves a trace, and every time a crime scene was entered, *something* was left behind. Without doubt, somewhere in this room, there was evidence which would point directly to the killer.

Close to the bed the pathologist snapped his case shut and stood with difficulty, too overweight to be on his knees. Seeing Steel he peered over his glasses and called out theatrically, "Well, we meet again Stainless. Come in, come close . . . come see Man's majestic handiwork."

He moved to one side and Steel and Moss saw the body. Or, the mess in which a body lay. As they moved towards the bed, the pathologist wheezed out, in an almost jocular tone, "Do you ever get the feeling Mondays should be banned Chief Inspector?"

Looking down, Steel felt a familiar jolt in his stomach and ignored it, but heard Moss's sharp intake of breath. Almost to the last inch, apart from where his bowels had evacuated, the sheets of the wide double bed were red with blood, and Lord Mitchell, his old body covered with cuts, lay red, naked and spread-eagled, wrists and ankles tied to the four bedposts.

"What can you tell me doctor?"

The pathologist gave him a grim smile. "Well, so far, I've counted eighteen *deep* wounds. There's more, but the body needs to be cleaned before I can be accurate. Most of the eighteen were deep enough to have him bleed to death – he would've died slowly – but," and he pointed to a deep gash in the neck, "this cut to the carotid was the killing one. You can be certain the killer was up to his armpits in blood at this point." He watched Steel absorb this, then continued, "Now, post mortem, there are these scores to the chest. All of which looks like they were made with a chisel or a sharpened screwdriver which, so far, your boys haven't found."

Steel and Moss peered into the chaos that had once been a High Court judge and could see two foot-high gouges scored deeply into the chest. "*Post* mortem?" asked Moss.

"That's what I said, my dear. Now, if you look at the penis, although it's difficult to see right now, there's a ligature tied tightly round it. When the body's clean I'll let the Examiners have pictures before I cut it off," and he smiled, "The cord that is. Right now I can't tell whether that was done before or after the killing blow but I can tell you he did have sex – or more precisely, he ejaculated – before he was killed; there's semen in the blood down there."

Steel was trying to organise his thoughts. "So, all this – the wrists and ankles tied, the ligature – was sexual?"

"*Steel.* How would *I* know? I can only tell you what I see, not how it came into being."

"I understand doctor. What I'm trying to determine is whether he knew his assailant or not."

14

Knox gave this a hollow laugh. "You mean there's a possibility the good judge had sex in this way and a third party did this?"

"A third party can be ruled out," Moss ventured, "if we can determine this was an activity which went wrong – it would be at the hands of someone Lord Mitchell actually knew."

"Again, I have no way of telling, although an assumption he knew his killer wouldn't be a wild one . . . but, I'll leave you to detect, Detective. Old as he was, he had sex – of some kind – and he was killed. I'll know more later."

"*When* was he killed?" asked Steel.

"Within the last twelve hours. Body temperature and progress of rigour suggests nine to ten. Look, I'll let you have my report as soon as . . . I know to you and me it's yet another body, statistic or whatever, but I do understand *who* this was. I'll be as quick as possible."

"Thanks, doctor."

The pathologist signalled to the mortuary attendants waiting patiently at the door, "I'm done here," and with a nod to Steel, he left.

Steel watched him go and turned to one of the Examiners. "Let me know if and when you find anything, right? Immediately – I don't want to wait on any paperwork."

Moss was looking down at the body, attempting to breathe deep, as Mitchell's vacant, sightless eyes stared past her to the ceiling. He seemed to have an angry look on his face. "There's something here sir; something I can't quite put a finger on . . . this is reminding me of something."

"Let's get out of here." With murder, Steel found that asking questions always acted as a shield from the awful truth before him. Now, with his appraisal of the *locus*, and initial questions asked, he needed to distance himself.

Moss resisted moving, although the way her heart was racing she was ready to run from the room. "Do these scores to the chest suggest anything?"

"No idea. Compared to the rest, they're very precise. They look like the start of noughts and crosses. Perhaps the killer got bored. Come on, let's go downstairs, we need to speak with Lady Mitchell."

"I can't imagine how she must have felt discovering this."

Steel looked at her; she would learn. "You could ask."

As they entered the high-ceilinged, thick-carpeted living room, with its dark, heavy antique furniture, polished surfaces, and the slow ticking of a clock, they were hit by a sense of stillness and, sitting at the heart of it, Lady Mitchell. The policewoman nodded at Steel and stood.

Coming into Lady Mitchell's vision Steel said, "Lady Mitchell, my name is Detective Chief Inspector Steel and this is Detective Sergeant Moss. I am sorry, but we need to ask you some questions."

Lady Mitchell, a slight bird-like woman, her face seemingly set in a permanent scowl, looked up, and Steel saw she was dry-eyed and very, very, still. "Please sit down Chief Inspector, Sergeant. Ask whatever you need."

"As I understand, you discovered Lord Mitchell this morning when you returned from Fife."

"Yes, that is correct."

"Can you remember at what time that was?"

"Yes, it was eight o'clock."

Steel glanced at Moss, "You're certain of that?"

"Yes, the car radio . . . Radio Four had just begun its news."

"I have a note you discovered Lord Mitchell at eight twenty-five and you called us at nine, Lady Mitchell." Moss heard softness in Steel's voice.

"You do? Yes, I'm sorry . . . I arrived home at eight and I discovered *that*, upstairs, later."

"And the twenty-five minutes?" Steel let his question hang in the stillness.

"I'm not sure Chief Inspector. Why?"

"Timings are important to us, that's all. So, when you discovered Lord Mitchell at eight twenty-five, you telephoned us at nine? Is that correct?"

"I don't remember."

"That's thirty-five minutes after you found Lord Mitchell."

"Well I'm sure you must be correct." There was a harshness to her voice now. "I *was* rather shocked to discover my husband murdered."

Steel changed tack. "I realise in your husband's position, he would have made many enemies over the years, but did you hear of anything recently? Anything unusual? Any threats your husband might have received?"

16

"Henry never discussed his work with me," and after a slight hesitation, "He never discussed *anything* with me; we had grown apart." She let the thought linger and Steel allowed the pause. "Yes, apart. I talked to him of divorce and he actually laughed at me." The stillness in the room had seemed to deepen. "He was a disgusting man . . . disgusting."

Steel said nothing, hoping for more, but she had retreated into self-contained silence. "We shall need to go through his papers Lady Mitchell, here and in his chambers. Now, is there anyone we should call? Someone who can be with you?"

"My daughter's coming for me. I shall spend some time with her in Crail until this . . . matter, is resolved."

Steel got to his feet. "Very well, Lady Mitchell. Please give the policewoman here a note of your address and a number where we can reach you. I *am* sorry for your loss."

Her head jerked up and she gave him a hard pitying stare. "Good Heavens, don't be *sorry* for me Chief Inspector – you may as well be sorry for a freed prisoner. I'm *glad* he's dead."

•

Steel and Moss walked slowly down the drive. He stopped and, popping a Rennies into his mouth, looked back at the house and the tall trees surrounding it and shook his head.

"Sir?"

"An eight-bedroomed house just for two people? *There's* a crime. Anyhow, what did you make of that?"

"A third party is a possibility."

Steel snorted. "What, he and Miss X are having sex, she comes home, finds him tied up and wreaks her revenge?"

"It's possible," Moss said, her voice dropping.

"Possible? Anything's *possible*, Moss. Where do you think Miss X is during all this – hiding in a cupboard, gone out for milk?"

"Could be *Mr.* X."

Steel laughed. "Good point, there's no telling, but I don't think there's a third party involved. Hopefully, Forensics will find something."

"Perhaps the sex play would've got him into a vulnerable position which would allow for a third party," Moss persisted.

"A *set-up* for a killing? Come on Moss, Grieve told me you were bright. That's *far* too convoluted . . ." he paused and looked back at the house, ". . . although, right now, it's all a bit convoluted. I'd say the killer is male, although a female could inflict that sort of damage, especially as the weapon appears to be something of the sharp chisel variety and the victim is tied up, unable to defend himself. And that . . . is that a male female thing in itself? Was it even sexual – or does it just *look* that way? We could be looking for Mr. X. *or* perhaps we leave Miss X and Mr. X out of it entirely because we've just spoken with the killer."

"She wasn't exactly the grieving widow, but wouldn't she visibly *be* the killer?"

Steel nodded; he was only thinking aloud, sounding out scenarios. "She called him disgusting, or was that what he was up to? I just don't see her involving herself in whatever the hell was going on in there and then killing him. She didn't have the time and I don't think there's enough hatred in her to do what we saw . . . she's dispassionate rather than passionate, and what we saw was the result of *some* sort of passion."

"Passion?"

Steel turned to her. "When you're working with me, Moss, you're going to have to pay attention. I *told* you, murder's a passionate crime. We're looking for someone who, in some manner, was close to the judge. There's degrees to close of course, but ninety percent of the time the killer is known to the victim. That fits Lady Mitchell but only in that she was his wife. There was perhaps a time when she could've, but I don't think now. And you're right, it would be written all over her if she'd killed him." He sighed. "Then again, there's those timings of hers . . ."

As they continued down the drive, Steel glanced at his new Sergeant; fast-track cop or not, she *was* meant to be learning. "What was your take on the bedroom?"

"Take, sir?"

"Yes, *take*. What did you get from it?" He saw she had no idea what he was talking about. "You've got eyes Moss, but you've got to understand what it is you're seeing."

"Sir?"

"The bedroom was single occupancy . . . a double bed but only one set of pillows. Out of all the items in the room, there was nothing there that was Lady Mitchell's. No jewellery, no items of clothing, no cosmetics. Nothing. A lot of couples have separate bedrooms but, *if* you've read the room properly, you'll not be misled by a wife or husband claiming a loving relationship where none exists and have them coming on to you as the grieving spouse.

"I wasn't exactly *expecting* the response we got from Lady Mitchell, but it fits. I doubt she spent *any* time there." He saw she had, eventually, caught his meaning. "It's not enough just to look Moss, you've got to learn *how* to look. You're a detective – don't take *anything* at face value."

"Understood sir."

Steel hoped she did. "This is not a time for sharp focus – Forensics'll do that – at this stage you've got to take everything in, even things that appear to have no connection. Question everything, learn something-"

"Answer nothing?"

" *What?* "

"Euripides, sir . . . a Greek dramatist . . ." and she faltered, feeling herself colouring.

Steel looked her in the eye; the very last thing he wanted was his new DS flaunting her university education. "I want you to *get* smart, not *be* smart, Sergeant."

They'd reached the gateway, standing by the ICV to take off their coveralls, when they saw a large red Mercedes sports car leaving the driveway of a house further down the empty street. Seeing the police vehicles, the driver slowed and glanced their way. In a fleeting moment Steel caught the face and Moss caught his look. "Someone you know sir?"

"A nudge from somewhere certainly. Maybe nothing, and it doesn't chime with Barnton. Anyhow, next step. Speak with Ken here and get a house-to-house started . . . d'you think you can manage that?"

Moss coloured and was about to respond, but bit her tongue.

"Grab as many bodies as you can. There's no chance of twitching net curtains in this area – most houses can't even see each other – but you never know, a neighbour *may* have seen something . . . dog walkers, joggers and the like. If Knox is right about the killer being up to his armpits in blood, then Forensics will either find he showered or had to

19

make a very discreet exit. I'm going to see Grieve and keep him up to speed.

"One thing. There will be press – I'm surprised they're not here already – but you can leave them to Ken; we have a good working relationship here. They'll know you're new, so when you're asked, just say there will be a press conference later. Nothing else. Got it?"

"Of course, sir."

He looked at her; a young officer in a new job with murder on her first day. Well, nothing in Accelerated Careers would help her now, she was in at the deep end and she'd sink or swim. "Any questions?"

"No sir . . . anything else?"

The judge's old body floated into Steel's vision. "Yes, if what's in there *is* sexual, the tying thing – bondage – what's all that about?"

Moss felt a small bubble of hysterical laughter rising and had to swallow the words, 'but we've just met'. "I'm not sure what we saw is actually *bondage* – that's S and M isn't it? – more a game, I think. Being completely vulnerable sexually or having complete sexual control over another – it's a turn-on . . . for some."

Steel looked at his attractive new DS and resisted any further questions.

THREE

STEEL WAS SIFTING THROUGH the first photographs from Forensics when Moss returned from Barnton. "How did it go?"

"Well, there are very few houses on the street itself, *or* on the neighbouring ones, and you were right about nosey neighbours; even if they were that way inclined, each house is a little private island."

Steel nodded. "Do you have a list of owners?"

"Ken printed out what we have so far. Uniform's still moving outwards, just in case."

Taking the sheet of paper from her he scanned its short length, "What's this one . . . Priority Private Equity?"

"That's where we saw the car leaving from earlier, sir. I did that one myself."

Mentally, Steel gave her a plus. "And?"

"You understand I've only discovered Barnton . . ."

"Yes. What?"

"Well, there was a different type of occupant from the other houses there . . . not an owner and ever so slightly hostile, unlike the rest. Nothing I could put my finger on, just a feeling."

Steel picked up the phone, "You got no other name?" and seeing Moss shake her head, he dialled. "Hello George, it's Steel, give me anything you have on Priority Private Equity, owners of a house in Barnton, would you? Soon as," and hung up. He turned back to Moss. "I've just been going through some of the pictures from the Crime Scene Examiners. Have a look."

Taking her time, Moss spread out the glossy photographs. Here, what had once been a living human was now frozen and reduced to part of a mute crime record. She came to the full-length shot of the judge the photographer had taken from above. In a sea of red, he was seen with a limb at each corner and she got the same nagging thought of being reminded of something.

Watching her, Steel said, "What?"

"I don't know sir . . . this just rings a bell."

"Guesses count."

"Sir?"

"Anything you can throw in counts Moss — there's never anything stupid except not throwing it in. Forensics are annoyed . . . so far they've found nothing, but that's science. For us, at *this* stage, a lot's guesswork with a few what-ifs thrown in for luck — pieces of a jigsaw to form a picture. So, if you have an idea — about anything — spit it out."

She shook her head. "Understood sir, but I can't quite get it . . . it'll come to me."

Steel nodded. "Okay. Now, those timings of Lady Mitchell's were bothering me so I twisted an arm and pulled her phone records. She made two calls before calling us."

"She did?"

"Yes. The first, at eight ten — a ten minute call — was to Smith McKnight Hughes, her lawyers, and the second, at eight twenty-one, to her daughter in Fife — a three minute call."

"She called us at nine."

"Yes, there's no telling what her movements in the house were, but she did say her daughter was coming for her from Crail. Her call to her daughter — her only call to her — was before eight twenty-five when she says she discovered Lord Mitchell, so why would her daughter — who she'd *just* spent a weekend with — be coming for her?"

"Are we going back?"

"Not right away, and it'll probably mean a trip to Fife now, which reminds me, we haven't heard from the Fife cops. Right now we need to see Dr. Knox, and there's a press conference set for three."

Moss got to her feet and as her eyes caught the full-length photo of the dead judge once more, she realised what had been nagging her. She turned to Steel and saw his half smile.

"You got it?"

"Yes, and sorry, it's nothing . . . this looks a bit like the Vitruvian Man."

"Say again."

"The Vitruvian Man. Da Vinci drew it. A man with his arms outstretched, describing both a square and a circle. The circle's how Mitchell was tied. As I said, it's nothing – I was just nagged as having seen it before."

"At this stage there's no 'nothing' – just another jigsaw piece. Let's get to the mortuary and you can tell me more about this drawing on the way."

•

As they entered, the brutal glare from the strip lights bounced off the white tiles and burnt into their eyes. Moss caught a faint lemon scent: an ineffective distraction from the strong antiseptic smell that had permeated the room over the years.

Clad all in green, Knox looked up from the corpse before him on the dissecting table. "We've got to stop meeting like this Stainless – people will talk."

As always, Steel ignored Knox's attempts at humour; there was life, then there was death – his job was finding the killer and humour played no part in it. "What more can you give me on Lord Mitchell?"

"There's a sheaf of photographs, but come, see for yourself," and with his rubber boots squeaking on the wet floor, Knox led them to the refrigerated unit. He opened a door and pulled out one of the shelves. Looking down at the body lying there, its old, now purplish flesh sagging off its already skeletal frame, Steel could clearly see the mass of small cuts which covered it along with much deeper ones and those caused by the pathologist's electric saws. He glanced at Moss and could tell she was having difficulty standing there.

"I was wrong in my count," the pathologist continued, "it was nineteen deep wounds – he was assaulted anally – along with, as you can see, *countless* smaller ones."

"Ideas?" Steel said, staring down at the body.

"Me?" asked the pathologist after a pause, "Or, are you addressing your Sergeant? Come closer my dear, your superior would like your input." He had not missed her hesitancy.

"No, *you*," Steel spat with some impatience; despite the fact this was all part of the job, he felt protective of Moss.

"Well, although there *may* have been some kind of 'game' at first, what you see is far from it. I think there may have been torture involved."

"Torture?" Moss managed.

Knox smiled. "Yes, my dear, torture . . . I would say the smaller cuts built up towards the deeper ones and over quite some time – there's chafing on the wrists and ankles. As you saw he wasn't gagged so he was very possibly pleading with his assailant."

"And the scores to his chest?" asked Steel.

"I have no idea. All I *can* say – affirm – is they were made post mortem."

Breathing heavily, Moss peered at the gouges on the chest; unlike the other cuts, both slight and deep, they had been made with some precision and were very deep. "There has to be some significance to these, sir."

"Yes. What are we looking at . . . eleven?"

"Maybe two, a Roman numerals thing? Or, two Is."

"Like the coffee bar?" Knox grinned.

Steel ignored this. "The ligature on the penis?"

"Oh, it was there before he died – that's all I can say. It could've been part of the game being played," and with a wink, "or maybe the old judge suffered from erectile dysfunction."

Steel sighed; perhaps it was just the job that gave the man his macabre take around death – *his* shield, perhaps. "Thank you doctor. We'll take the photographs and go."

"So soon?" Knox smiled, "I can't tempt you with anything else?"

Moss stepped up to him. "Actually, there is something. Don't *ever* call me 'my dear' again. I am Detective Sergeant Moss to you. I earned that."

24

Steel gave her another plus. "Right, press conference," and with a beaming smile for the pathologist, who now looked as pale as his charges, "Thanks again, doctor."

•

They drove back towards Fettes in silence before Moss broke it. "I'm sorry for that, sir."

"For what? I heard nothing for you to be sorry about."

Moss nodded. "It was unprofessional of me, but I've had that ever since I joined the Force and it crawls right up my back."

"What does?"

"The 'my dear' part. The 'what's a girl like you doing working in the police?' part."

For a few seconds Steel said nothing, remembering his outburst with Grieve earlier when he discovered he'd been given a woman as his bag carrier. He knew he wasn't much different, and actually *believed* women would never make good police officers. "What made you join? I mean, what with the graduate part, there must've been real choice for you."

"With respect sir, that's the same thing. Why *shouldn't* a graduate join the police?"

"Okay, call me old-fashioned or whatever, but the question stands."

Moss paused for a moment, watching the snow now beginning to fall on the city's streets, then said, "My father did."

Steel glanced at her. "Your father was a cop?"

She shook her head. "No, he was a drunk – a bullying, abusive drunk. I'd like to say it was on a Friday night but it was more like every night. One night, I was fifteen at the time, he came home and cut me in front of my mother. In his twisted head, I was a point to be made." Steel remembered her scar but said nothing. "A neighbour called the police . . . when they arrived I just remember the sense of restored order that came in through the door with them. It stuck with me . . . when I graduated, it seemed like a natural choice, that's all."

Inwardly, Steel was replaying drunken nights before his son. For a few chilling seconds he could feel the panic and hurt he must have caused in one so young, the invisible, and deeper, scars he had left on him.

"What about yourself, sir?"

Steel hated talking of himself and was thankful they were turning into Fettes. "That'll have to wait Moss."

•

Even if it hadn't been a slow news day, the combination of the murder of one of the small select band of High Court judges, and a murder in Barnton, of all places, meant the press corps had turned out in full. Steel had been right – this was front page news.

Moss stood off to one side to watch. Sitting behind a long desk were Chief Superintendent Grieve with a scowling Steel at his side and, adding his weight to the seriousness with which Lothian and Borders were taking the murder, Chief Constable Sir David Thompson.

Slightly apart, a press liaison officer started the proceedings. "Ladies and gentlemen, if we could have silence, Chief Superintendent Robert Grieve will read a short statement."

With a nod to Thompson, Grieve began, "At o-nine hundred hours, this morning, an emergency call was received at Force Communications Centre, Bilston Glen, from an occupant of number 69 Barnton Meadows, Edinburgh. Officers from Drylaw Mains Station were first to respond, arriving on scene at o-nine o-six hours, when the body of Lord Henry Mitchell of Warrender was discovered. This incident is being treated as one of murder and the Senior Investigating Officer is Detective Chief Inspector Michael Steel." Looking up, he finished with, "We *are* early into this investigation, but DCI Steel will answer any questions you may have," and sat back.

With that, the room erupted. Steel held up his hands, to be caught by several flashes from the stills photographers. "Please, one at a time," and spotting a face he knew from the Press Association, "Yes Andy."

"You say 'an occupant', could you be more specific?"

"At this moment, no."

"Was it Lady Mitchell?"

"I did say I could not be specific Andy . . . yes, Louise."

The pretty BBC Television reporter smiled her thanks. "Can you tell us *how* Lord Mitchell was murdered Chief Inspector?"

"Again, at this stage, we cannot say. What we *can* say is this was a particularly brutal crime, we are in the early stages of investigation and there are several areas which we are exploring."

Jim McEwan from the *Sun* asked, "Can the good folk of Barnton sleep soundly in their beds then, Chief Inspector?"

"Say again?"

"Well, you said it was a brutal crime. I was wondering whether residents should be warned to double-check their doors and windows."

Steel resisted a smile, doubting whether the *Sun* had a single reader in Barnton. "At this stage, there is no sign of forced entry, nor – again, at this stage – evidence of anything missing from the house." With a slight smile he added, "Though it wouldn't be a bad idea to remind your readership of home security, Jim."

A female voice asked, "Would it be fair to say you are far from an arrest Chief Inspector?"

Steel felt immediate heat and snapped, "Who was that?"

A reporter raised her hand. "Me."

"And me is?"

"Jay Johnstone. The *Scotsman.*"

A face new to Steel, and he'd never seen a more beautiful woman. In her mid-thirties with long, waved, flame-red hair framing a strong face, she sat poised and, for Steel, exuded quiet sex appeal. "Well, *Ms.* Johnstone," – damn it, why did I emphasise that? – "that question has no merit. We were informed at nine a.m. and now, some six hours later, we are following several lines of enquiry. We are moving forward with our investigation and," he scanned the room, "if there are no more questions, I would like to *continue* moving forward." Steel had had enough and got to his feet.

Mary Cohen from the *Daily Mail* threw in, "Do you know whether a replacement for Lord Mitchell has been named?"

Another pointless question. "I *think* that's something to ask of the Lord Advocate's Office, Mary."

As he reached Moss, he saw her smiling slightly. "What?"

"Nothing sir. There were some odd questions, that's all."

"Some damn foolish ones – what did you make of that 'far from an arrest' one? Given the killer wasn't found at the *locus*, am I meant to answer, 'no, we're close', in the very same day?

Just then, the reporter from the *Scotsman* materialised at their side. "Chief Inspector."

Steel turned; close up, she was even more beautiful. "Ah, Ms. Johnstone."

She offered her hand. "Please, it's JJ. I just wanted to apologise for asking a stupid question."

"They can slip out that way certainly." Steel was still annoyed.

She flashed him an open smile. "That's very forgiving of you. Again, I'm sorry. I interviewed Lord Mitchell recently – for a piece I'm writing."

"You did? When?"

"Just last week. Could I ask . . . was there any sexual aspect to the murder?" This blind-sided Steel, leaving him lost for words, and Johnstone gave him another smile, "Thank you Chief Inspector, you've been most helpful," and with that, she left them.

Now angry, Steel turned to Moss, "What *was* that? I feel like I was just ambushed."

Moss was watching Johnstone's elegant walk. Raising her eyebrows and shaking her head she said, "I'm not sure sir, but she must have something," adding lightly, "from her interview, that is."

"Come on," Steel snapped, "we've wasted enough time with this, let's get back to some *real* work."

FOUR

A COLD, WINTRY FRONT HAD BLOWN IN over Edinburgh from the North Sea, dropping a layer of snow on the streets, draining them of colour and making a monochrome scene of greys and white. Steel had difficulty driving in the wary lines of snarled traffic and, although he knew the snowfall could be gone within the hour, wondered why the city always seemed unprepared at this time of year. When he eventually arrived at Fettes, later than he'd wished, Moss was already at her desk.

"Morning sir."

Steel shook some persistent snow from his jacket and looked at her, wondering whether it was just her age that made her seem indecently bright and alive at this time of the morning. Even though he'd only had a couple of malts the previous evening, he felt hung-over and in need of coffee.

"We got the information on Priority Private Equity you asked for," but before he could respond, she added, "Have you seen the papers?"

Steel always made a point of not reading newspapers, and certainly not listening to or watching news, before work; it was his way of claiming his own time. He saw she had a stack of dailies on her desk. "No."

"There's big coverage, but you might want to look at the *Scotsman* first."

With a frown at her, he picked up the paper with its familiar masthead. On the left his eyes ran over 'P.M. To Host Edinburgh Euro Summit' and on the right, in heavier type, 'Murdered Judge Linked To Vice Ring – Exclusive: Jay Johnstone'. "What?" he let out, and sitting down heavily started to read. Moss waited in silence.

"What's this?" Steel exploded, "'Sources within Lothian and Borders Police yesterday confirmed the murder of Lord Mitchell had a sexual aspect to it.' Sources? *What* sources? That's irresponsible and damn-well inaccurate." He read on. "Hell, she writes of an escort, 'whose services were often used by Lord Mitchell'." Tossing the paper down hard on Moss's desk, he growled, "We'll need to visit the *Scotsman* and throw our weight about before the day's out."

To move him on, Moss said, "Priority Private Equity . . ."

Steel tried to push his anger away. "Yes, what do we have there?"

"It's a small company, based here, but with a lot of financial dealings – here and in Europe," and she passed the print-out from Records to him. "They're superficially a debt restructuring company with a large stake in developing, and leasing, commercial property. But, they *appear* to walk on both sides of the street; they've come to our attention – Finance's, anyhow."

"In what sense, both sides of the street?" Steel had attended a week-long course at Tulliallan Police College in Fife, run by the Financial Intelligence Unit. Then, as now, he was unable to grasp the labyrinthine way crooked money men could play with nothing, put it together to seem like something, and then make millions from the gullible. Crime was simple – black and white – but financial criminals baffled him.

"It's complicated sir but, on the legal side, they seem to make money whether a company they've invested in stands or falls."

Steel could almost feel his brain putting up shutters. He scanned the sheet of paper, reading the names of the principals shown at Companies House. "Well, well, Alan Prior."

"Someone you know?"

"Alan – Al – Prior is a well-known figure in Edinburgh; fingers in lots of pies. He's a slippery businessman, well-connected to movers and shakers here: politicians, lawyers – he's married to one – private bankers and the like. He's probably still as slippery but whenever his name comes up, 'no prior convictions' has always been the apt phrase.

"Some years back, the National Crime Squad had apparently linked Prior's name to one Billy McCann, a very active criminal here, who was getting his money mainly from prostitution and drugs. With his connection to Prior, NCS had him pegged as climbing a few rungs in the criminal ladder but before they moved on him, we nabbed him – more accurately, I nabbed him – for a robbery on a bonded warehouse."

"No communication?"

"What, between us and the NCS? No. Although they're meant to at least keep us in the loop. They were more than annoyed, but not as annoyed as me – we might've got Prior if they *had* communicated. In the end *they* lost Prior because they didn't tell us – *we* were after McCann and we got him."

"So, Priority Private Equity being owners of a house in Barnton?"

"Well, they're in property, but it goes to show – and this is right up NCS's street, with their stance of tackling crime from top to bottom – if you have an infestation of any sort, you can't be brutal enough about wiping it out."

"Sir?"

Steel leant towards her. "The face I saw when we were at Barnton – that was Steven McCann, 'young Stevie', Billy's younger brother and known to us. It seems Al Prior and the McCanns are *still* in bed together and, by the looks of it, quietly thriving." Steel paused and ran a hand over his chin. "Let's turn over the Priority Private Equity rock and see what crawls out."

Moss nodded. "Jay Johnstone's 'vice ring' . . . would there be a link to the McCanns there?"

Steel sat back with an long exhalation. "You reckon the escort service could be theirs? That's fairly close to home but you never know – we have a murder and almost next door, a known criminal. Peeling back the escort lid might yield something useful."

"What about the address shown for Prior's company?"

Steel looked at the sheet; the Registered Address was in Charlotte Square. "That's in the heart of the New Town – probably a lawyer's, but check it out."

Moss was scribbling notes and when she looked up, Steel continued, "As far as Lord Mitchell's concerned, we need to find out *why*, Moss – getting the why will give us the who. Let's find out everything we can about him – get to know him better than our own mothers – and we'll need to find out more about his past cases too. Trouble is, if there *is* a link there, it could go back years."

"Would someone wait before acting?"

"That someone could've just been released. It could quite as easily be someone who's spent the last fifteen years nursing a grudge. Let's try and narrow that down – find out who's been released over the past year."

Having mapped out their day, knowing full well none of it would follow any of the roads that had just been drawn, Steel looked at her, "Anything else?"

"Well, possibly nothing . . ."

"For God's sake Moss, I *told* you, 'nothing' always counts – the only time it doesn't is when we're passing papers over to the Fiscal. Go ahead."

She leaned forward, lightly brushing her fringe away from her eyes with her fingers and, today, Steel saw her as pretty rather than attractive. He knew he no longer had the eagerness he saw in her. He worked slowly on jigsaw pieces – ones that either fitted or didn't – and from sheer stubborn persistence, got his results. "I spent some time on the internet last night, following up on the Vitruvian Man."

"Right . . . and?"

"As I said, this may be nothing," and she held up a hand to acknowledge her continued use of the word, "but the point of that drawing is to show the perfect man. Perfect in proportions anyhow . . . I don't think there *is* a perfect man."

Steel glowered at her. "Just get *on* with it."

"Well, all the proportions in the drawing, the way a square, a circle and a triangle, hang together, are meant to show perfect – divine – proportions. Da Vinci was moved by deeper, hidden aspects, and drawn to mathematical codes. He put clues to a lot of this in his work."

"And this leads where exactly?" thinking to himself, There's nothing like an education; any more of this and she'll fall over.

32

"It could be – could be – something out of nothing. Despite the principles in da Vinci's drawing being sound, there's a whole slew of stuff about him on the web which has an occult nature to it – alchemy, magic and so on. Just part of that deals with 'the sacred power of numbers' – pure, fairly advanced, mathematics – and his drawing is all numbers.

"Now, if we take the two scores on Lord Mitchell's chest to *be* numbers, an eleven rather than something random, and if we assume he *was* tied in a way to resemble the da Vinci drawing, then the killer might've been working out some of this arcane stuff." She looked at Steel almost apologetically. "I know there's a couple of ifs in there."

Steel nodded, "More than a couple, but ifs can maybe open this up. Do you think the killer was leaving a message?"

"No sir. Assuming this idea has legs, whatever state of mind the killer was in – and it couldn't have been anything we know as sane – he may have been, in his head, *completing* some ritual with the scores . . . Dr. Knox did tell us they'd been made post mortem." She sat back, watching Steel absorb all this. "It's just an idea sir."

"No, at this stage it's an idea worth pursuing – those scores have to mean *something* and right now – although I *hate* the idea of this being somehow ritualistic – your take on da Vinci is as valid as my noughts and crosses . . . though only fractionally at the moment. Go a bit further with it, see if eleven means something, to da Vinci or anyone else; it may lead somewhere."

"Right sir. Where do we start?"

"With the everyday, Moss – murder and vice. I'm going to visit the *Scotsman* and speak with the News Editor. If Jay Johnstone – JJ – has got more stuff that's relevant to our investigation, I'm going to lean on her."

Moss smiled to herself; if she'd read him correctly, Steel would probably like nothing more than leaning on Johnstone. "I'll get on to Records, see what they have on Prior's company and what they can come up with regarding Lord Mitchell's past cases."

Steel got to his feet. He could see, with all the enthusiasm of a young officer in a new area, Moss was putting in the work – settling, like the snow on Edinburgh's streets. She wasn't Brian, but . . . "Where you staying, Moss? Sorry, I meant to ask last night. I can give you steers on where you can rent."

"I've actually hooked up with an old friend from University. She's a doctor at the Infirmary and has a large flat in Morningside, so I'm staying at her place."

"Do you know Edinburgh?"

"I've only ever visited – got shown around. Have you lived here long, sir?"

"All my life. Started out in Muirhouse, when the Billy McCanns of this world hadn't got a toehold there, joined the Force . . . been here ever since."

From his brief response Moss sensed direct questions would get her nowhere. "How did McCann get started?"

Steel perched on the edge of his desk. "How does *anything* evil get started? We allow it. The McCann family were a bad lot from the get-go. Billy went a usual route – shoplifter before his teens, on to shop-breaking, car theft and then, aged nineteen, an enforcer for a gangster named Doyle: collecting debts, and linked to stabbings and slashings. After Doyle was murdered, McCann went solo and, unknown to us, when the whole city was floating on heroin, he'd moved straight into being a high quantity drug dealer . . . making money on the back of other people's misery."

"Is that when he become known to us . . . beyond the petty stuff?"

Steel gave her a sharp look, "None of it's *petty*, Moss. That's how McCann took over an area that should've kicked him out – should've kicked the whole family out."

"Sorry, I meant-"

"I grew up seeing how the petty, as you put it, took over without anything being done and eventually, when McCann had hit his stride, decent people – those who couldn't afford to leave – were living in a hell he'd created for them where all crime was super-fuelled by drug users. His name popped up through a Customs sting in Glasgow but, by then, it was too late."

"Too late?" For a brief time Moss had worked with Liverpool's Drug Squad and 'catch them; jail them' had been the watchwords.

"McCann's bad but he's not stupid. He knew his time would be limited."

"And he was never caught? If he was a known dealer, why was he never-"

"What, set up? Isn't that just McCann in uniform? Bad's bad, no matter which side of the fence you're on." Although, as the words left his mouth, Steel recalled a similar weel-kent individual being stopped on the street and the officers simply planting a huge quantity of drugs on him. A practical solution: Edinburgh had one less drug dealer and *everyone* had been happy with that.

"No, I *certainly* didn't mean that . . . why was he never caught red-handed?"

He gave her the briefest of smiles. "Right . . . well, you'd need to ask our Drug Squad. As I said, he's not stupid. He never over-played his hand and there were always several layers protecting him. Even though Customs were doing the job we should've been doing, all they got were smaller fish, leaving him to take his money into other areas."

"And the drug dealing here?"

"It wasn't long before there was a policy change. It's still a problem but far less than it was."

Moss gathered her paperwork and got to her feet. "What was the policy change?"

"Possession meant you were a dealer, regardless of the amount, and the courts acted on that. In time, we turned the tide. Eventually I collared McCann, treading on the NCS's toes, but that was years ago. He's out now, supposedly managing a club in Leith, though that'll just be a front.

"Now, if the McCanns' connection to Prior is still there – and it looks like it, with you bumping into young Stevie in a house owned by Prior – then they're still looking to aim higher and Prior's still up to no good."

Moss nodded. "I'll see what I can find out in Records," thinking, even though they weren't on her list, if there was enough time, she'd look up the McCanns too.

FIVE

MOSS TOOK THE STAIRS, eventually reaching a basement corridor. Finding Records, with a superfluous sign, Authorised Personnel Only, she pushed inside to find herself in front of a counter with an office beyond. Here, the staff were civilian support and the whole room – apart from a large notice, which warned about breaches of the Data Protection Act (1998) for anyone who cared to read it – looked just like any other business office.

As she stood there uncertainly, a woman turned from her workstation. "Can I help you?"

Moss smiled, "Yes . . . sorry, I'm new. I have several things to look up."

The woman returned her smile and got to her feet, "Let's get you set up then." She looked Moss up and down. "You're X Division."

"Sorry?"

"X Division, dear . . . CID."

Moss felt as if she were back in secondary school, being questioned by one of her teachers. The bright-eyed woman was in her late fifties with a rosy face and tight perm, her ample figure clad in twin set and tartan skirt. All she needs is a strand of pearls and it could be Miss Fleming, thought Moss. The fact she'd called her 'dear' hadn't fazed her in the slightest; it even seemed natural. "Yes . . . I'm DS Moss, working with DCI Steel."

The woman gave this a wide smile. "Mike Steel . . . I *heard* Brian had moved on. How're you getting on with the History Man?"

"The history man?"

"Sorry dear . . . *one* of Mike's, how should I put it, qualities, is that he knows the history of, well, everything. Ask Mike any question on Edinburgh, or any crime in Edinburgh, odds on he'll have the answer," and with a laugh, "We could plug him in here." She turned to the terminal on the counter. "Name and current rank, dear?"

Now Moss felt she could be talking with one of her aunts. "Robin Moss. Detective Sergeant."

"Robin. That's a pretty name – born in December were you? Pleased to meet you . . . I'm Janet Tweedie and, for my sins, I head this lot." She tapped a few keys. "You're in luck; there's no other Moss in Lothian and Borders. Now, if I could see your warrant card . . ."

Moss handed it over and a few more keystrokes followed. "Right, you're now MossR2269X – that's the ID which shows on any searches you make – follow?"

"Straightforward. Do I need a pass code?"

"No dear, authorised personnel only, and that's you. And it doesn't matter about lower or upper case either," adding with a chuckle, "Some of your colleagues had to have that explained to them – thinking Sheriff Court and High Court – but I don't think that's you, somehow."

Moss grinned and shook her head.

Tweedie pulled out a sheet of paper. "I'll just fill this in for you and get your signature," and after some quick pen strokes she slid the sheet over the counter. "You've read, and fully understand, the DPA?" and without waiting for an answer as Moss signed, "Excellent. Now, what can we do for you?"

"Can I search Records myself?"

Tweedie smiled, "Of course you can dear . . . most ask us but we can't see what you can and we're not looking in the same way. It depends on what you're after, but you can do your own searches, fill out a requisition or simply phone us. We'll get to know you but some here *will* ask for your ID. The History Man, SteelM8513X, is one for phoning . . . the things I carry in my head."

Moss smiled at this, and could just imagine Steel's response to being known as a number. "I'm working on the murder of Lord Mitchell, so I need to look at the cases he sat on. After that, I need to look into a company, Priority Private Equity and, if I have time, two individuals by the name of McCann."

Tweedie shook her head. "Comfort yourself with knowing you'll be able to do the same to some poor DS or DC further down the line." She lifted the counter flap and with a "Follow me, Robin," took Moss through to two banks of computer terminals facing each other. "This is where you'll do all your record searches. You *can* search remotely but you'll need authorisation, or be one of the brass, for that.

"Now," and she moved the mouse so that the Lothian and Borders logo on the screen disappeared to reveal an authentication panel, "if you type in your ID . . ." And when Moss complied, a very uncluttered desktop appeared.

"These," continued Tweedie, pointing to the icons, "the Police National Computer, and the Procurator Fiscal's database are the ones you'll use most, although you might have need of SCD, the Scottish Courts Database, and NDNAD, the DNA database too. We have HOLMES for serious crimes and the Lothian and Borders database but that's been superseded by the PNC, so it's just a matter of time before it's removed."

"I've used the PNC before, though it's been quite a while."

"Well, there's been several recent updates, and we have the latest. All UK Police Forces are now linked together transparently, and it links with the SIS too," and to Moss's blank look, "the Schengen Information System – that's the Europe-wide database, and there's plans to link the whole bloody lot to the Americans' NCIC too." Moss smiled at her mild oath. "On top of all that, should you need it, you can hook directly from here into Interpol's I-24/7 encrypted communications system.

"Now, although you can access the Scottish Courts Database, we don't have details of a judge's work; their notes – they're with the Lord Advocate's Office and they get on their high horse whenever we ask – but, what with our work and the Procurator Fiscal's, you'll not be missing much. Just be warned this area is ninety-nine percent not a hundred. Now, what else was it?"

"A company called Priority Private Equity."

"You have any names to go with that?"

"Alan Prior goes with Priority Private Equity . . ."

Tweedie smiled. "Wait until you see the wildcarding we can do. If an individual's had as much as a traffic stop – if they've come to our, or any other Force's attention, in *any* way – we've got them."

She tapped in Priority Private Equity for Moss and within seconds a pane with two underlined links, Priority Private Equity_PPE and Alan Prior, appeared on the screen. Moss was about to ask Tweedie to follow the business link when the pane started to fill up with entries: AP Developments; AP Financial; AP Global Portfolio; AP Properties; Priority Developments; Priority Entertainment; Priority Financing, Priority Properties.

"Heavens."

Pleased to show off her department's abilities, Tweedie gave her a broad smile. "The link on the name means the person's either got a record, criminal or otherwise; has criminal associates, or has been suspected of criminal activity . . . you need to burrow."

"And the company links?"

"That means Alan Prior has, in some way, links to them all."

"But we only had him linked to Priority Private Equity."

"Where did you get *that* information dear?" Tweedie asked softly.

"DCI Steel phoned . . . I think it was someone called George."

Tweedie shook her head. "Both of them are old school; they think they can do it off the cuff. This," gesturing at the screen, "shows how wrong both of them are. I'll have words with George – he was probably working off the old Lothian and Borders database because he's used it for *ever*.

"Anyhow," she continued brightly, "you've got the hang of it. Just keep clicking away and, if you run into any roadblocks, well, I'm just over there."

Moss thanked her and clicked her first link.

•

Steel had left Fettes and headed north to Ferry Road, turning left towards

Barnton. It wasn't the smartest way to get to the *Scotsman* but he felt it was better, avoiding the traffic in the heart of the city as long as he could and giving him time to order his thoughts.

At the far end of Davidson's Mains – the Muttonhole, one of the many villages which Edinburgh had gradually swallowed – he reached a t-junction. To his right, the murder scene was less than a mile away. He turned left to skirt Corstorphine Hill and drive through Ravelston, aiming to hit the city at its west end near Haymarket; no doubt there would be plenty traffic there to slow him down.

When he called William Ritchie, the *Scotsman*'s news editor, Ritchie had said, "I was kind of expecting your call Mike. You know where we are."

"Top of North Bridge, right?"

Ritchie had laughed; the paper had moved to a new custom-built building in Holyrood Road, very close to the site where the new Scottish Parliament was being built. "Different paper, Mike."

"Certainly smaller, Bill."

Gunning the car to overtake slower vehicles in Ravelston he surfaced on Palmerston Place and was stopped in a line of traffic beside St. Mary's Cathedral. His ex-wife had cajoled him into Sunday visits there, her religion being the reason. It had been quite some time, but he thought he'd visit this coming Sunday – it was walking distance – and the Cathedral Choir was *his* reason. Ever since Richard Holloway, the "controversial" Bishop of Edinburgh, had spoken of retirement – was he falling or being pushed? – nothing of the religious side had touched him. It never had. And, although Holloway could be listened to on any day, it had always been the choir that had drawn him; exquisite voices shimmering and soaring in the great space, taking him where no words could. Especially words on the invisible.

Crossing the end of Torphichen Street, he glimpsed West End Police Station. A lifetime ago he'd spent some time working out of there, learning a lot of what was not formally taught, before climbing the rungs to end up in Fettes. He thought of Moss, wondering whether she would learn as much by coming straight to headquarters. Despite her experience in Liverpool, perhaps it would be a loss to miss learning Edinburgh's ways at the sharp shoulder of older hands, working out of a busy sub-station and tasting the darker rhythm of Edinburgh crime. Then again, cleverer heads than his thought differently, although he doubted whether any of them had done any real policing.

Soon he'd crossed the head of Lothian Road and descended past West Port, with its strip bars and lap dancing clubs, the so-called Pubic Triangle, and into the Grassmarket. It was gentrified there now; no more hostels for 'working men' and no more, "have you got the price of a cup of tea on you, son?" Ahead lay the narrow canyon of the Cowgate, still a ramshackle street which passed under George IV Bridge, no doubt next on developers' lists, and on into Holyrood Road where development was at full tilt.

Here, home of the new *Scotsman* offices, the run-down tenements for brewery workers and attendant warehouses – in what had always been a poverty stricken quarter – had been all but obliterated. The new Scottish Parliament Building, which would stand on ground profitably relinquished by a brewery, would be at the far end of the street, boldly challenging the old Palace of Holyroodhouse opposite – centuries apart but both dealing in power.

Every part of this street, just one segment of Edinburgh's latest New Town, seemed to be in development, and any lingering sign of poverty had been swept into hiding behind the city's ever-present genteel face.

Arriving at the *Scotsman*, he pushed through the revolving door, and, showing his warrant card to a security guard, asked for Bill Ritchie.

"Top floor sir," and pointing him to the lifts, "I'll let him know you're on your way."

Stepping from the lift Steel looked round; the building was safe-modern, all contemporary metal curves and glass. And, with the building's central area being an atrium, he could see no more than the outer edges of the lower floors and only a few of the workers in the hive. It's more like a corporate office than a newspaper, he thought, there's no character, no *noise*, although the wall of glass at the far end did give a stunning view of Salisbury Crags in the Queen's Park.

"You like it Mike?" Ritchie was walking towards him with his hand outstretched.

Steel shook his hand and smiled, "I feel I should be asking about my insurance policies or finding out about a loan, Bill."

Shirt-sleeved, Ritchie was a small, completely bald, man in his fifties, all tight energy contained in a neat frame and a lifetime in newspapers. He laughed, "It's a good move for us."

"Us, as in the owners, or the unions?"

"Now, now, keep your left-wing nonsense to yourself – the world's moved on, we're one big happy family here."

"Aye, *right*." Steel shook his head, "Do you not miss that vibration in the building with the presses running?" He looked about him. "Everything's changed," and as he caught sight of them again, "everything but the Crags anyhow."

Ritchie smiled. "You're getting old. It's adapt or die."

"You've been on a course," and turning to the matter in hand, "Today's front page Bill."

"Yes, come through," and Ritchie led him to his office. Sitting down behind a desk strewn with papers, he picked up the phone. "JJ? Chief Inspector Steel's here. Give us five and come up please."

He hung up with slow deliberation and looked across at Steel. "She wrote a good piece Mike. Left everyone else standing. We like that."

"She wrote, 'sources within Lothian and Borders Police confirmed the murder had a sexual aspect'. That makes it an inaccurate piece."

"Come on Mike, you know how these things are . . . we took a flyer on that but I'm told you more or less confirmed it."

"It's the more or less being less – I didn't *say* there was a sex angle to the murder."

"But she was right wasn't she," and Ritchie leaned back in his chair, "why else would you be here? You would've just ignored us. I trust my scribes – well, most of them – and she's proving to be a good addition." He gave Steel a warning look. "Before he was murdered we were about to run a piece on Mitchell anyhow. It was solid."

"That's as may be, but this is a murder enquiry Bill, and any information she has – you have . . . well, is it reliable?"

"You could take it to the bank and, as I said, we were running with it. We *will* back her and we're standing behind every word."

Steel nodded, knowing legal at the paper would've wanted every last word, every last punctuation mark, verified before giving a green light; after all, the man had been a High Court judge – best they didn't lose the paper over a story. Now of course . . . well, the dead couldn't be libelled. "What can you tell me of Jay Johnstone . . . JJ?"

"She's got pedigree Mike. She started here as a freelance, years ago, then worked quite some time with the heavyweights in London and did a stint as a stringer for *The Washington Post*. Frankly, if she'd wanted to she could've stayed in London, earned more."

"And?" Steel let the word hang.

Ritchie shrugged, "She wanted to be in Edinburgh," and he caught movement across the glass at the door. "That'll be her now."

Steel got to his feet and turned towards JJ as she entered. Today, she was wearing a stylish dark green suit over a paler green blouse, her long red hair pulled back into a ponytail, fully revealing her face. High cheekbones. Minimal make-up. A strong face, filled with purpose. If he were still a betting man, he would've laid a wager she was the most beautiful woman he'd ever met.

SIX

MOSS WORKED METHODICALLY through all the entries with Prior's name against them, making notes and hitting print whenever necessary. She didn't know Alan Prior, yet, but could already see a weakness there that might prove useful: his ego bled over every entry. Not for him the business anonymity of something like Edinburgh Finance as a company name – he had to have *his* name, or *his* initials, on every entity. Making a mental note not to be misled – the personalised naming could be a blind – she had turned to Lord Mitchell's past cases.

Steel had asked her to find out who had been released over the past year only, and that was just as well; Lord Mitchell had presided over the busiest of Edinburgh's criminal courts. Limiting her search to a tie-in of the Procurator Fiscal's database with the PNC, she started by wildcarding 'Mitchell' with 'release' and was immediately presented with an unmanageable list. She saw case after case come up on screen before hitting Escape and asking Janet Tweedie for help.

"Just give me five minutes dear."

As she waited, Moss pondered the odd term Procurator Fiscal, and reminded herself she still had to pass an exam on Scots Law, something all police officers had to do when transferring from any outside Force. Until now her knowledge had been limited to the Director of Public

Prosecutions and the laws of England and Wales, and as she rolled the word procurator around, she knew she had much to learn about Scotland. Idly, she hoped Mike Steel, the History Man, would be a guide to much of it.

Tweedie arrived, looked over her shoulder and pointed out her error immediately. "When you have a criminal judge's name, the word release is going to come up each and every time, dear. Isn't it?"

Moss sighed and felt herself colouring. "I'm sorry Janet, that's so obvious. Is there a way past that?"

"Yes, of course." She looked at Moss and recognised in her the desire to excel in all she did, even in areas like this. "Look, let me do this for you. You want everyone from Lord Mitchell's court who was released in the past year?" and getting a nod, "Okay, take a break . . . go get a coffee or whatever, I'll have this done in no time."

Thanking Tweedie, Moss got to her feet and stretched, feeling the eye-strain from staring at a computer screen for too long.

She avoided the lift and took the stairs quickly, pumping her heart, trying to shake off the stale drudgery of Records. Police-work was filled with this – jigsaws, as Steel had called them – little strange-shaped pieces of information which would build into . . . what? Hopefully, a solid picture that led somewhere. From the little experience she'd had, she knew that often it wasn't until the picture was there, and complete, before everyone could see it led nowhere except back to square one.

She found herself smiling, wondering how Steel was getting on at the *Scotsman* with JJ; he was rather obviously taken with the reporter, despite all his protestations about her irresponsibility and inaccuracies.

She had just got a coffee, and was scanning the room for an empty seat, when she heard her name being called over the intercom: *DS Moss contact extension eight three one immediately.*

She found an internal phone and dialled.

"It's Janet, Robin. You'd better get down here."

When Moss arrived minutes later, Tweedie looked up from the terminal. "Look."

Moss peered at the screen. In a very long list of names, one – Kenneth George McVicar – was high-lit and flashing red. "What's that one, Janet?"

"I got you a list of everyone released over the last year, and then went sideways . . . this McVicar wasn't released – he's an escapee."

•

"Now *that* – as you bloody well know – is not on Mike," Ritchie said sharply. Steel was probing for the actual source of JJ's 'vice ring connection' to Lord Mitchell. "No journalist can be made to reveal a source."

"She can be charged with obstructing a police enquiry – a murder enquiry at that."

"I *am* in the room, Chief Inspector," JJ said softly. She glanced at Ritchie. "I think – that is, if my source is willing – you may be able to interview her. I can't say for certain but with Lord Mitchell dead the game plan's been skewed. But, fair warning, it took some effort on my part to get them talking in the first place – I'm sure there's more than a few who'll be less than pleased that any of this has come out."

She crossed her legs, distracting Steel.

"Look," she said, "I've apologised for yesterday at the press conference . . . I – we," including Ritchie with a nod, "had our story anyhow – today's words were just topped off with a good headline, that's all." She leaned towards him and Steel caught the faintest trace of perfume; expensive, no doubt. "It was a cheap shot Chief Inspector . . . Mike. I'd rather not let it become a thing between us," and she gave him a dazzling smile, "Agreed?"

Steel nodded, "Agreed, but I'm trying to catch a murderer; any information you have is information I *need*." He knew they had a different agenda – caught or on the loose, murderers sold newspapers.

JJ sat back and the hem of her skirt inched back with her. Steel found *nice legs* running through his head. "I can apologise once again, but that's repetitive," and, with a smile, "I do try not to be repetitious in *anything* I do."

Watching their interchange, Ritchie cleared his throat. "Perhaps I could give you some background, Mike . . . JJ's been working on a specific story concerning vice in Edinburgh. Mitchell's name came up and she interviewed him. We have more to print . . . well, JJ and I have to talk but, provided her source is willing, I think it will be in *everyone's* interest if you're involved."

He moved a pencil and a sheet of paper on his desk needlessly, then looked up at Steel. "I'm *hoping* for . . . well, some sort of . . ."

"*Quid pro quo*, Mike," JJ completed lightly.

Steel sat back. They made a fine double act, and had obviously been discussing this very meeting before he'd even left Fettes. He knew how close journalists and the police could be and, from time to time, he'd used that closeness himself. "There are lines," he said, "I don't want them blurred."

"Of course," said Ritchie, and JJ gave a faint smile.

"So, tell me more, JJ."

She raised her eyebrows at Ritchie, who gave her a slight nod. "As Bill said, Mike, I've been working on this story for some time now. High placed vice, for want of a better phrase. That high place is a cross-section of Edinburgh's . . . well, ruling class: judges, lawyers, politicians and businessmen of various stripes. A cabal to be found in the city's top drawer. Their tastes are being fed by some shady figures and as I dug further, interviewed more people, Mitchell's name came up."

"You got his name from your source?"

"Yes, both directly and indirectly."

"How so, both?"

JJ received a tilt of the head from Ritchie. "Well, directly from my source, an escort, who's been to Barnton several times, and indirectly through a friend – a colleague – of my source," and seeing Steel's querying look, "You know how vice is in this city Mike – all the strata, from women on the street, up. My source knows a woman who manages a sauna and knew of Mitchell's use of escorts. But there appears to be an uglier edge to this."

"Uglier?"

JJ gave him a grim smile. "Look, we're all adult here . . . if people want to use escorts, well then, so be it," adding in a harsher tone, "Bloody hypocritical if you're a judge though."

"Again – uglier, meaning what?"

She paused, then let out a sigh. "What I've found is there's a taste for under-age girls *and* boys in Edinburgh. More correctly, a taste in certain circles within Edinburgh."

Steel sat back. There was no crime in using escorts – certainly foolish behaviour if you were a judge – but paedophilia was something else entirely; however, the thought that Ritchie and JJ saw a story with legs in their 'certain circles' involving children really turned his stomach. He was about to say so when his phone chirruped: an incoming text. He glanced at it and felt a hot pulse run through him. Keeping his voice even, he said, "I *need* to speak with your source JJ."

"I'll work on it Mike. We feel there's a *very* big story here."

Steel gave her a small smile. "Well, let's see . . . we have a murdered High Court judge who used an escort service – though I'll not say that warrants your 'vice ring'; you've mentioned the involvement of what you call shady characters – although you don't name them; and there's a possibility – possibility – of an organised group of paedophiles in, what *you* call, high places. I can see that you *would* call it a very big story. *But*," and he shrugged, "Well, the point is, apart from the murder, all I've got is your ideas on the rest. I work on fact. Speak with your source JJ – I want to interview them as soon as I can. As to the rest, as long as nothing's kept from us, I see no harm in having close contact with you."

She smiled, her green eyes narrowing. "None at all Mike."

Basking in the warmth of her smile, Steel almost missed a look behind it – a harder edge, something like that of a committed zealot. He rose to his feet, "I need to get back to Fettes."

He leaned in to shake Ritchie's hand, then gave his card to JJ. "Get in touch soonest. If there's something – anything – under-age endemic here, we'll stamp on it from a very great height, no matter *what* circle's involved."

Waiting for the lift to arrive, he pulled out his phone and read the text message again. It was from Moss – a simple message: *I think I've found the killer.*

●

Steel called Moss as soon as he was in his car. "What have you got?"

"A name sir . . . and he fits. He really fits."

"Right, save the details, I'm leaving the *Scotsman* now – I'll be with you shortly." He knew Moss would be pleased; if no arrest had been made at the *locus*, then seventy-two hours was all they had before the crime stood a real chance of slipping away from them. "Well done, Moss."

"Thanks sir . . . I got help." She heard his car starting. "How did it go with JJ?"

"I think we'll get to speak with her source. *Apparently* it ties in with another thread she's been working on, one we're going to follow up – crime in Edinburgh's high society."

"*Really?*"

"Don't get too excited. This is a story which does the rounds here every once in a while; a secretive inner group of Babylonians who run Edinburgh and who're up to no good, while we ordinary souls feed the machine, all for the privilege of keeping them in luxury. Mainly, if you listen to all that nonsense, pretty soon you'll feel you're falling down the rabbit hole. Remember, crime's fact, not fiction. I'll talk with you later," and she heard the line go dead.

Moss hung up; Steel had said mainly . . . She readied herself for his return by gathering her print-outs and notes together and re-reading everything.

Separating the pictures from the file, she looked again at Kenneth McVicar, Linda Croal, McVicar's common-law wife, and Malcolm, their eight year-old son; McVicar didn't just look evil, he *was* evil and, for the past seven days, evil had been on the loose.

Five years previously, McVicar had returned home, home being a high-rise flat in Pollock, Glasgow. As far as could be made out, he had spent the day taking all manner of drugs, enhancing their effects with trips to the local bar. When he reached home he had heard, so he said, Uriel whispering in his ear *Your wife and son are in league with the Devil and plotting to kill you.* When Strathclyde Police had smashed in the door – a neighbour alerting them to "horrible screams" – they discovered the naked bodies of mother and child, both dreadfully mutilated, and McVicar sitting calmly in a chair watching television with the sound off.

In one hand, McVicar held a full and untouched glass of water, in the other, a sharp and bloody chisel. Both the mother's and child's bodies were covered with multiple stab wounds and had been precisely scored with arcane symbols.

McVicar had appeared in a lower court from where he was remanded for psychiatric reports and, at the secure unit in the Royal Edinburgh Hospital, he'd been diagnosed as a paranoid schizophrenic. Later, in Lord Mitchell's court, he'd been found unfit to plead and sentenced to life imprisonment at The State Hospital, Carstairs; two deaths forgotten, and society safe from a very disturbed and dangerous individual – except it hadn't worked out that way.

Moss had never heard of either The State Hospital or Carstairs but it sounded like Broadmoor – a high security prison for the criminally insane. She knew those were the wrong terms, old-fashioned terms – inmates were patients and prison was hospital – but to her, reading the file and looking at the pictures, McVicar wasn't just insane, he was living, breathing, evil – the sort that *needed* locking up. Forever.

She was waiting for Strathclyde Police to fax through their report on McVicar's escape; with Steel not being at hand she hadn't mentioned the murder of Lord Mitchell.

•

Using every shortcut he knew, Steel made good time getting back to Fettes despite Edinburgh's traffic and having to negotiate another light fall of snow. As he walked in Moss was still poring over her notes. "Right, tell me what you've got."

She handed him the file. "Kenneth George McVicar. Age forty-four. Five years ago he murdered his wife and child. He was found unfit to plead and sentenced by Mitchell to life imprisonment in The State Hospital. He *was* there until a week ago, then he escaped . . . I'm waiting for Strathclyde to fax me their report on that."

"He *escaped* from Carstairs?" Unlike Moss, Steel knew the hospital and just how secure it was. "You sure he's our man?"

"Yes sir . . . look at the pictures."

Steel picked them up. He knew it wasn't the Job that hardened him, but there was always something that created a barrier – something which somehow allowed him to look at horror directly and be unaffected. At least, at the time. Sometimes these images would visit at night. It was then questions of what sort of world he lived in, and what sort of person he'd become by direct contact with it, would seep in.

51

He placed photographs of the mother and child side by side. "These symbols are giving you the connection?"

"Yes. I mean, I know we haven't worked out the scores on Lord Mitchell's chest yet, but they were quite deliberate. They were made with a chisel, same as McVicar used in Glasgow, and he was sentenced by Lord Mitchell."

Steel sat back, giving this some thought. "Would he have known?"

"Who? McVicar?"

"Yes . . . unfit to plead normally means there's representation in court while McVicar himself would've been snugly tucked-in elsewhere. Would he have known it was Mitchell?"

"The murder itself, the chisel, the symbols, Lord Mitchell," she pressed, "Everything points to an insane McVicar."

Steel nodded, "It would appear to. And you're waiting on a fax from Strathclyde?"

"Yes."

"Those jokers in Glasgow will take their time; we'll need to visit. I've no idea how *anyone* could get out of Carstairs . . . give the hospital a call and set something up. What about Priority Private Equity?"

Moss filled him in, passing over the awkward fact his original search on Prior's company had been less than thorough, although the print-outs clearly showed that. He skimmed through the sheets. "Why so many companies?"

"Protecting one against the rest perhaps. Tax reasons? We should really speak with Finance."

Steel was silent, then pushed the sheets and photographs away. "Well, until we visit Carstairs we're idle." He thought for a few seconds. "Let's take a trip to Fife."

"Fife?"

"Yes, we need to pin down Lady Mitchell on those times of hers."

"Seriously? You don't think McVicar's our man?"

He shook his head. "No, Moss, I'm not saying that. But according to the Fife cops, Lady Mitchell left her daughter in Crail before six in the morning. Which, given how quiet the road would be, and even if she's a cautious driver, puts her in Edinburgh a good hour before her eight

52

o'clock – perhaps a good *two* hours before the treble nine."

He looked at Moss, seeing something like disappointment cross her face. "McVicar probably *is* our man – he fits pretty well. You did good work . . . it's just I don't like someone – whoever they are – trying to mislead me. I want to get to the bottom of why she lied, and that's on my desk until I know. What d'you suggest . . . I should throw it in the bin because Lady Mitchell seems less likely to be our murderer?"

Chastened, Moss said, "No, sir. Of course not."

Steel stood. "Right, make the call to Carstairs, ask for the head of security, or whatever, and we can set off for Fife – it's pretty where we're going, you'll like it. On our way I'll fill you in on my meeting with Bill Ritchie and JJ. We'll watch how it goes, but there'll be some sharing of information."

It was then, knowing he couldn't really talk to Moss about JJ, that he missed Brian.

SEVEN

AS THEY CROSSED THE FORTH ROAD BRIDGE heading north, Moss took in the latticed ironwork of the three great red spans of the rail bridge downriver to their right. "That's simply beautiful."

Steel gave her a glance, "It's one of the World's wonders, Moss. Almost five thousand workers – briggers – took seven years to build it . . . fifty-seven lives were lost, though it's meant to be nearer a hundred."

Moss smiled at this: Tweedie's History Man.

"A fourteen year-old died," Steel continued, "He fell at the feet of his father, working below. *Imagine* that," shaking his head, "There's never a time I see it that I'm not impressed – awed by it – it's bold, confident Scottish engineering at its very best."

They continued north on the M90 in silence, then veered east on the A92 heading for Crail. Watching the countryside roll past, Moss said, "What do people do here, sir? Farming?"

"Uh huh . . . and there's *some* fishing. Trouble is, a lot of housing's been taken over by commuters – that, or for second homes. Upshot is, the locals can't compete on prices, so houses get sold to rich people, the likes of the Mitchells, and people whose families have lived here for generations – they leave." And Steel reflected on how there were all sorts of crimes; for him, the way people had been steadily robbed over the years of their ability to simply continue living where they'd been brought up, was one.

They arrived in Crail which, with its dainty pocket-sized harbour, cobbled streets and seventeenth to early nineteenth century housing, felt to Moss like dropping into a picture postcard. Easily finding Lady Mitchell's address they got out of the car, but before they could reach her door it was wrenched open by an angry young woman. "I've bloody-well had it up to here with you lot. Go away or I shall call the police."

Steel presented his warrant card. "We *are* the police, madam. I am Detective Chief Inspector Steel and this is Detective Sergeant Moss."

The plain heavy-set woman was in her forties, barefoot, wearing jeans and a cream cable-knit sweater, her shock of long dark hair wildly tousled, as if she'd just woken up. Hearing Steel, she blushed and, pushing her hair away from her face, peered at his card. "Actually, is that valid here, Chief Inspector?"

Steel gave this a mirthless smile. "Think of it like your Visa card – it's valid everywhere. I take it you are Lady Mitchell's daughter?"

"Yes. Antonia. Sorry, I thought you were the press," and she leant out to look up and down the empty street, "My mother's been bothered by them."

"A call to Fife Constabulary would fix that . . . I'd like to speak with Lady Mitchell."

She hesitated. "Well, come in. But I'll warn you, mother's very tired."

Steel shook his head, "This won't take long – only a couple of questions."

They were shown into a cramped living room, with furniture which seemed to fill every inch of floor space. Taking up what wall space there was were framed, amateurish, oil paintings: landscapes of a romantic, non-existent, never existing, Fife. Steel guessed the furniture would be overspill from Barnton, and the paintings the work of Lady Mitchell's daughter.

Lady Mitchell was standing to one side and, with a curt nod to Steel, she held out the telephone receiver, "This is for you Chief Inspector."

"For me?" Nobody knew he and Moss were there. He took the receiver from her. "Hello?"

"Chief Inspector Steel?" A slow, languorous voice, and Steel heard the unmistakable tone of an Edinburgh public school accent dripping innate

56

superiority – someone bred to presume his station in life meant others would always listen to him. "This is William McKnight of Smith McKnight Hughes – Lady Mitchell's solicitors."

"Yes, and . . . ?" Steel didn't like this one bit.

"I must insist that you have no contact with my client at this time, Chief Inspector."

"Insist? I am conducting a murder enquiry."

"Nevertheless, I *do* insist you do not question my client without my being present."

Steel could feel his temper rising, and was doing his best to rein it in. "I could insist myself, Mr. McKnight – we could formally interview your client at Police Headquarters."

"A word to the wise, Chief Inspector – that would be extremely rash of you, and I would not advise it. As to 'formally', *should* you wish to question my client, then you shall contact me and I will set an appointment. Any such appointment would *not* be at Fettes but here, in our offices. However – at *this* time – Lady Mitchell is not to be further upset and that is an end on it."

Steel was in two minds; he could simply ignore the man, taking the consequences, although now Lady Mitchell would no doubt be as tight as a Fife clam, or he could back off. He wanted to get to the bottom of those timings she'd given, but decided to retreat. "Very well, Mr. McKnight, I'll speak with you later."

Ignoring Lady Mitchell's daughter, who had one hand on her ample hip and the other out for the receiver, he hung up. He turned to Lady Mitchell, "We *shall* talk," and to Moss, "Let's go."

On the drive back to Edinburgh, Steel was silently seething, drumming his fingers on the steering wheel; then his mobile rang. He stabbed a button on the dash, "Steel."

"Just what the *hell* are you playing at Steel?" Even with the disembodied sound from the hands-free, Moss recognised Chief Superintendent Grieve's voice and heard fury.

"Sir?"

"I tell you to tread gently, I tell you I didn't want your heavy footfalls, and what do I get? You swanning off to Fife, barging in and upsetting

Lord Mitchell's widow, of all people."

Steel glanced at his wristwatch – they'd left Crail less than ten minutes previously; the phone lines must have been humming. "Upsetting? I barely spoke with her."

Grieve ignored this. "And I have to field a call from the Chief Constable – the *Chief Constable*, Steel – who's asking me if I know what my officers are doing. Know what? I couldn't tell him, and you know how that makes me look, eh?

"Foolish sir?"

"For Christ's sake, are you *trying* to annoy me? Not damn-well foolish – inept, man. *Inept.* I want you in my office as soon as you're back. You need to be on track."

Steel tried to say, "She lied to us," but the line was dead.

Moss, not knowing what to say, stayed silent. After a few moments Steel glanced at her. "At least you got your first view of the bridge Moss. And, you got to see Edinburgh's politics at work up close. *One* aspect of them anyhow."

They drove a few more miles in silence and then, with a shake of his head, Steel said, "She lied, and I don't like people who lie to me . . . whatever their reason . . . whoever they are. Despite McVicar, I'm not finished with Lady Mitchell."

•

Steel and Moss arrived back at Fettes to find Grieve fussing with the plant on his window ledge, his large hands delicately plucking out dead leaves and drizzling some water from a plastic cup on to the earth. Looking at it closely, he seemed satisfied and turned to them, "Well, sit down then." He'd obviously allowed his anger to vent on the phone.

When they'd settled he took his seat and, for a few quiet seconds, looked from one to the other. Leaning forward, he latched on to Moss first. "Being new, you have an excuse Sergeant. Although," and he picked his words, "well, you're part of a team here – I like team players – and, despite the difference in rank, your input is expected." He sat back. "Expected, Moss – you've got to speak up if you think the senior officer's going walkabout, eh?" This got a grunt from Steel. "*You* have a long career ahead of you . . . input and being a team player will take you far."

He turned to Steel. "As for you, Mike. What were you thinking? You know better and, as SIO, I *expect* better of you. Lady Mitchell is the widow of a High Court judge. A bloody *recent* widow, which seems to have slipped your mind. Christ man, you know the score . . . these are not the people we *lean* on, these are people who have the number of the Chief Constable's direct line – we stroke them."

Steel didn't appreciate being treated like a schoolboy, caught in some minor breach of school rules. Whoever and whatever Lady Mitchell was, she pulled her knickers on, one leg at a time, same as any other woman. "I *wasn't* leaning on Mitchell. She lied to us," he said flatly.

Grieve's eyebrows shot up. "Lied? How so?"

Steel took him through her timings, the confirmation by Fife Constabulary, and the calls she had made before making the treble nine.

Grieve sat back, his thick fingers interlocked over his ample belly, and absorbed this. "Well, you were right Mike," then looking at him through narrowed eyes, "you just went about it the wrong bloody way – one that got the CC on *my* back."

"We need to speak with her lawyers to set up an interview. She *has* lied to us though, and I want to know why. But," and with a glance at Moss, "there's a development which points in another direction entirely."

Grieve rocked himself forward. "What development?"

"Moss uncovered it."

Grieve turned to her, "Well then? Speak up Moss. For God's sake, I'm *meant* to be kept up to speed."

She laid out Janet Tweedie's help in searching through Lord Mitchell's past cases, the discovery of McVicar being an escapee from Carstairs, and ended with, "He appears to fit the bill, sir."

"I'll say, and very nicely too" said Grieve, buoyed now by knowing he had something to take to the Chief Constable.

Watching the dog chase the hare, Steel put in, "We're going to Carstairs tomorrow, early doors. I want to see whether there's anything he left behind that might suggest why he'd surface in Edinburgh rather than Glasgow. He *is* from Pollock." There was something niggling him about McVicar; he still seemed *too* much like a good fit for him. Despite everything, and especially considering the lie from the widow, he was a jigsaw piece with a very simple shape. If they ran with McVicar then Lady Mitchell's lie would be forgotten and that didn't sit well with him. He made a mental calculation: McVicar was more than enough for Grieve to sink his teeth into and take upstairs. For the moment, he'd keep quiet about his conversation with Bill Ritchie and JJ.

Grieve was much happier now. "Well done, Moss," and rounding on Steel, "See Methodical, that's what, and no bloody reason to go nosing around in Fife. You keep me up to speed on this McVicar, Mike – just as soon as you get back."

"I have an appointment tomorrow afternoon . . . the doctor."

"Doctor?" and then he caught Steel's meaning. "Ah, yes. Well I'm sure Sergeant Moss here," with a snappy smile towards her, "will be able to fill me in." He looked from one to the other, "Right then, off with you . . . and Moss, I'll expect a full briefing on McVicar from you – something to take to the Chief and keep him happy."

When they were back in their own office, Steel flopped into his chair. "And people wonder why I'm happy as a DCI – I couldn't be doing with all the politicking Bob Grieve has to do."

She could see Steel's anger was still smouldering. "Is the Chief Constable a friend of the Mitchells then?"

"He certainly moves in that social strata; sometimes it seems we're personal coppers for the bosses – a Praetorian Guard. There's those who have no voice, and then there's those who can instantly call on the likes of a Mister William McKnight and speak directly to the Chief." He shook his head at her, "See what's ahead of you? Anyhow, hopefully tomorrow, we'll see whether McVicar can be offered up as prime suspect. If so, watch and see Chief Constable, Sir David bloody Thompson, break the news – it won't be me."

Like the nudge of an old habit, he knew that it was at this time he and Brian would've headed for a pub to compare notes and bitch about their lot. "What are you doing this evening?"

"Taking Susan, my flatmate, to an aikido class," and with a grin, "throw her around and loosen her up a bit; her body's like concrete."

Steel had no answer to this; his DS wasn't just a different species, she was an entirely new breed to him. "Right, I'll see you tomorrow then.

Carstairs is about an hour away; let's hope when we get there we'll find something concrete to give Grieve."

EIGHT

THE EARLY MORNING RUSH HOUR TRAFFIC was creeping bumper to bumper into the city like a disjointed metal snake as Steel and Moss headed out of Edinburgh. Moss watched a car try to inch into a bus lane and duck back into line as a bus came up behind it, the driver leaning on his horn; this was the work before work, she mused.

Convinced McVicar was their man, she turned to Steel. "What do you hope to find at Carstairs, sir?"

"Something to persuade me on McVicar."

"You're still not?" failing to keep surprise from her voice.

He gave her a small smile. "Most escapees are found close to home Moss . . . my niggle is: Why has he surfaced in Edinburgh and not Glasgow?"

"But look at his MO . . . the murder weapon, the symbols carved into the bodies – made post mortem – that alone would make him a highly likely suspect. Add to that, his victim was Lord Mitchell, his sentencing judge," and her voice rose, "I really don't think it matters he's not from here."

They were stuck in roadworks that made Fountainbridge one lane, and the temporary lights were working fitfully. Steel glanced and saw her passionate certainty. Wanting to impress on her that in a murder inquiry there could never be shades of grey, he said, "Every part matters Moss. Right now, the chisel's only circumstantial and, remember, there were no symbols carved on Mitchell's body. If McVicar fits, I want him to fit perfectly and not have to be shaving off edges to *make* him fit. He is, or he's not, Mitchell's killer; let's not make him fit the murder, let's discover the facts that *show* us that."

As the lights allowed another two cars through and they edged forward, he saw her nod her head; she still wasn't convinced. Looking out at the snowy street he said, "This is where Sean Connery was brought up you know."

"Really?" One of her favourite films was *Entrapment*, a clever caper starring Connery with the striking Catherine Zeta Jones.

"Well," gesturing at the new buildings around them, "before all this, when it was just tenements for workers in the brewery and the rubber mill." He thought of Big Tam and how he'd translated his life but seemed to have kept himself true to the tight working class family upbringing he'd experienced here. "Yes, he came back one time and didn't recognise the place; couldn't find his way around."

Close your eyes, he thought, and, whether subtly or radically, Edinburgh will have changed when you open them; the city anyhow, not the landscape – that was eternal.

"No matter *what* you're looking at Moss, every part matters . . . don't ignore bits because they don't suit your thinking. You're probably right about McVicar. I just want more . . . more than a similar MO anyhow."

Eventually they'd cleared the roadworks and made it to Lanark Road. Flashing through the old villages of Juniper Green and Currie, now absorbed, peripheral residential suburbs of Edinburgh, they took the road for Carnwath.

As she watched the openness of endless fields on either side and leaden skies passing overhead, Moss said, "I *hate* prisons."

"Hospital, Moss. We'll, no doubt, be reminded of that . . . best you don't call it a prison."

"But it is, isn't it?"

Steel smiled at her persistence. "No. Hospital. It just happens to be a secure hospital containing some very dangerous people who are mentally ill."

She pondered this, wondering where the line separating danger and mental illness lay and where it merged. Certainly, with McVicar, the line had disappeared. "Is it an old institution?"

Steel shook his head. "Institution's wrong too. It was started in the thirties, to house so-called criminal lunatics from Perth prison so, yes."

"And the changes?"

"Things can change in a heartbeat. You're not expecting something Dickensian, are you?"

Moss didn't know *what* to expect. She realised, like most, her understanding of psychiatry was an ill-formed shadow; the criminally insane – or, correctly, mentally disordered offenders – and where they were confined were a complete blank for her. "No, I meant, where did the change from prison to hospital happen?"

"Ah . . . well the place was completed by thirty-nine – just in time for the war, so the Army used it. They handed it back, and eventually it became a maximum security hospital. It took 'til just recently to have it on one site – the road, and the railway, used to split it in two – now there's talk of a rebuild. Modern, Moss, and I'm told, modern in forensic psychiatry too – don't expect *One Flew Over The Cuckoo's Nest*," thinking to himself, At least I hope not.

They reached a rainswept Carnwath and within a couple of miles, saw the first sign showing The State Hospital. Before long the hospital buildings appeared off to their right, standing back from the road on a low hill.

The morning sky had become a glowering of grey rainclouds driven by high winds and, for Moss, as she took in the forbidding old buildings surrounded by vast high perimeter fencing, it all seemed fitting: this *is* a prison not a hospital.

Steel caught her thinking. "It's got a nickname – the locals call it the Penny." Seeing her blank look, he laughed, "Penitentiary Moss, sharpen up," and he wondered whether there *were* any penitents there – any who were atoning for the life they had led. Navigating his way into the visitors' car park, he made sure the car was locked and they headed for the modern reception block.

When they entered, they were met, not so much by numbers of staff, but by the presence of several security staff in a state of alertness. A young short-haired female security guard, dressed in a uniform of navy trousers and v-neck jersey over a crisp open-necked white shirt, approached. "May I help you?"

Moss was reaching for her warrant card as Steel said, "Detective Chief Inspector Steel, Detective Sergeant Moss from Lothian and Borders Police to see the Director of Security."

She wasn't impressed. "Did you complete a Visitor Request Application?" and Moss had a definite sense of being in someone else's domain.

"No, our visit was only set up yesterday. The Director *is* expecting us."

Scanning a clipboard handed to her by one of her colleagues, she gave a little nod, then held out a laminated page to each of them. "Do either of you have any of these items with you? If so, please place them – with your warrant cards – in one of these trays," pointing to a stack on the edge of a large, very modern scanner similar to those used at airports.

Steel and Moss went down the long list of items forbidden to visitors – knives, blades, razors, knitting needles and explosives seemed obvious, but ladders? Moss resisted asking whether any visitor had tried as she and Steel began emptying their pockets of mobile phones and wallets with bank cards and driving licences.

"You've no hand luggage with you?" Steel shook his head. "Then follow me please," and she led them beyond the scanner, where a full-body metal detector stood.

As Steel went through, Moss looked about her, seeing the ceiling-mounted cameras concealed behind domed Perspex; here at least there was every sign of tight security. A ping sounded from her right and she saw the staff room where a microwave had finished its timing. She gave the heavy-set security guard behind the metal detector a slight smile which he returned with an impassive stare.

When she walked through the metal detector an alarm sounded. Beckoning her forward with her fingers, the female security guard said, "Arms out to your side please," and she swept over her body with a hand-held scanner. It started to beep when it reached the level of her jacket's inside pocket and the woman looked at her, raising an eyebrow.

"Sorry, a pen."

Holding out her hand, she said, "I'll take that," and with a tight smile, "Too easily a weapon, Detective."

As first time visitors they were both photographed for the Hospital's database, and a machine printed out a sticky-backed pass with their picture on it. The female security guard made direct eye contact. "This must be worn at all times and surrendered when you leave. Your personal belongings will be locked up safely."

They were each then handed a personal attack alarm and, as Moss hesitated, the guard said softly, "While you're here, your safety is a priority for us Miss."

Moss had been in prisons before, but nowhere like this and, given how difficult it was to get in, she could well understand Steel's incredulity that anyone could actually *escape* from here.

Silent, they waited on one side for the Director of Security. It was a short wait, and very soon he arrived with two of his very well-built staff.

The Director was a short stocky man in his late forties with close-cropped ginger hair and what seemed like a fixed look of belligerence on his face. Despite this, he seemed more like an office manager rather than someone whose job it was to oversee the security of some of the most dangerous people in Scotland. With a scowl he offered Steel his hand. "Joseph Devine, Director of Security. I understand you're here regarding McVicar."

"Yes Mr. Devine. This is DS Robin Moss."

Devine gave Moss a curt nod. "Aye, we spoke yesterday . . . let me take you through to our Chief Executive, Eve Andrews," and, apart from him asking whether this was their first visit to The State Hospital, they walked in silence.

In her fifties, the Chief Executive was smartly dressed in a dark pinstripe suit over a dazzling blue blouse. With minimal but skilful make-up and wearing her hair up, she had the air of a senior businesswoman. "Good morning Chief Inspector, Sergeant . . . I hope you've come with news of my patient."

Steel warmed to her directness. "We *may* have news of his whereabouts

Ms. Andrews."

"A qualified answer. Please, sit down. Joe, could you get us some coffee?" and she tilted her chin in query to Steel and Moss. Both shook their heads and, as Devine poured two cups from the coffee maker, she continued, "So, what's the qualification Chief Inspector?"

"There was a murder in Edinburgh . . . it appears to have some similarities to the murders McVicar was involved in."

"*Damn*," she said softly, and caught herself. "I'm sorry . . . I *had* hoped nothing would happen following McVicar's escape. Who?"

"Lord Mitchell – a High Court judge."

"Oh my God." She gave the shadow of a smile. "Well double damn then . . . the last time anyone actually escaped from here was way back in the seventies – well before my time – that ended in tragedy too." She brought herself back on track. "I read of the murder – what makes you think McVicar?"

"A similar *modus operandi* – chisel . . . carving to the body."

Andrews' mouth was a thin compressed line as she shook her head. "Ever since I arrived, I've worked hard – we've *all* worked hard – to dispel some of the myths which surround the Hospital . . . the 'mad axeman locked away forever' thing the media is so fond of." Ever so slightly her shoulders sagged. "Now, with McVicar's escape, his possible involvement in a murder of a judge, it's going to set us back immeasurably . . . some of our political masters have very old-fashioned ideas on mental health." For a moment she had a faraway look, then said briskly, "Well, enough of us – what can we do for you?"

"Given McVicar's from Glasgow," Steel said, "I want to try and pin down why he went to Edinburgh. Lord Mitchell was his sentencing judge in-"

"It's unlikely McVicar would've known that, Chief Inspector. He wouldn't've *been* in court when the judge imposed a CORO on him," and seeing their blank looks, "Sorry – a Compulsion and Restriction Order, necessary by the Act."

"*That's* my point Ms. Andrews," Steel said, "McVicar's MO may chime, but I'd like to have a sounder connection with Lord Mitchell."

"I see."

"I understand Strathclyde Police visited. Did they, or, have you, discovered how McVicar escaped?"

"Aye," Devine put in, "Strathclyde Police visited right enough," his Glaswegian accent broadening, "But they didn't do anything *we* didn't do, and they didn't find out any more than *we* already knew."

Moss sat forward. "And *have* you discovered how he escaped?"

Devine puffed out his cheeks, then let his breath out with an exasperated rush. "You may as well say he walked through the wall; we can't find out how. At all."

Steel turned to him. "Considering Carstairs' security, that would be something of a mystery then."

Andrews nodded at this. "Mystery is the correct word. You have to understand that, currently, we have one hundred and thirty-nine patients in our care, but the usual ratio is flipped here – our staff to patient ratio is near enough three to one. We pride ourselves in knowing what each and every patient is doing, every minute of the day."

"But he's not here," said Steel. "Was there anything – anything at all – which even gave you a hint of him planning an escape?"

Andrews brought her fingers up to her head and very lightly stroked her temple. "A hint? Let me give you a *very* rough breakdown of our patients and how we run the Hospital, Chief Inspector. A good seventy percent of our patients suffer from schizophrenia. That was McVicar's original diagnosis, but changed by one of our consultant psychiatrists to a psychopathic personality disorder due to his substance and alcohol abuse.

"Of the total patient population, only one in four have committed murder and only the most violent patients remain locked up. Given McVicar's assessed risk level, he would've been able to have access to the grounds and our rehabilitation facilities, although monitored at all times. But, as to a hint Chief Inspector . . . no, I can't say McVicar gave us any hints he was planning to be elsewhere."

"And yet," Moss said softly, "you say you pride yourself in knowing what every patient is doing, every minute of the day."

Andrews gave her a slight smile. "Yes, although we do watch our patients closely at all times, we can't, so far, know what they're thinking. But you're right Sergeant, pride was perhaps the wrong word, one to be consigned to the past tense . . . it will probably get very dirty before too long."

Devine stirred and came to his Chief Executive's defence. "What Ms. Andrews is saying is, with the staff to patient ratio, and the code of security we follow, having no patient escapes since the mid-seventies *is*, in itself, a cause for pride.

"Understand too, our purpose here is not some, 'lock them up and throw away the key' regime, it's the creation of a secure and safe environment so therapeutic work *can* take place. We actually *believe* most of our patients can be rehabilitated."

Moss held up a hand. "I'm sorry. I didn't mean to belittle what you do in any way, it's just . . . well, *regardless* of what you do here, and in what way, McVicar's gone."

Steel nodded. That, for them, was the only thing of importance; the whole place could be Dickensian, or the most enlightened regime in the world – either way, McVicar had escaped. "Would there have been a time, or a situation, that McVicar could've exploited?"

Devine shot Andrews a anxious look. "Well, the way the wards are managed, and with the handover process we follow, it couldn't have been during a shift change."

"Why? How are the shifts managed?"

"There's three shifts per twenty-four hours, and a shift on a ward comprises a team leader and four others. The handover process itself has an inbuilt overlap so, at one point, there are ten staff on the ward."

"From the grounds then," and as Moss said this, she saw a troubled look pass over Devine's face.

"If it had been from the grounds he would've had to have pulled a David Copperfield trick and disappear before our eyes."

Andrews leant in, "We have had additional deliveries, and-"

"No, not then," Devine shot back.

"Additional deliveries?" Steel said.

"Christmas time, Chief Inspector," said Andrews, "we like to mark it . . . it helps some patients," and with a quick glance at Devine, "However, it does mean we have more traffic to – and from – the hospital."

Devine's voice rose, "We've been through that Eve – we're always *extra* cautious at those times."

For a moment there was silence in the room. Breaking it, Steel said, "Well, it remains a mystery then. I'd like to see his room."

Andrews looked to Devine, "Would that be a problem?"

He shook his head, "I'll need to rustle up some more bodies, but no," and turning to Steel and Moss, "When we're on the ward, or on our way to or from it, should anything . . . untoward, happen, I must ask you leave it to the staff to handle."

"Of course," said Steel, sending a silent prayer out into the universe.

When other security personnel arrived Devine phoned ahead, then led them from the management suite, out of the twenty-first century and back in time, to the building housing Ochil Ward, McVicar's home for the past five years.

Upstairs, on the first floor, permeated by a strong antiseptic smell, they were met by a long narrow corridor with single rooms off it. It was here that Carstairs' age showed. Each room was sealed by a heavy metal door with a peephole; cell rather than bedroom, prison rather than hospital. Ward staff had shepherded some of the patients into a communal area at the far end, and they could hear someone's voice raised in loud querulous complaint.

They stopped at McVicar's room and Devine pulled the heavy door open. "I'll let you go ahead."

Steel and Moss stepped inside, and as the door closed behind them with a clang, Steel felt a horrible trapped sensation rush at him. The cell itself was a simple narrow enclosure. On one side a single bed took up a wall, and against the opposite wall stood a wardrobe and a keyhole desk with some shelving above it. Secured, either to the floor or wall, everything had a tired, worn, look. Facing them was an old-fashioned barred and multi-paned shatterproof window through which the grounds and other buildings could be seen. The ambience was one of oppressive containment.

"Something to commit to memory Moss," said Steel, "You couldn't swing a hamster, let alone a cat. Who, sane or otherwise, *wouldn't* want to escape from this?" He pulled on the desk drawer and found it locked. "Tell Devine we need this open."

Moss pushed on the door to speak to Devine in a low murmur through the slit. She turned back to Steel, "The Nurse in Charge has the only key, it'll be a few moments."

Briefly, there were three people in a room too small for one, adding to Steel's claustrophobia. When the drawer was unlocked they saw it only contained a sketch pad. Moss lifted it out, placed it on the bed, and began to turn the pages.

McVicar's drawings were crude but powerful. Disturbed demonic faces, reminding Steel of the faces of church gargoyles, stared back at them. Each had been executed with multiple layered strokes, and each had text beside them completed in the same way.

Then, turning a page, they were face to face with McVicar's rough version of da Vinci's Vitruvian Man. They glanced at each other but said nothing.

Steel lifted the pad. "What's this Moss?"

In much smaller, more precise strokes, names and numbers were laid out. Every letter had a number beneath it. Moss brought it close. "This looks like – is – numerology, sir . . . each letter has its own number: A equals 1, through to Z equalling 26."

They peered at McVicar's work. The first name was Leonardo da Vinci and underneath that, the numbers added up to 146. "That's a 2, sir . . . you keep adding – 146 becomes 11 which becomes 2."

Below that, in smaller letters, McVicar had put his own name: Kenneth McVicar, and that, when each letter's number was added, also came to 146 – McVicar had wound his life and da Vinci's together.

"So, McVicar *is* our man, Moss. Your Vitruvian Man was something after all."

Moss only nodded and turned the page. This time there was no drawing, only letters and numbers. McVicar had written Mitchell's name over and over again and with different permutations. None of his workings had made a numerological 2 until he had written Lord Mitchell and then added an X. That had got him to 155, to 11 and then, to correspond with his own name and da Vinci's, a 2.

"Crazy as this is," Moss said, "it makes sense."

Steel looked at her. "Yes . . . two lines carved into Mitchell's chest to

72

make eleven, then a two, and an X to make the Vitruvian Man." He caught himself thinking madness must be sanity to the mad. He went to the cell door and pushed. "We'll need to take this with us, Mr. Devine."

Looking at the pad in Steel's hands, Devine said, "Is it confirmation?"

"I'm afraid so. There's no doubt in my mind that McVicar killed Lord Mitchell."

Now, all Steel wanted to do was to get the hell out of the place and breathe.

___

NINE

FOR A FEW MOMENTS STEEL AND MOSS SAT in the car in silence, each running through the experience of Carstairs in their minds. "What do you reckon, sir?"

"From what we just heard between Andrews and Devine, I think McVicar got away during one of those deliveries she mentioned, and I reckon Devine's going to get it in the neck – Director of Security and all." He gave Moss a small shrug, "Really, that's not *our* problem – how he escaped is immaterial – our problem is he's out," and with a sigh he turned the ignition. "Anyhow, if I never see this place again, I'll not mind. Let's get back to Edinburgh."

Moss had yet to assimilate her first ever visit to a secure hospital. Whatever she'd been expecting it wasn't what she'd just experienced, and she was vaguely unsettled by the thought. She nodded her agreement.

After they'd driven a short distance, Steel said, "You'd best phone ahead Moss – let Grieve know."

"*Me*, sir?"

He smiled. "Yes, you . . . you got McVicar's name in the first place. You can fill Grieve in when you get there, but it'd be best to let him know McVicar's our man . . . he'll want to tell the Chief." He punched in Memory + 5 on the hands-free.

Grieve's pleasure in hearing from Moss was palpable. "Well *done*, Moss – good work," and after a slight pause, "You there, Mike?"

"Sir."

"You have any doubts?"

Steel had many, but not on McVicar. "He's our man." He knew Grieve would be pleased; he was drawing fire from upstairs but now they had the name of Lord Mitchell's killer. Catching him was another matter, but Steel wasn't going to spoil Grieve's euphoria by bringing up the difficult part.

"Excellent, I'll have a word with the Chief. Give me all the details as soon as you get here Sergeant," and he cut the line.

Steel glanced at Moss; she was visibly pleased – a piece of police-work had worked as it should, and she could take some credit for it. A crime had been committed and, within two days, they knew who the criminal was; despite *his* misgivings, both parts had snapped together seamlessly.

They had reached the outskirts of Edinburgh when the phone rang. "Steel."

"Hi Mike. It's JJ."

"Hello . . . JJ." Moss saw Steel's features soften.

"I got in touch with my source. She took a bit of persuading, but I've convinced her to meet you."

"When?"

"Tomorrow morning. At the Regency Restaurant in the Imperial Hotel . . . nine o'clock, if that's okay."

"Aye, fine." He hesitated, then said, "Lord Mitchell's murder – I thought you might like some advance notice."

"Yes?"

"We have the murderer's name. Well, *alleged* murderer's name."

There was a longish pause with white noise static on the line, and Steel thought the signal had been lost, then, "You do . . . who?"

"Kenneth George McVicar. He escaped from Carstairs just over a week ago."

"Right . . . I read a piece in the paper at the time. How does he fit?"

"He used the same method that got him put away in the first place. That was for a double murder in Glasgow, five years ago. Mitchell was the

76

sentencing judge."

"The same method . . . can you give me more?"

"No, just the name and same method." He wouldn't give her details; she could do some spadework. "And, JJ?"

"Yes?"

"Don't be writing, 'sources within Lothian and Borders Police', okay?"

They heard her laugh; a pleasing sound that seemed to wash away the last vestiges of their experience of Carstairs. "Just how many apologies do you want to pull out of me, Mike? No, I'll use something like, 'it is understood'."

Steel said nothing; he would see. "Okay JJ, I'll speak with you later."

"Yes – I'll see you, briefly, at the Imperial tomorrow morning. And . . . Mike?"

"Yes?"

"Thank you."

They both heard the warmth in her voice and Moss saw Steel, for a moment, letting some sunshine in, his face momentarily filling with pleasure. She didn't know his past, hadn't enquired of anyone, but he probably lived alone; married at least once, no doubt. He wasn't *un*attractive, although getting some up-to-date clothes would help; he was stuck in a Marks & Spencer era from ten years ago. He was obviously drawn to JJ – who wouldn't be? – but, whether JJ was attracted to him, or whether she simply had an easy manner with – and on – him, she'd look for tomorrow.

"Will it be okay if JJ has this before the other papers, sir?"

"The *Scotsman* won't have anything other papers, or TV, won't get from a press release but, if JJ does her work, she'll have some details they don't. As long as we don't get the credit, it'll be okay."

Moss didn't say anything; she'd never worked with anyone from the press, and hoped he was correct. They were nearing Fettes, and she switched tack. "Your doctor's visit, sir . . . well, is it just routine?"

Steel gave her a faint smile. "Routine's the word. Send me a text message if anything important comes up."

•

"You don't like this Mr. Steel, do you?

Steel looked up from studying the swirls of the carpet at his feet. "No, not really." He was rarely called Mr. Steel, apart from here. Chief Inspector, this morning; now, Mr. Steel.

"Do you find a purpose in being here?"

"No."

The psychologist looked at her notes. "We have been meeting for quite some time, Mr. Steel. You find no purpose in our time together?"

Strings had been pulled. He knew that. The Police Federation had made sure he had kept his job *and* suffered no demotion, but he knew without these visits – these compulsory visits – he would've been out on his ear. "Purpose is perhaps the wrong word."

"Oh, I'm sorry . . . I thought my usage was correct. What word would you use in its stead?"

Steel looked at her. She reminded him of Miss Dobson, one of his primary school teachers – a thin-lipped, unsmiling face, fair hair pulled in place by a severe bun, and glasses that glittered at him, almost hiding the pale blue eyes behind, weighing him with the bedside manner of Little Red Riding Hood's wolf.

He shrugged, "I'm damned if I know what the purpose is." Reason, purpose: outside of work, Steel knew he had lost both. He had the Job – *that* gave him reason and purpose – but she wasn't asking for that.

"There's no limit on your visits here Mr. Steel. You do *appreciate* that? I have to . . . sign you off, if you will. The point is, you need to – must come to – how should I call it . . . an *understanding* of the past and your past actions. That is purpose enough. However, until you are in that place – really in that place – well, we'll continue to meet."

Steel understood past actions but saying, 'I abused alcohol then abused others' hadn't worked for her; she wanted the building blocks, not the wretched and sorry excuse of blaming something else. Anything else but him.

"It's an hour of my time Mr. Steel, for which I'm paid very handsomely. I'm sure you would rather be doing some police-work."

He wanted to shout *yes* at her; hurl it in her face. Yes, because the Job meant shaping some order out of the shapeless disorder that surrounded him every day.

And he could see then the Job was all that was left. There *wasn't* anything else. Anything else had been killed off and buried deep a long time ago; he saw a ghost of himself over a grave, tidily patting the earth with the back of a shovel. How could he tell this woman – this complete stranger – that these days, this present when he wasn't working, it felt as if he were surrounded by walls of grey watery fog, threatening to absorb him? How could he talk of the waves of unfathomable sadness which time and again would rush over him? Tell her that and he wouldn't last a week.

"You're not drinking now?"

"No," he lied easily; it was none of her damned business.

She made a note. "And, I believe you have a new Sergeant . . . a *female* officer. How do you feel about that?" She had segued from drink to females with ease. It could be the start of a song. An old song too.

Unresponsive, again he looked at the oil painting on the wall behind her head: a young child, with a frown-creased brow, was looking up and out of the frame and, entering it, was an old man's weathered hand. He found it unsettling and wanted to ask her what *its* purpose was – ask her what the purpose for everything was – but he knew there was no time for *any* of this; there was a psychotic killer on the loose. *That* was his purpose. It would do. For now.

•

Steel navigated his car into the private bay. As he stepped out, he realised he'd driven from the psychologist's office back to his house in the Dean Village on autopilot, unaware of his journey. He had just opened the front door when a chirrup from his phone alerted him to a text: *BBC News. Now. Moss.*

Finding the remote, he switched the television on. He'd missed the lead-in but was in time to see Chief Constable Sir David Thompson, with his flawless silver hair and suitably grave expression, standing in front of a large blown-up picture of McVicar. Fettes had moved fast.

Thompson began, "In connection with the murder of Lord Henry Mitchell, we are now actively seeking one Kenneth George McVicar, who recently escaped from The State Hospital in Carstairs." Pause; then eyes boring into the camera, "It must be stressed that no member of the public should even contemplate approaching McVicar as he is considered armed and extremely dangerous." Beat; now assuming his gravest expression, "*Should* any member of the public see McVicar, then they are strongly advised to either phone the number which is on-screen or the normal emergency number."

Thompson gave a slight nod and his press statement was over; there would be no questions and the feed went back to the studio. The newscaster gave a résumé of the murder of Mitchell, the piece ending with McVicar's face filling the screen and a repeat of the Chief Constable's warning that he was, 'armed and extremely dangerous'.

With the thought that Thompson seemed to be perfect casting for the role of a Chief Constable and the acceptable face of Lothian and Borders Police, Steel killed the power. With luck – a large slice of it – McVicar would be in custody shortly.

Picking up his phone, he called Moss. "Thanks for that . . . I told you the Chief would break the news," and giving her his address, "Head here tomorrow and we'll go to the Imperial together."

•

In a far different Edinburgh room, with its faint smell of cat urine, bare-board flooring and wooden slats nailed across and covering the windows, the television stayed on. It was the only light in the room and the remote wasn't working anyhow. McVicar narrowed his eyes and sensed something pure white bubbling up from deep within. He listened for the faintest voice of Uriel to guide him but could hear nothing other than a rushing sound filling his ears.

As he stared towards the television, committing to memory the name and the face of the policeman who had spoken his name, the glass of water beside him remained untouched. He had poured it from the tap but then thought better of it; who knew what poisons it contained?

TEN

"THIS IS QUITE BEAUTIFUL." Moss was standing at the large picture window of Steel's living room, looking out over the Dean Village, a diminutive and picturesque jumbled disorder of different building styles and heights embracing the narrow and slow moving Water of Leith, which cut it in two.

Her gaze ran upstream, over a metal footbridge and back to the cluster of warm red sandstone buildings that stood at its side and crow-stepped towards the sky. Opposite, a Victorian school butted into the old single-span stone bridge that stitched the village together, and high in the far distance she could see the graceful arches of the Dean Bridge, which seemed to further dwarf the village. Despite being five minutes from the city centre, this was rural.

"What's that?" Steel poked his head out of the kitchen, where he was making coffee.

Moss knew she'd passed some unspoken test in being told to meet him here. "I was just saying how beautiful this place is."

She cast her eyes over the room and saw no feminine touches. It was a lived-in room with nothing old, nothing new, and apart from a few framed black and white photographs on the walls, which looked vaguely familiar, there was little decoration. Yet the room wasn't spare; everything simply had its own spot, its own purpose. Functional. She took in the wall of bookshelves, with their stacks of books, DVDs, CDs and Quad hi-fi. She could get a better measure of her boss by reading some titles there, but Steel was coming from the kitchen with a mug in each hand.

"It is that. There's a nice riverside walk you should take – it'll take you all the way to Stockbridge. Get your flatmate – Susan? – to bring you here."

Moss took the proffered mug and sat down beside the window in an armchair which seemed to swallow her. "I will. Edinburgh's such a beautiful city."

"There are parts that would change your mind on that," Steel said, thinking of some of the older housing schemes, and some of the dwellings in them, littered with animal faeces, where, in the past, the occupants had stripped the skirting boards and doors for firewood. Places where you'd wipe your feet on the way *out* – out into an environment the very antithesis of beautiful. Places some people who'd lived all their lives in the city never visited; geographically, only a few miles away, but light years in every other sense. Edinburgh was, after all, in every thought and every stone, the city of both Jekyll *and* Hyde.

"In part, it *is* beautiful, though people see it with different eyes . . . Goebbels called it enchanting, and reckoned it would make a good summer capital for the Germans after they invaded."

Moss laughed at that; Janet Tweedie had been right to call him the History Man. "You lived here long sir?"

Steel sat down on an arm of the settee. "Yes – my wife and I bought it originally to fix up   . . . it didn't *quite* work out how I'd hoped."

She said nothing to this. "The buildings with the clock tower, is that just housing?"

"The Well Court? Yes, the building with the clock tower was originally meant as a community hall. The whole lot was built in the nineteenth century by the owner of the *Scotsman* to provide better houses for the 'working poor' to live in. You don't see many rich people doing that *these* days," and he shrugged, "although there's precious few poor here now."

Moss took a swig from her mug; her boss made a good coffee. "What are you expecting this morning sir?"

"I'm really not sure . . . hopefully something that'll move us forward. JJ's talked of 'vice rings' and so on, but that might just be journalese for one sad old man with a taste for escorts who should've known better. I'm more hoping for something solid on this under-age thing."

"How's vice handled here?"

"Differently from most places – one of the more enlightened things Edinburgh's come up with."

"*Enlightened?*" Moss couldn't even begin to think how anything to do with vice could be enlightened.

"Well prostitution's a fact of life," Steel continued, "Decades back, it was found that cracking down on it only made the problem worse. AIDS arrived when there was particularly heavy heroin use here, and drug users sharing needles spread that further. At the same time we were arresting any woman working the streets and, if she had condoms on her, the courts took that as evidence of prostitution. Trouble was, the women stopped carrying them and, in no time, Edinburgh became known as 'the AIDS Capital of the World'.

"So . . . ?

"Well, the city took a pragmatic view. What with trying to deal with innumerable injecting addicts, and knowing prostitution wasn't simply going to disappear, a decision was made to license saunas. It worked and continues to work – they get a public entertainment license for a few hundred and that allows us to inspect them. As long as there's no pimps, no drug dealing – and nothing under-age – they can continue."

Moss absorbed this; it was vastly different from Liverpool. "What about the women on the street then, or for that matter, the woman we're meeting with JJ?"

"They're opposite ends of the spectrum, Moss. If a prostitute has a drug problem she'll not be able to work in a sauna so the street's, normally, her only option."

"And the escort side – JJ's source?"

"Well the escort business is something completely different – escorts have to be able to blend."

"Blend?"

"They might not be hired for sex, they might be hired simply as a companion for a function and have to look . . . well, nothing like a prostitute," and he shrugged, "Blend."

Moss took another mouthful of coffee. "So we don't really prosecute prostitution then?"

"Oh, we do. If, for whatever reason, two or more women can't work in a sauna and are working in a house together, then that, by law, is defined as a brothel . . . they'll be arrested *and* prosecuted," and remembering the email he'd got from Grieve, "Do you not have an exam on Scots Law to pass?"

"So how's that any different from a sauna then?" ignoring the last.

"A sauna is licensed," and he smiled as he completed the circle. "As I say, enlightened pragmatism."

Moss shook her head. "Sorry sir . . . that's far from enlightened. To me, someone being able to *buy* another is morally wrong, and Edinburgh's simply colluding in that by licensing saunas."

Steel was taken aback. "*Morally* wrong?" His law was secular – moral wrongs were for the church not the police – and his natural inclination was to blame the society they lived in. After all, who among the women who worked the streets and the saunas would do so unless they actually needed to? "I'll grant you, as far as vice is concerned, we're more managing crime than policing it."

Moss frowned. "Then I have to simply disagree with that."

Steel wondered how on earth she'd be able to work with such ideals; there were too many situations where morality would be the very *last* thing needed. "You'll find 'morality' has *no* place in your work, Moss." He reached for his jacket. "Let's get going . . . save your questions on prostitution for JJ's source."

For the first time since she'd begun working with Steel, Moss felt a twinge of disappointment. Putting her unfinished coffee down, she got to her feet.

•

They parked opposite the Imperial Hotel in the wide street close to Haymarket Station. Before getting out Steel turned to Moss. "Don't take notes."

"Sir?"

"Well, if JJ needed to convince this woman to talk to us, I don't want her spooked from the get-go, especially in a public place talking to two cops. I'd rather have her talking openly."

It was early and, tucked into a corner of the Regency Restaurant, the sole customer was JJ. "Hi Mike."

"Morning JJ . . . this is my DS, Robin Moss."

JJ raised a hand and gave Moss a warm smile. "Hi Robin. Did you see today's *Scotsman*, Mike?"

Steel shook his head, "I don't read English . . . did I make an appearance?"

JJ feigned a sad face and slid a copy across the table. "You didn't even get a mention."

Moss scanned the headline: 'Carstairs Escapee Linked To Murder Of Lord Mitchell' and noted the 'Exclusive: Jay Johnstone'. Feeling slightly out of place as Steel and JJ leaned in to each other, she looked round the room, taking in the elegance of the columns, the sparkling glass dome and glass chandelier high above them. "This is all rather grand," she said.

Steel nodded, "The Imperial goes all the way back to a golden age of travelling, when posh folk used to have half a dozen servants in tow. It's had a few owners over the years but the latest have spent millions on it." He looked round. "Nice, if you can afford it."

"And you're telling me, you can't, Mike?" JJ asked, teasing him.

Steel smiled at this. "Perhaps I *choose* not to."

Moss gave JJ a surreptitious appraisal: a beautiful, confident woman, well established in her profession – one still dominated by men. Just like the Police, she thought, well aware there were only two female Chief Inspectors and one Superintendent in the whole of Lothian and Borders. She knew JJ would have had to prove herself – daily – and, seeing herself in a very similar position, she warmed to her.

The restaurant door opened and JJ said, "Here's Emma now."

Moss turned, and understood then what Steel had meant by blend. The slender woman who'd entered was about thirty, and dressed in a well-cut, simple navy pinstripe suit over a silk, high-necked, ivory coloured blouse. With very little make-up and her long dark hair swept back, she wore tortoiseshell framed glasses which set off and brought a seriousness to a naturally pretty face. There was no flesh on show at all and Moss, wearing a deep v-necked blouse, felt under-dressed. Whatever this woman really did, she would pass for a young businesswoman anywhere.

JJ introduced her as Emma Boyd and Steel stood to shake her hand. "Thanks for agreeing to see us Ms. Boyd."

Guarded, she said, "I'm really not sure how I can help you."

Steel gave her a smile. "That's okay, leave that to us."

JJ stood. "Sorry, I have to be elsewhere. Phone me later, Mike – I'd like to know how this goes." Moss noted how she'd closed the distance between herself and Steel as she spoke with him, and now the light touch on his arm as she was leaving. "I'll call you later Emma," and giving Moss a smile and a little wave, she left.

Steel turned to Boyd. "We just have a few questions Emma, but I'd like to ask you about Lord Mitchell first." They saw her hesitation, and he said, "Listen, don't be concerned. We're not interested in anything other than following up on some of the areas you've already discussed with JJ. I understand you met Mitchell on several occasions."

"I've been to his house . . . nine times, and I saw him three times at private functions."

"How did he contact you initially?"

"I'm online."

"You're not from here?" said Moss, who'd by now realised her glasses were plain glass: just one part of making the blend work.

"No, Surrey, but I work throughout the U.K. I'm only in Scotland about four weeks of the year."

"So," continued Steel, "Mitchell got in touch with you online. How does that work?"

"Well, there's a mobile number shown. Any client phoning me has to give me a name and number so I can phone them back. It's a safety thing."

"Safety?" said Moss.

"Yes, I work a buddy system; there's always someone else who knows where I am, who I'm with, and the number they've contacted me from. When I'm in Edinburgh, I use Jane Ingram . . . she's the manageress of a sauna here."

"Which sauna?" Steel said.

"Venus Leisure in Leith."

Moss sat forward. "In any of the times you were with Lord Mitchell, did he ever ask for anything in the bondage area?"

Boyd shook her head, "Never," adding, "I'm quite willing if a client wants that, but old Henry wasn't that way."

"How was he?"

"Pretty straight really. He'd book me for an hour and we'd have sex for about half that."

"The other half?"

"Oh, we'd cuddle and talk. A lot of my older clients are like that – you have to be a good listener."

"Talk of what? What subjects?"

"Nothing really . . . gardening was his main thing," then, realising what Moss was asking, "He never talked of his work if that's what you're thinking. I didn't even know he was a judge until much later, but he never talked of that."

Steel stirred. "So, you visit clients at their homes – do you work elsewhere?"

Boyd looked round. "Here mainly."

"Here?"

"For a huge hotel the Imperial's very safe, probably the safest in Edinburgh, and I'm very discreet. I stay here for about a week, maybe ten days."

"You said you'd seen Mitchell several times at a private function."

"Yes," and her brows knitted, "JJ said she'd told you about the under-age thing . . ."

"That's the reason we're here, Emma," Steel said. "Go on."

"Well, I've been booked for private parties, and at one of them . . . I was approached to see whether I knew any young girls I could introduce."

"And?"

"It's . . . despicable." She paused for a moment, and they saw her quiet anger. "I knew they didn't mean young, as in late teens." She glanced from Steel to Moss. "Look, I've made my choices, but this is *children*, for God's sake."

"Do you have a name for the person who approached you?" asked Steel.

Boyd shook her head. "No. Everyone's masked. It makes them anonymous; that's the whole idea. I'm sure most know each other, but anonymity is their kick and I never knew any names. Henry I already knew."

"And where were these parties held?"

"At a private house . . . hang on," and she reached into her briefcase to retrieve a hefty leather Filofax. Steel and Moss exchanged glances while Boyd flipped through a few pages. "Yes, it's Hawthorns and the address is 78 Turnberry Road, near the airport."

With a quick "Sorry" to Steel, Moss scribbled the address on a napkin. "What sort of parties are they, then?"

Boyd arched her eyebrows, a faintly amused look on her face. "Well, they're not Tupperware ones."

Moss coloured. "No . . . were they the sort where you might *expect* anything under-age?"

"Definitely not − everything *but* under-age, though there's a sort of private wing to this house and I was told it was off-limits."

"A private *wing?*"

"Yes. The house is a huge, rambling Victorian place in vast grounds. Ancient, with loads of rooms. It's been very expensively refurbished . . . top-flight kitchens, a cinema, saunas and steam rooms, and it's staffed like a hotel. There are all sorts of different activities in the rooms."

"What sort of activities?" Moss said, and Steel thought she just couldn't help putting her foot in her mouth today.

Boyd obviously thought the same as she rattled off a dry list. "Mostly couples partnering up with singles or other couples, group ones, women only ones. Some rooms where people just watched. You get the picture?"

Moss pushed the images away. "Yes. And this off-limits, private wing . . . you never got in there?"

"No. But there was one time when I dropped into the kitchens . . ."

"Yes?"

Boyd paused, thinking through her response. "I want to get this correct, don't want to shade it in any way because it was really brief. I went to the kitchens to get a coffee – to have a break in fact – and there were two young girls there, about ten and dressed . . . well, in the way I dress sometimes. I think they'd sneaked in to get something to eat. Anyhow, we surprised each other coming face to face. When the staff saw me they got them out of there *real* sharpish and I could hear them getting hell from someone . . . really laying into them he was. It was later I was approached and that gave me the creeps, but in any case – gut feeling – I knew I wasn't mistaken in what I'd seen."

"The people there," put in Steel, "what sort are they, Emma?"

"Well, even masked, without clothes we're all the same sort, aren't we?" She thought for a moment. "I'd say all of them are rich – that scent only the rich give off – and a lot of pukka voices too . . . you know, where house becomes hice. People like Henry."

"And you've only been there three times?"

"Since I was asked about introducing young girls I've always said I'm busy – didn't even want to be under the same roof after that. A pity actually, it was good money. Me and another were hired as party starters," and with a broad smile she added, "Not that we were really needed – some of the women there have the kind of appetites that put professionals to shame."

"You said, you and another . . . do you have her name?" Moss asked.

Boyd shook her head. "No, she was sent by Jane Ingram."

"Anything else you can tell us about this place or any of the people there, Emma?" Steel asked.

"No, not really," and she paused. "Well . . . "

"Go on," Steel prompted.

"This could mean nothing, there's possibly no connection, but I *was* approached later by a local. I can't swear to it, but I think he mentioned Hawthorns when he first contacted me. He booked me, for here, and it turned out he wanted to pimp for me. That's one thing I'll *never* have – I'll never need to have; I look after myself. I sent him packing."

"You say, local. Edinburgh? The type you'd meet at Hawthorns?"

"Edinburgh, yes; the type at Hawthorns, no. More working class with well-polished edges. Steven someone – I'll have his card," and she flicked through her Filofax. Seeing her collection of cards, Moss raised a querying eyebrow at Steel which he ignored. "Here we are," and she handed over the business card.

Steel took it from her, then got to his feet. "I'll need to hold on to this Emma," and to Moss, "I'm just going to phone Fettes, I'll be right back."

Moss watched Steel leave then turned to Boyd, "You said these private parties were good money." Boyd eyed her warily, and Moss shrugged with a reassuring smile, "It's okay – I'm just making conversation 'til my boss gets back."

"We got a thousand apiece."

"So, that would be good money? What do you normally earn?"

Boyd sat back. "Who *wouldn't* consider a thousand for a few hours' work good money? But I get your point. I charge two-fifty an hour so I can earn that in a day, but it might take longer, it all depends." Seeing Moss's expression, she added, "I *do* pay tax and National Insurance on that."

"Really?" Moss thought she could have a very long conversation with this woman.

"Yes, I'm registered with the taxman as a Corporate Therapist – everything's declared."

Moss was intrigued. "When did you start as an escort, Emma?"

"When I was at University."

Moss almost spluttered her coffee. "University?"

Boyd smiled, "That always gets people," and Moss had the feeling she enjoyed tripping people up with it. "Yes, I have a First in German – useful somewhere . . . Germany, I suppose. I kind of had to dare myself when I was really struggling to survive, never mind studying for my Finals. Now, in the space of ten years, I've got a savings account I wouldn't have had from anything else, and I meet some really interesting people."

"What sort?"

"A really wide range. It's mainly men, of course, though some couples book me," and giving Moss a coy smile, "some single women too."

Moss felt her cheeks grow warm just as Steel returned. "Sir?"

"George in Records should be sending something soon." He leaned towards Boyd,

"Thanks for your time Emma, we'll just keep you a few minutes more.

Is there a number where you can be reached if something else crops up – I take it the one on your website is current?"

"It is, but only for Scotland," and she fished into her briefcase to pull out her Filofax again. "Here's my card . . . use that number," handing one to Steel and, with a slight smile, sliding another across the table towards Moss.

Steel's phone chirruped and he scrolled through the message. "Okay Emma, I've got a picture I'd like you to look at. Tell me if this is the local who approached you."

She took the phone from Steel. "That's him. That's the guy who wanted to be my pimp."

Steel smiled. "You're sure?"

"Absolutely certain."

"Great. Well, we'll not keep you . . . I take it you're busy?"

She stood up and smoothed her skirt. "Ten-thirty, here – I need to check in."

With Emma gone, Steel turned to Moss and handed her the business card, which read: Steven McCann, Security Consultant. Her head shot up.

"That's right, young Stevie McCann, and she's just positively identified him." He gave her a triumphant smile. "But I've got better news than that."

"It gets better?"

"I had George run a check through the District Council's Rating Agency on Hawthorns at Turnberry Road."

Moss crumpled the napkin she'd been holding. "And?"

"The owners are AP Properties and the Principal is-"

"*Alan Prior.*"

ELEVEN

STEEL AND MOSS STOOD TOGETHER on the pavement, leaning on the car. She looked back at the Imperial. "Your thoughts, sir?"

"Pretty woman."

Moss rolled her eyes. "Pretty intelligent certainly. I meant on what she told us."

"Right. Well, I'm not sure we're much further forward."

"With a positive ID on Stevie McCann and knowing that Prior owns Hawthorns?"

"Well, Prior's *company* ownership may be just that. Does he actually visit the place? Know anything about it and what goes on there? And is there anything illegal happening there? Young Stevie trying to pimp Emma is nothing, 'though it would be good to give him a visit – lean on him. No, I mean the under-age thing . . . she really only confirmed what JJ told me. She's an eye-witness, but an eye-witness to what? A private wing and a couple of ten year-olds in a kitchen who may, or may not, have been inappropriately dressed. It's not much to go on, is it? . . . not enough to turn the place over."

He drummed his fingers on the roof of the car, deep in thought, weighing their next steps. Again, McCann and Prior had surfaced together and, like every cop, he didn't believe in coincidence. The link between them might be tenuous but it was there nonetheless.

First, close to the Mitchells' house, there's a house owned by Prior and lived in by Stevie McCann; next there's an escort who's worked at another house owned by Prior and she's contacted later by Stevie McCann. No, definitely no coincidence. The trouble was he would need to speak with Finance to get a better handle on *their* knowledge of Prior, and that could mean the whole thing being passed over to SCDEA, the Scottish Crime and Drug Enforcement Agency. Perhaps: they didn't have enough information. Yet. He stopped drumming and looked up to see Moss watching him, waiting patiently.

"With the appearance of one of Prior's companies, this has just got bigger; it looks like we've no choice other than a wee chat with Finance if they've already been looking at his equity company. Although, right now, I'd rather play it close to the chest. Let's take a trip to Turnberry Road first and see the place for ourselves."

Moss paused; visiting the house would be over-playing their hand. Perhaps this was what Grieve meant by speaking up if the senior officer was going walkabout. "That would be a mistake, sir."

"A *mistake?*" Brian would've simply opened the car door.

"Yes, we could look at it on a map."

"On a *map?*" Steel retorted. "Is that what you think passes for policing Moss? You've got to get your hands dirty . . . get your foot in the door."

Mustering her patience, and ignoring Steel's risible idea concerning her hands and feet, she said, "I'm *thinking,* a visit from us – especially as you said there's nothing there for us yet – would only put everyone on notice."

Steel paused for a moment then, with a terse nod, opened the door. "You're right, though I *would* like to see it. Let's get to Fettes and on the way," pointing to the glove compartment, "find it on the map."

They left Haymarket and headed west on Glasgow Road. As Moss unfolded the map, spreading it as best she could on her knees, Steel was trying to get his thoughts straight. The very *last* thing they wanted was to put either McCann or Prior on notice and what had been his response? – a knee-jerk reaction. She'd been right to stop him.

Having turned off at Roseburn to head through Ravelston, he pulled the car into the kerb. Moss looked up, "Sir?"

"You found it yet?"

Moss was following a road with her finger, "Got it. Wow."

"*Wow?*"

She folded the map to a more manageable size. "Just take a look at *that.*"

Steel looked and saw Hawthorns, appearing in a huge area of green. Peering closer, he said, "What's this? It's a damn lake – looks about the size of Princes Street Gardens and the house looks massive." Another house appeared beside the roadway; a gatehouse. If that was anything to go by, then the main house was beyond massive. "This really makes me want to drive there, but we'll get the plans from the Council later. Let's get to Fettes."

•

At Fettes they headed straight for Finance. Pushing the door open, Steel breezed in, undeterred by the clinical calm of the office. Spotting what he wanted, he strode over to a desk where a civilian support supervisor was working. "Morning. Chief Inspector Steel. Who's working on a company called Prior Private Equity?"

The woman looked at a list then, in a hushed voice, she said, "That would be John," and pointed across the room to a man sitting at a desk by a window.

Thanking her, Steel and Moss crossed the room and, pulling two chairs up to the desk, sat opposite him. The man looked up from his paperwork, surprised to see someone joining him. "Can I help you?"

Steel gave him an open smile. "Yes John . . . DCI Steel. I understand you're looking into a company called Priority Private Equity. I need some information on the company and its owner, Alan Prior."

He hesitated. "What's your interest sir?"

Steel remained non-committal. "Prior's name has come up in connection with another case. I just wanted to know where you're headed with him, that's all."

"I see," and he swung round in his chair to face his computer terminal. A swift flurry of keystrokes punctuated the near silence. "Priority Private Equity's just one of his companies . . . it's been flagged by Inland Revenue." He ran his eyes down the page, then turned back to Steel. "I'm sorry sir, what was your interest again? This is a parallel investigation with Crime Squad."

Steel didn't let his surprise show. "Yes, well we'll be seeing the Crime boys later. You were first on my list," he lied without skipping a beat. "It's probably nothing, but PPE came up as an owner of a house close to a murder scene . . . just part of the elimination process, that's all. It would be really helpful if you could give us a bit of background on your work."

"Well, as far as this department's concerned, we're working with the Revenue's Tax Inspectorate regarding PPE. Superficially, they're a debt restructuring company which works with ailing companies, making profits for its investors."

"Debt restructuring? How does that work then?" and Steel appealed to the man, "Any help you can give me, if you can keep it simple, would be really appreciated."

"Debt restructuring . . . well, to start with, PPE borrows money from lenders and adds equity from its own partners – rich individuals."

"Like you and me then?" Steel deadpanned.

John shook his head, "No sir. We're talking *very* rich individuals. Anyhow, with this combined sum, PPE buys all the shares in an ailing company, sometimes for as low as fifty pence on the pound. It then streamlines the company – replacing the management, selling off assets and reducing the workforce – making the company, somewhere down the road, very valuable for selling."

"And this is what Prior's doing?"

"What PPE is doing, yes. They claim to own pieces of over fifty companies. Here and in Europe."

"Sorry if I've missed something, but none of this sounds illegal," said Moss.

"No," he said, giving her an almost imperceptible shrug, "but there's been talk of investors being defrauded by PPE through sham transactions and shell games. That it routinely engages in transactions between its various funds – funds solely benefiting PPE – and that it's engaged in fake deals to disclaim liabilities but has held on to the assets at the same time."

"Talk?" Steel didn't like things without attribution.

"Yes. This originally surfaced from our opposite numbers in Scotland

Yard . . ." He was wondering now whether he'd said too much, and closed the file on his screen. "As I say Chief Inspector . . . ?

"Steel."

"Well sir, this is a parallel investigation . . . I really *would* prefer if you spoke with the Crime Squad."

Steel reached over the desk to shake the man's hand, "I fully understand John. We only want to cross our Ts and dot our Is. We'll go and speak with Crime now. Again, thanks for your help."

•

Back in their office Moss asked, "What was that about speaking with the Crime Squad?"

Steel smiled. "That was an unwelcome surprise. We will see them – just not now. I'm thinking, what with young Stevie close to the Mitchell house, in a house owned by Prior and now, Hawthorns – another house owned by Prior – if the Crime Squad are involved in some way, then there's every chance we'll have our investigation taken from us."

"And that would be a bad thing?"

Steel shook his head at this; she was missing what, for her, was a key point. "*You're* the one aiming high, Moss. That means you want results to carry with you as you climb – a track record of some good collars with your name on them. If Crime steps in with their size twelve hobnails, all we'll be left with is Lord Mitchell's murder, and that's as good as closed . . . or will be when McVicar's caught." He watched her absorb this. "Don't you *want* to take this further? – I mean you, personally, not just as a cog in Lothian and Borders."

She nodded. "Of course I do."

"Good. Part of being a DS is wanting to be a DI, who wants to be a DCI . . . it doesn't come by itself, you know – there's learning the job, then *learning* the job. Understand?" He gave her a mirthless smile. "Accelerated Careers won't teach you that Moss . . . won't help you at all if you don't get some good collars with your name on them."

Thinking, *Lesson over*, he lifted several newly arrived sheets of paper from his in-tray. "I see Forensics have come up with a preliminary on Lord Mitchell's house." He scanned down the sheets; "Blood in the bedroom's shower drain . . . Mitchell's only. Several non-matching fingerprints . . .

filed." He read further; "Now that's interesting. Apparently computer forensics found two secure folders on Mitchell's computer . . . one was his court work, a heavily encrypted folder, and another which had, according to this, 'simple password protection'."

"What was in that?"

Steel looked up. "One hundred and twenty-one pornographic images of minors. Male and female."

Moss frowned and sat back; paedophilia and the use of escorts didn't seem to go together. "Really?"

She took the sheet from him and started to read. "Odd . . . Forensics haven't given us creation dates for the files."

Steel took the sheet and squinted at the appended technical information. "Well, get on to them later and ask for a clarification of the dates for *all* the files on the PC – they'll love you for that.

"While you're at it, ask them what the hell, 'simple password protection' means. Is that simple to me, or simple to them? God, we may be after McVicar but this is *still* a murder inquiry . . . preliminary or not, this is slack work."

Moss agreed but said nothing. When she'd finished her note she asked, "You said later, sir?"

"Yes. If McVicar wasn't in the frame, I'd say now, but later'll do. And when you speak with them, throw your weight about – let them know if they'd been thorough they would've had a quieter life – and give them hours not days."

"So, what're we doing?"

"I was thinking we could do with a trip to Leith."

"Leith? What's there?"

"*Oysters* – Billy McCann's club. His base. It's time you met Edinburgh's leading villain and, if we find young Stevie there, we can rattle *his* cage too."

TWELVE

LEITH STANDS ON EDINBURGH'S NORTHERN SHORE, at the mouth of the Water of Leith as it spills into the North Sea and, depending on who's describing it, it's either Edinburgh's port or a proud entity all of its own. For centuries hard livings had been made from shipbuilding, trade between Poland, Germany and the Baltic, and whalers hunting far into the dangerous ice-filled waters of the Arctic.

It was a place with its own history and its very own mix of hard-working people who had always looked to the smooth-fingered city to its south with distrust. Over time, however, Edinburgh had swallowed it whole, and piece by piece Leith was succumbing to gentrification. Little enclaves of expensive specialist restaurants had sprung up for those who ventured there and, for a short time, there was cheap housing to be bought.

Year by year, however, the port's trade had dwindled. First through containerisation and then, with the need for larger vessels than the docks could handle, the Port Authority had eventually decided to relinquish the docks for development.

Yet despite what many would call improvements, there was still a dockland pulse which ran through the streets. The pubs may have been restyled and renamed, and the women who worked the streets and the incoming ships moved on, but the beating heart which had given them so much life was still there.

Moss was taking in the jumble of streets as they drove to McCann's club. "This reminds me of Liverpool . . . a sort of miniature version."

With a glance at the dense, blackened tenements, Steel said, "When I was younger, this place had a fearsome reputation," and he smiled, "There used to be some *very* rough pubs here. There was an area nicknamed The Barbary Coast with a pub called *The King's Wark*, though it was known as the Jungle, where, any night of the week, you could fight your way in *or* out, and then there was *Fairley's*, which used to have a puma in the bar."

"A *puma*? You're joking."

Steel shook his head and laughed. "No, I'm not . . . it would growl at the go-go dancers. It was well before my time, but I think their license was yanked." Moss tried to think of something from Liverpool to top this, but nothing, even in the wildest of apocryphal tales fed to wide-eyed rookies, came close.

Turning from the Shore, they crossed the river by Sandport Street, and ran into Coburg Street, parking opposite McCann's club, where a large pink neon sign above the door proclaimed *Oysters*. Moss sized it up as she got out. Compared to other premises sitting below the tenements with a run-down aspect to them, this corner conversion, which had absorbed the two shops on either side of it, was elegantly, and expensively, finished with impenetrable black glass.

They crossed the cobbled street to where two squat shaven-headed bouncers dressed in ill-fitting matching suits stood guard at the door. One nodded to them and Moss heard the other murmur, "Polis on their way in," into his two-way radio.

The entrance opened up to a bar on one side with a dark, spacious seating area beyond. A young bartender came forward and Steel said, "Tell McCann the police are here for him."

While they waited, Steel watched a pretty dancer with long black hair moving sinuously round a brass pole to Fleetwood Mac's *Black Magic Woman*. Clad only in the briefest of thongs and impossibly high-heeled shoes, her fluid body movements were in eloquent harmony with the notes Peter Green pulled from his guitar. She spotted him watching and with a little smile started to dance for him alone.

Holding the pole with one hand she swung out and round, gracefully dipping her body in a slow wide curve, the fingers of her free hand skimming the stage. Then, arching up, she threw her head back, tossing her long hair in a wild arc, and cupped her breast in her hand. As she slowly lowered her head, she gazed deep into Steel's eyes. Her direct eye contact was an erotic connection as dazzling as a shaft of sunlight out of darkness, and he gave her a small smile.

Moss came up from behind and stealing a glance at him said, "Your cup of tea, sir?" With her words, the dancer's spell which had captured Steel was broken, and she saw him momentarily flustered in her presence.

"More of a coffee drinker these days," he muttered.

Moss was about to say she hadn't caught that over the music, but thought better of it. While Steel made a show of checking his phone for non-existent messages, she continued to watch the dancer, now off in her own world and moving exquisitely to a deeper internal rhythm. Appraising her and her performance, she thought, What a stunning creature − a fabulous dancer.

"Well, well, if it's no' Stainless Steel . . . and he's brought Sapphire wi' him, too."

Steel and Moss turned as one. Apart from photographs, this was Moss's first meeting with William Edward McCann. Flanked by one of his men, he stood at just over six foot and was dressed in a well-tailored, expensive dark suit and open-necked ivory silk shirt − a bull of a man: barrel-chested, broad shouldered, with a thick neck. His face was smooth, pampered she reckoned, and his black hair fashionably cropped. He smiled, but it wasn't a smile that reached his eyes. They were hard, challenging and unblinking.

"It's been a while, Billy."

"Mr. McCann to you, Stainless."

The man at his side found that funny, laughing loudly. Loud enough to let everyone know.

Steel closed the distance between himself and McCann's laughing companion and, grabbing him by the throat, slammed him against the wall. Hearing the noise several people turned then, seeing trouble, got to their feet to leave. Moss readied herself, glancing quickly towards the front door where the bouncers stood. She hadn't expected anything like this.

With his back to McCann, and without releasing his grip or close eye contact with the man pinned to the wall, Steel said, "You are, and always will be, Billy McCann. I marked your card. Just you remember that."

"For fuck's sake Steel," McCann spat, "ye cannae jus' come in here and throw your weight around. Not *here*."

Steel thought differently. Easing his grip round the man's throat, he peered at him. "And what's *your* name, son? You're not a McCann I missed are you?"

The man licked his lips, and his eyes flicked towards his boss, but he was silent.

Steel released him and turned to McCann. "This thing's licensed, yes?"

McCann smiled, this time genuinely. "Easy. Johnny's my driver. The only license he needs he's got." He turned to Moss, his eyes very slowly taking her in, head to toe. "And who's this delightful young lady, Steel?"

"I'm DS Moss."

"Come now . . . despite your boss playing silly buggers, we're a' friends here. Do I no' get a first name?"

"That's only for *my* friends."

"Ouch," McCann said, pulling his face into a theatrical wince. "So, *Chief* Inspector, what can I do for you?"

"I'm looking for your brother."

"Stevie? You'll no' find him here. What d'ye think the wee eejit's been doin'?"

"What I know he's been doing."

McCann shrugged. "Think, know, you'll make it up anyway. I could gi'e him a message if you want."

Steel ignored this, poking at him, "Is this *your* club Billy?"

"Humble manager, that's all I am."

"So, the owner is . . . ?"

"A company, as I'm sure ye know. I'm just an employee, I manage it, and I think I do that well. *Oysters* is high class – we're no' like those places you'll find on Lothian Road and West Port. Look around . . . if you've no' frightened them off, you might spot the odd senior civil servant."

Steel held his gaze, but Moss took in the club. "No, I don't see any . . .

perhaps all the odd ones are at work."

McCann gave a deep laugh. "Oh, she's good Steel, I'd keep her if I were you. Especially now Brian's off to Dundee . . . a Detective Inspector I believe."

"And this is the only club you manage?" Steel said, refusing to rise to the knowledge McCann had flaunted.

"I manage a variety of entertainment establishments," McCann said, adding sharply, "All legitimate, licensed, premises – tax and VAT paid."

"I could check," but Steel knew these were empty words; there was no point in McCann having this front otherwise.

"You really should move on Steel. Everything that connected us is in the past," and he smiled at him, "water under the Dean Bridge, so tae speak. Instead of being an old-fashioned cop and wasting your wages – which, I'll remind ye, me and other businessmen pay – shouldn't ye be out there catchin' criminals?"

Moss could see this jibe had got under Steel's skin and was watching for another violent reaction, but he only said, "You let Stevie know I want a chat with him. I'll be back." And with a nod to Moss he turned to leave.

Watching them go, McCann called out, "Any time Stainless . . . just make sure ye bring Sergeant *Robin* with ye, I *like* having pretty birds in the club."

When they reached the car, Moss rounded on Steel. "That was assault."

He saw a fire smouldering behind her grey-green eyes. He knew this wasn't the way she'd been trained, but he and McCann had a history: cop and robber, cowboy and Indian, and if he could maybe stretch a point with her, good guy, bad guy.

"Really? You're going to tell me *how* to handle low-life Moss? Really? Tell you what, give me the Scots Law, chapter and verse, and maybe I'll agree with you." She said nothing and he gave her a faint smile, "For people like McCann it's a hello. Anyhow, I knew you'd back me up with your Tai whatsit."

"Aikido," she snapped, "and I was about to use it on *you*." She struggled to find more words for him, some that would express how wrong he'd been – and what did knowing Scottish law have to do with it, anyhow? – but, in the face of his blank expression, gave up with a loud exhalation.

Steel suppressed a smile, remembering the time Brian had just as violently disagreed with him. Of course, back then, Brian had simply taken a swing at him. "Are you done?" She said nothing as he opened the car door. "You better get studying for that exam if you still want to work with me," and then, with an open smile for her, "Remember one thing Moss: anger means they're unthinking . . . it *can* be useful."

They drove back to Fettes in silence. Steel knew only too well their disagreement was only part of that peculiar dynamic of enforced partnerships everywhere. It was rare to be in a successful partnership that was always smooth, especially as a cop. Thinking of JJ, he wanted to call her, bring her up to speed with their meeting with Emma Boyd, but it would be much better if he could visit her at the *Scotsman*.

He drove up to Fettes' front entrance to drop Moss off; he would call JJ when he was alone. "I've got a few things to do. Get on to Forensics and I'll see you later."

Moss got out of the car without a word and the door slammed behind her. Briefly, Steel watched her determined walk into Fettes – he knew she was upset with him but, well, they'd sort it out later.

He drove off, heading for the city centre through Stockbridge, and called JJ to tell her how little their discussion with Boyd had yielded. "I believe there's something there JJ, but it's not enough to act on."

"Really, you think so?" She hesitated. "Look, I'm tied up here right now and I have to be elsewhere later. How about meeting for something light to eat and you can explain that one to me."

He couldn't think of anything he would like to do more than spend time with her alone. "Where?"

"St. Patrick's Square? There's a good restaurant there. I'll see you at one, if that's okay."

Steel thought he knew Edinburgh's good restaurants, but none in St. Patrick's Square, the little three-sided rectangle of tenements surrounding a piece of grass with trees, set back from the busy arterial main road of Nicolson Street. "One's fine, JJ," he said and aimed the car towards the Dean Village. It wasn't really necessary, but he wanted to change – the smell of McCann clung to his clothes; dirty, like cigarette smoke.

Stepping from the shower he caught himself in the mirror and, seeing a foolish look there, told himself to act his age; she was a journalist he happened to be working with, nothing more.

Yet it had been longer than he cared to remember since he'd felt an attraction like this. There were many women he'd seen as attractive, but they had merely registered with him; he'd never acted on any of these attractions, and it had been a long time since any woman had played a part in his life. Too long really, but he'd learned to ignore his sexual side as if it were just another of life's impracticalities. Too complicated; too messy.

His marriage to Annabel had followed a depressing arc, from making love whenever and wherever they could, her lips hungrily seeking every part of him, to cold and separate sides of the bed where she wouldn't even give him a perfunctory goodnight kiss.

The loss of intimacy had been unbearable for Steel and eventually, through icy days punctuated by moments of sudden fire, what little survived of their relationship had been irrevocably devoured by one night of explosive drunken rage – a night that had ended with flashing blue lights at the door and a humiliating night in the cells. Inevitably, they'd staggered helpless into the bleak half-light of divorce. His drinking had never helped. His anger less so.

No woman should marry a policeman – they had *no* idea what they were marrying into; the Job was a heartless mistress, *never* taking kindly to wives claiming their time on husbands. The Job had eaten Annabel and their son – innocents, bystanders – alive.

And as he thought of them he saw the selfish reality, the deeper guilt, he chose to hide. It hadn't been the Job, not even the drink – it had solely been him, his actions. Thinking of his son he felt an all too familiar sadness wash over him; he had been a bad father, something he could *never* redress.

He stared at his reflection. Yes, it's alright to screw up your own life – that was free will, your own choice; you could do any stupid thing you cared to – but screwing up the lives of others, dragging them down into your own personal hell was, and would always be, unforgivable. He could hear a small voice rebuking him for being unremittingly hard on himself, but it was instantly drowned out by his father's words, "Your mess, your blame." Words, no doubt, stretching back countless generations of Steel fathers to Steel sons, all the way from Edinburgh to the Highlands.

He wiped away the condensation and, looking himself squarely in the mirror as he prepared to shave, pushed away any thoughts of JJ. She's a journalist I'm working with, that's all.

•

With difficulty, Steel found a place to park in St. Patrick's Square and as he got out saw JJ walking towards him, giving him a little wave and a smile he could feel at a distance. He watched her approach, red hair tied back in a ponytail, and wearing a soft waist-length green suede jacket with jeans over boots; she could have been conjured out of his psyche. Heads turned as she walked towards him; her presence was like that of an exotic bird with bright dazzling colours in Edinburgh's diurnal grey. Whatever resolve he had mustered earlier to treat this beautiful, intelligent woman solely as a journalist he was working with simply dissolved.

"Hi Mike."

"JJ."

"Let's eat at *Kalpna*," she said, pointing across the street to the part of Nicolson Street that made up the fourth side of St. Patrick's Square.

Steel looked. "Indian?" and as he read the sign, " *Vegetarian?*"

JJ smiled. "Don't tell me – you're a steak man."

"'Fraid so. Rare . . . the bloodier the better."

She threaded her arm through his and pulled gently. "Come on, you'll like this," and Steel, enjoying the sensation of her touch, allowed himself to be led.

When they were seated in the small restaurant JJ ordered a glass of white wine. "Drink, Mike?"

He shook his head. "No, I'll not."

"Is that, 'I'm a policeman and always on duty'?"

"Something like that."

Even though he knew next to nothing about the dishes JJ ordered for him – ignorance *was* bliss – his meal was perfect. Expecting fiery Indian flavours, Steel had been pleasantly surprised by the subtle and delicate tastes *Kalpna* conjured up. The place was a find.

But, really, he savoured her company. "What's your background JJ; Bill told me a bit, but how did you end up in Edinburgh?"

She smiled. "The third degree?"

"No, no, I'm just . . . curious."

"Well, I started here, on local papers, did some freelancing with the *Scotsman* . . ." and her features clouded. "I had a child, father didn't want to know, so I decided to head south – get in the big boys' playpen in London."

"A child?"

JJ looked down at the tablecloth and began drawing patterns on it with a spoon. "Yes, she . . . died. I was . . ."

Steel leant in to her. "I'm sorry JJ . . . I was just being nosey – it goes with the job." She nodded and looked up, and he saw her eyes were moist. "Emma Boyd?"

She smiled at him. "Yes, let's."

Steel took her through that morning's talk with Emma and sat back. "So, you see, it's not really much to go on."

JJ lowered her voice. "There's Hawthorns, and Jane Ingram who manages a sauna – she'll back up what Emma's told you."

Steel thought of the one hundred and twenty-one pornographic images of minors, girls *and* boys, found on Mitchell's computer. "Yes, and we'll need to interview her. It's good, but not good enough JJ," and he gave her an apologetic smile, "Not enough to warrant a raid, I'm afraid."

"Maybe I should just front it . . . knock on the door one night and ask for an interview."

"You should be careful," Steel warned, "you've no idea who or what you might be faced with *and* – very importantly – we don't want these people running for cover."

She sat back and studied him with narrowed eyes over the rim of her glass. "I envy you, you know."

"*Envy* me?" Steel didn't think anyone had *ever* said that to him.

"Yes. You have the ability to actually *act* against people who do wrong – get them put away. I can only write about it and I find that frustrating."

Steel smiled at this. "I get frustrated too . . . but I don't get to put them away, that's for the courts. Trouble is, there, where Justice is supposedly dispensed, all too often good – expensive – lawyers step in and people I *know* shouldn't be walking the streets are as free as you or me."

"Yes, *lawyers*." She placed her glass down hard and the spoon rattled in Steel's saucer. "Is there such a thing as a *good* lawyer, Mike? I often find myself thinking it would be better if people ignored the law, 'cause sometimes the law just doesn't work."

Steel laughed, "Then you'd have me to deal with. That sounds like anarchy."

JJ held up her hands in mock surrender and gave him a mischievous smile, her green eyes sparkling. "Guilty. I promise I'll come quietly. Or, do you want to use your handcuffs?"

Steel was silenced by her teasing.

"You know what I mean though," JJ continued seriously, "Edinburgh sets such great store on the majesty of the law: the history, the wigs – the damned *gravitas* – and people the law *should* protect end up *un*protected, and those who we need protection from are, as you say, free to walk the streets. Either that, or the law comes at us with people like Mitchell on the bench – a bloody hypocrite sitting in judgement over others."

Steel thought she was painting a one-sided picture. "I think, in *most* people's lives, the law tends to be something separate and it affects them before they know what's really happening. It can be a bit like a fast revolving door . . . they're sucked in and spat out before they know it."

She nodded and glanced at her watch. "Oh, Hell. I'm sorry Mike, I need to go."

Steel hoped his disappointment didn't show. "Yes, I've got stuff I should be doing."

Outside, JJ said, "I'll keep digging Mike . . . my story's definitely out there. There *is* a layer of this city – Lord Henry's layer – that needs a very bright light shone on it. I'm going to have a word with Bill, see if we can set up a stakeout at Hawthorns."

Steel saw the certainty on her face, a certainty she was doing the right thing, and thought, If there's anything I envy, I envy you that. "Be careful JJ," he cautioned, "in all ways – remember, we don't want these people spooked."

She gave him a warm smile. "I *will* be careful Mike. Keep in touch," and she reached up to him to give him a quick kiss on the cheek, her body lightly brushing over his chest. To Steel it seemed the most natural thing she could have done and he wished, wherever she was going, he was going with her.

He watched her walk away. With her ponytail flipping from side to side, and the graceful sway of her hips, he thought Jerry Lee Lewis must have had her in mind when he recorded *Chantilly Lace*. And, smiling to himself, he could almost hear Moss say, "Who's Jerry Lee Lewis, then?"

THIRTEEN

THE RAIN WAS HEAVIER NOW than when the old priest had first set out, and he was finding crossing the road difficult. There were so many cars these days and, for some reason he could never fathom, in bad weather drivers seemed to drive even faster. The fact his arthritis slowed him down in wet weather didn't help either.

Eventually there was a gap in the traffic, and he was able to reach the white line in the centre of the road. He had to pause for some time there, his eyes slyly catching the lap dancing club nearby, before a driver slowed to a stop and waved him across.

Reaching the other side he almost walked straight into Mrs. Fallon, who was fighting the wind for her umbrella. With any luck I'll be able to walk right past her.

However, Mrs. Fallon had spotted her priest battling both the elements and Edinburgh's drivers, and was waiting to intercept him. "Father McCartney," she called out into the wind, "Good morning to you. If you can call *this* a good morning."

"Ah, Mrs. Fallon," and he muttered the platitude, "All God's mornings are good."

"Just so, Father. Is this you getting your messages? You should've mentioned it to me."

The priest shook his head with "I can manage," although since his housekeeper had died he was managing less and less. He tried to disengage himself from the woman; not only was she a daily nuisance, the rain was even heavier now, and he could feel his clothes beginning to stick to his skin.

"You should make a list Father. I'd be happy to get what you need."

His little movements to disengage and pass her were not working, so he said, "I'll think on that Mrs. Fallon," and turned his back on her.

"I'll see you at noon," she called out after his retreating form.

Father McCartney moved on. He'd heard her but there was no way he was going to respond. Of all his parishioners – an ever-dwindling number, he reflected gloomily – Mrs. Fallon had to be the very worst. Without fail, she appeared at Confession every day, and every day had nothing to confess. Nothing of any consequence; certainly no sins. Eventually he had reproached her, reminding her that taking confession was a holy act and not something to be taken lightly. However, it was as if he had never spoken; the very next day there she was, waiting to confess.

Happy to get what I need? Could he tell her – any of his parishioners – what he really needed? A new life. A break from *their* petty lives. To be left in peace after serving the same parish for almost forty years. Dear God, the ability to simply go out for a couple of floury rolls for breakfast without being waylaid in the street. And that would just be a start. He knew he was at odds with his faith, but his irritation with his parishioners – he had no other word for it – appeared to have no bounds.

The inescapable questions to be asked at Mass: Who am I? Why am I here?, with their infallible answers: To know God, to love Him and serve Him, had ceased to have any meaning. Meaning for him was reminding Bishop Cairns, yet again, that a housekeeper was a necessity. After all, finding rashers of bacon *and* rolls for breakfast was very little in the way of life's expectations.

As he returned to his church, attempting to shelter the paper bag of rolls from the now driving rain, he knew he needed a sign. Something to show him, even now, he still could be blessed, washed clean and made whole. Something to show him there was indeed life beyond the Mrs. Fallons of this world.

112

Entering, he was in sight of the Host and he paused to genuflect; despite anything he thought these days, the groove his life had worn was deep.

From behind he heard a swishing sound and for one very brief moment it sounded like an angel's wing might sound. Perhaps God had at last heard his call for a sign.

The heavy brass candlestick moved rapidly through the air in a wide arc and connected with the priest's head, just behind his ear. As he fell to the cold black and white tiles, the bag fell from his grasp scattering its rolls, and a darkness he'd only dreamt of rushed towards him.

•

Moss was looking at the newspapers when Steel arrived. "Morning sir."

"Look, about yesterday . . . with McCann-"

"I over-reacted. I realise there's history between you and him. I was . . . well, it took me by surprise, that's all."

The previous evening she'd discussed their visit to *Oysters* with Susan, who'd listened, then said, "You know what it's like, Robin . . . there are prison officers who beat inmates, judges who overlook the truth because they believe the person in front of them isn't worthy. Hell, even doctors who don't respond to a patient's alarm – I've seen it myself. The thing is . . . what's *your* choice? How do *you* choose to act?" And, although Moss could've argued with what she saw as a rather bleak summation, she could see a workable truth in Susan's words.

To move Steel on, she folded a newspaper and handed it to him. "Have a look at this."

Steel took the paper from her and read: Edinburgh Businessman's Lucky Escape. He looked up, "What's this?"

"Alan Prior. Apparently, he was run off the road last night. Deliberately, according to that."

Steel read the short piece. "On the Dundee to Edinburgh road . . . bruised, but not badly hurt. This is going to be worth looking into. Especially if it *was* deliberate."

"I've already been on to Traffic in Tayside sir, they're sending us their report."

"Good work Moss." She was definitely an asset. He was about to elaborate on what she'd called the 'history' between him and McCann, to justify his actions with the fact that sometimes people do the wrong thing for the right reason, when his phone rang. It was Grieve, and he sounded far from happy. Clattering the handset down, he sighed, "The boss wants to see us."

Grieve was reading when they entered and, placing the sheet of paper carefully on his desk, motioned for them to sit. He looked across his desk at Steel. "What's this I hear about you poking around in a Crime Squad case?"

"Poke? I never *poke* . . . in anyone's cases."

Grieve leaned in and stabbed a finger at him, "One of these days your mouth's going to get you into *real* trouble. You know what I mean – explain yourself."

Moss glanced at Steel; he didn't seem fazed by Grieve, and she got the impression that, like old sparring partners, both had been round many a circle like this one before.

"If you mean getting information about a company from Finance yesterday, well until I did, I had no idea there *was* a Crime Squad case."

"Go on."

Steel laid it out for him. "On Mitchell's murder, one of the houses nearby was shown to be owned by one of Alan Prior's companies and the resident is Steven McCann – *Billy* McCann's brother."

Grieve sat back with his hands interlaced on his ample chest and his thumbs rubbing together. "And why are we interested in this *now?* McVicar's in the frame for Mitchell's murder, why are we interested in Prior and McCann?"

Steel danced close to the truth, knowing Grieve didn't really want the whole truth; it was just another problem he wanted off his desk. "Steven McCann's name came up when we interviewed an escort who'd been to Mitchell's house," and sitting forward before Grieve could interrupt, "I was doing my job, not poking around."

Grieve wasn't placated by this. "Well you were," he spat.

Steel threw out his hands, "How the hell am I to know if I'm treading on anyone's toes?"

Grieve shook his head at this. "I think just walking will do fine, Mike,"

114

and he rocked himself forward, "but what *I'm* left with is, you've not been cluing me in." He looked from Steel to Moss, "Pretty useless position, eh?" Neither responded and he slapped the palms of his hands down so hard on the desk Moss almost jumped. "*Eh?*"

Shaking his head he reached for the phone, "Let's see if Crime Squad can shed some light on this . . . DCI Rob Henderson might be just the man to help," and Moss heard a loud sigh from Steel.

With Grieve's eyes fixed on Steel, all three sat in silence until there was a knock at the door. On Grieve's "Come," Moss swivelled in her chair to see this new arrival almost filling the door-frame. With cropped fair hair, rosy cheeks, and as broad as he was tall, he looked as if he might be more at home policing a farming community rather than working out of a city headquarters like Fettes.

"Sir," and he saw Steel, "Well, if it's not the bad penny himself."

"You should try plainclothes sometime," Steel said.

Moss saw what Steel meant; though not in uniform, Henderson nevertheless looked every inch a cop.

"Right," said Grieve, "that's morning greetings over." He motioned in Moss's direction, "This is DS Robin Moss." She held out her hand which, as Henderson took it, felt as if it was being squeezed in a great bear paw.

"Good to meet you Robin. Don't let this bastard fool you . . . don't be doing all the work just for him to take all the credit."

"That's *enough* Chief Inspector," Grieve snapped, "Just remember where you are . . . both of you. This isn't the bloody playground."

Henderson squeezed himself into a chair, threw Steel a disdainful look, then turned to Grieve. "By rights, Superintendent McKay should be apprised of this meeting, sir."

Grieve rounded on him. "I don't need *your* advice Henderson. I'll speak with your Super if needs be," and he leaned in, raising his voice, "That is, if *you* think we should maybe be doing police-work by the book here at Fettes."

He picked up the sheet of paper from his desk, looked at it and tossed it aside. "Steel tells me he's done nothing wrong in speaking with Finance. Records show that a house in Barnton, close to Lord Mitchell's, is occupied by Steven McCann, a known criminal, and owned by one of

Alan Prior's companies.

"What Records *don't* show is any flag Crime Squad has a current interest in either McCann or Prior. Now, if Crime doesn't want any action to come at it sideways there *is* a procedure . . . one to be followed – *without fail*, if I'm not mistaken."

Hearing this, Moss realised it must have been Henderson himself who'd failed to flag the file with a Crime Squad interest.

Unsuccessfully, Henderson tried to hold Grieve's gaze. "I think that might've been an oversight sir."

"God's teeth, you're damn *right* it's an oversight." He paused, collecting himself. "So, clue me in . . . what's Crime Squad's interest in either McCann or Prior?"

"I thought the Mitchell murder was done and dusted?" Henderson was trying to recover the ground he'd lost. "Some nutcase from Carstairs, yes?"

Steel stirred. "Aye, bar the catching of him, that's all."

Henderson kept his eyes on Grieve. "As far as Finance is concerned, they're working with Inland Revenue's Tax Inspectorate and aiming for a Capone – a tax evasion prosecution, of Prior or Priority Private Equity. Maybe both."

Moss spoke up. "Yesterday we were told there was talk of investors being defrauded by PPE. And, that the case had originated from Scotland Yard."

"Yes, to both," said Henderson. "It sounds as if PPE's running all sorts of shell games between its various Funds. That and sham transactions. Finance was given the nod by the Serious Fraud Office."

"How did the SFO get involved in the first place then?" Grieve said.

"Well, apparently it started when a London paper got stomped all over for doing – attempting to do – a story on Prior."

"Stomped on by who?" asked Steel.

"Paisley Wark – Prior's lawyers here. His wife Jan's firm. The paper, the editors and the journalists were all served with injunctions and the threat of prosecution for libel, with a massive demand for damages thrown in for good measure."

"So they backed off?"

"At speed, given the current libel laws but," and he gave them a crafty smile, "all their research somehow accidentally landed on a desk at the SFO. I can see it now . . . some poor sod down there looking at it, wondering where to start, only to be ordered to get it off his desk, bump it to the Met and get it all sent north." He shrugged, "It's ours anyhow."

"Right," said Steel, proprietorial about criminal behaviour on his own turf, "but I'm getting lost. If there were sham transactions wouldn't that be obvious from their books? Do firms not have to report yearly?"

Henderson shook his head. "If you mean some sort of official oversight, no. Private Equity Funds don't need to disclose very much, if anything. In fact, many of their more . . . interesting aspects can remain private. Hidden. You can see the attraction for a guy like Prior, *and* for certain rich individuals."

"Okay, now I'm definitely lost. How come investors were not up in arms over this?"

Henderson smiled. "Welcome to modern finance, Steel – *most* of the investors make money, Prior, being Fund Manager, is making the most."

"What's the shorthand?"

"Out of the broken companies they buy – for next to nothing – PPE repackages the debt as Managed Funds. Basically, PPE sells the debt of these companies rebundled into what are known as collateralised loan obligations. CLOs buy assets at par and use cash flow to pay the debt holder and management first. The remainder goes to the equity investor who gets a better return depending on how much they've put in."

Grudgingly admitting to himself that Henderson *appeared* to be well-versed, Steel only said, "You lost me at collateralised."

"Me too," added Grieve.

Moss leaned in. "I think I get it," and was rewarded with a scowl from Steel. "It's a refined form of asset stripping, with the equity investor paying for buying the debt in the first place but standing to make a killing depending on how much they've put in."

"Well, sort of . . ."

"Thing is," Moss continued, "if PPE's doing something fraudulent, I can understand Finance's *and* Inland Revenue's involvement but," and she swivelled her chair to face Henderson, "that doesn't explain *your* involvement. Why would the Scottish Crime and Drug Enforcement

Agency be involved?"

Henderson smiled broadly, "Ah, give the lady a coconut," and gave her a stage wink.

Grieve nodded his approval at Moss. "Good question."

"You know about the Forth Development?"

"Fourth development?" said Steel.

Henderson curled his lip disdainfully. "No, *River* Forth, that great big wet area running to the north of Edinburgh."

"No, can't say as I have."

Henderson leaned back in his chair, stretching and threatening the buttons on his shirt. He clasped his meaty hands behind his head and looked at the others coolly, enjoying his moment of omniscience. "Forth Development is *the* next big thing for Edinburgh – it's the development of the riverside area, all the way from Cramond in the west to Joppa in the east. Ten miles worth. Granton and a bit of Leith is what's in play right now, but that's just the start. We're talking about the development of a completely new Edinburgh, and the cost? . . . billions."

"And Crime's interested in this, why?" asked Steel.

Henderson snorted at this. "Whenever there's money like that sloshing about, *especially* when it concerns the public purse and the private sector, there's interest for us. Prior's interest is in getting his nose stuck in the trough by raising finance, and using his development and property companies to get a big slice of the pie."

"None of which is illegal," said Steel, "But?" and he raised his eyebrows at him.

"Yes, the *but* is this development is attracting millions from abroad." He unclasped his hands and sat forward. "I'd like to track every pound and penny because I bet there'll be dirt on plenty but, currently, we're only interested in Euros from Holland."

"Holland?"

"You've heard of SARs?" Steel shook his head. "Suspicious Activity Reports. The Financial Intelligence Unit was set up as part of EU Regulations, and banks, accountants and lawyers are required, by law, to report any transactions they think are suspicious."

"Anything large you pay cash for? Any large deposits or withdrawals?"

asked Moss.

"*Any* large money transfers at all – the UK FIU receives about a quarter of a million SARs every year. Anyhow, the Dutch cops tell us *very* large chunks of money are coming from there into Prior's companies . . . those involved in the Forth Development."

"And these are not kosher?"

"Hard to say for certain at this time but, according to the Dutch, *some* of it smells like drug profits being laundered."

Moss sat forward. "If it *is* laundering, there's still no way we could prove Prior actually knows that. I take it the Dutch investors appear clean?"

Henderson nodded. "As a whistle, Robin. They have impeccable credentials," and he looked from her to Steel. "Nobody going to ask an obvious question?"

"*Is* there an obvious one?" asked Steel.

Moss, however, had put two and two together. "If the Dutch say the money coming into Prior's companies appears to be clean, although suspect it's drug money being laundered anyway, then they have an idea it's drug money from here because *that* explains Crime and Drug's involvement."

Henderson gave her a slight bow. "Two coconuts for the sergeant. Watch your heels Steel."

Steel ignored this; she was *his* sergeant. "Here, as in Scotland?"

"Better than that – here, as in Edinburgh. Want to hazard a guess as to what name might fit that frame?"

"Billy McCann," Steel and Moss said in unison.

Henderson sat back with a smile, while Steel let the idea of Prior, McCann, and billions of pounds fed by drug money, run through his head.

"So," Grieve said, "what are we talking of? Cocaine?"

"No sir," Henderson said, "cocaine's still coming into Europe via West Africa, but we're having more success disrupting that. Internationally, that is. According to the Dutch it's heroin. Here, on the street, the purity's very poor – about seventeen percent – but anyone bulk buying will be getting it at near enough ninety percent."

Grieve gave a long sigh; in his day it had been booze and cigarettes, and a damn sight easier to police. "Right Chief Inspector, I'll not keep you," and he held up a warning finger, "You'll find out who in Crime failed to flag Records with an interest and give them a quiet bollocking, yes? Let them know that, *this* time, they're lucky I'm not taking it further, eh?"

Henderson got up as rapidly as his bulk allowed, glad to be going unscathed. "Yes sir."

When he was gone Steel turned to Grieve. "Thanks sir."

"I don't just *sit* behind this desk you know, and I didn't get here without knowing a thing or two. Bloody Crime Squad . . . they act as if *they're* Lothian and Borders and everyone else can stumble around in the dark after them."

Steel made to get to his feet but Grieve said, "Sit where you are Mike . . . you too Moss. I'm not finished." He pulled the sheet of paper on his desk towards him and scanned it again, hopeful of seeing something different but it was still the same. "After your little jolly to Fife, the Chief received a letter from one William McKnight of Smith McKnight Hughes – Lady Mitchell's solicitors."

"What's this," Steel said, feeling himself becoming warm, "a *formal* complaint?"

"As good as. It's couched in nice polite terms but threatens . . . let me see: 'that, as lawyers for Lady Mitchell, we shall not hesitate' . . . 'over-zealous and unwarranted behaviour of DCI Steel', and *et cetera*."

He looked up at Steel. "So, the next step *will* be a formal complaint. A bloody *running* of the bulls in a china shop, eh?" and as Steel rose in his chair to respond, he waved a hand in front of him, "Don't bother Mike, just take this as a warning shot across your bows – one that, as you can see, the CC has heard, loud and clear. *Stay away from Lady Mitchell.* That's not me, that comes directly from the Chief. D'you hear?"

Grieve's stare bored into Steel. "Let's put her timings down to her getting a wee bit confused after finding her husband murdered, eh? Whatever, it doesn't matter . . . it's McVicar we want."

He looked at Moss. "See? You're still learning," and with a glance at Steel, "Properly, I hope. There's stuff you've got to take on board and stuff you've got to pitch over the side. A good officer learns the difference between the two."

Moss only nodded, and Grieve turned back to fire a last salvo at Steel. "This better not be in one ear and out t'other with you. Go on, get out."

When they reached their office, Steel exploded, "Bloody lawyers. She lied to us. Never mind Grieve with his, 'a wee bit confused', she lied. Nobody – no matter who they are or what fancy lawyers they can afford – gets to *do* that in a murder case."

Moss was about to reply when Steel's phone rang. He ignored it. After a few more rings it stopped and hers started. Picking it up she listened, then turned to a still fuming Steel. "Sir."

"What *now?*"

"McVicar . . . apparently he's murdered a priest."

121

FOURTEEN

WITH A NOD OF RECOGNITION, the PC hoisted the tape to let their car through. Both ends of the street had been closed, and a stoic phalanx of uniformed police were ignoring questions from the press and a growing crowd of gawpers who, despite the now sleeting rain, had been drawn to the flashing blue lights.

The street was two unremarkable rows of black tenements running between Lauriston Place and the 'pubic triangle' on West Port, broken only by the church which sat back from the pavement; an incongruous proximity of the sacred and the profane. Looking up at the flats, Moss could see what seemed to be a face at every window, occupants drawn by the knowledge something bad had happened on their doorstep.

Grim-faced, Steel stepped out of the car and caught sight of a young policeman, his face drained of colour, retching near the church's doorway. He crossed to him. "What's your name, son?"

The constable tried to pull himself upright but his body was still in revolt, and an older PC, watching his colleague with distaste, said, "Spiers, sir."

Steel gave him a nod. "Stand up, Spiers." With difficulty, the policeman managed and Steel saw his eyes were watering. Looking about him and lowering his voice, Steel said, "What the hell do you think you're doing?"

"Sir . . . it's *awful.*"

He reached for the young man's arm and turned him away from the street. "Awful is what you do. If you *can't* do that, get back to your station, get out of uniform, and go home."

The man blinked away the tears, his face now a bright red.

Steel paused, sizing him up. "Just remember *what* you are and remember what your uniform means. People look to you being in control. If you can't do awful do something *else*, and if you need to throw up when you do awful, do it somewhere else . . . not in plain sight. Right?"

Spiers remained silent and, in a quieter voice, Steel said, "Get yourself cleaned up son, and then get back here and do the job. It's that, or go home. Understood?"

"Yes sir." The young constable seemed to be pulling himself together.

Steel turned away from him and back to Moss, knowing – whatever it was – he had only put off *his* take on awful. "Let's get on."

At that point, the small door in the large arched doors into the church opened and a plain clothes officer stepped out to meet them. Shaking Steel's hand, and giving Moss a nod, he said, "DI Fisher, Torphichen. It's pretty bad. Let me take you inside."

They entered the vestibule and saw an elderly woman sitting on a bench sobbing uncontrollably, with a female constable at her side trying to console her. Steel raised his eyebrows in query at Fisher. "Mrs. Mary Fallon, sir. She discovered the body."

"Right," Steel nodded. "See if you can rustle up a cup of tea for her or something. You spoken with her?"

"Not yet . . . can barely get a word out of her," and he mimicked cup of tea towards the WPC.

"Don't let anyone whisk her away," Steel warned, "I'll want to question her."

"Of course," Fisher waited for them to clamber into coveralls and then, pulling on the mullioned door, stepped to one side to let them through.

The church was vast and cold. It would have been dark in there, but the temporary lights set up by the Crime Scene Examiners were two pools of blazing brightness casting high theatrical shadows on to the walls. Before them, at the end of the central aisle that ran between the rows of pews, they saw a photographer working around a large brass candlestick. A smear of bright red blood trailed from there, across the black and white tiles, and towards the alter.

Steel turned to Moss to see her dip her fingers into the holy water and with a slight bow of her head and a dip of her knee, cross herself. "*When* you're ready, Moss."

Moss shook her head at this. *Bless me, wash me clean, and make me whole* had been on her lips but, now, she was doubtful; perhaps she would never *be* what Steel might call ready.

"It seems he was hit here and dragged down there," Fisher said with a nod of his head. They looked into the pool of light and saw several Examiners and the bulky figure of Dr. Knox busily at work around what appeared to be an upright figure.

They walked down the side aisle and as they approached, the scene came into sharp, horrific focus – McVicar had crucified Father McCartney across his confessional.

The priest's arms had been tied-off at the wrists and a cord was wrapped around his neck, pulling his head upright. With his clothing torn apart, they could see his chest had been scored and, as they drew closer, the horror intensified; the priest's wrists had been nailed to the wood and a deep incision made across his forehead. From the loose flap of skin, blood had trickled down his face. In his evil, McVicar had mocked the Christ.

"Jesus," breathed Steel.

"*Sir.*" Moss felt a hot wave of nausea pass through her, her whole being rebelling at the unholy sight before her.

Knox turned to them. "Well, Chief Inspector," and with a nod for her, "*Sergeant* Moss. They're quite stacking up, aren't they? Two in one week and here, you might say McVicar's taken a biblical turn." He gave them a wide grin, "But I've got an easy one for you this time."

Steel said nothing; Knox's facetious way around death got right under his skin. Moss, however, couldn't help herself. "*Easy?*"

"Why yes, Sergeant Moss," Knox said, barely able to contain himself, "It's McVicar, in the church, with a candlestick."

"Tell me what you have Doctor," Steel snapped.

With a small shrug, Knox turned away from the body. "Well, he was hit over there – the alter candlestick being the obvious weapon – there's a massive wound behind his ear, and-"

"He was killed with that then?"

"No. Again, a chisel or the fabled sharpened screwdriver to the carotid artery. I'm in the right place, so God help me, I hope he was unconscious when this happened. He certainly wasn't dead."

Taking a deep breath, Moss moved towards the corpse and peered at the wrists; they'd been crushed with some force. Then she saw the type of nails which protruded from the priest's wrists and reeled back, her stomach lurching dangerously. "McVicar used a nail gun?"

Fisher nodded. "Yes. We found one between the pews with blood on it."

Steel was looking closely at the priest's chest: three precise, bloody scores, each about a foot long. "Are these the same as Mitchell's, Doctor?"

Knox twitched his shoulders and grunted. "I can't say for certain . . . but if you want an answer from me right now Steel, then yes, I'd say so – they're comparable," and he gave him a little smile, "In fact, you *could* say they're parallel."

Moss was beginning to feel faint; this was a holy place, yet evil had risen up to take command of it. "Did McVicar bring a nail gun *with* him?" Her question seemed to echo in her head, as if someone else had spoken, and she sat down slowly in a pew.

Fisher looked at her and saw her drop her head on to her chest. "There's work being done here Sergeant – I think he found the tool and improvised."

Moss only shook her head; she needed to get out of there – to walk away and keep on walking. She looked up at Steel and, beyond the priest's head with its rivulets of blood, saw the figure of the crucified Christ, high above the alter. "Sir."

Steel turned from his close examination of the corpse and could see she was sinking, her face ashen. "Go get some fresh air Moss." The horror had not passed him by – it promised more images for him to unwillingly carry and revisit at some dark moment in the future – but right now, he needed his DS at full strength.

She didn't move.

"*Now* Moss, and when you can, see if you can get something out of Mrs. Fallon."

Moss left the church and, taking several deep breaths, tried to centre herself. Closing her eyes she tilted her head back . . . the sleet falling on her skin felt good, and standing there alone for several minutes, she was able to regain some measure of what approached calm. *McVicar must be caught* was the thought that wouldn't stop running through her head, but it seemed to her that only blind luck would stop the mayhem now.

Composing herself, she stepped back inside; just as Steel had told the young constable, if she couldn't do awful, then she had no business being there. She walked across to where Mrs. Fallon sat hunched with the WPC and saw her hands clutching a mug filled with tea, her sightless eyes staring at the floor.

"Mrs. Fallon?" The woman's head jerked up at her voice, and Moss read deep fear in her eyes. You and me both, she thought. Giving her a faint smile, she said, "Mrs. Fallon, my name is Robin, I am a Detective Sergeant. I'm sorry, but I need to ask you some questions."

"It's Mary."

"Mary," Moss nodded slowly. "Can I ask you at what time you discovered the priest's body?"

"Father Patrick McCartney," she said, correcting her. For her it wasn't a body in there.

"Yes, Father McCartney . . . what time was it?"

"I came for Confession. Just before twelve."

"Was there anyone in the church? Did you see anyone leaving?"

"No. There was nobody here," and she looked up at Moss, "I saw him earlier, you know."

"Who?" Moss said sharply.

"Father McCartney . . . he was going for his messages. I can't help but think if I'd only stepped in to ask, this . . . wouldn't've happened."

Moss shook her head. "You can't think that Mary. You're in no way responsible."

"We are all responsible," Fallon said, her voice faltering.

Moss pressed on. "So Mary, at what time did you see Father

127

McCartney?"

"It would've been some time after ten. Aye, after ten."

"How long after? It's important."

"Let me . . . ten-thirty. Maybe five minutes either way."

"And he was *going* for . . . messages?" Moss said, perplexed.

Fallon nodded. "Aye, hen . . . his shopping."

"Right, Mary. Now, is there someone you can be with?" The woman gave her a blank look. "Someone who can comfort you."

Fallon's body trembled and tears welled up to brim in her eyes. "I'm on my own now. Father McCartney was my comfort . . . he wasn't just my priest, he was a beautiful man."

Moss caught herself thinking of the role priests played within their parishes: stern disseminators and watchdogs of the Word. Beautiful didn't fit. Glancing at the female officer, she said, "Well, I'll get someone to take you home." There were all kinds of victims of murder besides the dead and, placing a light hand on Fallon's shoulder, she said softly, "Take care of yourself Mary. We'll be in touch."

She stepped away from Fallon and was met by one of the uniforms. "Sarge, the priest's bishop is here." She looked beyond him to see a tall, thin man, rosy cheeked with a shock of white hair, standing expectantly on one side.

"Right, I'll deal with him."

She crossed over to the man. "Good morning, sir. I'm DS Moss, how can I help you?"

"Bishop Cairns. I must pray for Father McCartney."

Moss hesitated. "I'm not sure you'll be able to," and seeing the man's knitted brows and something like irritation flit across his face, she added, "This *is* a murder scene, sir."

"No, Sergeant, this is a church – Father McCartney's church. It is essential I pray for him."

Moss weighed her options and found she had precious few. "Please wait here sir, I'll speak with Chief Inspector Steel," and getting a curt nod from him, she re-entered the church.

Steel was sitting on a pew, far from the corpse, and deep in thought. To Moss it looked like he could be simply relaxing on a park bench. "Sir."

He turned to her, "You alright Moss?"

"Yes sir." She heard her lie – uttered with ease and here, in a church, before the Host – white lie or not, she had just sinned. "Father McCartney's bishop is here. He wants to pray for him."

Steel only nodded and got to his feet. "Timing, Moss . . . they're just about to remove the body." He looked round. "The Examiners haven't quite finished though . . . get him suited-up and bring him in."

When the bishop arrived he recoiled before the slack remains with a whispered "Holy Mother of God," and crossed himself quickly. He turned to Steel. "Thank you, Chief Inspector."

Steel gave a little shrug. "The Last Rites?"

Moss could have told him he was wrong, but that would've meant adding to what for her was already an intrusion; Cairns was right – this was a church, not a crime scene.

With a shake of his head the bishop said, "No, that is for the dying . . . I shall offer a prayer for the lately deceased," and seeing Steel's questioning look, "A prayer for the dead is one of the greatest acts of charity we can perform, Chief Inspector. I shall express the hope that God will free Father McCartney from any burden of sin and prepare a place for him in Heaven."

Steel had nothing to say to this but called out, "Everyone . . . could we have silence, please."

Bishop Cairns knelt, kissed his embroidered stole and slipped it round his neck, then made the sign of the Cross. Steel glanced at Moss and could see that, in her own private way, she was preparing herself too. He heard the first words, "Absolve, we beseech thee, O Lord . . ." and tuned out the rest; there was a murderer to be caught and nothing in this religiosity could possibly help.

Getting to his feet, the bishop thanked Steel, stressing his availability to help in any way and, with a murmured blessing for Moss, he left them.

Steel watched him leave with DI Fisher, then turned to Moss. "Before it's removed, I want you to look at the body again."

"Sir?"

"I want you to look at the body . . . *this* time, as a cop."

"I don't understand, sir."

Steel sighed. "Just *look*. Don't just use your eyes – use your head." He saw fear written on her face, and wondered whether she would ever get hardened to horror. He never had, but he was still there, trying to make sense of what appeared to be senseless; *somehow* she needed to reach a similar spot of her own.

In a softer voice he said, "You're being distracted by your emotions, Moss. Look at the body as a cop and you'll see it as evidence, not as a priest who's been horribly murdered. Young Spiers out there was right – it *is* awful. But, if you let *that* intrude – or allow yourself to be distracted by your emotions – you'll look but you won't see."

Moss still had no understanding, but turned to the priest's body. Somehow, in some way, the horror was diminished, although she still felt the urge to get as far away as possible. Staring at the corpse she tried to take in the knotted rope, the nails, the scores to the old man's chest, his bloody forehead, and the deep wound at the neck as if there were obvious clues – clues which could be the evidence Steel said she was missing.

Steel was watching her closely. "No?"

She shook her head. "No sir," and for a brief moment, saw a look of satisfaction on Steel's face. "What?"

"Nothing . . . you needed to see as a copper, that's all."

At first she felt a flush of anger, then realised what Steel had done, and in a quiet voice, said, "Yes."

•

He staggered down the steep hill which led from the New Town to Stockbridge. Earlier he'd tried to get a drink, but the bars nearby had been filled with Satan's daughters dancing for men with lust-filled eyes. Uriel had warned him not to stay.

As he was leaving one pub, two uniformed policemen were entering and blocked his exit. There were police everywhere.

"Just a moment, sir."

He stopped; in Glasgow the police never called him sir. "I've already been questioned," dropped from his lips, and he felt for the chisel in his pocket.

The two young constables had already had a long day, and he could see both of them were more interested in the near naked dancers.

130

"Right sir. Have a good evening."

He almost smiled at them; he *was* going to have a good one. Hearing Uriel whisper *Go*, he nodded and pushed his way out to the street, his eyes catching the still flashing blue lights from the street opposite.

Now, as he walked unsteadily down into Stockbridge, he wondered about those pills he had taken. A pub in Rose Street, a conversation with a youngster with an assumed hard man air, a dark lane, three flashing strikes with the chisel, and the drugs and the youngster's money were his. Perhaps he had taken too many.

The policeman's address had been easy to find; there he was in the phone book – D. Thompson, the man who'd used his name on television. Ann Street was more difficult, but after asking several people he knew how to get there.

Finding the house in the narrow, cobbled, almost fairytale street, he swung the gate open and made his way up the long path to the front door. A brass sign: Thompson. He smiled – brass, top brass, brassed-off – Uriel was guiding him.

He looked back towards the street. In the darkness, a strange pulsating white fog was emanating from the low ornate street lamps, but he could see no house lights.

Even touching the door should have tripped the state-of-the-art alarm but, making it mere worthless electronics, it hadn't been set.

Pushing the chisel into the door jamb beside the lock, he threw his weight against the door. It held. With another massive push he tried again, and the door burst open with a splintering crash.

Rushing into the house, he began seeking out Satan's helper. Uriel told him to kill anyone who appeared before him, but it was the brass he wanted.

Moving from room to room, with their soft, pretty things, he eventually realised the house was empty. A slow rage started to build and a keening white noise filled his ears. Finding himself in the kitchen, he began ripping doors open, stopping when he saw the cans of spray paint beneath the sink.

Uriel was in command, and he listened to his breathy guidance. Lifting a can, he went back into the living room.

Beginning on the wall facing the windows, he shook the can and, in foot high, dripping red letters, sprayed: Judge . . . Not . . .

The can sputtered – it had run out. Hurling it in anger across the room, it shattered the mirror above the fireplace and Uriel whispered in his ear, *Leave.*

FIFTEEN

MOSS WOKE IN A HOT SWEAT as a vision of the murdered priest jolted her from sleep. Realising where she was, she looked at the clock. Late. Not *too* late, just oh-my-God-I'd-better-move late. Naked, she stretched to open her body, pushing off the warm covers, then shimmied into her robe and headed for the kitchen.

Susan looked up from her paper as she entered. "Well, good morning, Miss Sleepy."

"You *could've* nudged me. I just hate being late."

Susan glanced at the clock. "You're okay. Besides, it's Saturday." She watched Moss busying herself, pouring a coffee and feeding a couple of slices of bread into the toaster. "What's your boss *actually* like, Robin?"

"Who? Stainless Steel, the History Man? Sometimes I get the sense of just being his sounding-board. I'm pretty sure, if he had a choice, he'd prefer I was male."

"But, apart from the occasional macho outburst of violence, a good cop?"

"Yes. He's old-school, treats me like a novice at times, but he's . . . right for me, I think. Yesterday he forced me to look at a corpse – as evidence . . . as a cop – and, until I did, I wasn't sure I could continue working as one."

"And now . . . ?"

Moss thought for a moment. "Don't get me wrong – I haven't worked murder cases before and, in one week, I've seen two really nasty ones . . . I'm bound to be affected but, well, I have to work through that, don't I? Do the job."

Susan nodded, thinking of the broken bodies that came before her. "We certainly do get to see some fairly horrific things, and he'll have seen more than his share." She poured herself another coffee. "What about that reporter he's met," and she gave Moss a wry look, "the one *you* called pretty?"

"JJ? Well, she is. You should see him in her company . . . he's *lost*. I don't know why he just doesn't make a move on her." She stared at the toaster as it made its ticking sounds and yawned. "Anyhow, there – I've told you about him."

A faint, pencil sketch, thought Susan. "Yes, but is he a stickler for time?" and with a little smile, "Will you get a row and detention if you're late?"

"Not sure," Moss replied, taking a gulp of coffee and willing the toaster to pop. "Saturday or not, I've never been late, so I don't know." She looked at the clock. "Going to squeeze in a shower, though . . ."

•

When Moss arrived Steel was slowly spinning from side to side in his seat in front of a large whiteboard almost covered with photographs of the McCartney crime scene. "Sorry sir – I missed the alarm."

Steel gave a little shake of his head. "You're here. Grieve's on his way in, and he's not sounding happy." He spun back to the whiteboard. "These bother me . . . there's something wrong here, and I can't get it."

"Wrong, in what way?"

"I don't know. Perhaps it's too early, but it's like I'm doing a jigsaw puzzle with a few bits missing . . . all the bits we have fit but, somehow, not as they should."

"I don't understand."

Steel gave her a faint smile. "It's okay, neither do I."

Just then Grieve appeared in the doorway, and giving Moss a cool "Morning Sergeant" he nodded at Steel, "A word with you."

In his office, Grieve circled his desk and sat down with a long sigh. "Sit down Mike . . . want to tell me about yesterday?"

"The McCartney murder?"

"What else? . . . I hear Moss couldn't hack it."

Steel sat forward. "That's nonsense. Where did you hear that?" Mentally, he marked DI Fisher's card; who else could it have been? "She wobbled, but she's just in the door, not even a week. Christ's sake Bob, you and I have seen plenty murders before – that was her second, and both were . . . well, as bad as anything I've ever seen."

"Maybe . . . then again, maybe I was wrong to make her your bagman."

"She's new, but she's getting there."

Grieve shook his head. "I need all my officers at full-strength . . . however long they've been here."

"She *was* – it was difficult for her, but she did the job, and did it well." Steel knew how Grieve thought; not only was he questioning Moss's abilities, he was questioning him as her superior. Where was *this* leading?

Grieve pulled a face, "Whatever you say Mike, but," and he reached for a folded newspaper, "now we're having to deal with *this*," tossing it half-way across the desk.

It was the *Sun*. Opening it, Steel was startled to see a large picture of himself almost covering the front page. The photograph had been taken at the start of the Mitchell press conference, when Grieve had handed over to him to field questions. His hands were up beside his face, his eyes closed, his mouth hung open, and he looked more than a little foolish – glaikit, his father would have said. In big, bold type the headline read: Murders 2 Cops 0, and under that, in smaller type, Lothian & Borders Police Lost At Sea.

"Christ."

"Christ indeed," Grieve snarled. "Let me tell you, you made no good impression on the Chief at that press conference – your attitude with the press was painful to watch."

Making a supreme effort to contain his anger, Steel said nothing. He noted the byline on this so-called story was Jim McEwan's; he'd deal with him later – there *would* be an opportunity.

"On top of that," Grieve continued, "the Chief got contacted – personally – by the Mitchells' lawyers because of you. Now this," and shaking his head, "You've got too damn close, too damn personal."

"Personal?"

Grieve stabbed the air between them. "I *told* you not to be heavy-footed on this, and what do I get, eh? You barge straight in, thinking what? That you're right and *somehow* that justifies *any* sort of behaviour. I don't suppose you bothered to inform Fife you were on their patch either," and seeing Steel's look, shook his head.

For a brief moment Steel wondered whether there had been further communication between William McKnight and the Chief Constable; was this Grieve covering his back?

Grieve leant forward, laying his hands flat on the desk. "I'm taking you off this, Mike. A Murder Squad will be set up until McVicar's caught."

"You're *what?*"

"You mishandle the press, you barge into the lives of people who should be kid-gloved, and," with a nod to the paper before Steel, "now this . . . and this is making *all* of us look bad. What else is on your desk right now?"

Steel felt heat coursing through him. "You can't take me off this case. It's mine – it was from day one."

Grieve slapped his palms down on the desk with a thwack. "You're *off*, and God damn it, don't you *ever* bloody tell me what I can or can't do, Chief Inspector – you're off, or you can go home. Now, what else do you have?"

Steel glared at Grieve. Keeping it vague, he said, "There's the vice angle I told you about . . ." and thinking of the conversation he'd had with JJ at *Kalpna*, "It came out of Mitchell's murder; we have a sauna manageress to interview."

Grieve paused, thinking. "Well, that's separate enough . . . just as long as you *keep* it separate and liaise with the Murder Squad if there *is* overlap. Follow up on that, and Mike . . . you're a DCI, don't make me have to ask you for daily progress reports and wonder if I should be looking over your shoulder to see what you're doing, eh?"

Steel got to his feet. "We done here?"

Grieve gave him a sad smile. "There you have it, in the proverbial nutshell – attitude. You're a good cop with a bad attitude – a walking bloody cliché. Yes, we *are* done here. Get out."

Moss looked up as Steel crashed through the door of their office and sat down heavily. "Sir?"

"We're off the McVicar case."

She was stunned. "*Off?*"

"Yes, a Murder Squad's being set up until McVicar's caught. Apparently, that's going to *look* better to all concerned . . . better than me as SIO, anyway."

"Why?" she asked, confusion written on her face.

Steel gave her a grim smile. "Get a copy of the *Sun*, that'll spell it out for you in nice monosyllabic words."

He turned to the whiteboard and looked once more at the pictures of the McCartney crime scene. "Better get these to Grieve, I suppose," and he paused, his hand halfway to the board. Turning to Moss he almost laughed. "This is *not* going to go over well."

"What's that?"

"This isn't McVicar's work."

"*What?* Of course it is!"

He tapped one of the photographs, "How many scores were made to the priest's chest?"

"Three, obviously."

"Yes, *three*. Why three?"

"*Why* three?"

"Yes, Moss, why. Apart from the weapon, both killings have widely different aspects, but the scores to the chest – the similarities in the killings – have been precise and, no doubt, Knox can tell us these ones, like Mitchell's, were made post mortem."

Moss was trying to grasp what he was saying; what, for him, was now straightforward. "Look," Steel continued, "it's simple, *we've* made it complicated. Mitchell was scored twice, McCartney was next, so he was scored three times."

He saw her bewilderment. "We *made* McVicar fit, Moss – a classic mistake – and we allowed ourselves to be misled with McVicar's bloody numerology and da Vinci nonsense. The two scores to Mitchell's chest *only* work if we look at them through the lens of McVicar's mumbo-jumbo. Or, looking at it the opposite way, three scores mean absolutely nothing if we try to apply our theorising on McVicar's 'two' to them."

He turned back to the photographs and, in a soft voice, said, "This isn't McVicar's work . . . it's someone else – and now he's got to three."

Moss stepped up to the whiteboard and stared at the photographs. What Steel wanted her to see now was not in nailed wrists, not in cords tying the priest, and not in the mimicked crown of thorns. The evidence was in the three scores to his chest, and she saw clearly three contributed precisely *nothing* to their reasoning for McVicar being Lord Mitchell's killer.

She let out a long breath. "If you're right sir, that means there's a 'one' we haven't found yet."

"Oh, I'm right Moss and yes, there *is* a 'one' out there. Somewhere. Find that and we'll be closer than we've *ever* been to the killer – a killer with *three* murders under his belt."

Steel rubbed his hand over his face. Looking at Moss, he thought of her being maligned for her work and how it might harm her. "At least we've reached this point within twelve hours, but we need to think through our next steps."

"Do we not just simply tell Grieve about this? Get everything handed over to the new Murder Squad?"

"Yes that's what we *will* do," and he gave her a smile; in time she would make a good copper, but she certainly didn't need any black marks against her now. "I'm just thinking of doing it the right way."

"The right way? Are there not rules on this?"

"Well you know what Douglas Bader said about rules."

"Who?" and then smiled at him, "What?"

"Rules are for the guidance of wise men and the obedience of fools."

Despite herself, Moss laughed, "That's not how *I* was trained."

"Well, there's training and real life, Moss. All I'm suggesting is we wait a while and then we – you – take this to Grieve."

"*Me?* Why?"

"You and I are off the case now. Grieve won't be happy, but it'll do *you* a power of good to bring your concerns about this being McVicar to his attention."

"Why me?" she asked again.

"Because, even though we've spent a week chasing the wrong person-"

"But he fitted."

"Like I said, we made him fit. So, when you point out your concerns, you'll be the one to get the praise, not me."

She thought again of Steel's insistence on jigsaw pieces fitting perfectly in a murder case, how he had kept on saying McVicar didn't fit. She had been the one to find McVicar's name. She had been the one to push on what she thought was an open door. Steel had said something niggled him about McVicar . . . and he had been right.

Getting to his feet, Steel said, "Trust me, Moss. This will be better coming from you."

She nodded. Above all, what she'd learned in under a week was that Steel *could* be trusted.

SIXTEEN

BILL RITCHIE'S OFFICE DOOR OPENED and JJ breezed in without knocking. He was on the phone, otherwise he would've given her an earful. She gave him a disarming smile and sat down to wait.

Tapping his pen rhythmically on the blotter before him, Ritchie was becoming more irritated by the second; JJ's entrance hadn't helped. "Look," he said, "just tell him to do it over, it's not good enough – not by a long shot." He listened to the response, then threw the pen on to his desk with some force. "Aye, well I'm not here to be loved, am I?" and slammed the phone down.

JJ's brow wrinkled. "Problems?"

"Goes with the job," Ritchie shrugged. He hesitated, then with the merest hint of a smile for her asked, "You heard anything on Lothian and Borders, JJ?"

"No. I saw the *Sun*'s front page, but I haven't spoken to Mike."

Ritchie thought of the man he'd known more years than he cared to remember. "Steel will be livid. No, not that – the Chief Constable's house was broken into last night."

"*What?* Was he there?"

"No, the house was empty. Thompson and family were staying with friends in the Borders apparently." He smiled. "Want to know the best part? . . . the alarms weren't set."

They looked at each other, then burst out laughing. "Oh my God," JJ said, "That has to be embarrassing. I wouldn't want to be the Community cop who has to take a statement from him . . . good story, though."

"They're keeping a lid on it . . . save Sir David's face. *I've* heard it was McVicar . . . the man's on a rampage in this fair city of ours."

JJ was incredulous. "McVicar? I don't think so. After murdering a priest, he goes after the Chief Constable?" She paused, thinking. "Who's your source on that, Bill?"

Ritchie's eyes twinkled, and he gave her a wry smile. "Never *you* mind. I've had a . . . a friendship going back over fifteen years. He's solid. It was McVicar."

"Fettes?"

"Aye, and that's as much as I'm saying. Anyhow, I want you to cover this – try and get a quote from Thompson, though I'll not rack you if you don't; he'll not want to talk about himself for a change."

"Who else has got this?"

"Nobody – I told you they're keeping a *very* tight lid on it; even the normal sieve is watertight. It'll be an exclusive for us. You." Ritchie sat back, regarding his star reporter – *current* star reporter – she had another front page exclusive today with Father McCartney's murder, scooping the others with details that could only have come from Mike Steel. The *Scotsman* was – for once – leading the pack, and he liked that singular position. "It'll be for the Sunday; do you no harm. Follow up on that would you?" His eyes narrowed with suspicion. "Anyhow, why are you here, I didn't know we had a meeting," knowing full well they didn't. "Is this something that can wait?"

"Not really Bill."

"Okay, I'll give you five. What?"

"Hawthorns."

Ritchie's brow knitted. "Remind me."

"The huge Victorian place Lord Mitchell used to visit? . . . Masked sex parties?"

"Of course. What of it?"

"I need to do a stake-out with a photographer."

"For?"

"To find out who visits – move my vice story forward."

Ritchie ignored her *my* and leaned back in silence, calculating costs, his fingertips drumming on the edge of his desk. Pushing himself forward, he picked up the phone and dialled. "Ian . . . can you come round for a few minutes? I need your input."

JJ sighed. "Is that really necessary, Bill? Can't you just assign a photographer?"

"Not for me to assign JJ, you know better. And I'm not going to get into anything with the Picture Editor over a story, no matter *how* good it is." He gave her a reassuring smile, "Slow down . . . you'll get what you need."

Within the minute there was a rap at the door and Ian Abbotsford entered. It looked as if he'd been sleeping in his clothes, then perhaps he had; it was hard to tell with someone for whom the word dishevelled could have been invented. With a nod and a smile for JJ he said, "What's up, Bill?"

Ritchie tilted his chin towards JJ, "It's her shout."

Abbotsford took a seat and turned towards her. "So?"

"I need to stake-out a house – find out who's visiting."

Abbotsford was a newspaper veteran of over forty years. After thirty years at the sharp end, he'd come off the road and into an editor's chair which, like his photography, he'd excelled in, winning several Press Awards for his choice, and use, of pictures. He knew there was nothing new under the sun, but nevertheless approached every job with undimmed enthusiasm. "Tell me more."

JJ laid out the story, what Hawthorns was, and – using Lord Mitchell as an example – told him of the type of visitors who could be expected.

Abbotsford mused on this. "You're not door-stepping the place?" and to the shake of her head, "Or hiding in the bushes?"

"We can expect security of some sort," JJ said, "Probably quite serious security, so this has to be discreet."

"Well, no doorstep, no hiding out in the grounds, and serious security – I'm not sending a snapper into *that* . . . sounds iffy for pics anyhow," and giving her a smile, "And I don't know whether we *have* any discreet photographers."

JJ ignored his pass at humour and stood her ground. "Look, I *need* a photographer."

Abbotsford laughed. She was a pretty woman and, when fired-up, fighting her corner, even prettier . . . there's something about redheads. He held up his hands in mock surrender, "Easy, now . . . you don't need a photographer, you need pictures."

"I don't follow," Ritchie put in.

"Well, from what JJ's said about the place, I doubt we could even get close, and we couldn't use the van – it'd stick out like a sore thumb. No, what I'll do is get a camera rigged up opposite the gate with a motion sensor," and turning to JJ, "That'll at least give you number plates, if not the occupants . . . will that work?"

JJ took this in. Hopefully, Steel would run the numbers for her and, from those, they'd have the owners. It was a start. "Perfect, Ian."

He gave her a small mock bow, "We aim to please, and yes, I'll get it set up. Might be able to run a test beforehand too."

JJ got to her feet, giving Abbotsford a wide smile and, for Ritchie, "I'll get on with that other thing, Bill."

●

"There has to be something that *connects* Lord Mitchell to Father McCartney." Moss was attempting to order her thoughts for a way forward.

Now off the murder inquiries – at least, officially – they had left Fettes and headed to Steel's house in the Dean Village in an effort to regroup.

"Beyond them being murdered by the same person, yes . . . assuming the murderer hasn't been picking people at random, anyhow."

"Could he be?"

"Yes, but I doubt it; brutal as they both were, the killer put some thought into each. Leaving aside the scores to the chest, which links them both to the same hand, I've a gut feeling Mitchell and McCartney *are* connected in some way – beyond being victims."

"A High Court judge and a priest?"

"*Seems* random, doesn't it? It'll help if we can come up with who number one was."

Moss was silent at this; they'd come full circle. Finding the first murder victim would, as Steel had put it, give them some sort of triangulation. The trouble was, the first victim might just add to the seeming randomness of the murders. Idly she thought, What if we find it's a teacher? A bartender? Where would that lead them? The bigger problem, however, was they couldn't be seen to be investigating the killings.

"How do we do this, sir? What's our next steps?"

Steel smiled. "Under cover of darkness. We've been told to work on the vice thread only, but what Grieve misses is that thread *is* connected to the killings."

An image of a scowling Grieve flitted across her mind's eye as she put her coffee down. "Some would say that's a stretch."

"Some would possibly be wrong then," Steel said smiling. Puzzles, of all sorts, had held an attraction for him ever since childhood, almost a natural precursor to joining the Force. For him, what was in front of them was simply a collection of jigsaw pieces. The picture was incomplete, but he knew – when he found the right way of looking at the pieces – the picture would be revealed. Somehow, the definitive answer to the question *How do these fit?* was staring him in the face. He laid out the pieces for Moss.

"Stevie McCann in a house near Mitchell's. An escort who visited Mitchell several times who, later, is contacted by Stevie McCann. And, the same escort has worked in a house, owned by Alan Prior, that Mitchell frequented. That may *seem* like coincidental connections to you Moss – and, so far, I can't see any connection to McCartney – but you've got to – must – treat coincidence with suspicion. It all ties together somehow."

"So, where do we start?"

"Investigating the connection between Mitchell, McCartney, and our mystery victim, has to be done on the quiet, because-"

"Definitely." Steel might be a good boss to work with, but being discovered looking into murders they'd been told to stay well away from would be more than prejudicial to her career.

Steel laughed. "I'm not missing anything, you know. If this – anything – goes pear-shaped, you can retreat behind, 'DCI Steel told me to'. Besides, we've got to look into the victims' backgrounds in a different way

. . . what is it connecting two seemingly unrelated people? Three, if we can find out who number one was. Get *that* connection and the murderer will be revealed. Right now, to us, Mitchell and McCartney *seem* to be disparate characters; to the killer, they're not."

Moss nodded her head slowly. Assuming the murders of Lord Mitchell and Father McCartney were *not* random killings, then Steel had to be right – both victims must have known their killer. "Again sir, where do we start?"

Steel put his unfinished coffee down and got to his feet. "We do what we're told. We follow the vice angle by visiting Stevie McCann, and then, Alan Prior . . . something'll turn up," and he smiled at her, "It usually does."

•

As they made their way to Barnton, Moss had the sensation of having first visited that select part of Edinburgh months ago; so much had happened since her first day with Lothian and Borders. "Do you think we'll catch whoever's behind these murders, sir?"

"There's two answers to that one."

"Two?"

"Depends on who I'm talking to. Possibly not, if it's you; yes we will, for anyone else."

She thought that overly pessimistic and told him so.

"Really? I thought, realistic . . . if we hadn't been misled into chasing McVicar, we would've stood a better chance. As it is . . . well, think about this: despite there being *another* victim out there – our number one – what if McCartney was the full tally? What if, for whatever reason, our killer had three to kill and now he's reached that?"

That possibility hadn't crossed her mind; pessimistic had been the wrong word. "So, if it's realistic to say, 'possibly not' to me, how can you say, 'yes we will' to others?"

"Because you're ignoring the unknown, Moss. If I'm right about the victims knowing their killer, that he was, in some way, settling a score, then there could easily be a fourth. Perhaps more." He gave her a faint smile. "Now, if I'm wrong about him, and these murders *have* been random, then we have a serial killer to deal with. Everything we know about serial killers suggests they speed up between murders. With less than a week between Mitchell and McCartney, we could expect another corpse by mid-week. Either scenario – the unknown – brings our killer out into the open, even if briefly, and there's a chance of him slipping up as he does so."

Moss pondered his logic; either seemed to work. Pressing him, she asked, "Okay, I get that, but how can you say we possibly won't catch him to me?"

"I've got a nagging feeling he's reached his tally, that's all. If he remains invisible, if he's made no mistakes at either *locus*, we stand very little chance of catching him."

Moss smiled. "A feeling? Does that constitute evidence . . . sir?"

Steel nodded, returning her smile. "To *me* it does – it will, to you, later on in your career," and seeing her quizzical look, "Forget the courts, Moss . . . forget the law, forget the public and the media. There's a point you'll reach – you alone – when you'll learn to trust the nudge inside you . . . an instinct you're right, an instinct that what you're doing will catch the criminal."

For a few moments, Moss absorbed this unexpected idea from Steel in silence. "And if you're wrong . . . if the instinctual nudge you get is wrong?"

Steel's shoulders lifted slightly. "Then you're wrong. But let me tell you, your own instinct, gut-feeling or whatever, is the very *best* tool you've got – nothing else comes anywhere close. Nothing," and as they turned into McCann's driveway, the car crunching over the expansive gravel, he added, "Even if you're proven wrong Moss, learn to trust that voice, it'll get stronger the more experience you get . . . a bit like faith, no?"

They got out of the car, noting the shiny BMW Series 7 and even shinier Mercedes SL600 convertible standing outside a four-car garage. "Is that two out of four?" Moss said, already faintly repelled by this display of conspicuous consumption. "Will he be out in the Ford Escort?"

Steel took in the large house with its extensive, well-tended grounds. It needed money, and lots of it, to have this, not just to buy, but to afford the lifestyle that went with it. This shouldn't be a preserve of an elite, he thought; privilege was something he'd abolish in his utopia. Although he didn't call it that. When he'd married Annabel, he had married, as the curious phrase had it, into money, which had afforded *him* a lifestyle well beyond his means, something he'd always had an uncomfortable feeling with, as if he was somehow undeserving.

Then he thought of the bribes he'd been offered over the years – Billy McCann had offered him fifty thousand when he'd arrested him all those years ago – that would've paved the way to a lifestyle like this, but not a *life*, not one he'd be happy to live anyhow.

Moss had pulled out her warrant card and was ringing the bell. As they heard distant melodious chimes, Steel thundered on the door with the side of his fist three times; the policeman's knock. To Moss's querying look, he said, "We'll get nothing out of this, we're only cage-rattling, see if any parts come loose – best he's on his back foot."

The door swung open, and Moss was face to face with the man she'd met on her door to door only five days previously. He was a younger version of his brother. "Steven McCann? I am Detective Sergeant Moss and this, is DCI Steel. We'd like to ask you some questions regarding a recent meeting you had at the Imperial Hotel."

McCann looked her up and down, and giving Steel a glance, granted her the flicker of a smile. "You'd better come in then."

He led them through a spacious wood-panelled hallway into the warm living room, tastefully furnished in modern style. "Take a seat," and when they remained standing, he said, "Should I have my lawyer present?"

"That depends on whether you think that's necessary, sir," Moss said.

McCann shook his head. "Naw . . . depends on what you have to say."

"You know the Imperial Hotel at Haymarket?" Steel put in.

"I've used it for business meetings . . . never stayed there," and with a smile for Steel, "too expensive, even for me."

"What business are you involved in?"

"Security."

"That's a small word for a large area."

Another smile. "Aye it is, isn't it?" As all three knew, a convicted criminal couldn't work in any area like alarm systems – his 'security' would be in providing muscle.

"Care to expand on that, sir?" Moss asked.

With another faint smile, McCann said, "Naw, I don't think so."

"You didn't have occasion to use that hotel to meet with an escort?" said Steel, "I'm also wondering whether by any chance that small word security covers prostitution."

Both Steel and Moss saw a slight change in McCann's eyes, his relaxed manner deserting him momentarily. "Prostitution? You're lookin' at the wrong person."

"You are aware it is a criminal offence to procure a woman for prostitution, or attempt to do so?" Moss said.

McCann shook his head but said nothing.

"We *could* continue our conversation at Fettes."

He looked up at her, "Then you'd have to *arrest* me, wouldn't you? Time I asked you to leave . . . that, or I'll need to phone my lawyer."

"On a Saturday? Wouldn't that be rather expensive, sir?"

McCann almost laughed at her. "Look around, Sergeant, d'you think expense bothers me?"

"A lawyer's really not necessary," Steel intervened, "We're conducting inquiries into prostitution in the Edinburgh area, and your name was mentioned."

"*My* name?" and he hesitated, thinking out his response. "Look, I've used the Imperial before, for business *and* pleasure, but anything a whore says about me is not on."

Whore had dropped too often from her father's ugly mouth, and Moss felt a flash of heat run through her. "I'll tell you what's not on, *sir* – attempting to sell another for sex is not on."

At that, Steel stepped back. "Thank you for your time Mr. McCann. Our inquiries are far-reaching, and ongoing, so we *may* have to speak with you again. We'll see ourselves out."

In the car, Steel turned to her. "Bit of a curate's egg there, Moss . . . you over-stepped a bit, but you did well . . . he'll be thinking twice and that works for me. A word of advice though – try not to make it personal."

Moss thought back to Steel's meeting with McCann's brother at *Oysters* – what was that if not personal? – but she pushed the thought away. "When scum like that offers his form of security to someone like Emma Boyd, calling her a whore, I can't take it any *other* way. I want to *nail* the bastard."

Steel smiled as he started the car, "Fair enough . . . I'd like that too." He drove off at speed, tearing great swathes in the gravel with the car's tyres, scattering stone chips onto the snow-covered lawns, and leaving pock marks like a shotgun blast.

SEVENTEEN

MOSS TYPED STEELM8513X with hesitant strokes; Steel had told her to use his ID, but she was nervous nevertheless. She glanced towards Tweedie. Janet had told her all searches were logged with the user's ID, but did that come up on her screen? Rejecting the thought as absurd, she typed Henry Mitchell plus Patrick McCartney. The little hourglass seemed to spin forever and then a pane opened: one hit in the Police National Computer.

Clicking on Mitchell to confirm she had the right man, she then clicked McCartney. With something like relief, she saw this Patrick McCartney was a career criminal, very much alive, and serving eight years in Barlinnie Prison after being sentenced by Lord Mitchell.

Burrowing further into the PNC, she moved into People Search. Typing Patrick McCartney again, she added his date of birth. Nothing – not a single entry in the whole PNC database.

"Are you getting everything you need, dear?" Tweedie was at her shoulder.

Feeling like a child being caught up to no good, she closed the pane, managing, "Just confirming something, Janet." This was faintly ridiculous. Despite Steel's assurances she felt she was doing wrong, and Tweedie would read that on her face as plain as one of her records.

"It's an easy system," Tweedie smiled, "but, if you're ever stuck, remember we can help."

Moss released a pent up breath. "Actually, there *is* something . . . is there an area of the PNC which lists unsolveds, Janet?"

"Unsolveds . . . ?"

"Deaths . . . uh, murders, perhaps."

Tweedie nodded. "That's unresolveds, Robin; URs – open cases. It's a rather sketchy area – suicides, suspicious deaths, and so on – but you can narrow your search. Right-click your People Search, get the UR tab and then refine it. There's far too many unresolveds in the UK, so it's best to start with Edinburgh and broaden from there."

Moss followed Tweedie's instructions and a pane with Name, Location and Date Range fields opened. Leaving the Name field blank, she typed Edinburgh. At Date Range, she hesitated; there had been two murders within a week. Limiting the search to a week prior to Mitchell's murder, she hit Enter. In seconds she had the result – there were three UR cases in Edinburgh within that timeframe: a suspicious death, a hit and run, and a suicide. Selecting all, she hit Print.

"Did you get what you needed, dear?" Tweedie called out over the sound of the busy printer.

Logging off, Moss gathered her print-outs together, managing a cheery, "Yes, I think so," and retreated guiltily out of Records, hoping her surreptitious search under Steel's ID would prove fruitful.

Back at her desk, she spread out the printed sheets, still with the strange sensation, for a girl from a good Catholic upbringing, that she'd done something wrong.

Then, from behind, and making her jump, came, "Where's Steel?" Grieve was framed in the doorway.

"I'm not sure, sir."

"Right . . . well, *when* you see him, tell him I want a word." Grieve paused. "I got your note on the McCartney murder."

"Sir?"

"Good observations, Moss . . . might still *be* McVicar of course, but good thoughts anyway; they've been passed on to the Murder Squad." He made to leave, then stopped. "I suppose you read the piece in the paper yesterday . . . about the Chief?"

"I did, sir . . . bit embarrassing for him."

"Quite. Steel's a friend of this Jay Johnstone, eh?' and narrowing his eyes, "Steel mention the break-in to you?"

"No sir . . . we were still working the McCartney murder. He'll have been as surprised as me."

Nodding his head, he looked at the papers spread out on her desk. "What're you working on?"

"Vice, sir." The lie was white enough.

"Right. Well, let Steel know I want to speak with him, eh?" and he was gone.

She let out another long breath and turned to her print-outs. A suspicious death: one Yvonne Cumming had been found dead on waste ground in Broomhouse, with a head injury. There was no evidence of her being attacked, only that she'd been drinking heavily earlier. A hit and run: one John Pride had been knocked down and killed in George Street. Witnesses had reported a car driving at speed which had failed to stop. A suicide: one Grzegorz Skłodowska, a Polish citizen, had been found mangled at the foot of a block of tenements in Easter Road, but neighbours had reported hearing a loud argument on the roof. All three had comprehensive notes from the Attending Officers, and all three were now languishing in investigative limbo. Steel would need to see these. She dialled his mobile, but when the call clicked over to his messaging service she hung up.

Her thoughts turned to the Father McCartney murder. Grieve was wrong if he thought McVicar was still in the frame; the three scores to the priest's chest had convinced her it was someone else.

Wondering what to do next, she thought of the steps the Murder Squad might take. If they now followed Steel's thinking and accepted McVicar *wasn't* the prime suspect they, likewise, would be hunting for some connection between Mitchell and McCartney. She tried to think what *her* steps would have been had she not been taken off the inquiry, and the first thought that came to mind was to look to McCartney's congregation.

She hesitated, trying to think this through. Was it even such a wise idea? She and Steel had already walked into an area they had been told to stay well away from. With an inner shrug, she picked up the phone, dialled the Archdiocesan Offices, and asked to speak to Bishop Cairns; there would surely be no harm in asking a question.

When she was put through, she began with, "Good morning bishop, this is DS Moss from Lothian and Borders Police . . . we spoke briefly on Friday?"

"Of course. How are you my child?"

"I'm well, thank you. I'm following-up on the murder of Father McCartney and was wondering whether you have a list of his parishioners."

"Why, yes . . . but I passed that to Inspector Fisher earlier."

Moss knew she should back off, but continued, feeling her chest constricting her breathing. "I wonder whether you could send me that?"

"Isn't that duplicated effort?"

"Ah . . . just investigating different angles, sir."

"Of course. Well, anything I can do to help. Give me your email address and I'll have my secretary send it to you."

Ignoring the hollow feeling that came from crossing a definite line, she gave him her address, thanked him, and headed for the canteen.

When she returned, vowing yet again to reduce her caffeine intake, at least at work – the coffee was awful, anyway – she checked her mail: one new mail with an attachment was waiting for her. Clicking on the attached file, she sent it to the printer.

Scooping up the printed pages, she scanned the list of names then slowly sank into her chair. The name Henry Mitchell had leaped out at her. *There* was the connection – Mitchell had been one of McCartney's parishioners. Feeling her heart beating faster, and resisting the impulse to punch the air, she read on, and saw the name John Pride.

John Pride? Hadn't she just read that name? Scrabbling through the print-outs of unresolved cases she'd found earlier in Records, she saw the same name against the hit and run in George Street.

For one brief moment the question, *coincidence?* rose in her mind, but when she saw that John Pride had been a judge, she dismissed it immediately. She had just found victim number one.

•

The soft knock signalled her ten-thirty appointment. Emma glanced in the mirror – a final quick check – and unlatched the door. It was open less than an inch when it burst towards her, smashing her in the face and breaking her nose. Blood spurted like a fountain and she fell backwards onto the floor. He was on top of her in an instant, straddling her, fists swinging. "You fuckin' *whore*," he screamed, "I'll teach you to open your mouth."

Shocked and in excruciating pain, all her survival instincts snapped into gear. Using every ounce of her strength, she drove her knee up between his legs, aiming for the ceiling, and heard a feral howl of pain.

Struggling free of their entangled bodies she crawled to the table. Pulling the cord, the phone fell to the floor, and she hit a button. "Help me," she managed, before passing out at the side of the bed.

•

Steel rushed into the office, holding up a hand as Moss began telling him what she'd found in Records. "Whatever it is, it can wait. Emma Boyd's been assaulted . . . we're going back to Barnton."

As they dashed for their car, Steel said, "Emma's been taken to the Royal – broken nose, broken cheekbone – apparently before they took her there, she told the PC to tell me it was Steven."

"McCann?"

"Yes, and we're going to *nail* him."

In the car park they were met by two uniformed officers waiting beside their vehicle. "Right," Steel said, "we're headed for Barnton Meadows to arrest one Steven McCann."

"Barnton?" asked one, "Sirens off?"

"Hell, no," Steel snarled, "I want as much noise and visibility as we can muster . . . let the good folk of Barnton know we're there and who we've come for – the scum living amongst them. And, when we get there, use as much reasonable force as is necessary, okay?"

The two cars raced to Barnton with sirens wailing and the full array of lights flashing, cleaving a path through slow moving traffic, and leaping through any red light they met.

Feeling adrenaline coursing through her, Moss was dying to tell Steel of her discovery. "I got some good information from Records and Bishop Cairns earlier, sir."

Grim faced, Steel shook his head at her. "Not *now*, Moss . . . McCann's the priority."

They arrived at McCann's house, throwing gravel in great arcs, some of the stones pinging off McCann's BMW. Steel leapt agilely from their car, strode to the door and began pounding on it with his fist.

As the door opened, the two uniforms rushed McCann and slammed him into the wall. Steel was in his face in an instant. "Steven Howard McCann you are under arrest for suspicion of aggravated assault. You do not have to say anything, but it may harm your defence if you do not mention when questioned something which you later rely on in court. Anything you do say may be given in evidence. Do you understand?"

McCann nodded and Steel said, "Cuff him," to one of the uniforms, and was pleased to hear a yelp of pain as the officer used reasonable force to bring McCann's arms behind his back.

Back at Fettes, with McCann booked in, Steel listened to Moss's excited explanation of how she'd found the third murder victim. He saw her animation as she recounted the steps she'd taken, read the certainty in her grey-green eyes and, for the first time, was actually glad Brian had moved on. Scanning the print-outs of unresolved cases, and the list of McCartney's parishioners, he looked up and gave her a broad smile. "Result, Moss. Good work."

"But what do we do with it, sir?"

Steel paused, running a hand over his chin. "You say Bishop Cairns had already given this parishioner list to DI Fisher?"

"Yes."

"Well, for now, we do nothing . . . Fisher, or whoever, will put two and two together – or *should* do."

"And if he doesn't?"

"We'll cross that bridge when – if – we come to it."

Steel's phone rang. Picking it up, he listened, then turned to Moss. "McCann's lawyer is here. Where do we have him?"

"IR Three."

"Right, let's get down there and bury him."

•

McCann was dressed in white coveralls, sitting with his wrists handcuffed and resting on the table before him. Looking up as Steel and Moss entered, a faint and by now familiar, smile crossed his face. Seated beside him was a lawyer Steel had never seen before. Over the years he had met many criminal lawyers, and it seemed they often liked to dress like their clients, as if they were one of them; slightly flash – one of the boys, but not really. This lawyer was in his late thirties, dressed in an immaculately tailored grey pinstripe suit over a crisp navy blue silk shirt, with a beautifully knotted yellow tie. With longish jet black hair brushed straight back from a wolfish face, he looked pampered, fit and tanned, and the tan was not from a sun bed.

Giving him a nod, Steel sat down opposite McCann and Moss sat by his side. She broke out two tapes, fitting them into the recorder, which started with a long beep, and turned to check that the ceiling mounted video camera was on. "Sir."

Steel gave the place, date, time, and identified himself, then turned to Moss.

"Detective Sergeant Robin Moss."

"And you are, sir?" Steel asked of the lawyer.

"I am Toby Greene of Paisley Wark, and I must insist my client is-"

"And your client," Steel interrupted, "is Steven Howard McCann," giving the lawyer a humourless smile, "To identify everyone present."

Steel looked at McCann. "Do you understand why you have been arrested, Mr. McCann?"

Greene leaned forward. "Chief Inspector, I must insist these handcuffs are removed. My client has-"

"Your insistence is noted, sir." Steel turned back to McCann, repeating his question.

McCann shook his head.

"For the tape please."

"No, I don't," McCann said, a half-grin on his face. "I know you . . . and her," nodding at Moss, "were at my door yesterday. This something to do with the same thing?"

157

"Where were you this morning?" Moss asked.

"A business meeting."

"Where was this business meeting?"

McCann smiled at her, but said nothing.

Steel eyed him; young Stevie was everything wrong with the society he lived in – a bully who enriched himself off others too fearful to resist. He glanced at the lawyer. Paisley Wark was Jan Prior's firm. Everything in him rebelled at this example of one law for the rich, another for everyone else. "Listen McCann, this is not difficult, but it will be if you don't answer our questions."

"Is that a threat, Chief Inspector?" Greene drawled.

"A statement of fact," Steel snapped. "Now where was this business meeting you say you were at?"

McCann smiled at him and leaned back, as relaxed as if he was sitting at home in his own chair. Moss wanted to reach across the table and slap him, to keep slapping him until the supercilious smile was off his face.

Sensing her frustration, McCann said, "Anger issues, Sergeant?" and with a smirk, "I know what'll help you."

Steel stirred. "You may care to explain to your client how long he could be held if he continues to refuse to answer our questions, Mr. Greene."

Greene looked at McCann and nodded.

"I was at a meeting with my lawyers this morning," he said, laying down his trump card with a broad grin.

"Are your lawyers' offices close to the Imperial Hotel?" Moss asked. She was rocked by McCann's answer; would a lawyer provide such an alibi?

"Everything in Edinburgh's city centre is *close* Sergeant," Greene said, "We are in Charlotte Square. I, myself, wasn't present at my client's meeting, but I can confirm Mr. McCann did have a scheduled meeting with one of our senior partners at ten-thirty this morning."

"Which senior partner?"

"Jan Prior."

"So, you don't know an Emma Boyd?" Steel put in.

"What, that . . ." and McCann stopped himself. "No, I don't."

"Ms. Boyd was the victim of a very serious assault, and you were identified as her attacker-"

"Can that be corroborated Chief Inspector?" Greene cut in.

Steel ignored him. When they'd arrived at Fettes fingernail scrapings and swabs had been taken from McCann and his clothing removed – any blood on those would be Emma's; corroboration would be unnecessary. He glanced up at the clock. "Interview suspended at one o-five."

A faint trace of annoyance crossed Greene's face. "Without any corroboration, I don't think you can hold my client, Chief Inspector."

"I can, and I will, Mr. Greene, that is, until I am wholly satisfied your client was not present when Ms. Boyd was assaulted."

"I must protest."

"Your protest is duly noted," and, with a nod to Moss, Steel stood.

Moss switched off the recorder and followed Steel out of the room. Getting well out of earshot, she turned to him. "What do you make of that?"

Steel shook his head. "Well, it's an alibi that had better check out, if-"

"But it's going to check out, isn't it?"

With a sigh, Steel said, "Yes. I'm pinning my hopes on blood evidence. And, if that comes up trumps, we can swing round on Greene – charge him with conspiracy." But he said this knowing full well lawyers rarely – if ever – left themselves open like that. Feeling his stomach churn with acid, he popped a Rennies into his mouth and bit down on it.

Later, in their office, the phone rang. Steel picked it up and listened. Having heard the man out, he tossed the phone back on its cradle. "Nothing Moss . . . there was no blood on his clothing, no positives at all. We're going to have to let McCann go."

"*No.*" Moss felt heat boiling up inside her.

Wanting to get some fresh air, Steel got to his feet. His job was to protect people like Emma, and when he wasn't there to protect, to catch people like McCann. He had failed on both counts.

His thoughts were as depressing as the rain mixed with sleet which was now steadily falling on Edinburgh's streets.

EIGHTEEN

STEEL PLACED THREE SHEETS OF PAPER on the table. Taking a marker pen, he wrote Pride on one, Mitchell on another and finally, McCartney on the last in block letters. He then numbered them 1, 2, 3, and added the brief details they knew about each underneath.

After their abortive interview of Steven McCann they'd left Fettes and made their way to the Dean Village. As far as Steel was concerned, they were still working the murders of Mitchell and McCartney and, despite the death of John Pride being logged as a hit and run, he knew – if investigated thoroughly – that death would be found to be murder too.

He tapped each page with his pen. "Pride. Mitchell. McCartney. They had a history together, but what?"

Moss said nothing, waiting for the History Man himself to proceed.

"There's *something* shared Moss; something that connects them all."

"Two judges and a priest? I doubt it'll be Masonic. If it exists, perhaps it's something so far back we'll never discover what it is."

Steel gave her a sharp look. "Don't let me ever hear you say *never* – that's not a word a cop uses. Besides, history's like a train . . . the present's the engine pulling history behind it," and he tapped the pages with his fingertips, "These three victims, with their history, are the carriages being pulled into the present – the killer did that. Whatever's linking these three men historically, the killer's *brought* that link into the present. We've got to find what connects them . . . what the coupling is."

Moss sighed. Grieve had told them, in no uncertain terms, their job was anything *but* the murders. "How far back in their history do we need to go?"

Steel sat back, thinking for a moment. "Maybe not that far."

"How so?"

"Well, with Pride and Mitchell being judges, we'll probably find they have very similar backgrounds. No doubt they both went to Edinburgh Academy and studied Law at Edinburgh University . . . perhaps they sat in similar courts. It's their more recent history we need to see. McCartney's a different matter, he's-"

"Are we certain of McCartney?" She wanted to revisit Steel's reasoning that the priest was indeed the third murder victim.

Steel eyed her over the rim of his coffee mug; he'd been the one to see McCartney as the third victim, and from that, Moss had discovered Pride as the first.

"*I'm* certain," he said. "If you look at the scores on Mitchell's and McCartney's chests as anything *other* than deliberate woundings – as being the result of random killings – then we have a killer acting in a way we've never seen before."

He saw a perplexed look pass over her face. "Every murderer has their own MO, Moss. Sometimes it's difficult to see – and, unfortunately, sometimes only discovered *after* we catch him – but their MO is their own signature. Like their fingerprints, it belongs to nobody else. Even if they're copycat killers.

"If you think that two – accurate – scores have a meaning, and that three – again, accurate – scores have a meaning, then tell me, if that's not *numbering* his victims, what is it?"

Moss tried to think of an answer, any answer, and gave up with a long exhalation.

"We're looking for a killer with a *plan*, Moss. This is not a madman like McVicar, this is someone who's self-controlled, someone who's thought out his killings. Someone who's been meticulous . . . someone capable of extraordinary brutality."

"But not with Pride's?" she ventured.

"Pride's murder, this supposed hit and run, wasn't random either – the killer probably used the only opportunity he had to kill him . . . it wasn't an accident but a thought out, cold-blooded murder."

Moss sighed again, pushing her fingers through her fringe. Steel was right, but they still needed a connection and, for her, something that gave meaning to the seeming meaninglessness of someone taking the lives of three people. Steel had said the killer's tally was perhaps three. If he *had* reached his tally, then did nothing, how would they ever catch him? "How do we proceed, sir?"

Steel gave her a small shrug; he'd had that question before him since realising McCartney was the victim of an unknown killer and not McVicar. From that moment on he'd been measuring darkness. How to proceed was the real question; all they had were three jigsaw pieces, with no picture to guide them, and no idea how they fitted together – not to mention the fact they'd been taken off the case.

Moss was running through her own thoughts; if these dissimilar men had been murdered because of something they shared, or something they'd all experienced together, what *was* it? Focus . . . nothing but a blank . . . and then, the slightest nudge from a distance, the hint of an idea breaking through. "Suppose we look at all three victims differently . . ."

"Go on."

"Well, rather than two judges and a priest, what if we see all three as judges?" She paused, watching Steel absorb this. "What if all three had, in some way, judged the killer at some point? . . . I know they're not meant to, but priests can often be seen as judges of people."

Steel let her idea run through his mind. Nothing surfaced to challenge it. All three men, of different ages, with differing backgrounds, *could* be seen as judges. She'd narrowed the possibilities. "You might be right. If they're all judges – if, at one time, they'd all judged the killer, sat in judgment over the killer, perhaps – then we'd have more of a thread to follow."

"We're still trying to find a needle in a haystack, though."

Steel laughed. "I thought pessimism wasn't an area for fast-track cops? This is not finding a needle in a haystack Moss, this is looking for the haystack. But . . . well, I think you may be right – all the victims were, in some way, their killer's judge. It makes sense." He placed his mug down on the table. "Let's put it to one side . . . let it simmer. Now, are there other connections they share?"

Both fell silent. Steel stared at the three sheets of paper before them and Moss watched him deep in thought. He looked up at her. "You know, I can't help thinking these murders and vice are somehow connected."

"In what way?"

"It started with Mitchell's murder when we found out he'd been using an escort. And then, who's living next door to Mitchell? Steven McCann. Who owns the house? Prior. Then we find out about Hawthorns . . . again, Prior's the owner. Emma Boyd gets badly beaten, and when we pull in McCann, his lawyer's from Prior's wife's firm."

"Right, a very strong connection between Prior and the McCanns, but nothing else. How does the McCartney murder connect with Prior?"

Steel looked at her and sighed. "I don't know, Moss . . . as far as we know, there's *no* connection between McCartney and Prior. But if Mitchell connects with Prior, is it a stretch to connect the other two to him?"

Moss laughed at this. "Well, *yes* . . . I can see there *could* be a link between Prior and Mitchell, but there's absolutely *nothing* to connect Prior with Father McCartney."

Steel held up his hands. "Okay, I'm being nagged by something, that's all." He looked at Moss; this might be difficult for someone with her beliefs to swallow. "Of course, there is *one* possibility of McCartney and vice connecting . . . you know, the priest and the choirboys sort of thing."

Moss felt herself colouring. "That's a . . . an offensive thing to say. We have nothing to even suggest that." Speaking ill of the dead priest – whether he was a judge of people or not - stood against everything she believed.

Steel nodded. McCartney wouldn't have been the first priest to have crossed that line; it could still be true, but he didn't press it. "Yes, nothing, just thinking out loud," and he reminded himself to explore the angle. There was still the not insignificant matter of one hundred and twenty-one pornographic images of minors on Mitchell's computer. Mitchell had been a parishioner of McCartney's; that connected them in murder – had they been connected in paedophilia too?

He looked at her; she was yet to learn the place for personal morality in police work. Gently does it. "Just a thought . . . did you ever get an answer from Forensics about the dates of the files on Mitchell's computer?"

"No, sir. Not that I've seen. I'll chase them up."

He stood, smiling down at her. "Right, let's visit Al Prior."

"Prior? Do we have a reason?"

"Reason? We're the police Moss, we don't need a reason," and he laughed at her puzzled expression. "Relax, I'm joking. We have our reason . . . remember he was run off the road coming back from Dundee. That'll work. I want to meet the man who's set to build a brand new Edinburgh on our coastline, *and* figuring so much in our contact with young Stevie McCann."

•

The remarkably pretty blond receptionist at Prior's offices took their warrant cards to examine. In a soft voice she called Prior's personal assistant to inform her the police were in reception.

Within the minute the PA, another pretty blond, though older, woman arrived. "How may I help you Chief Inspector Steel?" Moss glanced at the receptionist; efficient as well as pretty.

"We're here to speak with Mr. Prior."

Adopting a sympathetic tone, she said, "Mr. Prior does have a somewhat busy diary. Is there something *I* can help you with?"

Steel responded with his best smile. "It's a confidential matter, we can wait."

"Very well. I shall pass him a note, let him know you are here. In the meantime, can I have someone get you and Sergeant Moss anything . . . tea, coffee?"

Steel shook his head, and with a slight tilt of her head and a bright smile, she left them.

Moss saw Steel was appraising her as she walked away. "Stepford wives, sir."

"Say again?" Steel hadn't noted any submissiveness in the PA.

"The PA, and the receptionist, they look almost alike – a twinned unworldly perfection."

Always wary of women's opinions on other women, Steel smiled at this from her. "Someone's idea of perfection, certainly," and looked round. When these Georgian four-storey New Town houses had been built in the early nineteenth century, each had been for one family. These days almost all of them had been divided, if not sub-divided, into offices, but Prior appeared to have the whole building to himself.

He was struck by the hushed atmosphere. Nothing could be heard of the city centre traffic outside and the interior, which had been totally modernised, must have been soundproofed. He saw the receptionist was busy fielding calls, but reckoned he would need to be right in front of her to hear what was said. "Unworldly indeed, Moss."

Noticing a large antique table against a wall covered with small framed photographs, he wandered over. The photographs were all of Prior with well-known faces. There he was, a *serious* smile on his face, with the current Prime Minister; with the Leader of The Opposition; a shot of him with the previous American President; with a variety of film-makers – the makers, not the stars – and many familiar faces he'd seen on television.

"That's the last Pope." Moss had come up behind him.

He turned, looking to see if she was impressed; she had seen a pope, he had seen a possible connection with McCartney. "Do you think Prior's a Catholic?"

She shook her head. "This is just front, sir – ego – it wouldn't surprise me to see him with the Dalai Lama."

Steel nodded, pointing a finger at a photo of Prior with the smiling Tibetan leader.

Then, from a door behind the receptionist, Prior emerged with another man. Both looked happy – clearly a good meeting. Steel recognised the man; it was Edinburgh Councillor, William Kennedy, Convener of the Planning Committee.

Prior took Kennedy's hand to shake. "*Always* a pleasure to see you again, William," and walked him to the door, as if bidding a fond farewell to a house guest, "I'll get back to you."

Prior turned and, seeing Steel and Moss, his smile became a beam. This is a man who is definitely going to shake hands, thought Steel, and sure enough Prior crossed to them, his hand extended before him, welcoming them as if long lost cousins.

Steel felt the enquiring pressure on his knuckle. "Chief Inspector Steel, Sergeant Moss, I am so sorry to have kept you waiting," and dropping his voice to a conspiratorial stage whisper, though not Moss's hand, he said, "This is not about my unpaid parking fines, is it?"

In his late forties, Prior exuded a powerful and attractive charm; he was someone who would stand out in *any* room. His neatly cut black hair, greying at the temples, was swept back, and his clothing spoke of impeccable and expensive taste. With his slightly fleshy, lined face, deep complexion, almost hooked nose and sensual lips, Moss thought he might pass for a Venetian on the Rialto. Looking into his twinkling, deep blue eyes she could tell his charm and ever-ready humour would carry him far in dealings with many people, and in all sorts of situations. Much to her surprise, she found herself warming to him, and was reminded of her uncle from Mossley Hill, a person it was a pleasure to be with whatever the circumstances.

With a smile for Prior, Moss gently withdrew her hand. "No sir, this concerns a recent matter . . . the Dundee to Edinburgh road?"

Prior pulled a solemn face – this man is *good*, thought Moss – and ushered them into his office. She saw his little nod to the receptionist; he didn't need to say anything, calls would be held.

Skirting his large rosewood desk, Prior raised both arms to the seats opposite. "Please, take a seat. I *did* give a statement to Tayside Police on that matter."

"Yes sir," Steel said, "but we, in Lothian and Borders, like to look after our own."

Prior gave this a dazzling smile. "That's very gratifying Chief Inspector, but I doubt whether I can add anything."

"As I understand, this was a deliberate attempt to run you off the road."

"Yes. Two attempts in fact."

"At what speed were you travelling?" Moss asked.

"Oh, I'd say well within the speed limit, Sergeant," and leaning towards her across his desk, he gave her a sly smile. "*Perhaps* five miles an hour faster."

Moss was reminded of how one of her instructors at Hendon had warned her class of the inclusiveness many people attempted to get a police officer on their side. He was speeding, of course, but she said nothing.

"So," Steel said, "two attempts, but you managed to escape the other driver?"

"I *am* a good driver Chief Inspector and, luckily, I was able to leave at a slip road, though I hit the crash barrier."

Moss shifted in her chair. "Did you think the other driver was serious?"

"With two attempts? Definitely serious . . . eight thousand pounds' worth of damage."

"No sir, what I meant was, if someone *seriously* attempts to run you off the road, chances are – despite you being a good driver, of course – they'd be successful. Could this have been done to frighten you?"

Prior pulled his features into a deep frown. "I'm not sure I follow."

"Do you have any enemies? Someone who might wish to frighten you?"

"I'm a very successful businessman, Sergeant, I make enemies as I breathe – although none I can think of who may wish to *frighten* me. What would be the point?"

"Were you able to see the other driver, sir?" Steel said.

Prior picked up a pen, twirling it between his fingers, and Moss noticed the embroidered AP on the cuffs of his elegant silk shirt.

"No, it was dark, I'm afraid."

Steel nodded; something in his tone made him think he was lying. "What business are you involved in, sir?"

"Mainly finance, but well, any business that makes a handsome profit."

"And in making . . . such profit, there's nobody you can think of who might wish you harm?"

"Nobody, Chief Inspector."

"Well, sir," Steel said, by now confident Prior had not only seen the driver but more than likely knew him, "unless we get lucky, I think this unfortunate incident is one best put behind you."

"Just so," and he shifted in his chair as if about to stand.

Moss didn't take his cue; they weren't finished. "I believe you're involved in the Forth Development, sir?"

Steel played his part. "What's that?"

Prior put on his very best smile and got to his feet. "You don't know, Chief Inspector? The Forth Development is the flagship project of one of my companies . . . come, let me show you."

He ushered them into a room off his office with large framed plans on the wall, and a massive, highly detailed, three-dimensional architect's model, which dominated the space. With a sweeping flourish of his hand, he said, "*This* is the Forth Development, Chief Inspector."

Steel looked at the model, recognising the north Edinburgh coastline. "This is remarkable. And one of your companies is responsible for this?"

"Part of this . . . a large part." Prior smoothed his hair back, almost preening.

"I like how water is such a feature here," Steel remarked, "it makes me think of Holland."

Moss thought Steel dangerously close to over-playing his hand.

"Leisure is a significant aspect," Prior said, with a new, brittle tone to his voice.

"And housing? Will housing be a significant aspect? Or are all these leisure and commercial interests at the expense of houses?"

Prior bridled at this. "The mix was decided *years* ago by the City of Edinburgh Council, Chief Inspector." A small crack had appeared in his smooth façade. "You're surely not one of those who object to a development as grand as this for Edinburgh?"

"As long as it's for Edinburgh – the *people* of Edinburgh – I have no objection."

Prior looked at him, as if only now realising he and Steel had nothing in common. "That's a *very* old-fashioned idea. The world has moved on."

"It has?" Steel had seen how the world had moved on. He had grown up in Muirhouse, right beside this new strip of Edinburgh modelled before him. There had been places to work there, not marinas for the wealthy. In this moved-on world, the clock was being turned back and people were again being herded like cattle. "Moved on to what, sir?"

"To various destinations of enlightened self-interest," Prior was still smiling but there was no light in his eyes. "My companies *create* wealth Chief Inspector and, from that, ordinary people – the people you seem concerned with – benefit."

"The trickle-down theory? Surely *that's* the very old-fashioned idea – one that's been proven not to work," and Steel flashed a smile, "But, we didn't come to discuss the vagaries of economics, did we, sir? If you can think of anything – anything at all – that might help us find the person who attempted to run you off the road, please get in touch," and he handed him his card.

•

Looking out of his window, Prior watched Steel and Moss walk to their car. Unlocking a drawer, he pulled out a simple pre-paid phone and dialled.

"Yeah?"

"I've just had the police here."

Muffled laughter could be heard. "Aye, well? You've caught me on the tenth – a tricky enough hole – and I'm playing with a cop, right now. What did they want?"

Prior had not spoken to anyone about the trouble he'd had on the Dundee to Edinburgh road. "It was . . . a routine matter."

"Fuck's sake, Al. A routine matter? You're interrupting my game for a routine matter?"

Prior never liked to seem ruffled, always wanted to show himself in complete control. "They mentioned Holland, Billy."

"Holland? And ye say it was *routine?*" In the pause which followed, he could almost see McCann's angry face. Anger was uncontrollable emotion, and such loss of control disturbed him. He held the phone away from his ear. "How was Holland mentioned? Who was it?"

"A DCI Steel, with his Sergeant," adding in a lame voice, "He said part of the Forth Development reminded him of Holland."

The tinny, distorted laughter greeting this was almost welcome. "Stainless? Forget him. He cannae do anything, he's yesterday's man – a nobody. And saying the Development reminded him of Holland? What's got into you, man? That's *nothin'*."

Prior heard a muted, "Aye, in a minute," then, "Look, it's Baltic here . . . we'll meet up and you can tell me all about it, Al. Until then, *relax* – go for a manicure, or something. Dinnae concern yourself wi' Steel

. . . he's a wind-up soldier. He'll no' be able to make a move without being told to, and you and me both *know* he'll no' be told. Right?"

The line went dead and, in the sudden quiet, Prior looked at the phone and thought, Billy, you'd *better* be right.

NINETEEN

WHEN THEY WERE BACK IN THE CAR Steel saw his mobile was blinking but ignored it. "What did you make of Prior, then?"

Moss hesitated, thinking through their meeting. "He's very charming," which brought an explosive grunt from Steel, "and clearly vain, but d'you think he's really *connected* with the McCanns?"

"Definitely," said Steel, adding in a brusque tone, "and we've already got way too many connections to make that anything like a *sensible* question. With his, 'any business that makes a handsome profit', I think he's up to his ears with them."

Steel had already told her that, years earlier when he'd arrested Billy McCann, the National Crime Squad had had Prior in their sights. Major crimes, of the sort NCS handled, somehow didn't square with the man she'd just met. "He *seems* to be just a high-powered businessman to me."

"And you think businessmen can't be involved in crime, is that it? Ignore what people *seem*, Moss. We all put on a face for others – it's what's behind the face that matters. You *know* this. Anyway, most white collar crooks *I've* seen have been, in your words, charming."

Moss recalled Steel recounting his first meeting with JJ and Bill Ritchie at the *Scotsman*. He'd talked then of following up JJ's story on a secretive elite which ran Edinburgh – an inner circle of those in law, politics and business. Initially, that had been a 'vice in high places' story, but if there *was* such a circle, then it would be foolish to think it wouldn't operate in every aspect of life, including Prior's businesses.

Switching tack, she ventured, "Do you think it was wise to mention Holland, sir?"

Steel laughed at this. "Wise? I think it's wise to agree with everything I say when you're my DS," and watching her struggle for a response, "I'm joking . . . I didn't really talk of Holland, not in the sense you mean – Have you been financing drug runs from Holland, sir? – I just wanted to see his response."

"Yes, but given Crime Squad reckon that money coming into the Forth Development from Holland might not be clean, wasn't it risky?"

"But what was his response? From that point he became quite edgy."

More to do with his open hostility to Prior's pet project, she thought. "Maybe it was your left-wing views, sir."

"For *God's* sake, Moss, he's an asset stripper – his company goes in, and people lose their jobs – a few people get rich, a lot of people get poor. Tell me, what's right about that?" His father – a time-served engineer and life-long Socialist – came to mind. The firm he'd worked for had been sold to another in Glasgow, and in turn that had been bought by an investment company. Within the year the Glasgow firm had been 'rationalised' by the parent company, eighty-three men in Edinburgh had been made redundant, and his father, at fifty-seven, had never worked again. He had watched a once proud man lose his purpose and die, thinking himself a failure. "Left-wing, indeed," he snorted. "Anyhow, I tend to side with those who get their hands dirty from hard work, not those speculating with somebody else's money and gambling with others' lives.

"And let's face it, if there's criminal activity in the flow of money from Holland, that's an international concern. We're not going to see that as a meet at Edinburgh Airport with a bundle of used fivers in a brown bag, are we?" He watched her absorb this. "The Dutch area is Crime Squad's and Interpol's . . . brown bags at the airport is more Billy McCann's. Now, if I'd mentioned Hawthorns . . ."

He looked out at Charlotte Square Gardens, covered with a light dusting of snow, and shivered – it would be months before Winter finally left the city. The old trees were bare and black, rendering the gardens monochrome, and he wondered how often he'd seen the Job in the same way, reducing it to a simple matter of black and white.

"It's vice we're going to put Prior down for Moss – his company's ownership of Hawthorns, if it can be proved there's something underage happening there, *and* his connection with young Stevie, a tenant of another of his companies, who's deep into vice with his 'security' business."

Moss nodded but said nothing. Whatever the reality of Steven McCann's business, he had committed an aggravated assault on Emma Boyd then walked. More than anything, she wanted him charged with that.

"If we *can* connect Prior to drugs in Edinburgh somewhere along the way," Steel said, "then great, we will. But it's a big if, and we – you and I – stand a better chance with vice." He looked at her, and for a brief moment was reminded of himself as a DC. Back then he'd been freshly-scrubbed and nauseatingly keen to bring in every criminal in Edinburgh, to quash every crime at birth. "It's a matter of *choosing* our battles, Moss. We can't fight them all."

As flakes of snow began falling on the square, Steel thought of the Masonic handshake Prior had given. Was Prior's business – especially the Forth Development – yet another example of wheels within wheels, the very way some sections of Edinburgh had always operated? The history of the city itself showed a Masonic line running through it. He smiled to himself. Here he was, questioning the layers that might be seen, and those that might be missed, perhaps deliberately revealed or hidden by unseen hands, and he was parked in Charlotte Square.

At one time the square had been the furthest westerly reach of Edinburgh's New Town. He had been taken by a local historian's assertion that the distance between here to the Bank of Scotland in St. Andrew's Square, at the east end of George Street, when divided by the distance from Princes Street to the south to Queen Street to the north, was the value of pi, one of the fundamental measurements of the Temple of Solomon, and the very cornerstone of reason and intelligence to Masons.

"Sir?" She was becoming accustomed to his thinking silences.

"What?"

"Choosing battles . . ."

"Well, we can't do it all, and *you* must learn what can be achieved and what can't." The Job was difficult enough without looking for those who, for their own or others' reasons, would help or hinder him doing it.

The mobile rang and he punched a button. "Steel."

"Hi Mike." Moss smiled as Steel's mood visibly lightened at the sound of JJ's voice.

"Hi JJ."

"I tried to get you over the weekend . . . "

"Normally days of rest, JJ," Steel said with a smile.

"I was hoping to have a word with you after seeing the *Sun*."

"That didn't go over at all well at Fettes." He hesitated to say he'd been taken off the murders – that was newsworthy, and he wouldn't want to face her with a tricky dilemma. "Sometimes I wonder whose side the papers are on."

They both heard her sigh. "*I'm* on your side, Mike."

Steel knew only too well the curious dynamic between tabloid and broadsheet newspapers. Both fed off each other, even talked to each other, when there were no exclusives at stake but, in reality, they were the same, they simply put on a different face, reflected in either inflamed or rational reporting. "What can I do for you, JJ?"

"Are you alone?"

Steel glanced at Moss. "No. Sergeant Moss is with me."

"*Sergeant* Moss?" JJ laughed. "That's rather formal," and she yelled, "*Hi, Robin*. Anyway, I've been at the Royal to see Emma. I *did* want to speak with you after seeing that *Sun* piece, but since you're in such a grumpy mood, I'm not so sure."

"Grumpy? I'm never grumpy." This got a low *hmm* from Moss. "We need to speak with Emma . . . probably best we head for the Royal, now."

"Then we'll pass each other, I'm due elsewhere. So . . ." and there was a moment's hesitation, "What I was thinking, that is if you're free tonight, would you like to go out somewhere? We could go for a meal, or a drink."

Moss looked at him. JJ had just asked him out – at *last*, one of them had made a move – and his expression hadn't changed.

Steel, however, had been completely taken by surprise; he had *never* been asked out by a woman. Worse, he felt himself colour slightly in front of Moss. "Perhaps a meal, JJ," he managed.

"Great," and Moss heard the lightness in her voice. "Well, give me a call when you're free – I should be finished by four."

Agreeing to this, Steel disconnected and turned to Moss to see her broad smile. "What?"

"Nothing, sir. I think it's good . . . been waiting for it to happen in fact."

She'd been waiting? Was he so transparent? "We have stuff to discuss, Moss, that's all. Now, let's get to the Royal and see Emma."

Stuff to discuss, thought Moss; a real change is about to happen in his life and it's stuff to discuss? All in all, men were a strange breed, policemen even more so, and she was pleased a woman – especially a woman like JJ – had taken the initiative.

●

At the Royal Infirmary they were met by an older PC sitting in the corridor, outside the door of a private room. Putting his book down, he got to his feet with a wide smile. "Hello Mike, it's been a while."

"What's this, John," Steel said, "you still getting all the good jobs?"

The constable laughed. "Well, as my old mum used to say, 'If you're not doing this, you'd only be doing something else'. Mind you, if you ask me, this is a bit like closing the stable door, though nobody asked. Powers that be reckon, what with McVicar still on the loose, we can't be too careful."

"McVicar? McVicar's not behind this."

He nodded. "Aye. If he was, I'd not be here, and that poor young lassie in there wouldn't be either . . . she'd be down the road at the morgue." Then, with a grin, "Still, it gives me the opportunity to indulge my passion," nodding at a well-thumbed paperback of Trollope's *An Eye for an Eye*.

Steel introduced Moss, and as they shook hands, asked whether Emma had had any visitors.

"There was a friend just here – a pretty redhead – and a couple of our

177

lads from Torphichen, but apart from that, nobody . . . she's English, of course."

"And what's wrong with being English, like?" Moss asked, with an exaggerated nasal Liverpool twang.

"Ach, nothing at all Miss, but you're a Scouser, and that's not English now, is it?"

Emma was propped up in bed, her face swathed in bandages. She raised a hand, a feeble attempt at greeting, and in a quiet voice, said, "I thought I heard friendly voices."

"How're you feeling, Emma?" Steel asked.

"Like crap, though the painkillers help . . . did you get him?" She saw their expressions, and tried to shake her head, but gave up. "Why?"

"I'm sorry, Emma," Moss said, "he's been given an alibi," and she placed her hand on hers, "We *will* get him."

"You're certain it was Steven McCann?" asked Steel.

Emma nodded her head and winced. "Yes. It happened so fast, but yes, it was him all right." She started a laugh which turned into a groan. "Managed to hurt him though."

Moss looked at her bandages, remembering the prettiness they covered. "We can be thankful for that . . . were you expecting someone? Did you have an appointment?"

"Yes, my ten-thirty – an old sweetie." Behind the bandages, her eyes darted from Moss to Steel. "It *was* McCann."

"Sorry, Emma," Steel said, "we're just making sure," and he sighed at the violence women in Emma's profession – even careful women like her – suffered; another failure in his idea of what policing *should* be. "So, what now?"

"Get better, get home," she managed.

"Well, before that," Steel said, "We'll need to get a statement from you about being approached at Hawthorns. Okay?"

"Sure," she sighed. "I'm really going to miss John, though."

"John?"

Emma fluttered her fingers towards the door, "John . . . he's such a nice man. He reads to me."

•

The darkness had crept in as usual and by three o'clock was complete. Ever since childhood, he had loved winter nights in Scotland. The lights from shop windows and houses, the headlights of cars and buses, carving dark seductive shadows for him to slide into and disappear.

Now this darkness was a cloak for him as he glided along Edinburgh's streets. He had two hours left before the shops closed – more than enough time for him to pick the right one.

He had tried to focus his mind on the street where the policeman on television lived, but it was a memory which formed and then billowed out of range like smoke. He knew he had failed Uriel. He had listened for his voice, but the noise in this city – too loud for the holy whisper to be heard – had masked it. The sudden thought that Uriel had deserted him because of his failure buffeted him. Was there still a chance for him to prove his worth?

At this thought, a flash of light seemed to physically hit his forehead, and he felt his body being bathed in golden light which flared from his fingertips. Its power coursed through him, growing with such strength that he staggered against a railing in the street. The noise behind his eyes crackled in intensity, building to an almost intolerable pitch and then, with one blinding all-consuming flash, there was silence.

Far into the distance, yet close within his ears, he heard, *I shall never desert you.*

He pulled himself upright and listened. Nodding his head, he understood. He had failed to kill Satan's helper, but that man had helpers of his own – he could kill one of them.

From beside him, he heard, "Ye a'right, pal?" He turned to the man and saw his gaze was burning into the man's eyes as he backed away, fear now written on his face. He laughed as the man scuttled across the road, and then saw the shop sign he was looking for – a mortar and pestle; Uriel was leading him.

He crashed through the chemist's door, startling the young girl behind the counter, chisel in hand as he reached her. Invincible now, he vaulted the counter and, as the pharmacist emerged from the back, stabbed him twice.

The girl screamed and he grabbed her by the hair. "Shut it," he breathed into her ear and, pushing her ahead of him, made his way through to the cabinet he sought. Pulling on the doors, he realised they were locked. He looked back to the pharmacist, lying on the floor, moaning and holding his stomach – he would have the key.

There's no time.

Pushing the chisel between the doors he broke them apart with a loud splintering of wood and grabbed several bottles. He didn't need to read their labels, Uriel was guiding his hand.

Shoving the young girl away from him, he leapt the counter and ran to the door. In seconds he was back into the shelter of his deep, dark shadows. Pulling the first bottle from his pocket, he spilled out five tablets. They were blue; five would be enough. For now.

In the distance a siren wailed. He listened to what Uriel was saying under the noise and, nodding in agreement, moved out of the shadows as the siren grew louder.

With red and blue lights flashing their warning, the police car tore up the street on the wrong side of the road, scattering cars, before screeching to a halt at the chemist's. Both policemen were already running to the door as he pulled the chisel from his pocket.

It could have been near or far – time and distance were meaningless when he and Uriel were One – but within seconds he had pushed on the door and was inside. The young girl saw him and screamed. The policeman who had been bent over the pharmacist turned and stood, moving towards him. His hand moved at speed, the chisel connecting with the policeman's body, but meeting resistance. He heard the man's cry of alarm as the second policeman came forward.

The baton hit his head. He felt nothing, but heard the dull sound of impact. Laughing, he swung the chisel towards the man; Uriel's protection raised and surrounded him.

The second blow knocked him to his knees, and his body swayed. An inky darkness drew close and he tried to stand. With the third blow he was almost unconscious, but the golden light which suffused his very being, burst up and outwards as he rose triumphantly from his knees.

Stabbing the policeman in the neck, he brought his face close, his crazed eyes wide. "*Hah*," he breathed in the man's face before he slumped to the ground.

Cackling to himself, he reached the door and slipped out into the night.

TWENTY

STEEL STEERED HIS CAR INTO THE PARKING BAY, killed the engine, and paused in the warmth, thinking of his evening with JJ.

He smiled as he remembered his comment to Moss that he and JJ had "things to discuss". JJ had suggested they eat at what she said was her favourite tapas bar – yet another novelty for him – and, in tacit agreement, they'd got shop talk out of the way almost immediately. JJ had told him her Picture Editor had set up a remote camera at Hawthorns; he had told her – asking her promise to keep it to herself – he'd been taken off the murder inquiries. After that, they'd discussed everything but work, and discovered they had many shared tastes, their conversation lasting well beyond their coffees until an apologetic waiter told them they were closing.

Standing outside, JJ pulled Steel's coat together against the lightly falling snow then, gripping his lapels, reached up to kiss him. Eyes sparkling, she said softly, "This was good, Mike . . . phone me."

Sitting in the car, he could still feel the sensations of her lips on his, the curves of her body as she'd reached for him, and felt vibrantly alive. It was as if he'd been asleep for years, but now she'd awakened him, opening a part he'd kept under lock and key. Hidden. A part covered up by the Job, and buried by what he'd become since his divorce.

He put his key in the front door, and as he pushed it open froze on the threshold; there was something wrong, something out of place.

He listened, and from upstairs heard what sounded like a footstep. Holding his breath, he strained to hear, and out of the silence heard the sound of the sash window opening. A roan pipe ran within a foot of that window – whoever was upstairs had heard him enter, and was escaping into the alley between his house and the terrace of houses which dropped down the short steep hill towards the metal footbridge over the Water of Leith.

Dashing outside, he turned into the narrow alley leading to the rear of the terraced houses, surfacing through a series of steps on Belford Road, which skirted and ran above the village.

He was just in time to see a dark-clad figure disappear round the first corner. It was useless to shout, so he sprinted after him. By the time he'd reached the corner, panting, his quarry was half way up the steps. The man had almost made it to Belford Road, but luck intervened when he slipped on the snowy steps and stumbled. Steel heard him curse as he fell forward, and within seconds he'd ploughed into the man's back, knocking him back to the ground as he struggled to get to his feet.

The man attempted to wriggle free from Steel's grasp, but he had a hold of his jacket with one hand, and thrust his forearm across his windpipe in an effort to subdue him. "Police," he managed, his breath coming in short, sharp gasps; these few seconds of pursuit had shown Steel just how unfit he was.

The man pinned beneath him was in his forties, thinner than himself, with hair combed straight back and a bushy moustache on a thin face. He was wearing a tie, which seemed incongruous. Keeping a good grip, Steel stared at the man – there was something familiar about him. "Are you one of McCann's?"

The man grinned, and his eyes flicked over Steel's shoulder.

The blow struck Steel behind his ear and seemed to radiate from there, spreading through his body and, as he slumped on top of the man, he felt hot breath on his neck and heard a whispered, "Wrong in *all* ways, chum," from behind and lost consciousness.

•

"So where do we stand exactly?" The man looked over his glasses at the three men sitting around the large, perfectly square table. He was seeking reassurance from them, something to ward off the nagging feeling that something was not quite going right.

Every week all four met, to sit at this table in the oak-panelled drawing room of one of Barnton's oldest houses and discuss their ventures. They had convened here for years and, although they used aliases, they knew each other intimately; there was nothing any one of them didn't know about the others' lives. There were no notes before them; each man carried their collective information in his head and, as each knew what the others knew, there was no need.

North, the man to the speaker's right, looked up. East had always been a worrier – not a bad thing, but pointless, he felt. Meticulous plans were made and, when executed in similar fashion, there was no need for worry. He could use a drink – his own little foible; the others abstained – but that wasn't permitted until their meeting was over. "As we stood before, nothing's changed," he said. "Why?"

East nodded slowly. "I'm getting soundings of interference from-"

"Interference?" the man opposite North said.

"Police involvement," East said. "Well, nosing round the edges."

"Then rest easy. Their business is not ours, and you *know* there'll be no interference from that area."

"Yes . . . but Fettes isn't everything, there *is* an international aspect."

West had listened to this brief interchange between the other three with growing impatience. At sixty, he was the youngest of the group and, although he would trust each man here with his life, there were times when he saw them as old women who could nag a simple thought into a problem. "This comes from where?" he asked East.

"Prior's becoming a face within Fettes again, and there's his needless involvement with the McCanns too. It worries me . . . we might suffer if Prior becomes someone in the spotlight."

"And you'd suggest what?" Prior *was* a problem – too flashy, too visible, and his dealings with the McCanns reckless – but, with several layers in place, they were more than just a safe distance from him, they were completely separate. Even when handling their investments – partial investments, no man here could ever be called foolish – Prior had no knowledge of who they were or even that they existed.

East sat back with a sigh. "I'm not suggesting anything . . . I'm only saying we should be watchful."

"We are . . . always," South put in, "and our friends at Fettes keep us fully informed. Nothing Prior does can affect us – nothing that can't be addressed before either he, or the police, even make a move." He looked at East and saw concern on his old friend's face. "If Prior does become a liability – in *any* way – he can be dealt with."

North positively hated the flashy flamboyance of people like Prior; their disgusting vanity aside, they attracted unwanted attention. "Yes, we can break his little so-called group of companies – overnight, if needs be – leave him with nothing."

East glanced at North. Behind that almost avuncular look lay a ruthlessness that, at a deep level, had always disturbed him; perhaps it stemmed from his lack of discipline with alcohol. "That, I hope, will be unnecessary, but we should be alert . . . if Prior's behaviour becomes a problem – a threat to our concerns – that the police can't control, then yes, we shall act."

North mulled this over. East's concern hadn't lessened. "Perhaps we shouldn't be worried, but more attentive. I'll have a word at Fettes," and looking round, "Is there anything else?" He saw the others shake their heads. "Then, unless a situation arises which *necessitates* an earlier meeting, we shall meet again in a week's time." He could almost taste the Macallan's.

•

Steel came to, and for a few disoriented moments couldn't place where he was. Managing to prop himself up, he saw there had been a heavy fall of snow, but had no idea how long he'd been lying there. He was frozen, and his head felt as if it had been hit by a brick. Feeling gingerly behind his ear, he found wetness and, when he looked, saw blood on his fingers.

For a moment he sat on the step, trying to come to terms with what had happened. Glancing at his watch he reckoned he'd been lying on the steps for about half an hour. He checked his pockets – his wallet was still there. Either the burglars – there had to have been at least two – had been frightened off by his arrival or they had already managed to clean him out.

Holding on to a railing, he hoisted himself to his feet, feeling nauseous as his head spun, an excruciating pain stabbing behind his eyes. He reached his front door and realised he must have left it open when he'd given chase. Great, he thought, good police-work there . . . let's hope I *did* frighten them off.

Collapsing into an armchair, he reached for the phone to dial Fettes. Identifying himself, he asked which detectives were on shift.

"DI Harrison and DS Morton are in the building, sir."

"Patch me through to DI Harrison, I need to report a crime."

•

"You're sure you don't want that seen to, Mike?"

Steel shook his head; a mistake, as another wave of nausea passed through him. "No, Kenny, if you say it doesn't look bad, it'll heal okay by itself."

Harrison smiled, "Where there's no sense there's no feeling?" Closing his notebook, he looked round, taking in the expensive hi-fi units and television. "You must've disturbed them at the outset. The window upstairs seems to be how they got in – unless someone's passing, they'd be hidden in that alley – best to look at getting that more secure," and he laughed, "There, I've done my community bit." He got to his feet and held out his hand. "I'll write it up, Mike, but you know as well as I do there's not much chance of catching them . . . that is, unless you remember the face you saw." The thin, sharply featured face, nudging him with its familiarity, seemed to swim before Steel's mind's eye for a brief moment, then it was gone. He gave Harrison a little shrug.

"Right, if you *don't* want me to run you to A and E, I'm done here."

Thanking Harrison, he shook his hand and showed him to the door. When he'd gone, Steel wandered aimlessly through the house, feeling all the worse for being on the receiving end for once. Earlier in his career, as a DC, he had often followed up on burglaries and, almost without fail, victims had used the word, *violated.* Here, years later, he knew exactly what they'd meant, and could only imagine how he would have felt if the place *had* been ransacked.

Harrison had been right; his arrival had probably coincided with the burglars', and he'd disturbed them before they could begin their thieving. Small things, such as his collection of small antique boxes, which could have been slipped into a pocket easily, had been left, while larger items like the television would have needed a vehicle.

He sat down, struck by the thought that if a vehicle was involved, the only place to park would have been outside the house, not on Belford Road, which would have meant a lengthy walk up snowy steps, and the risk of being seen. And, if they parked outside, where the street was a mere lane – blocked off by a stone bollard to stop vehicles using the short, steep hill which ran past the terraced houses – then their vehicle would have been obvious to anyone.

He tried to replay his return home. His mind had been filled with JJ but, like all detectives, he pictured scenes as a matter of course. Obviously, no vehicle had been parked in the Resident's bay, or in the lane, so that meant it had to have been parked in the oddly shaped space – the only available space – which lay at the back of Drumsheugh Baths, the old Victorian, Moorish influenced swimming pool on Belford Road. He tried to pull this to mind but couldn't see it; *had* there been an unknown vehicle parked there on his left when he arrived?

Again he tried to think this through; something didn't add up. The man he'd chased was in his forties, and, although he couldn't swear to it, the – English accented – voice of whoever had hit him sounded around that age too. The burglars hadn't been youngsters then, looking for easy, perhaps drug, money, but practised hands. This had been thought out, planned, and that bothered him.

With time on their hands the burglars could have cleaned him out, wherever their vehicle was parked, but nothing was missing, and that could only mean he'd arrived home at almost exactly the same time they'd broken in. That struck him as a coincidence, and the more he thought about it, a wild, unbelievable, one.

With his mind beginning to clear, he took his time and retraced his steps, pausing in each room to take things in. Nothing even seemed to be disturbed, which both lent credence to him arriving home at the very time the burglary began, *and* to the absurdity of the idea. He was missing something vital but couldn't see what it was.

He found himself back in the small box-bedroom, his home office, from where the burglar had escaped, and stood there taking it in. There was a small bookcase, a chair, and an old desk on which his rarely-used computer stood.

Pulling on the drawers, he saw nothing of any consequence; again, everything looked undisturbed. Powering-up the computer, he looked in the start menu for last used items; nothing new there – his last used item consisted of some notes made the day after the Mitchell murder.

The Mitchell murder? A distant alarm bell began to sound. He lifted the small pile of papers beside the computer and riffled through them. Then, taking his time, he sat in the chair and went through the papers again. No, what he was looking for was definitely not there.

He looked at his watch. It was late, but perhaps not too late, and he wanted an answer, now. Picking up the phone, he dialled Moss's number.

"Hello?" It was her flatmate, Susan.

"It's DCI Steel, Susan. I'm sorry to phone so late . . . is Moss there?"

He caught the smile in her voice. "*Robin?* Yes, hold on."

Steel heard her put the receiver down and walk away, and a few moments later, Moss picked up. "Sir?"

"I'm sorry to disturb you at home, Moss."

"That's okay, we were just watching the end of a film . . . what's up?"

"Do you remember when we were going through the murders of Pride, Mitchell, and McCartney? Here in the Dean Village?"

"Yes."

"And I wrote their names, and details about each, down?"

"Yes, sir. On three separate sheets."

"You didn't take those, did you?"

This got an emphatic, "No, sir . . . I wouldn't."

Moss heard Steel's long sigh, then a silence which spoke of several thoughts coming into his mind at once. "I've had a burglary, and the only things missing – the only things I *know* to be missing – are those sheets of paper."

TWENTY-ONE

STEEL WOKE EARLY TO SET ABOUT what he suspected would prove a fruitless task. He put Wayne Shorter's *Odyssey Of Iska* on the CD player and selected *After Love, Emptiness*. Taking his time, with Shorter's sinuous sax floating and following him through the house, he went from room to room, looking at everything anew. He wanted an answer, but deep down felt it would elude him. Something else could be missing but, in what seemed to be an undisturbed house, how would he know?

Why on earth would someone break in and steal three sheets of paper? kept running through his mind. And why these particular sheets of paper? The three names, and what they meant to each other, only had relevance to him and Moss.

Weighing the possible consequences, he made a discreet call to a DC he knew on the Murder Squad, and found they were still investigating the murders of Lord Mitchell and Father McCartney in tandem. And, despite Grieve having passed on Moss's observations on the murder of Father McCartney – that he might be the third victim of someone other than McVicar – they had yet to make a connection between Mitchell, McCartney and Judge Pride.

Their failure to make that connection concerned Steel, and he knew he couldn't keep his thoughts to himself much longer. Soon – very soon – he would need to bring this direct connection to the Murder Squad's attention especially as, or so it seemed, whatever tree they were barking up was the wrong one.

Moss arrived, and while he made coffee he took her through the previous night's events. Troubled, she sat down, nursing the hot brew. "You're *sure* you held on to those sheets, sir?"

"Absolutely . . . since last night I've gone over and over that. I remember coming home and seeing them lying on the table. I took them upstairs and placed them beside my computer . . . I can *see* them there." He wasn't even sure why he'd done that, why he hadn't thrown them away.

"But why would someone want to steal something like that?" Moss was as perplexed as he was.

"I'm damned if I know."

His mobile rang, and with "I'll take this," he wandered through to the kitchen.

Hearing laughter and Steel's lighter tone, Moss didn't have to guess who the caller was. Once again, she felt a satisfying glow; JJ had made a move when Steel looked like he would have danced around her forever. Getting to her feet Moss stood at the window, looking over the Dean Village. A light flurry of snow was falling, conjuring a fairytale scene, like a child's snow globe, before her. This part of Edinburgh really is beautiful; come Spring, I'll bring Susan here.

Steel came through smiling. "Right, grab your coat, we're headed to the *Scotsman*. JJ's got pictures from Hawthorns."

•

As they waited for JJ, Moss took in her surroundings. She'd been in a newspaper office only once before, at the *Liverpool Echo*, when Merseyside had been working on a growing problem of knife assaults. To her the *Echo* had *felt* like a newspaper while here, although she could see people were busy, there was no real noise, and none of the distinctive smells she took to be part of the industry. She turned to Steel. "Is the *Scotsman* printed here?"

Steel shook his head, then Moss saw his face light up – the lift doors had opened and JJ was walking towards them.

With a dazzling smile which seemed to bathe Steel, JJ reached for his forearm to give it a gentle squeeze. "Morning, Mike," and turning to Moss, "Hi, Robin. I'll take you up to Ian, our Picture Editor."

They took the lift to the top floor, and Moss couldn't help but notice how close JJ stood to Steel. Soon they were in the Picture Editor's office, a chaos of colour and monochrome images with every available space covered by photographs, and JJ introduced them.

Abbotsford held up a thumb drive, "I put this together for you," then pushed it into his PC. "Everything's been edited for close-ups of the number plates, and I've deleted the occasional passing car, and any duplicates."

"You're keeping the originals though?" Moss asked, already contemplating what they might need for evidence.

Abbotsford nodded. "We back-up everything as a matter of course but, for this, I've got my own drive."

A multi-paned browser opened on his screen, and one by one each picture on the drive appeared. Every picture was a perfectly legible shot of both rear and front number plates.

"How many shots are there?" Moss asked.

"A hundred and twenty – sixty cars in all."

Steel peered at the screen. "Is there a way of knowing the time?"

"Yes . . . hang on." Abbotsford selected an image and double-clicked. A number plate filled the screen, then he cursed and held up an apologetic hand. "Sorry. My mistake . . . the originals have a timestamp on them, not these cropped shots."

"That's okay," Steel said, "You'd be able to get a time if we need it though?"

"Sure."

Moss's memory was jogged by the pornographic images of minors found on Mitchell's computer. "How can you tell when a picture was taken, Ian?"

Abbotsford swivelled in his chair to face her. "Well, with digital cameras, there's exif information," and seeing her blank look, he laughed. "Sorry . . . exchangeable image file format . . . it's metadata, part of the file – data about data – and shows when the image was created, what camera and lens were used, and a load of other stuff . . . GPS too, if you want. So, yes." He saw her absorb this. "Be careful though, exif information *can* be removed – doctored even – and," with a nod to his screen, "although duplicates *normally* carry the same info as the original, the creation date and time *can* be different."

Moss smiled her thanks while Steel looked at her, wondering why she'd asked.

"So," JJ said, "this is a start, yes?"

Abbotsford gave JJ a small nod of agreement. "Well the camera's still in place," and, looking from her to Steel, "How long do you need?"

This was clearly an excellent resource for determining exactly who visited Hawthorns. "As long as we can," Steel said, "I'm expecting to see a few duplicate visits."

Abbotsford closed the browser, pulled out the thumb drive, and held it out towards Steel. "Someone'll let me know though . . . yes? That's a pretty expensive piece of kit out there unattended."

"There could be a really big story at the end of this, Ian," JJ interjected.

"A few days, maybe a weekend," Steel said as he took the drive. "Thanks for your help, Ian . . . we'll find out who owns these cars, then take it from there."

JJ walked them out of the building, and Moss asked Steel for the car keys so he and JJ could have a few moments alone. Sitting in the car, she glanced back at them. JJ was dressed in an elegant, black trouser suit with a short bolero jacket – a long legged beauty – and with her arms around Steel's waist, her long red hair cascaded down her back as she looked up at him. She was laughing as she said something to him; better still, her boss was laughing too.

•

Back at Fettes, Steel had patched his computer into the Driver Vehicle Licensing Agency's database in South Wales. As Moss went through the pictures, one by one, Steel fed the numbers into a search box, noting the registered owner's name and address.

Some of the names produced were unknowns to him but most were not, and the list he was compiling contained a healthy cross-section of Edinburgh's movers and shakers. Here were politicians – including, he noted, Councillor William Kennedy, the Convener of the Planning Committee – bankers, and businessmen. They were mainly men, but not all, and it was no surprise to him when Prior's name came up, nor his wife Jan's – both with matching black BMW 7s and personalised number plates, AP1 and JP1.

He looked twice at the next name before him. "Give me that number again."

Moss repeated the number and Steel sat back. "Have a look at this, would you . . ."

She got up from her chair and came behind him. Onscreen, she read the name Robert James Henderson, with a registered address in Falkirk. "Sir?"

"That's *Rob* Henderson – DCI Henderson of Crime Squad, to you and me."

"That can't be. Are you sure? It must be another Robert Henderson . . ."

Steel shook his head. "I know his address. He's lived there for years. I don't like him, as you've probably gathered."

"Yes . . . why?"

"Crime Squad, Moss – all of them bend the rules but, with Rob Henderson, it's as if there are no rules to be bent."

Steel's phone rang, breaking the silence that had fallen between them, but he continued to stare at the screen, deep in thought, and ignored it. He wasn't sure what the full implication of this discovery meant. Not yet anyway. As his phone died, Moss's began to ring and, skirting the desk, she picked it up.

"Yes, sir . . . Of course . . . Chief Inspector Steel's with me now." He watched her as she laid the receiver down rather shakily; it looked like bad news.

"What is it?"

"We're wanted upstairs. Now."

"Upstairs?"

"That was Grieve . . . he's waiting for us in the Chief Constable's office."

With a scowl and a muttered "What now?" Steel got to his feet. Grieve with the CC sounded ominous. His hands reached for his tie to straighten it, but he stopped himself. Reaching into his pocket, he found his Rennies, and popping one into his mouth crunched down on it.

They walked to the lift, and as they waited Steel turned to her. "Whatever this is, if it's something bad, remember to stick with, 'DCI Steel told me to do it', right?"

She gave him an uncertain nod. "Have you had any dealings with the Chief before, sir?"

"Rarely – I usually avoid him if I see him coming. He's part of that upper echelon who haven't had their hands dirty in decades. He's more of a politician . . . working cops normally don't run into him."

Both fell silent as the lift arrived to take them to Fettes' top floor, where they made their way along the carpeted corridor to the Chief Constable's office.

The Chief's secretary, a near-legendary woman in her late fifties never known to smile, looked up as they entered. Pulling her glasses down, she narrowed her eyes at them over the rim. "You'll be DCI Steel and DS Moss?"

The old dragon, Steel thought, she was more accustomed to arranging the Chief's social calendar than anything. She knew who they were alright. Giving her a broad smile, he said, "That's right, Cath."

He was pleased to see her cheeks redden as she pointed with her pen at the chairs against the wall. "Sit there." Getting out from behind her desk, she knocked on the door to the inner office and pushed it open. Steel listened to her soft murmur and, after a small pause, heard the familiar voice of television and radio. "Send them in please, Catherine."

When they entered Steel saw an unhappy Grieve, staring at his shoes, sitting to one side with another man he didn't recognise. "DCI Steel and DS Moss, sir . . . you wanted to see us."

The Chief Constable eyed him up and down, then turned to Grieve. "Bob?"

Grieve cleared his throat. "DCI Steel, you'll remember I spoke with you – just three days ago – regarding your involvement in the murders of Lord Mitchell and Father McCartney?"

"Yes sir."

"Do you remember what my orders were?"

"I'm not sure whether I could recount them exactly, sir."

Grieve glared at him. "This is *not* the time. You *do* remember I instructed you to cease all investigations into those two murders, as all investigations were to be handled by a Murder Squad that was being set up?"

"Yes sir."

"And yet you failed to follow my orders."

Steel thought fast. Nobody knew he and Moss had continued to work on both murders, so how could Grieve know? Unless . . . could it be the DC on the Murder Squad he'd talked with this morning? He knew the man well, and had been very discreet, so rejected the thought.

"DS Moss and I did in fact continue working on a *vice* matter which arose from Lord Mitchell's murder, sir . . . there may be a blurred line."

The Chief Constable scowled and weighed in. "Forget your damned *blurred line*, man." Then in slow, clipped tones said, "I *know* you Steel. I had to field a letter from a prestigious Edinburgh law firm concerning you. Now did you, or did you not, follow your superior's order?"

In for a penny, in for a pound, Steel thought. "I did follow Chief Superintendent Grieve's orders, sir," and he saw Thompson glance at the unknown man.

"And you can confirm this, Sergeant?"

Whatever this meeting was really about, it was likely heading towards a disciplinary matter, so before she could speak, Steel said, "Sergeant Moss followed *my* orders, sir."

At that, Thompson sat back, appraising her. "You're new here, Sergeant . . . a graduate on Accelerated Careers. Am I right?"

In a firm voice she said, "That is correct, sir."

"So, what I'd say to you is this . . . you would do very well to remember both your training *and* your aspirations. Am I being clear?"

"Yes sir."

Steel sought to take some sort of command of a situation already well out of his control. "Sergeant Moss is an exemplary officer sir, an invaluable asset to the Force . . . but, if I may, this would appear to be a meeting in which I feel there should be a representative from the Police Federation present," and he saw a sardonic smile appear on the face of his third, silent, inquisitor. "I think I am entitled to both that," and with a jerk of his head to the man, "and also to know exactly *who* is present today . . . and why."

The man sat forward, every trace of his smile wiped from his face.

"This is Commander Bruce of the National Crime Squad," Thompson said.

The NCS? London-based, yet here? And in a flash of recognition, Steel placed the face of the man he'd chased from his home. He *had* seen him before; Tulliallan Police College in Fife, perhaps four or five years back, a Detective Inspector, if he remembered correctly. *That* was how they knew of his and Moss's continued involvement – last night's burglary had been an NCS fishing expedition.

He felt a righteous anger rising. "And just *what* involvement does Commander Bruce have in *this* matter, sir?"

"That's *enough*, Chief Inspector," Grieve snapped.

Thompson's cheeks flushed and he shuffled some papers. "You forget yourself, Steel. You don't get to ask questions here."

For a moment there was silence in the room. Steel sensed some kind of stand-off in play, and all three were looking at him as if he might say something more.

Thompson finished his shuffling, and looking at Steel, said in an icy tone, "You are an experienced officer DCI Steel, and yet, despite such experience, you failed to follow a simple, direct order from a superior officer. In the meantime – that is, until a further meeting can be held with a Federation Representative present – you are on leave with full pay forthwith."

He turned to Moss. "Sergeant Moss, I accept you had no culpability in this matter; CS Grieve will assign you new duties in due course," and looking from her to Steel he dismissed them with, "That is all."

Thompson sat back, matter dealt with, but Steel wasn't finished. Taking two strides towards their London visitor, he thrust out his hand and, taken by surprise, Bruce took it to shake.

Steel, however, didn't shake the man's hand, only held it in a tightening vice-like grip. In a soft voice, almost a whisper, he said, "I'll be seeing you later, Mr. Bruce."

TWENTY-TWO

STEEL AND MOSS WALKED BACK TO THE LIFTS in silence. She couldn't grasp what had just happened and needed to speak with him, but one glance told her it would be best to wait.

Steel pressed the call button and paused, staring at it, then stabbed it a couple of times. The lift eventually arrived and, once inside, he turned to her. "I'm sorry, Moss," and held up a hand to silence any reply. Feeling his stomach churning, he knew this was the wrong time to discuss anything, let alone what they'd just been through. In front of an outsider, no less.

The lift reached their floor, and Steel held the door for her. "I'll call you later, we have to talk," and when she stepped out, giving him a concerned nod, he pressed for Ground.

Leaving Fettes at speed, he drove towards the city centre. He needed to think, but his house, somewhat tainted for him right now, would be the wrong place; he would go where he knew his mind always cleared.

Navigating swiftly through the city, taking all the short cuts he knew, he surfaced on the Cowgate and sped down Holyrood Road. He glanced at the *Scotsman* building as he passed; seeing JJ would be something positive, but that could wait. With a momentary pause at the end of the street, he turned into the Queen's Park.

The road which runs through the park round the dormant volcano of

Arthur's Seat is one-way, and within minutes he had gunned the car through an almost complete circle. Pulling into the kerb at the final downhill section, he killed the engine and stepped out.

Edinburgh was being hit by the infamous East Wind straight off the North Sea but, in his present mood, Steel didn't even register the needle-sharp cold. He felt as if he'd been dealt a sucker punch, well below the belt and, as he replayed the scene in the Chief's office once more, he was angry in a way he'd never experienced before.

With his breath making white vapour clouds before him, he took a few steps on to the slippery snow-covered grass and looked over the distant, sprawling city. The Salisbury Crags, small stratified cliffs, rose to his right, and he could make out several hardy souls walking on the Radical Road, which skirted their base. Far in the distance the castle could be seen dominating the Old Town, and the leaden sky, overcast and promising more snow, was pierced by the spires of Edinburgh's numerous churches, pointing to the heavens like God's accusatory fingers.

This view always lent some distance between him and what he thought were his problems. It was a timeless and ancient prospect, one which always seemed to calm him; a place where he could regain perspective when his life seemed out of kilter.

The last time he'd stood here had been when his divorce to Annabel had been finalised. That, too, had hinged on simple sheets of paper — a few lines unceremoniously bringing twelve years of marriage to an end — and it was here he had gained a clearer perspective. Nothing lasts. Were those sheets of paper, pilfered from his house by the NCS, and the way he'd been handled by Grieve and the Chief, yet another nudge — it was not in his nature to call it a sign — that it was, once again, time to move on?

As he took in the jumbled panorama of buildings, sea and sky . . . *which writer had summed up Edinburgh from here?* . . . he allowed his thoughts to tumble through his mind and, slowly, felt himself calming. The distant buildings before him meant nothing; they were impermanent. Only the lie of the land — carved that way, millions of years before, by a great ice age — had some kind of timeless reality for him.

He took a deep breath; he really had no choice, and it was quite straightforward. Regardless of how any subsequent meeting at Fettes might go, he was a cop, something criminal had happened, and it was *his* job to correct it. He smiled to himself. This was him, years ago, when he'd joined the Force, when all he could see were whites and blacks. Moss would understand.

After a few more silent moments looking out over the city, he got into his car, turned on the heaters full blast, and picked up the phone. "Give it half an hour, Moss . . . I'll see you at the Dean Village."

•

"Surely not . . ." Moss had listened to his reasoning, and still couldn't grasp what Steel had laid out for her. ". . . that would mean a conspiracy to pervert the course of justice."

Steel gave her a thin smile. "Back to the law books with you. I think, an attempt to defeat the ends of justice, is what you mean. It's not that, but it *is* a conspiracy."

She threw out her hands and sat back. "What, between a Chief Constable, a Chief Superintendent, and a Commander of the National Crime Squad?"

He looked at her; she was young, but not *that* young. "You've never come across corrupt cops?"

"No. Well, yes . . . I've *heard* about them. But the Chief, Grieve, and Bruce, together? That's," and she sat forward, searching for the right word, "inconceivable."

"Come *on*, Moss – *anything's* conceivable," and he saw her holding on to her incredulity. Perhaps she was thinking that in his shock and anger over this morning's meeting he'd simply dreamed up this scenario. He tried a different tack. "What do you know about the NCS?"

"Very little," she admitted with a shake of her head.

"Well, the NCS was formed out of Regional Crime Squads . . . ours used to be in Morningside, a hive of crime."

"*And?*" ignoring his attempted humour about Edinburgh's most genteel of suburbs.

"One of the Regional Crime Squads – the South-East Regional Crime Squad, who called themselves "the groovy gang" – were, in fact, a South London *mob*."

Steel recalled how every police force had been rocked when – from this one Regional Crime Squad alone – over fifty corrupt detectives had been removed, and most had been prosecuted. "The papers had a field day . . . it was, as they put it, a scandal, and they referred to them as, 'the best police force money could buy'. Regional Crime Squads are no more, but do you *really* think some rotten apples didn't manage to survive into the NCS? Who knows about Commander Bruce?"

She could see the possibility he might be right. But Bruce, the Chief and Grieve acting together still seemed beyond belief. "Okay, but a conspiracy to what ends, sir?"

Steel was silent for a few moments; he'd been unable to answer that question himself. "It's beyond me," and before she could say anything, "though clearly someone doesn't like the connections we've uncovered. Beyond that . . ." and he shrugged.

Moss sighed and got to her feet. "I don't think I'm firing on all cylinders. I need another coffee . . . you?"

He smiled, pleased at the way she was making herself at home, but shook his head; his stomach was still rebelling and the Rennies weren't coping.

In the kitchen Moss poured herself another mug and tried to order her thoughts. She had already put herself at risk by continuing to investigate the three murders with her DCI but, now, he was her, *suspended* DCI.

By now, after all they'd been through, she felt she had Steel's measure; this was a good man and, despite his flaws, a man of integrity, even wisdom. Common sense told her the supposed burglary and the Chief's knowledge they'd continued working on the murders, having been told not to, had to be connected. But the notion of a conspiracy involving top cops was something else altogether. Whatever she did in the coming few days, she would need to be careful.

Steel was standing at the window when she returned. "What can *I* do, sir?"

Without turning to face her, he said, "Whatever's safest, Moss . . . you have a career ahead of you – a long one, I hope. Do whatever's safest." He felt a twinge of guilt as he said this; he'd told the Chief she'd been following *his* orders, but, nevertheless, she'd put herself, and her career, in harm's way because of him.

He turned to her. "I think I *will* have a coffee," and made for the kitchen, still with a jumble of thoughts in his head.

Returning with a fresh mug he sat down opposite her. "Has Grieve spoken with you yet?"

"He came in later. Asked me what I was working on," and to Steel's querying look, "I told him I was working on vice . . ."

"Good . . . I know Bob, he'll let you run with that for some time before he'll hook you up with someone else." He leant forward, speaking in a low voice, "Somehow, all of this is connected . . . the vice, the murders. Damned if I can see it, but there's got to be something which connects it all."

"You mentioned Prior, before."

"Yes. There's just too many times his name comes up when-"

"Hang on," Moss interrupted, "*there's* the connection between Prior and the three we were in front of this morning . . ."

"What?"

"Hawthorns."

Steel frowned. "Hawthorns? What connection?"

Moss smiled – for once, she felt she was ahead of her boss. "What name had we *just* come up with when we were going through the pictures from the *Scotsman?*"

Steel's frown deepened. "Rob Henderson."

"Exactly." She'd found two of Steel's jigsaw pieces and, to her, they were a perfect fit. Leaning forward, and resting her chin on her fists, she looked up at Steel from under her fringe. "*So* – let's just suppose – DCI Henderson goes to Hawthorns, not as a visitor – a user – but undercover? The Crime Squad *could* be in the middle of its own investigation of Prior right now – part of the investigation into PPE."

Steel absent-mindedly reached for the wound, now hardening into a rough scab behind his ear. She could be right. "That doesn't explain the NCS breaking into my house."

She shook her head. "It might. Remember Grieve gave you a roasting over what he called 'poking into a Crime Squad case'? Steel nodded – he was beginning to see the pieces himself. "You told me yourself that when you arrested Billy McCann, you'd stepped on the NCS's toes, because they were after him *and* Prior. Somehow they knew we were still investigating the murders, when we'd been told not to – couldn't that 'somehow' be the break-in, and the theft of those sheets of paper?"

Steel got to his feet and stood by the window again. Moss was bright and her theory held water. If Crime Squad *had* placed Henderson in Hawthorns, or the NCS had advised that course, then it could quite easily be part of something larger – *larger* making a wandering line between Prior, with his Forth Development and ownership of Hawthorns, and Billy McCann with his suspected connection to drugs from Holland, and whatever else he was up to as a "humble manager" of *Oysters*.

With him and Moss following a vice angle to the murder of Lord Mitchell, perhaps the NCS, for *their* reasons, had needed them well out of the way. Letting the Chief know they were still investigating the murders – having been told not to – had been an expedient, not to mention cynical, move.

He turned back to Moss to see her smiling. "Well, did I get it right?" she asked, and her smile got broader.

Steel let out his first laugh of the day. "It makes *some* sense, Moss . . . I'm not quite sure we could call it complete sense, but it does seem to fit a couple of larger pieces together."

She gave him a small tilt of her head in a faux bow. "And I should continue working on vice . . . because?"

"Because I'm certain all the pieces we've been stumbling over – the murders, Hawthorns . . . *Prior* – all connect, and vice seems to be the key to it. Speak to JJ about this – be cautious though, remember she *is* a reporter – but if we continue to follow the vice angle, I think we're going to get a much better understanding of what the hell all these separate pieces of the jigsaw are."

She looked at him and paused. "What should I say to JJ about you, sir?"

"Tell her I've been sent on leave, but nothing else," and his face grew more serious, "Be careful, Moss . . . if you're right, there'll be heavy aspects to all this."

"I will," and with a wide smile, "Nothing else?"

At first Steel was mystified, then realised what she meant. "Ah . . . tell her I'll phone her later."

Moss had real difficulty finding a parking space anywhere near the *Bean Grinding* café, and simply gave up, leaving the car on a yellow line.

When she eventually made it there she saw JJ waiting for her at a window table. Holding up an apologetic hand, she said, "Sorry, it's impossible to find a parking space in this street."

JJ smiled at her. "It's okay, Robin . . . what with the Parliament being built, Holyrood Palace, *and* us at the *Scotsman* . . ." She shrugged, then gave her a questioning look, "So where's Mike?" and seeing hesitation cross Moss's face, added, "Not that it's not nice to see you of course."

Moss held her breath for a moment, then exhaled with a loud sigh. "He's been sent home on leave."

"He's *what?* What for?"

Remembering Steel's words on being cautious with JJ, and mindful of never having worked as closely with a reporter before, Moss said, "Apparently for not following an order. It's nothing, and it'll probably blow over."

JJ shook her head. "Mike will be *far* more than upset." She flashed a smile at a passing waiter, and arching her eyebrows at Moss, "Coffee?"

Moss thought she'd probably had more than enough today, but nodded, "Please."

"So, was there anything useful from those Hawthorns pictures?"

Delving into her bag, Moss pulled out a spreadsheet and held it halfway towards JJ. "These names are between ourselves, okay?"

"Agreed," JJ said, and took the sheet from her. Unfolding it, she ran her eyes over the list, and Moss saw her eyebrows raise a couple of times. "Some unexpected names here."

"But some expected ones too?"

"The usual suspects, as they say . . . I see both Prior and his wife are here."

Moss leant in towards her. "What's your next step with these, JJ?"

"What's needed is another reference point – these names alone are not enough. Visiting Hawthorns is no crime, although I can't imagine wanting to," and she gave Moss a conspiratorial smile, "It's all a bit too decadent – and exhibitionist – for me. No, somehow, I've got to find who has a taste

205

for children . . . who the perverts are." She looked down the list again. "Didn't Ian say there were sixty pictures on the thumb drive?"

Moss sat back; a half-truth would be best. "That's all I have, JJ. Have you heard from Emma at all?"

"Yes, I phoned her. She's on the mend, but she's still very shaken."

Moss saw Stevie McCann's face swim before her. "I want McCann . . . that evil bastard shouldn't be walking the streets."

JJ pursed her lips. "No chance his alibi won't hold up?"

"None. It's watertight."

Folding the spreadsheet and placing it in her bag, JJ said, "You know Robin, sometimes it's a simple matter of pulling the right lever . . . get the *right* one and the whole edifice falls."

"The boss was going on about me choosing my battles, but if I knew how to get Stevie McCann with one blow, I'd do it."

JJ took a sip of her coffee and looked off into the busy street. "Sometimes it's better to ignore the also-rans and go straight to the top," and, turning back to Moss to look directly into her eyes, "If you kill the heart, the body *will* die."

"And the top is . . . ?

"Alan Prior . . . without a shadow of doubt. One way or another, he's at the heart of all of this. Go after Prior, Robin, everything else will come tumbling down."

For a brief moment Moss glimpsed a different side to the intelligent, attractive woman sitting opposite her. This was the tough reporter, hardened from peering into probably some of the worst human deeds and wresting stories from them.

"The boss reckons Prior to be pretty central-"

"*Another* thing we see eye to eye on."

"-but I'm not so sure . . . perhaps all he is, is just a clever, albeit shady, businessman," and she hesitated, giving JJ a shy grin, "Actually, I found him attractive."

JJ reached across the table and placed her hand on Moss's, giving her an indulgent, sisterly smile. "Ah, but it's the clever and attractive ones we have to watch out for – no matter *who* they are," and glancing at the time, got to her feet. "Sorry, I need to go. Thanks for the list, it's a real step forward . . . I'll get in touch with Mike later – do something to cheer him up."

Moss watched her through the window as she crossed the busy street, and thought, JJ you've no idea how much you've cheered him up already.

TWENTY-THREE

AFTER MOSS HAD LEFT TO MEET JJ, Steel pondered her theory on Rob Henderson. No matter which way he came at it, it looked like a perfect jigsaw piece, fitting precisely into what they already knew as fact. And, he knew, if the Crime Squad *had* placed Henderson, that would explain their need to ensure nobody did anything to draw any unwanted attention.

Steel shook his head; if the man had only flagged the files with a Crime interest, he and Moss would've trod *far* more carefully. Although Hawthorns itself would probably be safe to operate in, undercover work was a dangerous river to swim in, and there was no telling what might be stirred up if a target ever got wind of police involvement.

He got to his feet and, selecting the second movement of the *Symphony of Sorrowful Songs*, stood at his window to watch the river rushing by in full spate. As Dawn Upshaw's powerful voice surfaced, he realised his anger had almost evaporated, but not quite. Rob Henderson may have made a simple human mistake, but the NCS's actions were a different matter altogether.

Replaying the chase that ensued when he'd stumbled on the break-in, he knew he'd need to find a way of dealing with Commander Bruce, and then there was the Chief Constable to think of too. In his whole career he'd never been sent on leave and, whatever choices the Chief had made, they'd been based on the NCS's illegal actions.

Just as he was beginning to wonder what he might do with his enforced free time, the doorbell rang, and rang insistently – someone leaning on the bell. He glanced at his watch; it was far too early for Moss to be returning from seeing JJ. Opening the door, he was surprised to find DS Grieve's bulk filling the frame.

"Sir?" Steel was nonplussed.

"Enough of the sir," Grieve said, with a shame-faced expression, and as Steel stood to one side to let him in, "This isn't official – I'm not here officially – but I need to speak with you."

"About what?"

"I want some answers," and he looked round, "D'you still keep a good malt?"

Steel nodded; whatever this visit signified, it definitely wasn't official; he'd never known Grieve to take a drink during the day. Thinking he'd like some answers too, he poured a couple of drams.

Grieve threw his coat down on the back of a chair. "What's that noise?"

"Górecki."

"Bloody mournful sound, prefer Daniel O'Donnell myself . . . can we switch it off?"

It's meant to be mournful, you old philistine, Steel thought, as he aimed the unit's remote to silence the CD. Grieve was taking in the room. "This is very nice, Mike . . . it's a shame you and Annabel never made a go of things."

"What?"

"Sorry, old habit. Sheila and me, well we thought you were a good couple, right for each other, you know."

"That was ages ago, and there's been a lot of water under the bridge since then. Anyhow, we were more like cat and dog." This is surely not a social visit, he thought.

Grieve eyed the glass Steel was holding out to him. "Bloody hell Mike, I said a drink, not a taste, eh?"

Steel looked at the whisky – it *was* a daytime measure – and went back to the bottle to double up what he'd poured.

As he took the glass, Grieve said, "You could've been more than a DCI you know. And what with the connections you had with Annabel's family, you could've climbed much higher," and he raised his glass, "Slàinte."

Steel took a sip of the small whisky he had poured himself, still wondering – especially after this morning's meeting – why the hell Grieve was here. "As I said, that was a long time ago. We've both moved on."

"And you have a son, eh? How's he?"

Christ. "I haven't seen him to know."

Grieve shook his head at this. "Just the other day I was saying to Sheila I like to see families put first in our line of work."

Steel immediately thought of the families that had been rendered null and void by the Job; in his experience, Bob and Sheila Grieve were the oddity, not the norm. "Work tends to put families last Bob – you know that. Anyhow, I'm pretty sure you didn't come here to talk about me and Annabel, and how I could've been more than a DCI. What was-"

"And you're hooked up with this Johnstone girl from the *Scotsman* now?"

"Seeing each other. I don't know about hooked up."

Grieve's brow puckered. "That's been one of your problems Mike . . . Annabel, this Johnstone girl – bright things with their own careers – not copper's wives. Wrong stock, eh?"

Steel almost laughed out loud. He wasn't the most enlightened person – in fact, Grieve had called him a dinosaur not too long ago – but even to his ears, his boss was sounding like something from the fifties. Keeping an even tone, he said, "I'm fairly sure JJ would be unhappy to be called either a girl, or stock."

"Just my point, Mike. The girl's got a different attitude to a copper's wife. JJ indeed . . . not that I'm judging her."

"Really? . . . Why are you here Bob? It can't be just to talk of my choice of women and drink my whisky."

Grieve held out his glass. "Yes, I will have another . . . I want some answers, Mike. What happened at that meeting with the Chief?"

Steel sat back in his chair. "You were there, Bob."

"Look, I was simply called in – your superior officer, eh? – but I was given a fait accompli, along with an unwarranted bollocking, by the Chief," and with a pained expression as his mind came to it, "Why can't you just follow orders, Mike?"

Steel felt himself becoming hot. "For Christ's sake, are we going to go over old ground? I *was* following orders, just not the way you – or the Chief – wanted, that's all." He thought of Commander Bruce. "How did you know we were still looking into the murders?"

"I didn't. Like I said, I got called upstairs and the Chief told me you and Moss were still investigating them, after I'd told you not to . . . made me look damned foolish I'll tell you."

Steel thought back to his earlier conversation with Moss. "And where did the Chief get that information?" He knew he could weigh in with his thoughts on the NCS, but held back. "We were working the case but, as you know, one thread – here, vice – can lead to a whole bloody tapestry."

"No, it leads to treading on toes – a speciality of yours."

"Crime Squad's?"

"No man, the Chief's. He's set great store on this investigation of Prior and McCann. Rob Henderson made a mistake by not flagging Crime's interest in Prior's company, but it was the Chief's toes you were stomping on."

"Okay, but where did he get the information Moss and I were still working the murders?"

"I was hoping *you* could give me an answer to that. I know cases don't come at us, all neat and tidy – I'd've just given you a rocket for flying solo when I'd asked you not to – but that's my point, how did the Chief get wind of this, when I didn't?"

Steel finished off his whisky and sat back, bumping up against the need to tell Grieve that the NCS had broken in and stolen his notes, such as they were. "How much involvement do the NCS have in Hawthorns?"

Grieve glowered at him. "Well *I* don't know, do I? What I do know is Crime, along with Inland Revenue, are investigating Prior . . . him, his companies, everything his companies own, *and* his connection with the McCanns. The Chief thought this was too big for Lothian and Borders to handle – stupid sod that he is – and invited them in as advisors.

"Henderson's been placed there, supposedly as an investment banker with Deutsche Bank – if you can believe that of him – but, apart from that, I know nothing."

Steel shook his head on hearing confirmation of Moss's theory directly from Grieve. He weighed up his options, wondering where this might go. "You know I had a break-in?"

Grieve nodded. "Yes. I bumped into Kenny Harrison – he told me about it. Nothing taken, eh? I heard you disturbed them," and he gave Steel a sharp look. "Why? What's that got to do with anything?"

Steel paused, looking at Grieve; they'd been through a lot together. "This is an unofficial visit, right?"

"How many more times? Yes . . . why?"

Taking a deep breath, Steel said, "The NCS were behind it."

Grieve laughed, then stopped himself. "My God, you're serious."

"Listen, Bob, you need to keep this unofficial – keep it between us, for the time being, anyhow. I know that-"

"But I thought nothing was taken. You're trying to tell me the NCS broke in here, stole nothing, and-"

"I *am* telling you. Moss and I had been discussing connections between our vice investigation and the murders . . . I made some notes on the murders and that's what was stolen. Nothing else."

"You can't be serious about the NCS being involved, Mike."

"I am serious. I recognised the one I chased – been on a seminar with him at Tulliallan. We never talked, but when I tackled him, I *knew* I'd seen him before."

Grieve got to his feet and began to pace. "I can't have this . . . you're telling me that police officers have taken part in something illegal, and I'm supposed to keep it to myself . . . do nothing about it?"

Steel saw that, where Grieve had been somewhat mellow with a couple of whiskies warming his insides, now he was fired up. "You have to keep this unofficial, Bob. It's water under the bridge but, if you want to know how the Chief knew we were still working the murders, it's down to the NCS."

"I'm not *having* that, Mike," Grieve said, his voice becoming loud. "It's not on . . . I can't just stand back when one of my own officers gets this sort of treatment. And from bloody outsiders too."

Steel held up a calming hand. "You *must* keep this to yourself. If you don't, there's every chance Crime's case could be screwed, and then we'd *all* end up with egg on our faces . . . anyhow, how would you bring it up with the Chief?"

Grieve had stopped his pacing and was looking out the window, mulling over what Steel had said. "Some view, Mike . . . Look, I get what you mean, but I can't just do *nothing* now, can I?"

Steel sighed, "Yes, you can. Nothing good can come of you raising this. Not now." And he thought of Moss. "There's one thing you *can* do . . ."

"What's that?"

"Moss. She's still working the vice angle. Leave her alone, let her run with that; don't transfer her to someone else."

Grieve's eyes narrowed. "And, as you tell it, the vice angle she's working on ties in to the murders?" He shook his head as he fully grasped what Steel was saying. "For God's sake man, she's learning all *your* bad habits, isn't she?"

"She's a good copper, Bob – or will be if she's left alone to be one. Let her run with the vice investigation . . . I've not thought how, but I'll deal with Bruce and his sidekick. Somehow."

Grieve pursed his lips, thinking. "I'm not sure I *want* to know how you'd deal with Bruce but, if you think it'll help, I can drop Moss off my radar . . . for the time being anyhow – that couldn't be open-ended. And you, you'd better make sure the Chief doesn't get wind of any continuing involvement with Moss – keep your head down."

He gave Steel a shrewd look. "But – listen up – I want you to bring me up to speed with everything you and Moss have been working on . . . you might care to remember I *am* your superior officer, eh? Enjoy your supposed gardening leave, but I need to be clued in."

He took a deep breath, filling his broad chest. "You're a good cop Mike, but you go your own way, *far* too often. I need you to remember protocol. Which reminds me . . . I got contacted by your psychologist – she tells me you've missed a couple of sessions."

Steel looked at him in surprise; only Bob Grieve could bring up missed counselling in the middle of this conversation. "Seriously? They're a complete waste of time, everybody's, not just mine, and I *have* been rather busy with actual police-work."

Grieve shook his head at this. "Protocol, Mike – doing things the right way, eh? – it's the bit you *always* seem to miss, but leave it with me . . . I'll find a quiet way to make them go away." He placed his empty glass down. "As to this other matter, I don't like what you're telling me. Not a bit of it . . . it's a bad business when coppers think they're above the law. Nobody's safe with that."

Steel gave this a grim smile; he couldn't agree more. "So, one for the road, or are you driving?"

•

Steel was in his kitchen, looking for something – anything – he could cook, half-listening to Radio 3's *Live In Concert*, when his doorbell rang. Closing the fridge door on its uninspiring contents, he sighed. It had been quite a day and, unless it was Grieve coming back for another round, he reckoned it would be something like the bloody Jehovah's Witnesses. Could an evening get any more gloomy?

He opened the door and was taken aback to see JJ standing there, smiling, her head slightly tilted to one side. "Excuse me sir, I was looking for a policeman."

Feeling his spirits lift, he smiled at her. "Was it any particular policeman you were looking for, madam?"

"Yes – *very* particular – I was looking for one on leave . . . can I come in, or should I continue my search for this mythical creature out here in the freezing cold?"

Steel stood to one side. "I'm sorry, come in," and now he grinned, "we can form a posse and look for your policeman together."

Interlacing her fingers behind his neck, JJ reached up to kiss him. "I've brought my toothbrush . . ."

TWENTY-FOUR

JANET TWEEDIE WAS BALANCING ON the edge of a desk, nursing a raspberry tea, as Moss settled herself at a computer. "So how are you getting on with our History Man, Robin?"

Moss smiled up at her. "So far, it's been . . ." and she searched for a word to sum up her experience adequately, "*interesting.* I'm beginning to catch on to some of his ways of thinking, *and* his quirks, but really, I'm glad to be working with him – he's a good DCI." She thought better of mentioning the small matter of Steel being sent home on leave; it would be round Fettes soon enough.

Tweedie eyed her; over the years she'd seen many young CID officers come and go – very few female ones, though – and could well imagine how Steel would be interesting to work with. "Well, from what *I* know of Mike Steel, he's certainly got his . . . idiosyncrasies, but you know what? Most experienced cops – those I've spoken with, anyhow – respect him. He can be a deep one at times, but he's all about the job . . . getting it done," and with narrowed eyes, she drifted off into memory. "Righting wrongs, is what Mike Steel is about. These days, that would be called old fashioned, but he's respected for it."

She gave Moss a faint smile. "He's had his share of troubles though . . . used to have a proper temper on him, got him into *all* sorts of bother," and she cast her mind back to one infamous occasion when he and his wife had one of their explosive rows – they were common knowledge at Fettes – and Steel had ended up in the cells. "Then again, who's perfect in *this* world?

Tweedie nodded to herself, "All I know is, if I was ever in a tight corner, Mike Steel – out of the lot of them here – is the one I'd turn to." She pushed herself back on to her feet and smoothed her skirt. "Will you listen to me . . . I'm holding you back with all my blethering," and with a smile she returned to her desk.

Moss logged on, thinking about what Janet had said. When she compared Steel's MO with what she'd learned at Hendon and in Liverpool, yes, he was in many ways old fashioned and, at times, unorthodox. But his way of working – his jigsaws – came from deep experience and that, for her – the more she learned – was what mattered more than anything else. Today, without him, she felt curiously vulnerable, and hoped his enforced leave would end soon for both their sakes.

Double-clicking the PNC icon, she typed Steven Howard McCann. Within seconds a pane opened showing his arrest record, but that wasn't what interested her. Two business entities were shown: SHM Security and PA Entertainment.

Following the link for the security company, it only showed an address in Charlotte Square, Edinburgh and not, she noted, the address in Barnton where she'd first come face to face with him.

Moving to the second link gave her the same result.

With a sigh, she turned to Tweedie. "What do I have to do to get more information on a company, Janet?"

"What result are you getting, dear?"

"Just an address."

Tweedie got to her feet again and looked at the screen. "Well, to us, that means the business itself is clean . . . it comes up because of its connection with a known offender." She leaned in to peer over Moss's shoulder. "Looks like someone should look at what sort of security this one offers . . . can't imagine he'd be able to offer anything to the likes of banks."

Moss shook her head. "Security meaning muscle, Janet, and if I can find out more, I'll probably find he's mainly in the business of providing it for working girls as well as bouncers at bars and clubs."

Tweedie drew her mouth into a perfect O of comprehension, then with a brisk nod to move things on, "What were you after?"

Moss was after more than an address. She couldn't forget McCann's demeanour when she and Steel had brought him into Fettes. He was an arrogant criminal, one who thought himself untouchable, and who'd walked after his blatant assault of Emma Boyd. She wanted *anything* that could be used to bring him in, and *keep* him in. "I'm not sure, Janet – something more than just this."

"Try the Companies House database," she suggested, "that'll give you the principals of the company, financial reports, and a lot more too. Though, fair warning, often the names shown are just some third party – someone you can address mail to – a company secretary, or whatever . . ."

She could see Moss had no idea how to proceed. "D'you want me to get this for you, dear? It *is* what we're here for." Moss gave her a grateful nod.

Within minutes, the printer was kicking asthmatically into life. With a smile for Tweedie, Moss retrieved the sheets and scanned them. The principals of both companies were identical: Steven H. McCann and Tobias I. Greene. Sitting down slowly, she looked at the information again, and was nudged by the PA in PA Entertainment. Could PA simply be a reversal of AP? Was PA Entertainment yet another one of Prior's companies, another example of the name reflecting the man's ego?

Pulling out her notebook, she flicked back the pages. On the day she had started with Lothian and Borders, Records had found the actual owners of McCann's house in Barnton to be Priority Private Equity – one of Prior's companies. Finding the page, she read the address of that company: 17 Charlotte Square – the same address as McCann's two businesses. "Can you get me the occupants of an address, Janet? It's in the New Town . . . Charlotte Square."

Within seconds, the printer came back into life. Collecting the sheet, Moss saw four different companies listed, but only one stood out – Paisley Wark, Jan Prior's law firm.

She sank back in her chair, and then it hit her – Tobias I. Greene was Toby Greene, the lawyer from Paisley Wark who'd arrived at Fettes after they'd arrested McCann. Her first thought was to contact Steel, but she dismissed it; there was more information to be mined first.

Looking at the PA Entertainment data, her eye ran down the page, pausing at an entry for a subsidiary called Venus Leisure Ltd., and she sensed a circle being completed.

Flicking through her notebook again, she found her entry for the day she and Steel had first met Emma at the Imperial Hotel. Emma had mentioned a woman called Jane Ingram, a manageress of a sauna in Leith and, sure enough, the name of that sauna was Venus Leisure.

Getting to her feet, she thanked Janet for her help – it was time for her first ever visit to an Edinburgh sauna.

•

Steel woke and looked to his radio alarm. He stretched, knowing he'd never slept as late, or as deeply, in years. Perhaps this was something he would just have to become accustomed to as long as he remained on leave.

Rolling on to his side, and leaning on his elbow, he looked down at JJ beside him. How could he ever become accustomed to *her*? Last night they'd discovered a perfect mirror in each other for their needs and desires; there was something deliciously, even wildly unpredictable about this extraordinary creature who'd entered his life – *accustomed* simply didn't belong in the JJ lexicon.

She was lying on her side, facing away from him, and slowly he pulled the sheet down to uncover her. In tousled disarray, her waves of red hair fell down the graceful sweeping curve of her back to the delightful roundness of her buttocks, and he felt himself becoming aroused.

In a soft, sleepy voice, she grumbled, "I'll catch cold, you know," and reached back for him. Gripping him with her long fingers, she arched her body, and giving a little laugh, murmured, "Breakfast?"

Steel heard his mobile ring from the living room, but ignored the distant sound as he reached for JJ, parting her hair and kissing the nape of her neck.

•

Moss listened to Steel's robotic voicemail greeting. She hesitated, then left him a short message; she could catch up with him later.

When she'd started with Lothian and Borders, she'd toyed with the idea of getting a GPS system to help her find her way around Edinburgh's myriad streets. Today, without Steel, she was relying on a quick study of her A–Z, and despite making one or two wrong turns, was soon at Venus Leisure.

The days of cars-for-all were a long way off when these tenements had been built; now, however, the street was jammed with parked cars, and she had to leave hers some distance from the sauna. Like Billy McCann's club *Oysters*, this was a conversion of a large corner shop below the tenements. Heavy curtains covered the windows, hiding the interior from prying eyes, but as she walked towards it she could only wonder what it was like to actually live in the streets nearby – it couldn't be residents didn't know what trade was on their doorstep. Then again, she recalled Steel telling her Edinburgh had no red light area, and if saunas were *supposedly* tolerated, then the likes of Venus Leisure had to appear somewhere.

Pulling the heavy wooden door open, she found herself in a small reception area with another door facing her, and a glassed-in reception to her left. Behind the glass, a young man in his twenties with a sallow face pitted with acne put down his paperback, squinting at her with curiosity; was she a wife or girlfriend of one of the sauna's punters? "Can Ah help ye?"

She slapped her warrant card flat against the glass. "Police. I need to come in."

The young man said nothing, but pressed a button and picked up his book. The door in front of Moss buzzed, and she pushed it open to step inside.

This larger reception area had been decorated in someone's idea of American Regency Revival with dark red, striped flock wallpaper and deep red velvet armchairs around three sides of a large, dark wood table. The table was covered with euphemistically named top-shelf magazines and, mounted on the wall, with its sound off, was a large flat screen television showing a pornographic film.

An attractive, dark-haired young woman – late teens, early twenties, Moss guessed – appeared briefly in the doorway to the sauna proper. When she saw Moss she pulled her robe tight over the skimpy black slip she was wearing and disappeared.

Moss turned to see the young man still reading his book. She waited several seconds more. "I want to speak with Jane Ingram."

Without looking up, he grunted, "Who?"

"Jane Ingram, your manageress."

"No' in," he said, flicking to a new page.

This was a game Moss had neither the desire nor the patience to play. Grabbing his wrist, she pushed it down hard on the table and took the book from his hand. "When will she *be* in?" The young man shrugged, and that was enough for her. "Tell you what, get on the phone, and *get* her in – tell her the police are here."

He looked her up and down. "Why *are* ye here? We've a'ready . . . " and stopped himself.

"Already what?"

"Never mind . . . s'pose Ah cannae get her?"

Moss sighed and brought her face closer. Lowering her voice, she said, "You'll get her because, if you don't, I'm going to get more police in here, and you'll face an inspection – a very long inspection, which might take all day, and see *you* spending a night at the local station. Now . . . *get her.*"

Cursing under his breath, he picked up the phone, dialled, and all was quiet for a few moments. "Hi Jane . . . yeah, sorry. We've got the cops here – well, one cop – she wants tae speak wi' ye." Ingram's response, as Moss could hear, was a much louder stream of words. "Well *Ah* dinnae ken, do Ah?" and passed the receiver to Moss.

"Hello, Ms. Ingram. This is DS Moss from Fettes CID – I need to have a word with you about Emma Boyd. It's important and needs to be now, but *not* on the phone."

Whatever the woman's attitude with her receptionist, Emma's name produced the desired effect. "Gi'e me half an hour an' Ah'll be there."

Moss held out the receiver to the young man, but had to wait as he buzzed the inner door open for a man who'd arrived. Seeing Moss he hesitated. "Everything alright here?"

"Yeah, hunky D, Mr. G – you'll be wanting to see Candice?" and getting a nod, he pushed a button on an intercom. "Candy, you have a client . . . Mr. G."

He swivelled in his chair to take the phone from Moss. "Ye waitin' then?"

Moss had already taken in her surroundings. The DVD showed three entwined people, with intimate close-ups she really would have preferred not to have seen; even worse, the impassioned performers were stupefyingly bad actors. The heavily thumbed magazines on the table would hold no interest for her, and now, in frothy pink, Candy had appeared to meet her Mr. G. – a dreadful mismatch of an attractive, young, perfectly proportioned, scantily dressed woman and a grey man, easily old enough to be her father. "Yes, I'm waiting . . . not *here* though, I'll wait outside."

"Right," he said, and picked up his book to resume reading.

Outside, filling her lungs deep with cold air, she had not gone more than a few steps when a car slowed to her walking pace. A man leaned out of the window. "A'right, darlin'?"

She looked at his leering, unshaven face; that did it. Walking briskly to his open window, she pushed her warrant card in his face. "Do you know it's an offence to kerb crawl? . . . Well, *do* you?"

The man spluttered, "Look, I was only-"

"Get out of here, you worm . . . and if I ever see you – or your car – anywhere *near* here again, I'm coming after you. Understood?"

He didn't need to be told twice and sped off. Too disgusted to bother taking the car's number, Moss was soon in her own car, and settled herself to wait for Ingram. Having rarely worked vice in Liverpool, she felt faintly disturbed by this close contact with Edinburgh's open business of sex for sale.

She didn't have to wait long. A bright blue Lexus sports car turned slowly into the street and double-parked outside the sauna. Ingram stepped out and Moss appraised her. In her fifties, with her blonde hair scraped back into a tight ponytail, she was dressed – too tightly – in black leggings and knee-high fur boots, with a bright red, silken waist-length jacket over a white blouse and, even at a distance, Moss could see an excess of heavy gold jewellery. She sounded her horn and got out. Ingram turned, saw her and hurried over. "You the polis?" and getting a nod from Moss, "Follow me . . . I cannae talk here."

Moss followed the Lexus out of Leith, along Ferry Road, and into genteel Trinity, to park in a quiet residential street. Ingram walked back to Moss's car, opened the door and got inside. "Sorry, Ah jus' cannae be seen wi' the polis."

"Why not, Ms. Ingram?"

"It's Jane . . . the people I work for," and she smiled, "sorry, they dinnae like cops."

When she smiled Moss could see she was quite attractive, and would've been pretty when she was younger. "Who do you work for, Jane?"

"I dunno – it's a company."

"PA Entertainment?"

"Aye, that's right," and she glowered at Moss. "Why d'ye ask, if ye a'ready know? – I thought this was aboot Emma."

"Did you know she's been assaulted?"

Shock and alarm crossed Ingram's face, giving Moss her answer.

"Ah'm sorry tae hear that – Emma's a really nice lassie, she's been a right pal to me," and then in a small voice, "It's a . . . dangerous business."

"Want to know who assaulted her?" and Ingram gave a little nod. "Steven McCann, Jane. He put her in hospital with a broken nose and a broken cheekbone."

Ingram's eyes were casting from side to side, and her fingers began to beat out a tattoo on her knees. "He's a bastard, right enough, but I cannae help ye wi' that . . . ye understand, eh?"

Moss understood, yet failed to understand how fear so often got the better of reason; her way had been to always stand up and fight her corner. "I do, Jane, but right now, that's not what I want to talk to you about. Emma told me you'd supplied girls for a private function at a place called Hawthorns."

Ingram's fingers were now beating in double-time. "And that's why young Stevie hit her?" Moss nodded. "I jus' dinnae ken . . . Ah'm no' really sure Ah can help ye, y'know?"

Moss knew she was losing her. "Relax, Jane. Emma told us she went to Hawthorns several times, that you supplied girls on a couple of occasions, *and* she used to visit a Mr. Mitchell in Barnton too. It's not that we-"

"*Lord* Mitchell? Yon judge frae the High Court?"

"Yes. I know you supplied the girls, but it's not that, Jane . . . I want to know whether, at any time, any of your girls talked about supplying younger girls – children – at Hawthorns. Was that ever mentioned by any of your girls?"

Ingram thought for a moment, weighing her options. "Aye, one lassie telt me she'd been asked one time . . ." She now had a dreamy, faraway look in her eyes, and in a soft whisper said, "Ah've met some right evil bastards in my time, but those goin' for kids, well . . ." and she tailed off, then shuddered, "hangin's too good for them. I just hope there's a special place in Hell."

Moss knew she'd reached a point where she shouldn't push too hard but, hearsay or not, Ingram had just corroborated Emma's story. Talking to the girl who'd been approached would be the next step; then they would have *two* witnesses, and could go on to deal with Hawthorns. Keeping her voice soft, she said, "I'm going to have to talk to her," and seeing Ingram inching away from her, "We're talking about *children*, Jane."

Ingram's head went down. "Aye, Ah ken . . . it's just, well mah life wouldnae be worth nothin', if it came oot Ah'd spoken wi' ye."

Moss put her hand on Ingram's forearm. "I'm going to speak with my boss, Jane. He'll want to speak with you," and she squeezed her arm, "but that can be anywhere – somewhere where you'll *know* you're safe." She looked at Ingram and saw a hint of tears in her eyes. Continuing in a softer voice, "And then, we'll *need* to know which girl was approached. You do understand, Jane? Every day we stay blind to who these people are a child is being harmed . . . yes?"

"Aye, ye're right but, right now, Ah'm scared . . . Ah've gotta think."

"Of course," and Moss handed her one of her cards. "That's me, Jane. You can always reach me at that number – leave a message if I don't answer."

She looked at Ingram, hunched over beside her, and, in an even tone, said, "I was abused by my father," and as Ingram's head shot up, she held up her hand, "Not sexually – physically. But, if we, *you* and *me* Jane, can stop one more child from being damaged – maybe for life – it's worth it, no?"

Ingram nodded her head up and down. "Aye." And, at that moment, Moss thought she *would* hear from her again.

As she watched Ingram walk back to the Lexus, back to the life that made expensive cars and God knows what else available, she reminded herself not to rush her fences. Perhaps it would better to simply *hope* to hear from her later. Nevertheless, she'd discovered there *was* a corroborative witness to the paedophile element at Hawthorns. It was a real step forward.

It was time to speak with Steel – he would be pleased.

TWENTY-FIVE

HEARING SUSAN COMING HOME from yet another night shift, Moss pushed back from her computer, wondering where the first part of the morning had gone.

With exhaustion catching up with her, Susan flopped on to the couch and raised a hand. "Morning, you. What are you doing home at this hour?"

"Trying a different tack work-wise," and she watched Susan yawn then stretch from her fingertips to her heels. "You look shattered . . . how was work?"

Susan attempted a smile but was defeated by another yawn. "Fourteen hours of dealing with traffic accidents, heart attacks, assaults and attempted suicides? Not bad really, it was a relatively quiet night."

Moss could see she was in need of a break. A long one. Perhaps Greece, where they'd spent two glorious sybaritic weeks island-hopping? "Have you never thought of getting out of A and E?"

Susan gave this a weary smile. "No, it's the front line . . . nothing else comes close – you're alive, y'know? – and I couldn't even imagine doing just the one thing, day in, day out. Anyhow, why *are* you here?"

Moss was unsure of that herself. She'd phoned Steel to bring him up to speed on her meeting with Jane Ingram and, although he'd called it 'good work', advising her to give Ingram twenty-four hours then lean on her, he'd seemed less pleased than she was.

"I'm trying to get another angle on this Alan Prior character I told you about, and I've plumbed our databases . . . He's dirty, yet *somehow* he manages to always appear like some buccaneering businessman rather than a crook."

Moss glanced at the computer, and in a low voice, said, "He's at the heart of everything," hearing JJ's voice: 'Kill the heart, the body dies'. "*Anyhow*, I really thought I might get something else from a straight web search."

Susan was overtaken by yet another jaw-breaking yawn. "And . . . ?"

Moss shook her head, and stared at the screen. "Nothing. All I can find are business links, and – *if* he appears elsewhere – it's to point to some story celebrating how charitable he is. He's got the best PR money can buy . . . I was hopeful there'd be something giving me the less 'public' side of the man."

Susan yawned again, this time getting to her feet. "Sorry, Robin, got to shower, and I've *got* to sleep." She looked at the open webpage. "You should try that Archivalweb site, Google's a bit current. Maybe you'll find what you're looking for there." Then, giving Moss a quick hug, "I'm off . . . have a good day."

Moss heard Susan start the shower, smiling as she struck up Annie Lennox's *Money Can't Buy It* in a heroically tuneless voice, then navigated to Archivalweb.

The first three links she found on the site were useless, and she felt she'd already seen a version of them anyway, but the fourth gave her a jolt of recognition – she'd been aware of this information, but it had slipped her mind completely. In front of her, like a webpage in fragments, was a small, disjointed piece from an independent news site on how the *Telegraph* had been served with injunctions over its, attempted, reporting on Alan Prior.

Reaching for her coffee, she recalled DCI Rob Henderson mentioning this when he'd explained the Crime Squad's investigation of PPE, one of Prior's myriad investment companies. If she remembered correctly, the injunctions, launched by Jan Prior's law firm, Paisley Wark, had stopped the paper's investigation stone cold, someone had forwarded all their information to the Serious Fraud Office in London, and then the SFO had bounced everything north to the Crime Squad at Lothian and Borders.

The links on the page were inactive, and knowing she couldn't ask Henderson for any information, she tried a search using permutations of Alan Prior and injunctions, but came up with nothing.

She sat back, faced with a straight choice: either she could phone the SFO or the *Telegraph* . . . it might be easier to get answers from the SFO.

Eventually, after two false starts and one interminable hold, she was put through to a Section Head. He listened without interrupting then said, "I'm not sure who would've dealt with that Sergeant, but I can ask around, see if I can't find which team it was – but in a case like this you *are* reliant on someone's memory."

"I was hoping you could help, sir."

"Well . . . a few points you should bear in mind. Even if we *did* receive this information, we deal with fraud . . . who's to say the documents you're enquiring about actually laid out something fraudulent? Next, we work mainly with the City of London Police . . . if we received these documents, we would've passed them on to them." He paused as he realised he was not making her work any easier. "Unfortunately, if the information mainly concerned, uh . . . activities *outside* the City, then they, in their turn, would've passed them to Scotland Yard, and then – sorry – in all likelihood, because of who the central player is, someone there would've passed them on to you."

Moss's sense that she could be on to something was giving way to a sinking feeling; she would've been far better phoning the *Telegraph*. "It does seem a bit of a *very* wild goose chase but, well, *if* you come up with any information, please get in touch," and she gave the man her phone number and email address.

"I'll contact you if I find anything helpful, Sergeant . . . good luck to you."

She glanced at the clock; she would phone the *Telegraph* later – better to show face at Fettes, especially with Steel not being there. She was reaching for her coat when her mobile rang. Unknown Caller lit the screen, and she hesitated, letting it go to voicemail – it was probably yet another telemarketer. When the little icon showed she had a message however, she dialled. Coming through on a crackling, static-filled line, she heard: *Is this DS Moss? Mah names Carol . . . Ah work wi' Jane – Jane Ingram – phone me back, right?*

Wondering whether Ingram had prompted this woman to call her – was she the corroborative witness they needed? – she called the number.

A bright voice answered. "Hiya, this is Sindy."

"This is DS Moss, from Lothian and Borders CID. I just got a call from this number. Someone called Carol?"

"Aye . . . sorry, that's me – Ah work wi' Jane at the Venus. I need tae speak wi' ye – Jane's been beat up."

Moss felt a jolt run through her – Steel's *give her twenty-four hours* had been far too lax for Jane's safety. She asked where they could meet.

"Ah'm at the Venus, right now . . . it's the best place tae meet."

Surprised, Moss asked, "Are you sure?"

"Aye. Definite."

"Right Carol, give me half an hour, and I'll be there," and, still wondering about the girl's safety at the sauna, she added, "If anything happens before I get there, phone 999, okay?"

Thirty minutes later, Moss was pulling up outside Venus Leisure and, when she entered, saw the same young man on reception.

"You again?" he complained, running his fingers over his pockmarked cheek. "Whit noo?"

"I want to see Carol . . . Sindy."

He shrugged, muttering, "Ah'm no' gettin' involved," but buzzed her through nevertheless.

A pretty young woman with a mass of dark curls framing an almost doll-like porcelain face with coal black eyes and full, bright red, lips was sitting on one of the over-stuffed chairs. Her robe was open over a miniscule red satin slip, which was possibly one size too small for her. Getting to her feet, she said, "You Moss?"

Moss nodded.

"Come doonstairs, naebody'll bother us there," and turning to the young man, "Eric, Ah'm no' here . . . ye understan'?"

He held up his hands. "Ah'm wishin' Ah wisnae here neither."

Moss followed Carol downstairs. The whole cellar had been expensively converted into something stylish and modern, in contrast to the flocked wallpaper tackiness upstairs. At the far end stood a large custom shower and, beside it, a wooden rack filled with neatly folded, fluffy white towels. She could see no sign of an actual sauna.

Carol opened the door of one of the six rooms. "We can use this one," and Moss followed her inside.

Dominating the over-warm deep red room was a large double bed surrounded by wide cheval mirrors with a ceiling-mounted mirror above. To the side was a small cabinet with a large selection of oils and talcs and, mounted on the wall, a large television, obviously taking a feed from the DVD player upstairs.

"Can we switch that off?"

"Aye, sure." Carol killed it with a remote and sat down on the edge of the bed. "Maist o' yon stuff's pathetic, but the punters like it."

"How's Jane?"

"Regrettin' she ever spoke wi' ye."

Moss could well understand that. "Who was it, Carol? Who beat her up?"

"Jane telt me, young Stevie did, the bastard."

"Steven McCann?"

Carol nodded.

"And you're not concerned? I mean, Eric upstairs knows I'm CID."

"Eric's yon three monkeys in one, and that shite Stevie McCann doesnae bother me," Carol spat. "Doesnae matter who, or what, he – or his brother – is, if he as much as laid a finger on me, ma brother'd kill him." And she shot Moss a fierce glance, "An' Ah mean, kill him – he kens that fine."

Moss appraised this pretty, feisty girl; it certainly wasn't bravado. "Let's hope Steven *doesn't* come to any harm then. Are you the woman Jane told me about . . . you were approached at Hawthorns?"

"For bringin' kids there? Aye . . . yon's disgustin'."

Moss weighed her options. "Look Carol, as far as Hawthorns goes, we'll need to take a statement from you . . . we can't act without it. It's the only way we can put a stop to what's happening there." She thought of

McCann. "Did Jane *ask* you to phone me?"

"Well, Ah didnae even ken aboot ye, until Ah went tae the Royal. Jane telt me she'd spoken wi' ye . . . aboot Hawthorns an' a'. Gi'ed me your card."

Moss caught sight of herself in one of the mirrors, her face serious. "Listen Carol, I came here because of your call. For you to make a statement, I'll need to be with another officer. I can come back later, or meet you somewhere else – the choice is yours – but I *will* need to take a statement from you."

Carol glanced up the clock. "Ah'm aboot to become Sindy. Ye can phone me, aye? . . . we can, well . . . mebbe meet."

"I will do, Carol." They would need to get that statement very soon.

Moss made her way back upstairs. Just as she was about to leave she noticed a camera mounted high above the door; she'd missed that on her earlier visit. Turning to Eric she asked, "That's not a dummy, is it?"

"Naw . . . motion sensitive . . . records a'body comin' in and oot."

Moss stepped in beside him. "Where's the recorder?" Eric pointed below the counter. "Wind it back for me."

He sighed. "Tae whit?"

"To whenever your boss arrived."

For a brief moment he didn't move, but Moss leant towards him with a glare – she was used to dealing with scallies like Eric – and he pushed the rewind.

Intermittently, the screen showed figures moving in jerky motion. Then, two figures were seen, both from behind. First there was Jane Ingram, closely followed by a male figure Moss took for McCann. She took over from Eric and jockeyed the player between rewind and play, and at several points, saw McCann's hand rise to Ingram's back and push her.

Rewinding the tape further, McCann's arrival – now face-on to the camera – could be seen. She paused the tape, and looked closely at his face; was it her imagination, or did he really look angry?

Ejecting the tape, she turned to Eric. "I'll need to take this."

"Naw . . . wait a minute. D'ye no' need a warrant, or somethin'?"

She did, but Moss rounded on him. "You could be charged with obstruction, Eric. Do you want that?"

A few moments later Moss was getting into her car, clutching the tape. Yet another trip to Barnton was on the cards, but first she needed to visit Jane at the Royal.

•

"Your client is only helping us with our enquiries, Mr. Greene. He's not under arrest."

McCann's lawyer leant his immaculately dressed body across the desk towards her. "This is nothing short of harassment, Sergeant, and once you have finished with this . . . pantomime," his lips curling with distaste, "I shall be lodging a complaint with your superiors."

Moss felt herself rising to this ridiculous, but not unexpected, statement. Pantomime indeed. She had gone to the hospital to speak with Jane Ingram, but it had been a one-sided conversation; Ingram had been unable – or simply unwilling, Moss couldn't be sure – to speak with her. Co-opting an enthusiastic young DC in Fettes, now at her side in Interview Room One, she had then gone to Barnton to ask – very politely, she thought – that McCann come with them to Fettes, to assist them with their enquiries into a serious assault.

Moss shuffled her papers, pretending to read, taking her time. It was a purposeful delay, to make McCann anxious, but glancing at him now, she saw that familiar supercilious smile as he sat watching her from under hooded eyes. It was a smile she wanted to erase, permanently, but she was having her doubts and, not for the first time, wished Steel was with her today.

Nodding at Greene, and speaking clearly for the microphone, she said, "I'm sure I don't need to tell you that lodging a complaint on behalf of your client is quite within your rights, Mr. Greene. However, as far as we can ascertain, your client was the last person to be seen with Ms. Ingram, who has been hospitalised as a result of an assault. We merely wish to question Mr. McCann formally. Now, I would like you both to watch a video-"

"A video which was illegally obtained," Greene drawled. "Seriously, Sergeant Moss, are you really going to go down this route?"

"I myself obtained this video this morning from an employee of Venus Leisure, where Ms. Ingram works," and she looked down at a non-existent note, "as a . . . manageress. I simply asked for it, and it was handed to me. Willingly, and a receipt was given. Now . . . I would like you, and your client, to watch this video," and for the recording, "Mr. McCann and Mr. Greene are now being shown the security tape from the Venus Leisure sauna."

"What are we supposed to be looking at, Sergeant?" Greene said.

Ignoring him, she asked McCann, "Can you confirm the man on this tape is you?"

McCann nodded.

"For the recording please."

He gave her a theatrical sigh. "Aye, that's me."

Moss wound the tape forward to where McCann and Ingram were seen leaving together and hit pause. "Now, Mr. McCann, who is the person you are seen with here?"

McCann laughed. "Why are you asking?"

"Just answer the question."

With a shrug, he said, "That's me and Jane Ingram, the manager."

Moss inched the tape forward. "And what do you see now?"

"What is this? It's the same people."

"Good." She moved the tape forward frame by frame. "What I now see, Mr. McCann, is Ms. Ingram in front of you, and you are pushing her forward," and she turned from the screen to McCann, "fairly aggressively, by the looks of things."

McCann turned to his lawyer, his voice rising in complaint, "Are you just gonna sit there while this . . . she makes up stuff?"

Greene raised a calming hand. "What I see is my client-"

"This is an interview of Steven McCann, sir," Moss snapped, "I'm not interested in your opinion. Now, Mr. McCann, what *I* see is your arrival at ten o-eight, and four minutes later, you leaving, forcefully pushing Ms. Ingram ahead of you."

"I needed to speak to her, I didn't want to do it on the premises."

Moss gave him a small smile. "Really . . . *on the premises*? You're telling me you needed to speak with your manageress and you couldn't do that *inside* the Venus sauna. Is that correct?"

McCann nodded, and Moss saw his arrogant self-assurance was ever so slightly deserting him. "For the benefit of the recording, Mr. McCann has just nodded his agreement." She flicked a page of her notes, pausing again. "Where were you after leaving the Venus sauna, Mr. McCann?"

"I . . . I dunno. I don't keep a diary."

"So, you had no meeting with your lawyers *today*, then?"

Greene sat forward. "I must strenuously object to that question."

"Noted, Mr. Greene. Now, Mr. McCann, where were you?"

A pregnant pause filled the room for a few moments, while McCann adopted an exaggerated pose of searching his memory. "Oh, aye, that's right . . . I went shopping. Jenners."

"So you'll have receipts?"

"Receipts?"

Clearly, he wasn't at his sharpest. "Receipts for purchases. That is, if you want me to believe your story of going shopping. A receipt would carry a time on it."

McCann paused, then gave her a triumphant smile. "I didn't find anything I liked."

"I see. Well, I'm sure when we review Jenners' security footage, we will be able to place you there fairly accurately."

Greene stirred. "Really Sergeant Moss, you are simply browbeating my client, I-"

"Browbeating? Rather than beating – the beating Ms. Ingram suffered?" and she looked directly at the lawyer. "I would have thought, given Ms. Ingram is, in fact, your employee, you would be more concerned." She saw a nervous bob of his Adam's apple. "I have got that right, Mr. Greene – you *are* part-owner of Venus Leisure, are you not?"

Greene's face flushed; she had hit a nerve. "That seems like a conflict of interest to me, sir," and she gave him a chilly smile, "professionally, I mean."

The silence that followed was broken by a knock, and a uniformed PC entered. "Sorry Sarge, I have a note from Chief Superintendent Grieve for you."

Moss unfolded the single sheet of notepaper: *There's a development. See me. Now. Room 23.*

Attempting to make the best of this interruption, she arched her eyebrows, and glared at McCann for several seconds. "We'll take a fifteen minute break," and glancing up at the clock, "Interview suspended at two twenty-five p.m."

Moss switched off the recorder, feeling prickly waves of irritation flood through her. While not really expecting McCann to suddenly confess, she had been boxing him in, leaving him little room for manoeuvre. *Damn Grieve . . .* a break at this point would only allow McCann and Greene to regroup.

Walking briskly along the corridor, she found the room, knocked and entered.

Grieve was perched on the edge of a desk with his arms crossed, staring at the floor. Looking up at her, as he swivelled in his chair, Steel said, "Hello, Moss."

TWENTY-SIX

MOSS WAS INCREDULOUS. "I have to do *what?*"

"I told you," Grieve growled impatiently, "let him go."

This was the final straw, and her face flushed, the scar along her jaw standing out white against the red. "McCann's guilty of – at least – two serious assaults, there's *no way* I can let him go."

Steel smiled to himself; she was fighting her corner, fighting for what she thought was her case. It wasn't, of course, and her mistake was in making the fight personal.

"Have you anything solid to charge him with?" Grieve left a small gap for her. "*Anything?* There's much bigger fish to fry here, Sergeant," and with a nod to Steel, "your DCI will explain. Now get back to IR One, thank our Mr. McCann for his time, and let him go."

Moss's annoyance at having her interview interrupted had transformed rapidly to anger, then into an overwhelming sense of impotence. Momentarily, a disturbing vision of her father's face jumped before her. "Two women have been assaulted by that coward. I'll be *damned* if I thank him," she retorted.

Grieve slammed the palms of his hands on the table, and the sharp noise echoed round the room. "You'll damn-well do as you are *told*, Sergeant," glaring at her.

In the silence which followed he breathed deep, calming himself. "Look . . . I understand how you feel," and with a nod to the monitor on the desk, "From what I've just seen – *and* from what Mike's told me – I'd say McCann's guilty of assault on the Ingram woman, but having him in here is counter-productive right now."

He paused, trying to find the right words for her. "I think the choice the Chief made . . . well, it's left us in a bad position." His eyes flitted from her to Steel. "That's between us and these four walls, eh? Going after Steven McCann might jeopardise the bigger picture.

"You're not clued-in yet. But you should know your work on this Hawthorns place is a significant part of that bigger picture." Getting to his feet, he turned to Steel. "I should've been elsewhere a quarter of an hour ago, Mike . . . see that McCann's gone, and then," with a nod to Moss, "explain how things stand with your Sergeant."

With Grieve gone, Steel looked at Moss, her stunned stare boring a hole in the carpet. "Get back to IR One and conclude your interview. There's no need to say anything other than we're still investigating the assault . . . tell Greene, if we need to, we'll interview his client again. Short and sweet, and I'll see you upstairs after. Okay?"

In one vigorous movement Moss stood and pulled her jacket together.

"That's short and *sweet*, Moss . . . you were doing good work there – with very little to work with – but Grieve's right, there *are* bigger fish than young Stevie to fry."

Moss gave him a curt nod, "Sir," and left to make her way back to the interview room, with her old Liverpool mantra, 'catch them; jail them', sounding in her head.

Ten minutes later she was back in their office. Dropping into her chair, she spun round to face Steel. With her finger tapping his desk in emphasis, she said, "There's nothing I want more right now than to knock that smile right off McCann's face."

Steel leaned back in his chair, locking his fingers behind his head. The criminals he had caught, yet walked – normally, with the help of clever, expensive lawyers – crowded in on him. "If young Stevie's the only one who gets away from you in your career, you'd be working somewhere quiet in the Highlands with Northern Constabulary, not here. We *will* get him – for something – but not right now."

She let out a long exhalation. "I don't suppose I could get a promise on that out of you?"

Steel gave her a knowing smile, and shook his head.

"So, what's the bigger fish to fry? Are we going to pull McCann in later?"

"Slow down, there's a lot you need to know. Let's get out of here and get a coffee."

As they headed for the car park, Moss had only one question for him. "So, you're not on leave now?"

With a twitch of his mouth, Steel said, "Sort of . . . yes."

She thought, *Good*, but said, "What do you mean, sort of?"

"Grieve visited me yesterday . . . to talk about our meeting with the Chief. He's been placed in an awkward position by Thompson, and he's told me to stay well out of his way; gardening leave until the raid on Hawthorn's over."

Moss nodded, although she didn't understand – particularly Fettes' internal politics – and on the drive to the Dean Village found herself still being distracted by thoughts of young Stevie. He had walked – twice now – and that burned her up. Despite Grieve's orders, there had to be some way she could nail him.

Back at Steel's house he busied himself making a pot of coffee while Moss stood at the living room window, taking in the now familiar wintry scene, and feeling a calm slowly descend like the intermittent flakes of snow falling before her. Idly she wondered whether Steel used this view in the same way, or whether he was simply accustomed to it.

Steel handed her a mug with a sympathetic smile. "You okay now?" He liked that she'd locked horns with Grieve, hoping nevertheless she appreciated that being a DS was having a foot on a very low rung on the ladder, Accelerated Careers or not.

She'd calmed down, but was far from okay. "So what's this choice the Chief made?"

Steel settled in his seat and took a sip of coffee. "Involving the NCS. Choosing personal glory over doing the job right."

Her eyebrows arched into her fringe. "What do you mean?"

"Not letting the right hand know what the left hand's doing . . . a typical bureaucratic foul-up," and he smiled, "Grieve fouled-up too."

Nursing his coffee, he sat forward. "Out of a long list of mistakes, the first was Rob Henderson's, when he failed to flag the Crime Squad's interest in Prior's PPE. You *were* right about him, by the way."

"I was? . . . Hawthorns?"

"Uh huh – he *was* placed there. He had the cover of being an investment banker with some German bank . . . Deutsche Bank. Though how anyone would take Rob Henderson for anything other than a copper is beyond me." A disquieting vision of Henderson, naked apart from a mask, ran through his mind. "The idea was for him to trail his skirts, to get close to Prior personally with disaffected talk of, 'the bank gets all the profits, but I only get bonuses'.

"Anyhow, as you know, Crime Squad's working with the Tax Inspectorate on PPE, and that originated with the NCS getting information on Prior from some London newspaper – information they passed on to the Crime Squad."

"Yes, that was the *Telegraph*. I was following-up on that, and I spoke with the SFO . . . trying to get more on Prior," and she wondered how long it would've taken her to follow all the steps that led from the SFO to the NCS.

Steel was surprised. "You were? Come up with anything?"

Moss shook her head.

"Well, Crime Squad's now got solid information from their Dutch counterparts that drug money *is* being funnelled, via PPE, into the Forth Development," and giving her a grim smile, he leaned further forward conspiratorially, "with Billy McCann up to his neck in it.

"The Chief got wind of all this and bloody-well *invited* the NCS in, to liaise with Crime Squad." He gave a little shrug. "It's a big case, Moss – drugs from Holland, impropriety in the Forth Development, with a local villain and a big wheel businessman thrown in for good measure. Although, big or not, we don't need a bunch of London mavericks invited in to do our work for us.

"Of course, it'll be Lothian and Borders that drops the hammer, and the star when that happens will be Sir David Thompson," his eyes flitted across

240

the television's blank screen, "I can almost see the interviews now . . . if it goes well, he'll make it seem as if *he* pulled it off himself."

Moss took a swig of coffee, placed her mug down, and got to her feet to look out of the window once more, allowing this information to sink in. She saw a small child running ahead of his mother on the metal footbridge to slide on the snowy surface; it seemed like a scene from a Brueghel painting – something very distant from a place like Hawthorns.

She turned back to him. "So, we come along, stagger into a case that should've been flagged as a Crime Squad one, and you get whacked by someone from NCS, because of that?"

"Almost. The burglary was because somehow the NCS learned we were still investigating the murders . . . perhaps they were tipped off. Anyhow, in that, we were seen as a threat to the Hawthorns operation."

"Why weren't we just told the NCS were active here?"

Steel laughed. "In one sense, we were. Although, they're not active, they're here as advisors . . . which covers a multitude of sins. But *anyway*, a combination of us – me – not wanting to pay attention to Grieve, *and* what I still say is a connection between Prior, vice, and those three murders, led the NCS into playing cowboys – it was their quick fix," and his eyes narrowed, "I'm not finished with Commander Bruce, though . . . he doesn't get to fix *anything* that way. Not here."

Moss sat down opposite him. "And what was Grieve's foul-up?"

"Ach, a simple one: after I was sent home on leave, he asked you what you were working on-"

"I think I said vice . . ."

"Yes, but he didn't see the connection between that and the murders, and you didn't correct him. Anyhow, everybody's pleased you didn't, because now you've found the girl from the sauna who worked with Emma at Hawthorns."

For Moss the picture was still cloudy; it would be more accurate to say she'd stumbled on Carol. "And that helps how exactly?"

Steel smiled at her. "Come on, Moss. You're the fast-track cop. We've got a statement from Emma and we need to get one from . . . what's her name?"

"Carol . . . Sindy when she's at work."

"Right. Well, with statements from Emma and Carol that they were approached *at* Hawthorns by paedophiles, the place can be raided *at the same time* as Crime Squad move on Prior, Billy McCann, and whoever else is in their sights."

Steel saw her struggling to absorb this. "Don't you see? . . . *your* work's been instrumental. It was good police-work – you did well."

Obstacles seemed to confront Moss whichever way she turned; doubt assailed her, and she knew doubt was a poison. Her mind was filled with images of two ten year-old girls at Hawthorns, Emma and Jane lying in hospital beds, and most troubling for her, Steven McCann's smile.

"So, what about Steven McCann? In the midst of all this, the bastard gets to walk?"

Steel gave her a small shake of his head. "Not quite. The thinking was having him in could make others nervous, and . . . well, right now, that wasn't wanted."

Moss sighed; young Stevie had gotten right under her skin, and she wondered whether she'd ever manage to choose her battles. "What do we – I – do now, sir?"

"You've got to meet our Child Protection unit. With two witness statements on the paedophile aspect within Hawthorns, that'll trigger a raid on the place – all being well, synchronised with raids on Prior and Billy McCann." He gave her an encouraging smile, his eyes sparkling. "Lots of arrests, Moss."

"All being well?"

"It's a Crime Squad show now. Once we have Carol's statement, and Child Protection are primed, there's nothing left for us to do. We're out."

She reached for her coffee, but it had gone cold.

•

Moss felt despondent as she drove back to Morningside. She knew they would play a very small part in the next few days; there was an important witness statement to be taken and then, when that was in hand, a meeting with the Child Protection Unit. But after that, what? With Crime Squad leading, they would play no part in the planned raids, no part in taking down Al Prior and Billy McCann.

Steven McCann nudged her again. She *owed* it to both Emma and Jane to nail him, but knew Steel, and Grieve, were right; she, and they, would just have to wait. And as McCann's sickening smile appeared before her again she wondered what, if anything, she'd done wrong, and whether what she had done could've been done differently.

Halted at traffic lights in Tollcross, she looked round. Piles of snow were banked up beside the pavements and the road was patchy with dirty brown slush. One thing very few people told you about living in Edinburgh was having to deal with its maritime winters. That, and the fact that here, at four in the afternoon, it had already been dark for an hour. If she and Susan could at least plan on going somewhere – *perhaps* Greece – her gloomy mood might lift, although she knew that was shaped less by Edinburgh's climate, more by Steel saying, *we're out.* She felt at a loose end, as if her energies had nowhere to go.

Her eye caught the posters at the Kings Theatre. The panto was still running, and she smiled as she recalled Susan calling it a rite of passage. Not for going as a child, but for revisiting when she was older. Perhaps a couple of tickets for *Jack and the Beanstalk* would knock out her blues and cheer her up, and she almost laughed out loud as she thought, *Oh no it won't.*

The driver behind her leant on his horn; she'd been sitting there meditating on green, and the car skidded in the slush as she gave it too much acceleration. Giving him an apologetic wave, she continued towards Morningside, thinking to stop at *Gourmet Pasta* in Church Hill for some freshly-made pasta.

Home, she turned the heating up a notch; this was her first Edinburgh winter, and the unexpected dampness had permeated her bones. Taking the mushroom ravioli through to the kitchen, she poured herself a small glass of claret, and went through to the living room to power up her computer.

Checking her mail first, she was surprised to see a message from the man she'd spoken with at the SFO. He had written to apologise for their last contact, and had – *personally,* she noted – made his own enquiries. He'd tracked the information they'd been given by a journalist at the *Telegraph*, and included a live-linked email address for an editor at the paper, who was, he assured her, waiting to hear from her.

With a smile, she rattled off a quick reply to thank him for his help, and then, taking her time, composed a message to one Joseph Helms, Night News Editor at the *Telegraph*.

The cursor hovered over Send as she re-read and re-thought what she had written. All in all it was a somewhat useless task; the papers themselves had been passed on by the Met to Lothian and Borders ages ago. However, she remained curious about Prior and, remembering Steel had told her curiosity was the best quality of a good detective, she gave a little shrug and clicked Send.

Reaching for her bag, she pulled out her work folder and saw a sheet from Forensics which laid out their findings on Lord Mitchell's computer. She'd had no time to go through this until now and, taking a sip of wine, sat back and began to read.

In the preamble there were several lines detailing the methodology used to move the computer from Barnton to the lab for analysis – live at a specific temperature, with an uninterruptible power source and something called a mouse jiggler – which meant less than nothing to her but, further down the page, the date and time shown against the folder containing pornographic photographs of minors rang a distant alarm bell.

Opening her rapidly filling notebook, she flicked to the day they'd received the pathology report and read her entry. What she saw didn't make sense. Glancing at the clock she saw there was still enough time to call Forensics.

Identifying herself, she asked to be put through to K. Forbes on extension 390.

"Kevin Forbes."

"Hello, this is DS Moss from Fettes CID. I got a computer analysis from you on-"

"Case number?"

She gave him the number and waited. When he came back on the line, he said, "You were the DS who gave us grief over this particular case."

With an inward groan, she remembered: when they'd received the preliminary report from Forensics, Steel had told her to throw her weight about for what he'd called slack work.

"You told us the information was needed right away, Sergeant – within hours, if memory serves – and yet, here you are, a *week* later with questions."

She chided herself, both for catching someone obviously at the end of their work day, and with the fact she'd probably been too free with Steel's instructions. "I'm sorry, it's a murder case," she ventured, "that was possibly just the heat of the moment," and, although she hated doing it, she ducked behind a lame excuse, "I'm new with Lothian and Borders, and my DCI told me to get a fuller report from you . . ."

Forbes appeared mollified by this. "Bosses . . . they get you to do *all* their dirty work, eh? So what questions did you have?"

Moss breathed a sigh of relief; it was always better having everyone working on the same side – it was just a waste of energy otherwise. "Well, it's really only one question."

"Fire away."

She ran her eye down the page. "It concerns the folder you have marked as LB_HM51. Could I confirm the date as being January third?"

"Yes. Although that's correct for the folder, not the contents, which I see we've date-listed for you, and they're from last year to eight years earlier."

"Right. But the folder's time . . . are you certain of the time?"

"Sergeant?"

"Sorry, I didn't mean that. It's just the date is the same day as the victim was murdered."

"The date is January third and, as you can see, the time is one fifty-one a.m."

Moss glanced at the paper before her. "Could you hold for a moment," and she flicked the pages of her notebook, finding her entry noting Mitchell's time of death: even though Dr. Knox had not been precise, he'd placed it as being *before* this folder had been created.

For a moment, she was immobilised, unsure of what she was reading. Puzzled, she looked between her notebook entry and the time shown on the forensics report. It could only mean one thing: the killer had placed this folder on Lord Mitchell's computer *after* he had murdered him.

"Are you still there?"

"Sorry, I was just checking something . . . you're certain of this time?"

She heard his deep sigh. "Sergeant Moss, *I've* had a long day. I'm sure *you've* had a long one too . . . there is no room for error here. In *our* line of work, things are, or they are not. The date *and* time for that particular folder are as you can read on our report."

Apologising to him once again, Moss wished him a good evening and hung up. She was aware this was significant information, but couldn't quite grasp it. Why would the killer take the time – at the murder scene – to place a folder on Mitchell's computer? And in an instant she saw the answer: the killer had *wanted* them to find it, and his only reasoning for doing that was to mislead – to make out Mitchell was a paedophile.

TWENTY-SEVEN

AS IT CRUNCHED ROUND THE DRIVE the car's headlights swept over the house, briefly catching the stony, malevolent face of one of the gryphons at the front door. Tonight, there was yet another meeting and this one had been hurriedly arranged too. "Have we *ever* been here during the day, James?"

His chauffeur flicked his eyes to the rear-view mirror. "Certainly not since I've been driving for you, sir."

He smiled to himself; James had been driving him everywhere for nearly twenty years. The Silver Wraith drew up beside the portico and, belying his age, James leapt nimbly from his seat to open the door for him. "I've no idea how long I shall be, James. This might be quick, but one never knows."

James only nodded; five minutes or five hours, it was immaterial to him. This man had rescued him, had rescued his whole family; he would wait for him until Hell itself froze over without even thinking of it.

As the car door closed behind him, the front door opened and pale yellow light spilled out over the flagstones. McKetterick held the door for him as he hurried out of the chill January air. "Good evening, sir."

"Good evening, are the others here?"

"Yes sir, they are waiting for you."

He shrugged himself out of his coat and made his way through the entrance hall to the usual room, which tonight was warmed by a large log fire. The three men, who'd been waiting in silence, looked up as he arrived. Slipping into his chair, he looked round at the others and held up a hand. "My apologies . . . trouble with a merger in Japan. I had to instruct a government minister."

East gave him a thin smile and a small shake of his head. "We are four, and it is for me to apologise; our meetings are generally not so close together." He sat forward, and after a short pause, said, "It was necessary; I've had some disturbing news."

"What news?" North asked.

"One of our friends at Fettes was in touch with me earlier." He looked round the expectant faces. "Apparently, the police have a raid planned."

"Raid? Of what?" West asked, shifting in his seat. Despite their ease of avoiding police attention, it disturbed him they were anywhere close to any of their activities.

"Hawthorns," East said, and hearing their collective sigh, added, "along with Prior and his pet thug McCann."

"When?" North asked.

"It's not been set yet, but I think we can count on it happening soon."

"*Prior*," North spat, "Why do we tolerate the man?" It was a rhetorical question; they all knew he was, in his small way, useful.

"How does this affect us? Is the Forth Development at risk?"

"Not in the slightest."

South sat forward. "Remind me, what's our risk?"

"We have just over eighty-five million sunk into the development. That's at twenty-five percent over five years. It would be a ripple, nothing significant. But if Prior gets caught up in this, we can turn it to our advantage," and East looked round. "We'll simply form another company and swallow his share."

He regarded the others solemnly. Between them they controlled billions of pounds in ventures worldwide, and even if, somehow, it came to the loss of the Forth Development – and he didn't think it would – eighty-five million would be a setback, not a loss. "No, regardless of what we think of Hawthorns – and those who . . . use it – there are individuals there who *must* be protected."

Each man gave silent assent, thinking of who East meant. Despite their open sexual proclivities, there were men, and women, who visited Hawthorns who were key players in many fields; people they used.

A log sighed and shifted in the grate, spitting out sparks.

South stirred in his chair. "Why has this arisen now?"

"Apparently," East said, leaning in, "there's a paedophile element in Hawthorns."

North shuddered. "Animals."

"But useful animals," East countered.

"And this has been discovered by the police?"

"Yes, a young Detective Sergeant is the one to have, if not uncovered it, to have brought reliable witnesses forward."

"Is it too late? . . . Do we buy him off? Have him promoted, or what?"

"He is a she, and yes, it's too late. A stupid, cack-handed, attempt was made to nip this in the bud but that's only succeeded in complicating matters. No, what I propose – why I called this meeting – is that we do nothing. Let the pieces fall where they may, but," and he looked round the other three, "we warn our assets – let them know they should avoid that particular appetite, at least at Hawthorns, for the time being."

"Should Prior be warned?" South asked.

"God, no," East said. "Let him twist in the wind. Hawthorns was always his – *and* his wife's – peculiar little folly," and as he thought of them, he added, "His ego could stand a dent or two, and if the police action were to break him and his companies, then, as I say, we'll absorb that slack."

The others nodded.

"So – and without informing them why – we warn those who are necessary to us, now?" South asked.

"Yes."

North was disturbed by this news; his third marriage had produced twins – a boy and a girl – who were now ten. "Does that include those who might be part of this paedophile activity?"

"Unfortunately, we can't be certain of who they are," East said, sitting up in his chair. "and, that is a *serious* oversight. In future, as part of our profiling, we must know such things – it's a vulnerability we can use. However – right now – this is not a judgment call based on morals, but on business. Morals don't come into it, do they?"

North said nothing; decades ago he had made his own choices. East was right.

"We are agreed then? Warn our assets, and do so as soon as possible?" and reading no disagreement on their faces, "Again, my apologies for calling this meeting at such short notice, but I am certain you now understand why."

All four got to their feet; despite the hour, each had many contacts to make. North stepped outside into the dark for his car, and hearing the rumble of distant thunder, thought through the names of those he would need to contact. First though he needed a whisky or two to wash away the bad taste of this news about Hawthorns.

•

Darkness was his friend; it had always been so. Tonight, cocooned within it, he wandered the streets attempting to finish the task which Uriel had set him by killing Satan's helper. However, all he could remember was the street he sought had a girl's name, and he was hopelessly lost in the strange city.

Overhead the thunderstorm which had rolled over Edinburgh was growing in strength, and when he listened for Uriel, the peels of thunder and the buzzing static inside his head masked even a hint of his majestic voice. Perhaps the tablets he'd taken were to blame; there was no clarity as before, and even their effect could only be felt in the far distance.

Resting against the wall of a blackened tenement, he looked along the street to distant traffic lights, seeing them slowly change from red, to amber, to green. Then, surprising him, they stayed on together, flickered for several moments, and went out. Bewildered, he stared into the darkness and as he did, the lights began running through a rapid cycle, their rays lighting and flashing across the wet cobblestones, then stopped. Red. The colour grew in intensity, washing through him – becoming part of him – and the noise in his head receded. From deep within the ensuing silence, soft at first, he heard his master repeating one word over and over again: *Come.*

Seconds later, he was standing beneath the traffic light, bathing in its red glow. Perhaps Uriel would guide him to the street where he had failed before. Now loud in his head, as if he were standing beside him, he heard his master's instruction: *This way.*

Gliding along the dark, red-drenched streets illuminated by flashes of lightning, he followed the voice, unaware of time or, now, even of purpose; he was Uriel's to instruct. It was then he knew that trying to kill Satan's helper was too dangerous; his master had a different plan for him.

Turning a corner, he was surprised to find he was now on a busy street packed with shoppers, and, looming on one side, a great rocky fortress lit by multiple flashes of lightning. The shops' lights blazed menacing yellows and whites, but he felt Uriel protecting him with a glowing, pulsing, red. Close, he heard his master clearer than ever before: *Here . . . come to me.*

In the distance he saw a great stone spire soaring into the night sky, a crimson-streaked crescent moon hanging to its left, and to his half-thought question, he heard Uriel's loud *Yes* reverberate in his head.

As he hurried across the street, he collided with a man rushing in the opposite direction, and when he heard, "Watch where you're goin' pal," he reached for the chisel. He saw a look of recognition in the man's eyes, but Uriel commanded him onwards and, pushing past him, he reached the far pavement. He didn't see the man pull a phone from his pocket.

Minutes later he was standing before the towering edifice which straddled a massive statue. Now, from the topmost point, the red light grew in intensity as it rolled over the stone in waves to reach him. Entering the surrounding gardens, he circled the structure looking for a way to reach the top where Uriel waited, and at the rear saw a small projecting entrance. As he approached, the statue at the base began to glow with white pulsating light and the dog at the statue's feet lowered its head to look at him with baleful glittering turquoise eyes.

Ignoring both, he entered the wooden structure, and a man came forward shaking his head. "I'm sorry sir, we're just closing." He stabbed him with two quick chisel strikes and pushed his limp body to one side. Hearing Uriel's command *Come to me*, he crossed to the stairs and began to climb.

His breathing was laboured when he reached the first level, and he paused in the room there, seeing a carved wooden panel – an elaborate coat of arms crafted for someone famous – within which, a mermaid and a savage supported a shield. The savage ignored him, but the mermaid lowered the mirror she held and looking at him with piercing ruby eyes, said, "The moon shall fill her horns again." Then, turning the mirror in her hand, a red beam flashed from it across the floor to the steps, "Watch weel, Son of Uriel."

The steps were becoming steeper, the gap through which they passed more constricting, and, although his breath was now shallow, his legs were strong, and he didn't stop at the second platform but pushed himself on to meet Uriel. But when he reached the next level his lungs were on fire and he had to pause. Looking out over the city which was bathed in blood-red light, and being struck by lightning bolts, he looked down and, far below, saw the flashing blue lights of several police cars. Uriel's urgent *Danger* filled his ears.

The final steps were so steep he found he was using his hands to climb as much as his feet, and the walls were so narrow he felt as if he were burrowing into the stone itself. But, with one final push, he reached the top landing. Lightning flashed on all sides, its white forks cleaving through deep red clouds.

High above, within a billowing cloud, Uriel waited. The gap between them had been closed but was still too far, and from behind he heard the crackle of police radios approaching. "Master?" and hearing Uriel's answer, he nodded and climbed on to the stone parapet.

Stretching his arms wide he reached upwards.

Briefly, his entire body was illuminated with white light as a blast of lightning hit his outstretched fingers, and he plummeted to the ground two hundred feet below.

TWENTY-EIGHT

STEEL LEANT AGAINST THE DOOR JAMB and watched JJ moving lightly round the kitchen as she prepared breakfast. She was wearing only his shirt, and for a fleeting – absurd – moment, he wished he could watch her like this forever. She *belonged*, somehow. Smiling to himself, he doubted this was a thought he could, or should, mention.

JJ gave him a quick kiss as she passed. "I'll just bet you normally make do with coffee."

Steel smiled; he was a more than passable cook. "Sometimes. Although, I have been known to open the odd cornflake packet."

She shook her head at that; too often she'd done the same, the rhythms of her job setting its own demands. "Well, at least this morning you'll get a proper breakfast."

He crossed to her, and wrapping his arms round her waist, pulled her close, feeling the warm curves of her body through his shirt. "I could eat *you*."

JJ leaned back in his arms then turned to look up at him, her green eyes sparkling with mischief. "Now would that be a *proper* breakfast?" Seeing him about to respond, she tapped him on the chest with an elegant finger. "Shoo . . . you're distracting me."

Steel kissed her again and, lifting his coffee, wandered into the living room. Running his fingers along one of the CD shelves, he pulled out *The Lark Ascending* and slid it into the player's drawer. As the first notes of the violin mingled with the noises from the kitchen, he realised for the first time, in a very long time, he was relaxed. Happy? That was perhaps a stretch, and he knew his happiness had nothing to do with others, but he sensed that, whatever part it was that had kept him separate and untouched for so long, it was very distant at that moment. JJ had rekindled him, filling a space he hadn't really been aware of. Hearing her call out, "Almost there," he felt *close* to her. Perhaps, for now, that was enough.

Standing at the window, watching a flurry of light snow briefly obscure the village, he wondered how Moss was doing. She'd been upset over letting Stevie McCann go, and he wanted to talk to her about her meeting with the Child Protection Unit, to let her see she was playing a far more important part in Grieve's *bigger picture* than she thought. He took a long swig of coffee; he'd phone her – although, catching a glimpse of JJ in his shirt, later would do.

JJ came through from the kitchen carrying two plates and placed them on the table. "There are whopping big holes in your fridge."

Sitting down, Steel cut into the fluffy mushroom omelette. "I think there's a few rashers of bacon and some black pudding there."

JJ laughed. "What? You *want* me to poison you?"

"I could never be a vegetarian."

"Hitler was one," JJ said, laughing, and then her features clouded. "This raid on Hawthorns, Mike . . . am I really going to be stopped from covering it?"

"Stopped? No, of course not. But if you mean actually being there, then yes, all media will be stopped. Anyone going anywhere *near* Hawthorns, or any of its visitors, between now and then could jeopardise everything – they'd probably be arrested. Besides, it's not up to me; DCI Henderson's the one to deal with."

She swept a long lock of hair back from her face. "We – you, Robin, and me – got it to this stage. I kind of feel cheated."

"You're not the only one – Moss feels let down. You'll get an exclusive when-"

"Yes, but I want to *be* there, Mike. I want to *see* that bastard Prior's face when his empire crumbles about him."

Steel let out a sigh; she was hard to resist. In all ways. "I'm sorry, JJ, I know we've taken it this far, but it's a big operation, one the Chief wants to go without even the hint of a hitch. I'll give you everything I've got, but that'll be after the raid."

"Crumbs," she said, giving him a mock pout.

"Hardly," Steel said with a smile. "You've interviewed Emma, and Carol, from the Venus sauna?"

"I interviewed Carol yesterday, Emma when she was in hospital."

"Well then," he said, sitting back, "when I give you the names of anyone found in the house – especially in the house's wing – you've got a powerful front-page story. One that nobody else will match."

JJ chased a mushroom round her plate with her fork. "I know, but . . . well, you know how it is, Mike. We get so close in what we do; it's hard just to sit and watch."

Steel nodded; he always got close in the cases he worked. Some he'd never been able to let go, even those which had been closed. He was about to say so when his phone rang. He looked at JJ, and shook his head.

"You're not going to answer that?"

"I'd rather spend time with you."

JJ smiled and tilted her head on one side. "But . . ."

"But I'd better answer it." He got to his feet and picked up the phone. "Steel."

"Morning, sir."

Steel winked at JJ. "Morning Moss. What's up?" He listened for a moment, then thinking of somewhere, far from Fettes, to meet, said, "Let's get together at Montpeliers, in Bruntsfield, then. Give me a half hour." JJ gave him a wicked smile, and undid a button of her shirt. "Well, make it an hour."

JJ arched her eyebrows at him and laughed.

•

Moss scanned the *Scotsman* crossword again. Fourteen across: A Roman poet peers into the void; four letters – one an S, if she had seven down correct – had her stumped. She glanced at her watch. Steel had said to give him an hour, and she'd been there almost two. Through the windows she watched passers-by hurrying through the snow as her fingers tapped a restless tattoo on the table.

She was spotted by her server who came across to her table. "Another coffee?" and when she hesitated, "A drink, something to eat?"

Moss shook her head. "Just a coffee, please," vowing yet again to rein in her consumption. This morning, despite the short brisk walk from Morningside, she felt stiff, almost hung-over, and knew she had to get a grip on her personal life. This was nothing new. Back in Liverpool, after she'd left training at Hendon anyhow, she'd learned that working as a policewoman was a disruption to most personal things, like keeping up with family and friends, seeing the latest films and watching her diet: living what most people called a normal life. That had been exacerbated when she became a DC, and now, as a Detective Sergeant, in a new city, with a new boss, she sensed that even the idea of paying attention to herself was slipping. She definitely should have been practising aikido with more regularity – she was nowhere near ready for her next exam, out of the kyu grades to become a yudansha.

The server arrived with her coffee and, placing it down before her, he paused, giving her a warm, winning smile. "Been stood up?"

She looked up at him in surprise, struck by the thought that, nowadays, this was another aspect of her personal life she ignored. He was handsome, in a young sense, and reminded her of some of the boys she'd been at University with. Discounting the pathetic, and pointless, approaches of some of her male colleagues, it had been years since anyone had chatted her up. If that was what he was doing. With a thin smile, she said, "No, I don't *get* stood up," and she noticed Steel's arrival. "You'd better bring me another cup. Make it a Colombian."

The server followed her gaze, and seeing Steel making his way towards her, he blushed. "I'm sorry . . . just making conversation," and hurried off to get another coffee. Moss smiled at his retreating form and hoped she hadn't offended him. Some detective, she thought – perhaps he was just being pleasant, just doing his job.

Steel sat down and Moss could see how relaxed he was; his garden leave was obviously beginning to work for him. "Sir. I've just ordered you a coffee."

"Thanks. Did you hear about McVicar?"

"McVicar? No."

"I was just speaking with DI Fisher from West End . . . apparently he jumped off the top of the Scott Monument last night – closed Princes Street."

Moss slumped in her chair. "I thought we were going to get lucky and catch him." Knowing this would close any current investigations, this news gave her no satisfaction; demented or not, McVicar had simply evaded justice by taking his own life.

Steel shrugged. "I'm not sure about getting lucky – I think you make your own, and despite your notes following the priest's murder, the Murder Squad was still looking at him as prime suspect." He shook his head, "Whistling tunelessly in the dark. Anyhow, what's this about Mitchell's computer?"

Moss took him through the conversation she'd had with Kevin Forbes at Forensics about the folder of pornographic images they'd found on Lord Mitchell's computer. "He was adamant their date, and time, were both correct. Which can only mean, judging by Dr. Knox's time of death, the folder was placed on Mitchell's computer *after* he'd been murdered."

Steel sat in silence for a few moments, absorbing this, and breakfast with JJ seemed like days ago. "So, the killer did that, then?"

"Short of there being a third party – there at the same time – it's the only answer I can come up with."

Steel sat back. "You'd better pass that on to the Murder Squad. I've no idea what this folder means, but there has to be *some* relevance. If the killer placed it there, he's a cool one – it would've taken time. And what did he mean by it?"

"Pretty obviously, to mislead us. To make us think Mitchell was a paedophile."

"But, why? Why would the killer do that?"

Moss shook her head. "I don't know. Perhaps to . . . well, to make us see him in a bad light."

Steel ran a hand over his face. "Again, why? What purpose would it serve? He murders Mitchell, then places a folder of pornographic images on his computer to mislead us? It doesn't make any sense. That is, unless he *was* a paedophile, and murdered because of that."

"I don't know about that, sir. He had a taste for escorts – Emma said he was quite straight, sexually – but he did *visit* Hawthorns. We don't actually know whether he was in the paedophile group that uses the wing, but it seems – to me, anyhow – children wouldn't be his taste."

Steel frowned. "You could be wrong, but I don't think so. Anyway, pass it on to the Murder Squad, perhaps it'll help them." He took a sip of coffee. "What else have you got on today?"

"I'm getting a statement from Carol . . . the girl from the Venus sauna."

"Where you meeting her?"

"It's set up for Fettes at one. Then I've got to see a DCI Scullion in Child Protection."

Steel nodded. Carol's statement corroborated Emma's, and with those in hand, the Child Protection Unit would trigger the raid on Hawthorns and, from that, the raids on Prior and McCann. "I'd like to be with you when you take Carol's statement, but I'd rather it wasn't at Fettes."

"But it's set, sir."

"Humour me, Moss. Give her a call and ask her if she can go to the cop shop in Queen Charlotte Street. It's nearer the Venus than Fettes, anyhow."

Moss pulled out her mobile and scrolled through her numbers.

As she dialled, Steel picked up her *Scotsman*, scanning her attempt at the crossword. Hearing her, "Thanks Carol, I appreciate your help," he looked up.

"Okay?"

"Yes. She's happy with that . . . says she knows quite a few of the cops there anyhow."

"I'll bet," Steel said, giving her a small smile. "You're not to know, but a lot of Leithers see Edinburgh as a foreign city – it's always better to ask them to go to the local shop. Fettes can be a bit intimidating anyhow, especially for a working girl from Leith."

He pulled out his mobile. "Give me a second," and he dialled what was, for him, a well known number.

"DI McLean."

"Adam, it's Mike Steel."

"Mike. Long time no hear. How're things in the Premier Division?"

Steel smiled; Fettes could be remote for cops too. "Fine, Adam. A quick courtesy call . . . I need to take a statement from a witness . . . better, all round, if I take it at *your* house."

"No problem, Mike. When?"

"This afternoon at one, and if I can get it typed up straight away . . ."

"What? You frightened of chipping your nail polish, or something?"

Steel laughed. "It's a rush, that's all."

"Nae bother, Mike. I'll have one of the civvies primed. How long, d'you reckon?"

"Half an hour. Tops."

"Fine. I'll let the Desk Sergeant know to expect you."

"Great, I owe you one."

Steel heard his ready laughter. "Let me guess – a ticket for the next Hibs home game?"

This was an old, long-standing joke between them, and Steel laughed. "Yeah, yeah . . . second prize, a Hibs season ticket."

"Right then, I'll see you."

"Aye, see you, Adam. Thanks," and Steel hung up. Looking at his watch, he said, "We've got time, but when we're done here, let's get down to Leith. Oh, and by the way, your crossword . . ."

"Yes?"

"Your seven down's wrong – fourteen across is Ovid."

•

Moss walked to the door with Carol while Steel chatted with Adam McLean. Looking out, she shivered. The falling snow, driven by a stiff wind coming off the North Sea, was now almost horizontal.

She turned to Carol and was again struck by the transformation in her. Instead of the frothy, scantily-clad sex worker – and what work that must be, she thought – she saw a young woman conservatively dressed in a dark trouser suit, more fitting for work in the nearby Civil Service headquarters.

"Thanks again, Carol. You've been a real help."

Carol pulled her gaze away from the wintry street. "Aye, well . . . anythin' that'll stop thae sick bastards goin' for weans, ken?" and she gave

Moss a quick, worried look. "Ah'll no' havetae testify, or nuthin'?"

Moss hadn't thought about the next steps. As far as she was concerned, Carol's statement, added to Emma's, were simply necessary tools for them. A raid on Hawthorns could go ahead and, until it did – and paedophiles were caught, and charged – she had no idea how the prosecutors would act. She gave Carol a quick smile. "That's not down to us. I doubt it, but I can't say for sure." Seeing concern flit across the young woman's face, she added, "I'm sorry, that call's made by the Procurator Fiscal's office, not by us."

"Well, Ah'd prefer no' to," and with a quick grin, "For mah reputation, ken?" and then her brow furrowed.

Moss reached for her arm, and gave it a small squeeze. "You did the right thing, Carol," and seeing her doubtful look, "Don't worry. I think when this is brought to court neither you nor Emma will need to be there."

Steel joined them, and thanking Carol again, he asked whether they could give her a lift anywhere.

"Naw, Mr. Steel . . . Ah'm goin'tae grab a taxi roond the corner, an' see mah brother," and without another word, she pulled her scarf tight up under her chin, and stepped out into the snow.

Steel watched her go. "Everything alright, Moss?"

Moss's shoulders twitched. "She's worried, sir, that's all."

Steel knew only too well how Carol would be feeling. "She'll be thinking she's grassing, but she needn't be worried. The one thing that excuses witnesses talking to us is when children are involved. Then, people have an almost medieval idea of justice. It's why paedophiles and their like – the Rule Forty-Three prisoners – are separated in prison." Much good it does them, he thought. The medieval hand had a reach much longer than a court of law; there would be accidents, and worse, ahead for anybody found in Hawthorns' wing when they found themselves imprisoned.

Shrugging that off – he too had thoughts on justice that could be medieval – he said, "Right, you're sorted. I'll run you to Fettes and you can meet Jim Scullion."

Driving carefully through the snow, they navigated their way from Leith in silence, and when Steel turned the car from a slippery,

260

unploughed Great Junction Street on to Ferry Road, Moss said, "Anything I should know about DCI Scullion, sir?"

Steel shook his head. "He's a good cop. But he's . . . well, a man of certainties," and he grinned, "I think you'll have a lot in common."

Moss gave him a quizzical look; there was obviously more to Scullion than Steel was letting on, but she didn't pursue it.

When they reached Fettes, Steel killed the engine and turned to Moss. "With these statements, the raid on Hawthorns will happen very soon. Crime Squad's been waiting on you, but they've been getting Prior and McCann lined up in their sights too. Rightly, they see this as a three-pronged action, but Jim Scullion's the one to set the wheels in motion."

"Understood, sir." She did, feeling professionally and emotionally involved, yet divorced from the impending raids. "And if I need to speak with you?"

"I'm spending some time with JJ, but I'll have the mobile on."

As long as you answer, Moss almost said as she stepped out of the car.

Steel watched her walk away; everyone should have to meet a Jim Scullion in the Job – the man's certainties were now becoming eccentricities and, although he was by no means unique, Scullion was well on his way to legendary status within Fettes.

As Moss pushed through the glass doors he smiled to himself; she was turning into a good Sergeant, and he didn't doubt for one second he'd hear from her later.

•

Making her way to the fourth floor, Moss found the Child Protection Unit and, as she entered, the first thing that struck her was how quiet the offices were. There were no raised voices, no sounds of an office at work. A young officer lifted his head. "Yes, can I help you?"

"DS Moss for DCI Scullion."

He pointed to a door, returning his gaze to the computer screen.

Hearing a "come" from her knock, Moss pushed the door open. Scullion was seated behind a desk overflowing with stacks of documents. In his late forties, everything about him said neat; the very opposite of his desk. Clean-shaven, with precision-parted jet black hair, he looked as if he'd just arrived from the barber, and under his waistcoat his shirt looked as if it had just been pressed. The only thing which – strangely – failed to match this overall neatness were his unruly, bushy eyebrows.

Raising his head from the document before him, serious brown eyes shot her an impatient look. "Yes?"

"DS Moss, sir."

Scullion's stony look melted in an instant. "Ah yes, Moss . . . excuse me." He stood, and pulling his jacket from the back of his chair, slipped it on, and, straightening his tie, reached across the desk to shake her hand. "As you can see, I wasn't ready for you today. Please, take a seat."

Moss sat down, aware Scullion was weighing her. "I have two witness statements for you, sir."

Taking them, Scullion said, "Hawthorns, right?" and to Moss's nod, he sat back and eyed her critically through unblinking eyes. "Tell me about yourself, Sergeant."

Moss was surprised, but gave Scullion a short summation of her career.

"A fast-track policewoman then. Maybe *my* boss one day. And you're working with DCI Steel," adding enigmatically, "There are too many greys in Mike's life." He paused and gave her a quick smile. "That was perhaps not the first question to ask of you. Tell me, what do you know of Child Protection?"

"Very little, sir," and she thought it best to stick to the matter in hand. "I know these statements will trigger a raid on Hawthorns, and that's a good thing."

Scullion gave this a slow nod. "'A good thing'. Yes." He eyed her keenly. "Now, would you say that's good as opposed to bad, or good as opposed to evil?"

"I . . . I'm not sure, sir."

Scullion sat forward. "You're too young – too inexperienced as an officer – to be *un*certain, Sergeant." Seeing her confusion, he continued, "I'm sorry, my presumptions are to the fore. I see you're wearing a cross. Are you a *practising* Catholic?" Moss could only nod at this swift transition. "Yes, I know, we're not meant to ask, are we?" and he lowered his voice to a conspiratorial whisper. "I'm a practising Christian, though that's got nothing to do with the price of fish.

"Very recently, I forwarded a case to the Fiscal concerning a priest of the Catholic persuasion. Now I ask myself, whether – to the church in Rome – a priest who is charged with sexual abuse is bad or evil," and he raised one bushy eyebrow at her.

Moss knew the Church's position on errant priests had been to hide the problem from view, then simply move the priest to another parish, a response that had not sat well with her. "We only have the law, sir . . . I mean, what constitutes an offence."

"That's just a starting point," he snapped. "Yes, offenders – against what *you* call, the law, are – hopefully – caught and prosecuted. It used to strike me the same way when I was arresting people for doing bad things to children. Now I see that differently. Now, I see evil abroad."

He gave her an open smile. "Are you thinking there's an edge out there, and I've slipped over it? That my job's finally got to me?"

Something like that was beginning to form in Moss's mind, but she said nothing.

"Well," he continued, "it has, but in a different way. This *woefully* understaffed unit does everything it can to bring bad people to justice . . . although, *I* call them evil rather than bad." Gesturing between himself and her, he said, "*Our* bad is between legal and illegal, right and wrong, if you will; *my* bad goes beyond that – believe me, the moral bankruptcy I have seen *allows* for evil, Sergeant."

Steel had been right when he'd said DCI Scullion was a man of certainties but, to her, when people broke the law, whether they were good or bad – saintly or evil – simply didn't matter.

"Do you know what the biggest trigger for the sexual exploitation of children is?" Moss shook her head. "In a nutshell, it's when power meets vulnerability. Now, I have no idea *who* we might arrest at Hawthorns, but I do know they are, in their own way, powerful people. And when such people allow evil to ensnare them, then vulnerable children can do nothing *but* surrender."

In a soft voice, Scullion continued, "Don't get me wrong, Sergeant, these are not bad people, these are evil people with a special place waiting for them in Hell," and tapping the witness statements she had brought lightly with his fingertips, "Calling them bad is a distortion of both English and the truth."

Moss realised she was ill-equipped for a conversation like this, a conversation Steel hadn't prepared her for. Scullion seemed like a modern-day prophet calling down hellfire on the perpetrators of child abuse. "I *think* I get your point, sir," she ventured.

Scullion gazed at her. "I hope you do. Anyway, all of that is them . . . there is, of course, us. You've heard of Dunblane?"

"The shootings? Of course." The deaths of a teacher and sixteen young children – fifteen five year-olds, and one six year-old – had seared her.

"Yes . . . the shootings. Lothian and Borders weren't directly involved. It was Central. Five years *prior* to that dreadful evil hatching itself in the world, Central's Child Protection Unit investigated Thomas Hamilton, the killer. They forwarded their report to the Procurator Fiscal for consideration of ten charges, and what happened? *Nothing.* No action was taken," and he shook his head slowly, his eyes fixed on some distant point. Then, in a low voice, "Ten charges . . . sixteen young lives. I sense a Masonic hand.

"You're familiar with Burke's, 'All that is necessary for the triumph of evil is that good men do nothing'? Well, not on *my* watch. Not on my watch. Unfortunately, *I* can't punish these people at Hawthorns, but I can make damn sure I make no mistakes, either in the catching of them, or in how I hand them over to the Fiscal's office."

Scullion leaned over his desk towards her, and in almost a whisper, said, "Here, there will be *no* triumph of evil, Sergeant," and Moss saw his brown eyes shine with a zealot's inner certainty.

He paused, straightened in his chair and then, in an even tone, said, "Thank you for bringing me these statements, Sergeant Moss," and dismissed her with a nod. "Good work."

Moss got to her feet. "Sir."

Waiting for the lift, she felt she'd been thrown in at the deep end by Steel without him giving her any idea of just how deep that end was. Scullion's neurotic neatness was clearly the offset of the man's inner turmoil. He was far too tightly wound. If there was an edge out there . . . well, Scullion might not have slipped over it, but he was clinging to it with his fingernails.

There was nothing on her mind now other than phoning Steel. To say what she didn't know, but she'd think of something. As soon as she left Fettes she rang him, and let out a long exasperated exhalation as his answering service kicked in.

Staring at the phone, the feeling of wanting to throw it as far as she could swept over her, and then she laughed out loud at the absurdity. What an idiot I am, she thought – a right divvy – of *course* Steel could've been with me . . . he had *wanted* me to meet with Scullion alone.

Shaking her head as yet another layer of Steel was revealed, she ended the call without leaving a message.

TWENTY-NINE

COMMANDER BRUCE HELD HIS PINT GLASS up to the light. "What *is* this? The Jocks are meant to be hard drinkers. This tastes like bat's piss."

DCI Stalker laughed. "How d'you think it'll go tonight, boss?"

Bruce squinted at his watch. Tonight would see some action, at last, and then he'd be able to leave this God-forsaken place. "As far as *I'm* concerned, the drugs side's the important thing, and I'm worried about this shower fucking up with McCann." He peered gloomily at his glass. "As to the rest . . . if they get a few nonces from the raid on this house, Hawthorns, that's all to the good, but the investigation of Prior and his company, well, that's going to run and run. In all likelihood, he'll walk."

Wide-eyed, Stalker looked at him. " *Walk?* Nah, boss."

Bruce gave a little shrug. "I hate financials, Stalky . . . bloody hate them. He'll be fined, maybe spend a twelve-month if we're lucky, but we'll not do him . . . *really* do him. No, if they take down McCann, it'll be a result in my book."

Stalker thought back to their last job, when they and Customs had intercepted a container ship at Tilbury filled to the gunwales with five kilo bags of cocaine. "This all seems a bit Mickey Mouse to me, boss. I mean, they're not going in tooled-up to bring down a gang, just a local bad boy with a club." He looked quizzically at Bruce. "How *did* we get involved again?"

Bruce eyed Stalker. From a certain angle, with his greasy hair combed straight back from his thin, sharply featured face, his bagman reminded him of one the ferrets his old man used to keep – a bushy moustached one. "'Cause they asked us Stalky, didn't they? That Chief Constable looking for a bit of glory, I reckon. And we're not involved are we? We're only here as advisors, see?"

He tried his pint again and, pulling a face, placed it back on the table. "That's the trouble with the Jocks – all these provincial outfits . . . they always think they can do it themselves, then they get scared of their own shadows, and when push comes to shove, they ask for *our* advice." He gave a barked laugh. "Although, that DCI – Farmer Rob – *he's* a good listener."

"Still, we had a bit of action with Steel, eh?" With his lips curled back over his discoloured teeth in the semblance of a smile, Stalker now presented the disturbing image of a grinning ferret.

"Well, *you* did . . . I just got to whack him."

Stalker laughed. "Tap him, boss. Tap him."

Bruce looked round the pub, beginning to fill up with a noisy after-work crowd. Glancing at his watch again, he got to his feet. "I'm going back to the hotel, freshen up a bit, I'll see you back at Fettes, about seven. Right?"

"Right you are, boss," and Stalker took another pull on his pint; bat piss or not, it was alcohol.

Bruce pushed through the doors out on to the street, and pulled his coat tight about him; that's another thing about this bleeding country – always cold, and now here's a fog rolling in. Making his way into the lane running behind the street, where the rental car was parked, he pulled out the keys and pressed the button. He saw the car's lights responding with a flash, but didn't see the man pressed deep in the dark shadows of the doorway he'd just passed.

At an unhurried pace the man closed the distance and, coming up behind Bruce, punched him hard in the kidneys.

As Bruce fell to the ground the man followed him down, grabbed him by the hair, and lifting his head, slammed it into the cobblestones.

Bruce was out cold.

Rolling him over, the man rummaged through his pockets. Finding his wallet, he flicked it open, smiling when he saw the warrant card identifying Bruce as an officer of the National Crime Squad. Slipping the wallet and car keys into his pocket, he fished for the small bags of heroin and stuffed them into Bruce's coat pockets.

Getting to his feet, he looked round warily and, stepping back into the shadows, pulled out the pay-as-you-go mobile and dialled 999.

"Emergency. Which service do you require?"

"Polis."

Within seconds, he was connected.

"Ah wantae report a crime . . . some bastard tried to sell me drugs."

"What is your location, sir?"

"Ah'm in Rose Street, in the lane just behind the Robertson's pub."

"Is this person still in the vicinity, sir?"

"Oh, aye, he is that. Ah jus' came intae the lane, for a pish like, and this bastard appeared . . . Ah gi'ed him a doin'."

"If you would stay where you– " but the man ended the call. He looked down at Bruce sprawled on the wet cobblestones and, with an emphatic nod, turned away.

Finding a dumpster on the corner, he dropped the wallet, car keys and mobile from his gloved hand. As they clattered to the bottom the first patrol car's sirens could be heard wailing in the distance, and he smiled into the night.

•

Sir David Thompson's jaw was clamped shut as he looked at the two men sitting opposite. The build up to Operation Northside had made him all the more nervous for a successful outcome. It wasn't the biggest operation Lothian and Borders had run but it *was* his, and now, with the clock ticking, Commander Bruce of the NCS had failed to show.

Thompson picked a non-existent piece of fluff from his immaculate uniform sleeve and, fixing the Londoner with a stare, snapped, "So where *is* Commander Bruce, DCI Stalker?"

Stalker had answered this earlier, but raised placatory hands. "I'm sorry, sir, I have no idea. I'll go to his hotel, see if I can find out what's happened . . . it's not like him."

Thompson pursed his lips; it was certainly not like any of *his* officers. He turned to DCI Henderson. "Well . . . Rob, it would seem Bruce has left you to run the whole show yourself," and he raised his eyebrows, "I take it that's not a *problem?*"

Henderson heard the unspoken, *if this goes wrong, you get to carry the can* in the Chief's question, but knew better than to voice anything. He was annoyed Thompson had even asked the NCS for advice and wondered, again, why he'd thought it necessary to bring in outside advisors; Bruce had been a loud-mouthed, intrusive nuisance, getting under everyone's feet. *He* had no problem with the man going missing – why would he? Crime Squad was far more than capable. "Commander Bruce's absence this evening is regrettable, sir, but the operation won't be affected."

Thompson leant his elbows on the desk and steepled his fingers before him. "Understood, Rob . . . it's just . . . well, if you're certain, we move on. How many officers are taking part?"

"Sixty-five in total, sir – majority for Hawthorns. Social Services are also involved, for any minors at the house, but they'll stand off until it's been secured."

"Armed?"

"Yes sir, each team has Authorised Firearms Officers in the lead units."

Thompson fingered his tie. "What about Prior's house and this club of McCann's?"

Henderson longed for this meeting – by no stretch could it be called a briefing – to be over. He wanted – needed – to talk with the teams taking part, those doing the job, rather than his Chief Constable who, judging by his nervousness, only seemed concerned with how the operation might reflect on him. "I foresee no problems with either, sir."

Thompson sat back. "Very well Chief Inspector. I'll let you get on. Do keep me informed."

Keen to get out of the Chief's office, Henderson took his cue and stood. "Thank you, sir."

•

"Right, everyone. Listen up." Henderson's loud voice cut across the chatter in the Incident Room. Now, with his tie undone, and his tight shirt coming loose from his belt, he had a harried look. "You've been through this with your Team Leaders but, as we're all together, let me take you through it one more time."

Henderson stood to one side so that everyone had clear sight of the photographs of their targets, the blown-up maps, and a large schematic of Hawthorns itself, taped to the whiteboard on the wall.

"Operation Northside has three targets this evening – Alpha, Bravo and Charlie, for those of you who've mastered their alphabet." This brought a collective groan. "Alpha is Hawthorns," and scanning the room, "Who's got Alpha?"

Steel and Moss had squeezed into the back of the room, and Moss studied those who raised their hands. These officers, in their dark tactical clothing, were the sharp, heavy end of modern policing. She knew these men and, she noted, three women, had received psychological testing and specialised, highly sophisticated training but, to her, they simply looked like modern day gladiators spoiling for a fight, fretting to be let off the leash as the adrenaline began to build. All of them knew their task for the evening ahead. All of them had an enough-with-the-talk look on their faces.

"Okay. We'll not be ringing any doorbells – there, or anywhere else – especially at the gatehouse. Sergeant Murray?"

"Six officers are detailed, sir. We'll ram the gate and – immediately after that – hit the gatehouse."

"Right. First task is to quickly disable comms – we don't want anyone there warning the main house."

Murray nodded; he knew his part, and didn't need reminding.

"The rest of Alpha team," Henderson continued, "will be going in hard, but dealing softly with the main house occupants. Let me remind you, there will be some *very* important people there – people who, no doubt, will be found in compromising positions."

"Way-hay," rose from the back and got a small ripple of laughter.

Henderson glowered towards the source of the interruption. "Above all, we will be *professional*, Quinn. I'll hear no word coming back that any of us fouled-up in *any* way. Is that understood?

"The main house – Alpha Two – is a distraction," and he thumped the house schematic with a meaty fist, revealing a damp patch of sweat under his arm. "This wing – Alpha One – is our primary target. If you think we're being careful in the main house, here we'll be wearing kid gloves." He turned to the man standing to one side. "DCI Scullion's team will secure Alpha One . . . Jim?"

Shirt sleeved, with cuffs neatly folded back and tie impeccably knotted, Scullion stepped forward. "Thank you, Rob." He paused, slowly scanning the assembled ranks, looking into their faces. "As *some* of you know, I'm from Child Protection; count your blessings if our paths haven't crossed. Our target tonight is this wing, which we now know is being used by paedophiles."

He glanced across to where Steel and Moss were standing. "We have DS Moss to thank for all the work she's put in on this."

Everyone turned to look at her, and Moss felt uncomfortable being singled out. She still felt she hadn't done anything special, but gave a sheepish smile as Steel winked at her.

Scullion's brown eyes shone as he gazed over the room. "Tonight, we're taking down some *evil* people. Many of you have children, but I want to stress what DCI Henderson has just said, we'll deal with these people wearing the softest kid gloves. I want everyone – not just the officers under my direct command – to be clear on that. Woe betide any officer who as much as puts a scratch on one of these animals. We have our job to do but, as I don't have to remind you, that's just the first step – I don't want any high-priced lawyer, later in court, saying we overstepped the mark."

He paused again, thinking of the night ahead, but had nothing to add. "Rob."

Henderson nodded and stepped forward. "Now, Target Bravo – Alan Prior's house in Gamekeeper's Road, Cramond – is straightforward." He pointed to the blown-up map behind him. "You'll park up here. According to Intel, the gates to his house are normally open of an evening . . . if they're closed when you get there, drive through them.

"Target Charlie is *Oysters*, Billy McCann's club in Coburg Street,

Leith. Here, you'll park up in East Cromwell Street. Now, unlike Alpha and Bravo, we may have a slight difficulty here – while it's his so-called office, it's also a club. There will be members of the public there – not *too* many, I hope – but nobody is to be allowed to leave. Nobody.

"We're timed for nine p.m.," and he glanced at the clock, "just over an hour and a quarter from now, so we've only got about thirty minutes, max. Once I'm informed each team's in place, absolute radio silence will be maintained until you receive a Go from me, and even then, there will be *no* chatter – your Team Leaders will be live-miked, and they're the *only* voices I want to hear." He glared across the room. "You know to leave any personal mobiles here. Anyone using one tonight . . . well, the Chief will have your job, and I'll be *more* than happy to help him throw you out.

"One last point: resistance levels. Prior is low, as is Hawthorns. With Oysters you can expect *some* aggro. Remember though, none of that is holy writ – be careful at all targets."

Henderson looked round the room slowly. "Northside is *very* big. We're going to break up a paedophile ring, take down some big players and, at least, disrupt a drug line. Take another look at your targets, ask questions of your Team Leader if you have *any* doubts on what you should be doing," and he drew himself up, "Above all, be professional, do the job, and good luck."

As the officers broke up into smaller groups, Steel turned to Moss. "I think I'll stay, see how this turns out."

Moss hesitated. With nothing for her to do, she felt displaced, somehow adrift. "Do you think Steven McCann will be scooped up in this?"

Steel knew the Teflon-coated younger McCann was weighing on her mind, and she was still taking it personally. "We *will* get him, Moss. Great if it's tonight, but it'll be sometime soon, you can bank on it."

Moss thought back to her time as a DC in Liverpool. There, she'd come across outright villains, some very violent gangsters, all the way down to the small time crooks who ran cheque scams and shoplifting gangs. All of them were known, yet many of them had avoided being caught, left free to walk the streets year after year. Some of the cops she'd worked with had grown old during that same time. It was a scenario without resolution, like a perpetual game of cowboys and Indians. "I think I'll just go home, sir."

Steel watched her leave. She needed to toughen up, stop taking the Job personally. He knew all about making it personal, knew too you could be bent out of shape if you did. He wondered whether he'd ever been as soft as Moss and, for a brief moment, glimpsed his younger, rookie self; yes, perhaps he had.

He hoped Operation Northside would net young Stevie for her; it was no more than she deserved.

THIRTY

TEN PEOPLE WERE SQUEEZED into Fettes' small communications suite, each remote from the raids, but all wanting to feel as if they were somehow taking part. Steel managed to push himself to the back of the room and DCI Henderson, noting his arrival, scowled at him but said nothing.

Static crackled from the multi-band radio, and Henderson snapped, "Can't that be squelched?" at the communications officer.

The woman nodded, "Sir," and adjusted the knobs before her. For a few moments there was silence, and then a wave of white noise swept through the room.

"Christ," Henderson muttered, "Let's *try*, shall we?"

The three teams had left Fettes in a fleet of unmarked vans, heading north to Turnberry Road, Cramond, and Leith. Now all Henderson needed was a call from each to let him know they'd arrived without incident.

Despite his dislike of the man, Steel had some sympathy for Henderson. No matter how well any operation was planned, there was always a chance the unexpected would play its hand. All it would take for Operation Northside to fail would be an accident on Edinburgh's now foggy streets, or the breakdown of one of their ageing vehicles. And Henderson didn't have just the one raid to command, he had three.

Running his hand through the stubble on his head, Henderson looked at his watch. Seventeen minutes before the Go. He glanced up at the clock above the comms desk then back at his watch; he had to hear soon.

The tension in the room was growing by the second. Everyone was hunched forward, staring at the speakers, willing the Team Leaders to make their first call; then, as another wave of static rose, they heard "Bravo in place."

"Thank you, Bravo," the comms officer responded, and what seemed only moments later they heard "Alpha in place." Everyone waited in silence, and the second hand ticked out three more interminable minutes before they heard "Charlie in place."

Henderson pulled his gaze from the speakers and back up to the clock as the red second hand nudged forward. Less than ten minutes left. This would be the longest time of the night.

•

Moss turned the key in the lock and flicked on the hall light. She was greeted by a deep silence from the empty flat, and wished Susan wasn't working tonight. If she'd picked up the term correctly, it would've been good to have a blether with her. On everything and nothing.

Dropping her bag on the couch, she went through to the kitchen and looked into the fridge for something that could be microwaved. Selecting a chicken korma, she peeled off the plastic top, peered at the contents, and hoped it tasted better than it looked.

As she set the timer, she realised it was almost time for the raids to begin and, with a creeping sense of anxiety, wondered whether she should've remained at Fettes with Steel.

She lifted the bottle of claret; there was very little left and, if she was going to drink, one glass of wine certainly wasn't going to work. Reaching for a bottle of water, she went through to the living room to switch on the television and, scanning the programme guide, sighed – there was nothing there to distract, let alone hold her attention tonight.

The microwave pinged, and thinking she could perhaps send a few mails to those who – no doubt – thought she'd dropped off the edge of the world, she powered up her computer before going through to collect her meal.

Setting the plate down on her desk, she took a sip of water and launched Thunderbird. There were four mails waiting for her. Marking the offers for Viagra and printer ink as spam, she saw the third mail was from her aikido sensei: a short message asking her to call him. The fourth made her sit up. It was from J. Helms at the *Telegraph*, a single line: *Give me a call. Any evening.* Noting the number, she took a forkful of the chicken dish. It tasted worse than it looked, and probably breached the Trade Descriptions Act, so pushing the plate away she picked up the phone and dialled.

"Night Desk."

"Ah yes . . . could I speak with Joseph Helms, please."

"Speaking."

"Hello Mr. Helms, this is DS Robin Moss with Lothian and Borders Police."

"Sergeant Moss. I got your mail. Must say, it took me back a bit."

"Do you remember working on that story, Mr. Helms?"

"How could I forget? And it's Joe." To Moss's ear, he sounded much younger than she'd imagined a News Editor might be. "Yes, it was like a train wreck . . . a lot of pressure was put on us and the Editor at the time."

"That was from a law firm, here in Edinburgh?"

"Yeah. But the owners got involved too. At one point we all thought we were going to be sacked."

Moss realised she had very little knowledge of the structure of newspapers. "Was that odd, Joe? The owners being involved?"

"Well, the owners at the time were an American company, and–"

"American? What's their name?"

"Coltbridge Corporation. They owned quite a few newspapers, here and in the States."

"And they wouldn't normally be involved in something like the story on Mr. Prior?"

"Oh, no. Coltbridge was the money side, they didn't get involved in the day to day running of their titles. We have a Managing Editor and an editorial board . . . why keep a dog and bark, y'know."

Moss scribbled a note; she would need to find out whether Prior or any of his companies had links to the American company. "So, it would've been odd . . . the owners getting involved?"

"Yes, it was," and Helms paused before continuing, "Look, whenever there's any sort of exposé in the works, newspapers kind of *expect* an approach from lawyers flexing every legal muscle and coming at you with a kill-the-first-born attitude."

"But this was different?"

"Well, with the owners entering into it, yes. Don't get me wrong, a Mexican stand-off is more normal than you might think. When you write negatively about an individual, or a company – especially when you detail wrongdoing – you're going to get threatened with lawsuits. It's expected. But out of the blue, Coltbridge was coming at us too, telling us to spike the story."

"So you backed off?"

"We had no choice. We were prepared to fight off the injunctions – legal had cleared us – and we would've published had it been the usual threats, but with the owners leaning on us we couldn't do a damn thing."

Moss paused to absorb this. "What was the gist of your story?"

"Simply, Prior's a crook, and his companies, with their promises of at least a twenty percent return per annum, are all smoke and mirrors, not worth the price of their letterhead. We'd done the work, it's a shame we couldn't publish."

Moss nodded in silent agreement. "When you say we, who was involved with you? If it's possible, I'd like to speak with them too."

"Well, apart from some background research by others, me, Howard and Jenny were the main reporters."

"And are Howard and Jenny still with the paper?"

"No, they've both moved on. Howard owns a pub in Babbacombe on the South Coast – the retirement he always dreamed of. I'm sure he'd be pleased to speak with you. I can get you his address if you'd like."

"Yes, thanks. And Jenny, has she retired too?"

A burst of laughter came through the receiver. "Our firebrand? No, she's nowhere near retirement. If you were going to pick one out of the three of us who'd hand everything over to the Serious Fraud Office, it wouldn't've been me or Howard. No, Jenny had a real bee in her bonnet about Prior. It was like his greed offended her at some deep level. Howard used to have huge stand-up arguments with her about making it personal."

Moss made a mental note to speak with her before Howard. "You don't happen to have an address for her, do you, Joe?"

"Yes, but Jenny's working in your neck of the woods."

"She *is?* What's her last name?"

"Johnstone. Give the *Scotsman* a bell and ask for JJ."

•

The second hand was counting down the last minute and, to Steel, it seemed as if everyone in the communications suite was holding a collective breath. At the ten second mark Henderson stepped forward and picked up the desk microphone. Gripping it tightly, he watched the clock, and when the second hand reached twelve, he pressed the button. "Control to Alpha, Bravo, Charlie . . . Go."

All three Team Leaders responded, and for a brief moment everyone could hear the noise of vehicle engines roaring into action. Henderson placed the microphone down lightly, and looking round the small crowd gave them a quick, humourless smile. "Geronimo."

Seconds later the room was filled with piercing cries of "Armed police. Stand still. Armed police," and then, rising above the cacophony, an almighty crash followed by what sounded like metal screeching upon metal.

Henderson lifted the microphone, then hesitated. If it was something bad he'd hear soon enough; the last thing any of the active teams needed at this point was someone sitting comfortably in Fettes, asking questions. Though, feeling his heart thumping in his chest, he knew he was far from comfortable; one day – after he'd retired, no doubt – Lothian and Borders would become properly modernised and have video links for raids.

"Alpha Team Leader to Control."

Henderson drew a deep breath. "Go ahead."

"Lead vehicle damaged, sir. The gates-"

"The gatehouse, Sergeant Murray," Henderson growled; damage to a vehicle was the least of his concerns.

"The gatehouse, and communications, are secured, sir. Two persons – one male, one female – detained."

279

"Thank you. Contact me when Alpha One and Two are secure."

Henderson placed the microphone down, and Steel caught him gently clenching his fist before him. So far so good.

Seconds later, the radio crackled back into life. "Bravo Team Leader to Control."

"Go ahead, Bravo."

"House is empty. Repeat, house is empty."

"Thank you, Bravo."

Several of those in the room exchanged glances. At this stage, Prior's house being empty could mean he was at Hawthorns; fingers crossed it didn't mean he'd been tipped off. The Bravo team would secure the house and grounds and, executing the warrant, ensure Prior's home office, any computers and communication devices remained untouched for Forensics.

"Charlie Team Leader to Control."

Oysters. "Go ahead."

"Target secured, sir. One injury. A doorman. Thirty-five people detained."

"William McCann?"

"Sitting on his hands, perfectly still, sir. Hasn't said a word apart from asking for his lawyer."

"Good work . . . let me know immediately if Alan Prior's one of your thirty-five."

A wave of static came through the speakers, drowning the man's reply, and the comms officer adjusted the dials before her.

"Say again, Charlie Team Leader."

"That's a negative, sir. Alan Prior is not, repeat not, at this *locus.*"

Henderson gave this a small, tight nod. "Alpha Team Leader, did you get that?"

"Yes, sir. We're entering the main house now. I'll let you know, as soon as I can." His words were almost drowned out by the crash of the hand-held ram bar – the big key – smashing Hawthorn's front doors open, and shouts of "armed police" mingling with the first scream of the night.

Henderson sat down heavily. With Bravo and Charlie secured, Hawthorns was now the last piece to drop into place. No one, himself included, had any way of knowing to what extent tonight would be deemed a success but, above all, he hoped the wing, Alpha One, would see the capture of many of the paedophiles who frequented it.

Again, there was nothing to do but wait. Henderson ran a hand over his brow and felt dampness on his palm. Swivelling in his chair, he caught Steel's eyes and acknowledged the positive nod he received. He lifted his coffee cup. It was cold, but that didn't matter.

Seven minutes later, the radio burst into life. "Alpha Team Leader to Control."

Henderson spun back to the microphone, spilling some coffee. "Go ahead."

"Alpha One and Two are secure. Alan Prior in neither. Forty-three people in Alpha Two, including *Jan* Prior, have been detained."

"And Alpha One . . . ?" Henderson needed to know this target, this specific part of the combined raids, had gone well.

"I'm in here now, sir . . . we've detained eleven people." There was a pause, then Murray said, "We need to call in Social Services."

Bad news as well as good. Henderson felt a queasy ripple in his gut. "How many, Sergeant Murray?"

"Five, sir. Repeat, five minors on the premises – one boy, four girls," and at that moment everyone in the communications suite heard a shrill yell, followed by a crashing noise like a door splintering apart. Murray's voice rose. "What? Oh, Christ, get him off. Get him *off*," then silence.

Henderson hunched over the microphone. Keeping his voice level, he said, "Control to Alpha Team Leader."

Soft white noise hissed from the speakers.

"Control to Alpha Team Leader."

"Sorry, sir," Murray's echoing voice seemed to fill the room. "We've had some trouble."

"Trouble?" Nothing could go wrong. Not now.

"Yes, sir . . . DCI Scullion . . . he just head-butted one of the detainees, then gave him one hell of a kicking before we could stop him . . . it's very bad, sir – we're bringing in an ambulance."

•

Unsure about the information she'd just been given by Joe Helms, Moss sat very still, staring at the phone and cracking the empty plastic water bottle in her hand.

What *if* JJ was Jenny Johnstone? People changed their names for *lots* of reasons. And Steel . . . did *he* know? When she'd talked about following up on Prior with the SFO he hadn't mentioned it, and she knew he would have, then if not before. And why hadn't JJ mentioned it herself?

Moss cast her mind back to the press conference following the murder of Lord Mitchell, where she'd first seen JJ. Steel had been annoyed by a question from the press corps, and asked who it was. JJ had introduced herself then as Jay Johnstone. Moss shrugged; Jenny to Jay was insignificant, and Jay Johnstone to JJ was not only an easy contraction, it suited her. Nevertheless, something was nagging her although, as yet, she couldn't quite put her finger on it.

What she found disturbing was not only had JJ not mentioned working for the *Telegraph* previously but, more to the point, she hadn't mentioned working there on a story concerning Alan Prior.

She knew she should discuss this with Steel, but hesitated as she reached for the phone. Right now, Operation Northside would be in full swing and, even though he wasn't involved, she knew trying to talk to him during the raids would be pointless. Besides, simply telling him what she'd discovered about JJ wouldn't exactly be helpful – she needed more.

Leaning back in her chair, she stretched, wondering where she could get something that would give her more insight on JJ, and her gaze fell on the stack of old newspapers Susan had piled up beside the fireplace.

Getting to her feet she crossed the room and, riffling through them, pulled out every *Scotsman*. When she had them in order, she looked at the stories carrying JJ's byline. Remarkably, given so much had happened since, the first was from only eleven days ago: *Murdered Judge Linked To Vice Ring*. Recalling how incensed Steel had been when he'd read that, she read through the piece slowly, then placed the paper to one side and picked up the next.

It didn't take long for her to read through all of JJ's pieces, but she was still no further forward. All she'd gleaned was confirmation of JJ's qualities as a reporter. With a sigh, she tossed the last paper into the pile and went through to the kitchen. As she was slicing cheese for a sandwich she thought of Steel again. Tomorrow she'd have to talk to him about JJ, a thought she didn't relish.

Cleaning the sharp knife reminded her of the scores the killer had made on his victims' bodies, and she shuddered; the vision of those scores would stay with her forever. Then, like a flickering light seen from a distance, she was nudged by a line she had just read in one of JJ's pieces. It was one of Steel's nudges. Putting the sandwich to one side she hurried back into the living room and picked up the pile of newspapers.

Finding the right paper, she read through JJ's piece headlined: *Carstairs Escapee Linked To Murder Of Lord Mitchell*, and felt a twitch of embarrassment – it was she who had led everyone to McVicar, wrongly as it turned out – then she slowed to re-read one sentence. The information was clear enough, but it puzzled her. JJ had written: *It is understood that Lord Mitchell's body was marked in a similar way to McVicar's victims, with scores to his chest.*

She frowned. As far as she could recall, the information that Mitchell's chest had been scored had never been released. And she remembered clearly JJ phoning when they were on their way back from Carstairs, but Steel hadn't told her then either.

She was beginning to get a very bad feeling about this. How could JJ possibly know about the scores to Mitchell's chest? She knew contacts were everything to a reporter – had Dr. Knox told her?

At that moment the flat seemed even more silent; she knew now she needed to dig much deeper into JJ's background. Turning to her computer, she opened a remote connection to Fettes, but when she typed in her ID a warning box appeared on screen: *Unauthorised User. Your attempted log-in and IP Address have been recorded.*

Looking at this in silent frustration, she remembered Janet Tweedie telling her approval was necessary for remote connections. For a few moments she wondered what to do, then, trying Steel's ID, smiled with relief as the now familiar Fettes desktop appeared before her.

Double-clicking the PNC icon opened the database, and she typed in Jennifer Johnstone, leaving the location field blank. A long list of names was returned, but none was close to JJ's age. Then, although she knew the database was smart enough to include diminutives and aliases, she tried Jenny and then Jay, but with the same result. So, neither Jennifer, Jenny –

nor Jay – had even been guilty of as much as illegal parking.

Tapping her pen rhythmically on her pad, Moss sat back and pondered her next step. She looked at the Scottish Courts icon. It seemed doubtful anything would be there, especially as the PNC had given her nothing, but she double-clicked the icon, opening the database, and navigated to the Search Judgments page.

Johnstone brought three results. The first two could be discounted immediately, as both referred to a town of that name. However, when she clicked on the third, then began reading the page, she felt a small electric shock run through her, followed by a chill, like cold fingers gripping her shoulders.

Before her was a three year-old Opinion of the Court, delivered by Lord Mitchell, in the Appeal by Jennifer Johnstone against Alan Prior. She sped through the preamble concerning the support of a minor, WJ, decided earlier in the Sheriff Court, but when she reached the lines detailing the Sheriff Court's action, and the order that had been entered, she realised she'd been holding her breath.

Reading the Sheriff's name, she let out a long, loud exhalation. The Sheriff in the lower court had been John Pride.

Judge John Pride. Lord Henry Mitchell of Warrender. Murder victims one and two.

THIRTY-ONE

STEEL LEFT FETTES WITH A FEELING OF warm satisfaction. Apart from failing to apprehend Alan Prior, the raids had been a success. Then, with a jolt, Jim Scullion came to mind. Every cop had come close to meltdown at some time or another and, when it came to arrests, some *chose* to hop backwards and forward over the line, but Scullion seemed to have snapped completely at Hawthorns. Barring a miracle, he was finished, and the Job had taken yet another good cop.

It was still Crime Squad's show, and he hadn't waited for the bus-loads of detainees from the raids. He'd noted the names of those detained at Hawthorns: a rich tapestry of Edinburgh's so-called great and good, most of whom were taking a do-you-know-who-I-am? approach, and a motley collection of staff and customers from *Oysters*, with Billy McCann at the head of the list. Most importantly, eleven paedophiles in Hawthorn's wing had been arrested, and all of them would be charged that night.

Rob Henderson had many long hours ahead of him if he chose to deal with all those detainees. Steel knew, if it were up to him, he would've simply thrown everyone in the cells, regardless of who they were, or what they could be held for, and let them sweat it out for the night; allow the darkest fears to build in their minds.

Billy McCann was definitely going down. Henderson had told him of the bright trail they and the Dutch police had traced, leading directly from a Chinese gang in Rotterdam to Leith, and tonight, Team Charlie had found a huge cache of money, false passports and weapons at *Oysters*. He found himself grinning. Apparently McCann had been silent apart from asking for his lawyer, but Toby Greene had been one of those swept up at Hawthorns; McCann would need a different lawyer now.

It was a pity young Stevie hadn't been detained anywhere; Moss would certainly be disappointed, but he'd have a chat with her later, try to reassure her they *would* collar him, eventually.

He turned off Comely Bank Road to make his way up Orchard Brae. With a rise in temperature most of the snow had gone, but swathes of patchy fog now lay over the city. He thought of JJ. It would be a perfect end to the day to reach his house and find her there, but he knew she'd be busy. He had tried calling her before leaving Fettes but her mobile had been switched off, so he'd left her a simple voicemail: a list of the eleven names of those arrested in Hawthorns' wing. She certainly had a powerful exclusive ahead.

The car slid on a patch of impacted snow as he negotiated the bend in Dean Path on his descent into the village. Correcting it, he reached the narrow stone bridge, and was about to turn up the lane to his house, when Alan Prior came to mind again. He hadn't been at any of the raids' targets, so where was he? Perhaps he *had* been tipped off and, with a new passport and a briefcase full of bearer bonds, was already on his way to somewhere safe and warm in South America. He peered through the windscreen at the murk; right now, South America would be a good choice for anyone.

Choices. It struck him the targets chosen for tonight's raids made sense, but one place had been missed – Prior's New Town offices. He glanced at the dashboard clock . . . Ach, what the hell? and began the climb up Bell's Brae and out of the village. Prior's office was only a few minutes away – he may as well take a look.

At the top of the brae, where the road surfaced at the end of the Dean Bridge, he made an illegal, and dangerous, right-hand turn into a bank of fog, and headed for Charlotte Square.

When he reached the square he had to drive slowly. As well as some remaining patches of snow, the fog was dense here, lending the street a mysterious, somewhat sinister, aspect, like a scene from a *Jack the Ripper* film. Slowing to a crawl by Prior's office, he saw the solitary BMW 7 outside with its lights off. Parking opposite, on the gardens side, he made his slippery way across the road.

The car had been carelessly parked at an angle and, with the driver's door ajar, an insistent alarm was chiming atonally. Avoiding the door handle, he pulled the door open cautiously to peer inside and saw blood on the seat. Whatever was going on here, it surely wasn't good.

Steel reached into his pocket for his phone, and cursed; he'd left it in the car's cradle. Then, just as he turned back to cross the road, a large dog bounded out of the fog, barking loudly, startling him and making him jump; not so much *Jack the Ripper*, more *The Hound of the Baskervilles.*

From some invisible spot on the pavement ahead, came, "Rex. Come here . . . stupid dog," and out of nowhere an elderly man, wrapped against the cold, emerged wraithlike from the fog.

He was as surprised as Steel. "I'm so sorry. Don't worry, he's okay – bark's much worse than his bite. Come *here*, Rex."

Catching his breath, Steel said, "Police. Do you have a phone?"

With a nod, the man reached into his pocket.

Steel took the phone from him. "Did you see anything here . . . the car?"

"Yes. Earlier . . . on the first part of Rex's walk. It was hard to see in this fog, and I was a bit far off, but there were two people . . . I think one of them was drunk."

Steel nodded and dialled Moss's number. A pause: voicemail. "Moss, it's Steel. I'm outside Prior's office in Charlotte Square. There's something wrong here, I'm going to investigate. Get here if you get this."

Handing the phone back with thanks, Steel made his way up the front steps; this sudden whim of his seemed to be leading to some kind of reckoning. He pushed on the door, and, finding it open, stepped inside, seeing light spilling from the room he knew to be Prior's office. Making his way as softly as he could across the entrance hallway he reached the door, and with a light touch from his fingertips, and growing apprehension, pushed it open.

A blood-stained Prior, barely recognisable from the sleek, immaculately groomed tycoon of a few days earlier, was tied to a chair with tape across his mouth. His wrists and ankles were bound with rope and his shirt ripped open, exposing his chest. Blood trickled from both nostrils, and there was a livid, bloody wound at his temple.

He stepped forward and Prior's head came up – so not dead, then – and he gave Steel a look of recognition, which rapidly turned to one of alarm.

Steel caught a slight movement to his left, just before a massive blow hit the side of his head. White light exploded before his eyes, then a deep darkness embraced him as he struggled to hold himself up, before sinking to his knees and falling face first at Prior's feet.

•

Moss leant on the horn to push a car out of her way as she accelerated dangerously down Lothian Road. She had no idea what faced her, nor whether she could handle it. Her heart was racing and she half hoped a patrol car would catch her speeding and come after her.

Her mobile had rung while she'd been trying to sit still and find the calm to comprehend what she'd just learned about JJ. Unknown Caller had lit the screen and initially she'd ignored it. To her surprise it was Steel. In his voicemail he'd said something was wrong, but he couldn't know just *how* wrong that something was. Not only was JJ connected to Alan Prior, she was directly connected to at least two murder victims, and now Steel was at Prior's office.

She flashed her lights rapidly at a bus pulling away from a stop, but the driver was still coming out in front of her, and when she touched the brakes she felt the vehicle drift out of her control as it hit a patch of stubborn snow. Struggling with the wheel, and shifting down gears to avoid braking again, the car's headlights pierced a patch of fog, catching the other side of the road. It was clear and, whispering a prayer, she turned the wheel and pressed the accelerator.

The rear of her car slewed, missing the bus by inches, but now she was speeding head-on towards a car that had turned off Princes Street. This is *not* my time, she thought as, to the accompaniment of loud horns, she whipped the wheel to her left, fish-tailing back to the right side of the road and jumping the lights, which had just turned red. A matter of seconds later she'd turned off Princes Street and was pulled up in the comparative hush of Charlotte Square beside Steel's car.

Moss crossed the street and paused at the BMW, just long enough to see the blood. She'd no idea whether Steel had phoned this in before going in to investigate, so taking a deep and – hopefully – calming, breath, she called Fettes, asking for the Duty Inspector, and tried to explain. It was an explanation that was taking far too long, and the man seemed to be annoyed a mere Sergeant was telling him what to do. Moss ended the call abruptly by telling him to send a couple of patrol cars.

At the office's front door she hesitated, took a deep breath, and entered. Seeing a bar of light from underneath an office door, she approached cautiously and, with an awful sense of foreboding, pushed the door open.

The sheer horror before her made her recoil instinctively and, as she took it all in, she felt her stomach drop and her heart beginning to hammer like a steam piston.

Prior and Steel were both tied up. Steel was propped up against a table with tape covering his mouth. His head lifted as she entered, and Moss could see an ugly wound at his temple that had bled profusely.

Prior was seated on a chair, staring sightlessly at her, unquestionably dead. His head had been tied upright and his neck showed a deep, bloody gash at his carotid artery. With his shirt torn open, she saw his chest had four deep, parallel scores. Bundles of banknotes had been stuffed into his opened mouth and, with Moss's stomach already heaving, it looked as if Prior was vomiting money.

She was startled as JJ materialised from the shadows, moving quickly to Steel's side. With her flame-red hair in a ponytail, she was dressed in jeans and trainers, a thermal jacket over a dark green t-shirt. She looked as composed – and as effortlessly beautiful – as always, except, tonight, in her hand was an old, wooden-handled chisel, stained with blood.

Moss found herself transfixed as she stared at JJ. There was a hard glint in JJ's eyes – something Moss had never seen from her before, even at her most passionate, and she caught a slight movement from Steel; a warning shake of his head.

JJ gave Moss a wary look. "Such a shame you had to come," she said softly.

Moss moved forward slightly, and JJ brought the chisel's point to Steel's neck. "Whatever you're thinking, Robin, don't."

Moss stepped back a pace, bringing her hands up, palms out. " *Why*, JJ? Or is it Jenny?"

"Jenny. Always has been," JJ said, flashing a sardonic smile. "For, why" and she paused. "Ever come to the end of a long road, Robin? That point when you *know* there's nowhere to go that might be called forward, where it's impossible to go back, with no escape roads to your left or right." She gave Moss a quick, thin smile. "Ever been there? Have you ever reached that point where you know you have to do *something*, or else you'll die?"

"But, *this?*" gesturing towards Prior.

JJ gave a small shrug. "He was the last . . . should've been the first."

Moss knew, whatever happened, she had to keep JJ talking. She tried to remember the classes at Hendon that supposedly dealt with situations like this, but her mind was blank. "And Pride, Mitchell and McCartney?"

JJ gave this a harsh laugh. "Judge John Pride . . . I thought you'd missed him. That's where it started – where I *thought* it had started."

"What started?"

JJ lost focus for a moment. "Claiming it back . . . me and this thing," pointing the chisel at Prior's corpse, "had a child together." Her eyes misted over. "I was young, my daughter needed help, and I turned to him for-"

"Turned to Prior?"

JJ nodded her head contemptuously towards the dead man. "Yes, Prior. My daughter was seriously ill and needed treatment, treatment that couldn't wait for the NHS, and I contacted him for help. Before I knew it, my life had been turned upside down. I lost my job, lost my so-called friends – I *had* to leave, to live in London and, my daughter . . . she died slowly."

For a moment, Moss caught the grief and hurt that lay behind the insanity of JJ's actions, and could almost empathise with a woman so shamefully mistreated by such a loathsome man. She knew about trying to talk someone down, but had no idea how to do so when madness was underscored by such fierce intelligence and driven by such a consuming sense of injustice. Glancing at the chisel, she saw it was looser in JJ's hand.

290

Keep talking. "How did you go from that, to this, Jenny?"

"I reached a point in the road – the end of that particular road – where I'd had enough of his relentless interference in my life. All I'd asked for was *help*. I was *so* naïve – you wouldn't've recognised me – and I thought, fight back. My stupid mistake – then – was thinking I could fight back by using the law."

Moss looked to Steel, but his eyes were downcast, and he seemed to be drifting in and out of consciousness. "Judge Pride?"

JJ gave a grating laugh. "Judge Pride, brought out of retirement to act as a Sheriff, and fuck me over in the process? Yes. Follow the money – Pride was *paid* to fuck me over."

"And Mitchell?"

"Ask yourself this, Robin – why would a criminal judge sit on a civil appeal? Was it the court's busy calendar or a payment from Prior?" Moss knew JJ wasn't waiting for an answer. "Judges should be made to conform to a set of rules, no? – *some* sort of oversight. It can't be hard to have their performances monitored by some kind of matrix, can it? But these are judges – *Edinburgh* judges, for God's sake – too high and mighty to be judged by anyone, though they can be bought by the likes of Al Prior to judge *me*.

"When I interviewed Mitchell, he didn't recognise me – he wanted me, though, and that made it easy." The hardness in her eyes had become positively flinty. "He babbled like a little boy at the end."

"And that was justice?"

JJ batted Moss's words away with a short humourless laugh. "*Justice?* You're a cop, and you talk of *justice?*" Her head pushed forward, and with a tilt of her chin, "I went looking for justice, and all I got was law, and those who buy the law. Law? Justice? I found out, the *very* hard way, they're just words Robin. What's the line? . . . 'The Law is still, in certain inevitable cases, the pre-engaged servant of the long purse'? Well, I'll tell *you*, justice can be found in *this*," and she waved the chisel before Moss's face. "This is *my* pre-engaged servant, and it has its *own* certain inevitability."

Moss wondered where the hell the patrol cars were; she could keep talking, but there was a point ahead – an inescapable point – where there would be no more talk, no more time. Something in JJ had irrevocably snapped its moorings and, tonight, there could only be more danger ahead. "And Father McCartney?"

JJ shook her head. "A man drowning in a sea of his own hypocrisy. I'm Catholic. Was, until my daughter died at Prior's hands. When everything went wrong in Pride's court, I turned to McCartney for help, and all he gave me was scripture and the catechism. Then, when I found he was taking money from Prior too, well, he *had* to die. He was the worst of them all – I turned to him not for my sake, but for my child's."

Moss felt a cold shudder run through her as she remembered Father McCartney's church, and the persistent vision that would forever haunt her of the man crucified across his own confessional. JJ might *appear* rational – even argue a lucid justification – but Moss knew she was dealing with a madwoman. *Where were those damned patrol cars?*

"So, you did all this simply for revenge?"

JJ's green eyes were wide and unblinking. "*Revenge?* Oh no, Robin, revenge is so . . . *petty*. I came for retribution . . . yes, retribution, and that's what I've delivered."

Moss ignored this. "And where do we go from here, Jenny?"

JJ's eyes narrowed. "Like I said, it's a shame you had to come." She looked down at Steel, and laid a soft hand on his shoulder. "Such a shame all round. I would've been gone. Mike would've come to with Prior for company and been none the wiser. But you had to come, and I . . . I have to go."

"I can't let you, Jenny. You know that. You've murdered four people."

JJ brought the chisel to Steel's neck again. "Are you sure about that, Robin?"

Deliberately keeping her eyes off Steel, Moss said, "I'm sure. And I can't let you hurt him, either."

JJ hesitated for a moment, as if calculating odds, then lunged at Moss's stomach with the chisel. Moss quickly stepped forward and off-line, swivelling on her feet so that, for a split second, they were facing in the same direction, forming a perfect mirror image of each other. Rapidly wrapping her nearest hand over JJ's strike hand and pulling it over her stomach, she immediately swivelled back, maintaining a sticky hold over

JJ's hand and cupping it with her free hand from below.

She heard the sharp crack as JJ's wrist broke, and the noise of the chisel hitting the floor; perhaps not a perfect wrist lock, but an effective one.

If JJ felt pain she certainly wasn't deterred and, emitting a low crazed moan, was now clawing at her with her free hand. Briefly, training advice from years ago flitted across Moss's mind: never fight a madman, nothing is predictable.

Moss spun away from JJ, avoiding her attack. This time she was in no doubt; there was no possibility of subduing JJ and, as she rushed her again, Moss again stepped off-line and jabbed her straight fingers into her throat.

JJ was still trying to attack but couldn't breathe; the combined force of her forward momentum and Moss's strike had flattened her windpipe. Almost in slow motion, she sank to her knees and then crashed, face first, onto the floor.

Handy, thought Moss, quickly grabbing JJ's wrists behind her back, pulling roughly on the broken one, and cuffing her.

Turning to Steel, she squatted down beside him and, with a broad smile, ripped the tape from his mouth. "Impressive, Moss," he managed, just as four uniformed policemen burst through the door.

THIRTY-TWO

MOSS STRETCHED HER LEGS OUT in front of her and yawned. By her side, the cup of something described as coffee had gone cold. It had been a long day, and a *very* long fortnight since her first day with Lothian and Borders. She smiled at a pretty, sloe-eyed nurse hurrying past, and wondered whether *she* ever had any doubts about her work, her vocation. And was being a Detective Sergeant even a vocation, or was it simply a step on a career?

Looking down the long corridor, she saw Susan walking towards her, her crisp white coat open, stethoscope dangling round her neck. With her fair hair pulled loosely away from her face, and very little make-up, she looked tired under the harsh lights. Moss thought of Greece again; we must get away, if only for a week.

Susan's face shadowed with concern. "How are you, Robin?"

"Tired." Perhaps it was concern that made work a vocation? "I feel I could sleep for a week. How's my History Man?"

"Well, he was banged up, but he wants to go. I'm never happy about letting anyone leave after a concussion – especially one that results in loss of consciousness. I'd prefer to have him stay, a night of observation, but I can't *keep* him here."

Moss nodded, but she'd drifted, listening to Susan's refined Edinburgh burr. Right now, her rolling *prefer* and *observation* were pleasant, melodious sounds in her ear. Steel's desire to leave was only what she expected of him. "I could always handcuff him to the bed . . . he's alright, though?"

"He *appears* to be, but he shouldn't really be on his own. There's no one, is there?"

Moss shook her head. "No," and an image of flame-haired JJ floated across her mind's eye, "not now."

Susan sighed. "Well, could you run him home, Robin?" Moss nodded. "Okay, give it five minutes, then come along to the Emergency Suite. He's still a bit fragile, but he'll probably be alright at home. I'll send him away with some painkillers and a recitation of the dire warnings about ignoring any post-trauma symptoms."

Moss couldn't imagine Steel ever being fragile. "When do you finish?"

Susan gave her a wan smile. "Seven . . . eight, maybe. Who knows? We always *hope* for a quiet night."

"I was just thinking of Greece."

"Greece?"

Moss got to her feet. "Getting away, you know. You and me."

Susan's smile lit her face, wiping away the tiredness in her eyes. "That sounds the stuff of dreams, Robin. Yes, let's plan it," and she gave Moss a hug. "Five minutes. And you, you take care, d'you hear? You've been in the wars too."

Moss watched Susan walk away; taking care was the very least of her concerns somehow. Remembering Emma and Jane, in the wars and in this same hospital, she wondered whether the raids had swept up Stevie McCann. Linking her fingers together, she raised her arms above her head and stretched; probably not – for a fleck of scum, McCann seemed to lead a charmed life.

Walking over to the vending machines, she rested her forehead on the glass and stared at the contents; yet another terrible coffee would probably waste five minutes.

•

Steel was being helped into his jacket by a nurse fussing around him when Moss arrived. "Ready to go, sir?"

"I'm not sure I needed to be here in the first place." Steel grunted.

Moss pointedly looked at the large bandage on the side of his head, and raised an eyebrow. "Really? Well, let's get you out of here."

They walked to the car park and, with Susan's warnings fresh in her mind, Moss was watchful of every step Steel took. When they were settled in the car, she said, "You'll be home in no time, sir."

"I'd like to go through the Queen's Park first . . . if that's okay."

This was in the opposite direction, and Moss thought his request more than strange. Perhaps he needed a little more time before returning to a place he had, in part, shared with JJ. "Of course."

In silence they drove the few miles through mostly deserted streets and, as they passed the *Scotsman*, Moss glanced at Steel. She half expected a comment from him, but he was staring out of the window, lost in his own world.

She had driven almost round the whole park, wondering why Steel had asked to be driven here, before he said, "Stop here, would you."

They'd reached the point where the road dipped towards the exit beside the Commonwealth Pool and, as she pulled to the side, Moss could see the looming, dark shape of the Salisbury Crags to her right, silhouetted against the sky.

Steel opened the door. "Give me a moment."

"You alright, sir?"

"Just need a bit of fresh air," Steel muttered.

Moss watched him walk on to the grass. There were still patches of snow here and there, and she thought there would be hell to pay with Susan if he fell on her watch. Zipping up her jacket, she got out, plunged her hands deep in her pockets, and perched on the car's wing.

Steel pulled his collar up and looked out over Edinburgh. The sky was clearer now, and the moon seemed close as its light glanced the very edge of the Crags. Houselights were twinkling in the nearby yet distant city, each illuminating a story, but each too far away to be read from here. It was a thought which comforted him. Looking up, he could just make out the starry clusters of Orion and the Plough. Edinburgh was going through yet another shifty change as Winter appeared to be in retreat, but he knew it was only going into hiding.

He pondered change; really, everything was in a never-ending state of flux. Billy McCann would disappear for a long time but criminals, like nature, abhorred a vacuum, and someone – another sociopath, no doubt – would take his place. Perhaps young Stevie would take over, or would this be the time some Glasgow villain fancied moving in? Hawthorns? Well, Hawthorns would probably continue, despite the public shame, and prurience, in the wake of tonight's raid. The eleven paedophiles they'd arrested would be jailed with the hope their network would be penetrated, and more arrests would follow.

He scanned the horizon, seeing moonlight glitter off the River Forth, forever slowly running to the sea, lighter against the darkness of the area near its edge where he'd grown up; the Forth Development would continue too. Despite the amount of money – the mostly dirty money that had been funnelled through PPE – and regardless of his prominence on Edinburgh's stage, Al Prior had only been a small player. There were bigger players – hidden players, somewhere – who would doubtless see their profits out of the venture; another passing episode in the sweep of Edinburgh's history.

Thinking of Prior brought him back to JJ. The next time he'd see her would probably be in court, and he shrank from the thought. But then again, like McVicar before her, she would probably be found unfit to plead and end up incarcerated in Carstairs. Darkly, he wondered how Bill Ritchie would deal with *that* exclusive.

In her madness JJ seemed to think she'd knocked him out cold, but he'd been conscious while she delivered her final, lethal retribution. His impotent horror and revulsion as he listened, helplessly, to her whispered words for Prior, and the awful sounds as she murdered him, would remain until his last breath.

Steel knew, for all her actions – and *evil* was the only word that came to mind – JJ had been in the right; a shocking thought that assailed him and lingered too long for comfort. Not for the first time, justice had gone missing, only to be redressed by JJ in truly awful fashion. He knew he had very few beliefs, but he did believe in the law, the whole system of justice that had failed her so dreadfully and, once again, had been shown as anything but infallible. What would *he* have done under similar circumstances?

"I'm getting a 'why' moment, sir." Moss had walked up to stand at his shoulder.

Steel shrugged a half smile, and then remembered the lines that had eluded him the last time he'd stood here. "You know what Thomas Carlyle called Edinburgh, Moss? . . . *This accursed, stinking, reeky mass of stones and lime and dung.*"

Moss gave him a sideways glance; even now, after everything that had happened to him, the History Man was quoting philosophers. "Sorry sir, I don't follow."

He gave a tilt of his chin towards the city. "Whatever this is – accursed or not – the question *why* suggests choice, and . . . well, we don't have any. It's what we do; it's the Job. And if we don't do it, there's *only* darkness left down there. There are no why moments, though they do touch us from time to time. If you *really* questioned what we do, start to think that way, you're in the wrong job." He turned to her. "And you're not in the wrong job, Moss – you did well; not many sergeants get to close three murders. You'll be alright."

Oddly, Moss felt both pleased and embarrassed. She looked away from Steel and out over the city that was now her adopted home, and thought of three jigsaw pieces – herself, the Job, and Edinburgh – and, despite her doubts, the fit seemed close to perfect. The other pieces in her life, those barely-shaped ones, well, in time, she felt they would fit too. One piece she would make certain of, one that would be put in its proper place, was Stevie McCann: God willing, I'll nail him.

She looked at him again. "I never thought of revenge as a motive for the murders."

Steel gave her a small nod. "I told you, way back at Mitchell's murder – your first day with me – to look for *why* it happened. Looking for why leads to *who*." He shook his head slowly. "Revenge may very well *be* a kind of wild justice when you've been badly wronged Moss, but it's a sickness too. It must have eaten her alive, piece by piece, day by day," and his voice dropped. "Every day the sickness would've taken a little bit more from her . . . taken her away from who she really was."

Moss glanced at him; every exhalation was making white vapour clouds before him. "I'm sorry . . . you know . . . about JJ."

Steel saw JJ's animated face very clearly then, her alluring green eyes only dancing with pleasure, with no hint of the relentless inner turmoil that had driven her for years. Without doubt she *was* the most beautiful woman he had ever met. Their relationship, if it could even be called that, had been formed over only a matter of weeks – far too short to really hurt him – but for their few brief times together they'd connected at a level he'd only imagined existed.

He felt a brief shiver of something like regret pass over him in one sad wave, then vanish. Although he didn't hold on to it, he knew, like all the dark phantoms he carried, visiting him when least he wanted, JJ would return again and again.

"Me too, Moss . . . me too."

cx

Also by David Hutchison – *Deacon Brodie: A Double Life.*

Based on the true story of one of Edinburgh's most infamous sons, and set in 1788, this novel is available as either a paperback or e-book.

When respected Gentleman and City Councillor, Deacon William Brodie, chases his love of gambling, he is drawn into a double life and soon the respectability of day gives way to a life of crime at night.

Betrayed by an accomplice, and revealed as a "*Gentleman by day, thief by night,*" Brodie escapes to London where he is helped to leave for Holland. Eventually captured in Amsterdam and returned to Edinburgh, he is then faced with a trial before a city where once he was a leading citizen.

In Edinburgh's High Court, Brodie is found guilty and sentenced to be hanged, but his closest friend has a different idea and, in full view of everyone, he takes his riskiest gamble yet . . . his life for the turn of a card.

cx

Lest You Be Judged is independently published by

FRANKLIN ƒ PUBLISHING
GREENFIELD USA

Printed in Poland
by Amazon Fulfillment
Poland Sp. z o.o., Wrocław

48794893R00172